THE CROWN PRINCE

THE FORGOTTEN KINGDOM SERIES

FOUR GEMS. FOUR REALMS. ONE FORGOTTEN KINGDOM

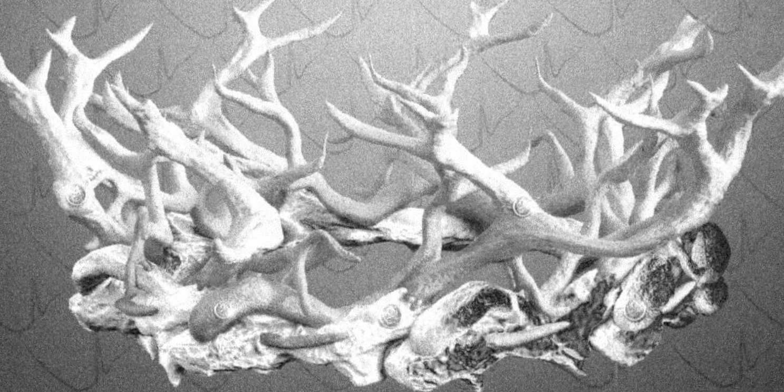

USA TODAY BESTSELLING AUTHOR

LICHELLE SLATER

THE FORGOTTEN KINGDOM SERIES

The Four Stones of Tern Tovan
(Prequel to The Forgotten Kingdom Series)

The Dragon Princess
(Sleeping Beauty Reimagined)

The Siren Princess
(Little Mermaid Reimagined)

The Beast Princess
(Beauty and the Beast Reimagined)

The Phoenix Princess
(Snow White Reimagined)

The Crown Prince

Receive the prequel to *The Four Kingdom Series* for FREE by signing up for my newsletter:

https://mailchi.mp/78ba88ee86a2/lichelleslater

ASHWRYA
DRAGON MOUNTAINS
WEEPING WOODS
DARNING FOREST
CORNESH
ARINGTON
KASTEN MOUNTAINS
TISWIL
DRAKESPINE MOUNTAINS
CHORSE
ZELIG
FILONE
AVARE
TOST
ANDORIN
SLOVAL
HANDLIN
SERVAD
MANDON FOREST
WHITE CLIFFS
GRISWIL
CASTLE BAY
PORT MERE
DELPHI
LAYTON
PORT OF GILLSBERRY
TERRICINA
PORT SOUND
CORINTH
SIREN'S
GATE
N
S
E
W

Edited by Maria Rosera

editor.paisleypressbooks.com

Cover Design, Interior, and Formatting by Melissa Stevens

theillustratedauthor.com

To Pamela Burke
May 1933 – August 2020

I have so many fond memories with you—canning beans in your kitchen, sleeping in the basement with all of the beds, playing in the irrigation water, and playing the piano with you.

I remember spending time playing Dominoes, Phase 10, and other games all while watching "The Price is Right." I remember big family dinners (my favorite of which was Christmas dinner).

I recall singing "Rida, Rida, Ranka" and that one time I drove you to Park City to listen to the Utah Symphony and my car blew a head gasket.

Going to Spud Harvest.

Swimming at the pool.

Sitting and just talking for hours.

I am going to miss you so much, Grandma.

I know you're happy to be with family on the other side.

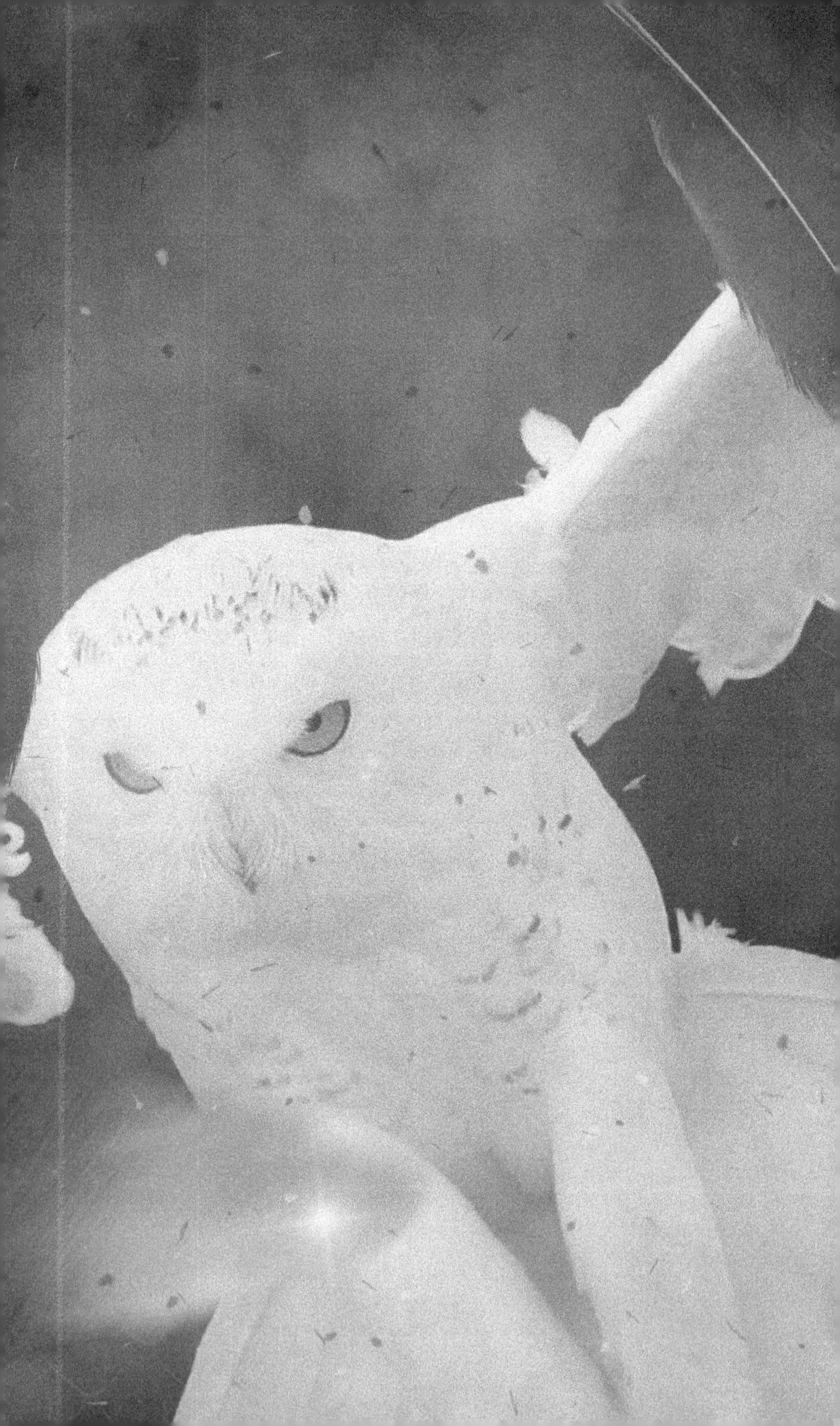

ONE

The dusty smell of stagnant books, worn leather, and ancient ink filled my nostrils. The sun's rays filtered through the thick panes of glass, lighting every particle hanging in the air from movement for the first time in ages.

Having just restored the four stones to their place and uttering the spell to release all of Fidsa from the curse, my father stood across from me. A father I hadn't seen since I was a toddler. A man so dangerous and selfish he had laid a spell on the four stones to "help" each realm in his kingdom, only to rupture the very fabric of time and nature, banishing them all to a different state. Servad, the capital city in the land, had been frozen in time. Griswil, Arington, Zelig, and Terricina had been trapped in never-changing seasons, and their people forgot all about Servad.

My father leaned against his desk. His golden hair poured over his white robes, and his eyes patiently watched as he waited for the answer to the question he had asked me: Did Selina have her heart back?

Unsure if I should trust him, I didn't answer right away. Selina had raised me to believe my father was selfish, two-faced, and power hungry. Nothing I'd seen proved otherwise. Not only that, but I still didn't know if the information I'd learned was accurate—that Selina's heart resided in my chest.

Finally, I shook my head. "No."

Tovan studied me silently before giving a nod. He swiped the stones and deposited them into his pocket. "Where is Hazel?"

"I think you should answer *my* questions now," I said firmly.

He turned back to me. The light from the window made his golden hair glow from the light of the afternoon sun. "We have a lot to catch up on. Tell me. Was it Selina alone who raised you?"

"What else should she have done when you abandoned me?" I needed to calm down. My flurry of emotions at meeting my father for the first time wasn't helping me to keep a level head, and I certainly didn't know how I should be feeling.

"Abandoned you?" he repeated. He shook his head. "Is that what she told you?"

I narrowed my eyes. He was an excellent liar, indeed.

"Gerard . . ." He looked like he wanted to reach out and touch me, but he must have read the expression on my face warning him not to.

I folded my arms across my chest. What was taking Selina so long to get here?

"Where is Hazel? Your mother?" Tovan sat back down on his chair.

"Don't know," I lied. "I want to know the truth, though. Why did you stop Selina's spell and fracture time? Why did you create the stones in the first place? And why would you give up the power of the throne?"

"You have been deceived your entire life," Tovan answered sadly.

A growl built up in my chest and I opened my mouth to snap back a retort, but a hand touched my arm. I looked down to see Princess Ismae's hand. I'd forgotten I dragged her through the mirror from the fairy realm with me. I still didn't have a clue why.

Just a few minutes ago, we were in the fairy realm. Tavia, the princess of Zelig, had attacked Selina and attempted to kill her, using the aid of every prince and princess she could rally to her side. I could remember few details, that Selina had attempted to take Tavia's heart and I had been somehow involved in the fight.

My head throbbed, and I wondered if I had hit it during the fight. I knew I had been on Selina's side, but details of the battle were blurry.

Shaking my head, I lifted my gaze to Ismae's brown eyes.

"Listen to his side," she urged softly. "There may be things he can teach you that you didn't know before. Maybe you can connect some dots with what you *have* been told."

Her smile calmed my flare of anger enough I turned back to the man who helped create me. "Speak."

"You could introduce me to your friend." Tovan leaned forward, but I blocked him. "I never would have abandoned you," he said with certainty. "You're my son, my eldest, and we both loved you. We lost our first child. How could I ever abandon you?"

I recalled reading about that loss in his journals. Both he and my mother had struggled to accept the death of their unborn child and felt such exceeding joy when they became pregnant again.

But how could I possibly know what that felt like? What *any* kind of love felt like?

Tovan's gold eyes pierced into my heart, and I turned my gaze away.

"When you felt threatened, you left me behind," I said firmly. "*That* is called abandonment."

"No. I sent you and your brother and sister away to keep you safe, Gerard. When I made the stones, my intention was to help each country handle their problems without being required to come to the king for every fear and worry in their land. If you read my journals, you would know that."

I scoffed.

"They needed to be able to help themselves with minor situations. When the king of Arington activated his stone . . ." He heaved a sigh. "Chaos erupted. I knew something was wrong with the stones. I had suspected it before giving the stones away, but I never thought my own mother would do something so . . ." He inclined his head in thought. "Callous. I collected the stones immediately. After examining them, I finally sensed the underlying spell that had been fabricated on top of my own enchantment. I was foolish."

I smirked. Finally, he admitted it.

Tovan continued, rising to his feet and crossing to the window. "I tried creating a cleansing spell to return the stones to their initial state. I should have found new ones altogether, but I feared that someone would stumble upon the corrupted stones and use them for evil. I confronted my mother about her spell too." His hand brushed against his pocket and he faced me.

"She told you that you never should have attempted such a lofty spell. You were hardly experienced," I finished for him. "You shouldn't have been attempting those spells in the first place."

Tovan raised a brow. "I was a Tern at the time, Gerard. I'd had several years of learning and experience under my belt. I believed magic can evolve and benefit all. I helped advance this city beyond anything others have seen. Carts that need no horses, thus helping the poorer families who can't afford a horse to get their wares to the market. I made a sewing machine to help sew magic into fabric to enchant a cape to fly, a dress to be cool in the summer, and so forth. Of course, they were lofty aspirations, especially when my mother used to think the same way. Selina was the first to bring enchanters to help build the city of Servad in the first place."

My brows met. "Selina?"

He nodded. "Then everything changed overnight . . ."

I frowned. "You're saying her heart was taken that long ago?"

His smile was sad. "By your stature, I would say you're . . . eighteen? Nineteen?"

"Nineteen."

"You were barely three years of age when she changed. If you were only three the last time I saw you, standing just there"—he pointed to a spot behind me—"it has been sixteen years." He turned his gaze to me.

For a moment, I remembered those eyes.

I crouch beside a puddle, my bum brushing the damp blades of grass while I watch the glassy eyes of frogs floating on the surface of the water, their plump bodies lying beneath the muddy surface.

A frog to my left lets out a long, low croak, and his throat puffs up. It is dusk and the mosquitos enjoy flying around me and trying to steal bites of blood.

I hear my father's footsteps before he kneels in the mud at my side. "What are you looking at, Gerard?" he asks.

"I'm just watchin' va frogs. Dey are so cute!"

"Want to catch one?"

I look up at my father, up into golden orbs smiling back at me. "Will catching dem hurt dem?"

"Not if done correctly, no." He rolls back the sleeves of his white and gold robes—one day he tells me I will have some of my own—then slowly lowers his hand into the water. His sleeve brushes the surface, dipping into muddy bubbles, but he doesn't care. He never does. "The trick is

to move fast enough they can't get away." He moves his hand beneath the surface and snatches a frog around the belly, then holds it out to me.

I grin and wrap both of my hands around it. Its skin is bumpy, yet slick, and surprisingly squishy. It suddenly squirms to get away, and I squeeze tighter to hold on.

"Easy, not so hard," Father says abruptly.

I loosen my grip, and the frog plops to the ground and hops off.

Father laughs and coaxes me closer to the puddle. "Go on. Your turn."

For hours, we play in the mud, just me and my dad, until long after dark. But the darkness didn't matter.

My daddy is the sun wizard.

Finally, he scoops me up into his arms and carries me into the palace and up to our floor. When we enter the room with a warm fire, Mother is sitting on the couch with my baby brother in her arms. My baby sister is asleep in a nearby crib.

As soon as my dad sets me on my feet, I run over and poke my little brother's face. "Mafias, I can't wait till you're big like me!"

"Honey, you need a bath." Mother wipes off the mud I trailed on Mathias's face. "You look like you had a lot of fun. Tell me what you did with your daddy."

As suddenly as the moment arrived, it was gone. Pain in my brain pulsed, like it might implode, and the light in the room had rings of pink and blue around them. I clamped my eyes shut, rubbed my forehead, and took a big breath.

"Do you remember?"

When I finally peeled my eyes open, Tovan's lips played with a knowing smile.

I shook the fragment of memory from my mind. It had to be magic, and I wouldn't give into it. "How was I taken from you?"

"You burst in while Selina and I—"

"Fought over the power?" I snorted.

"Over the stones and the power within them, yes. I couldn't risk harming you, though. In desperation, I cast a spell, returning the stones to each kingdom, hoping I could at least get them out of her hands for a while. At the same moment, she cast a spell I didn't hear. Before I knew it, nature and time fractured. The last thing I remember is Hazel scooping you up into her arms. Selina tore you from her, and . . . that is it. Until now."

We looked at each other for a few moments in silence.

I recognized the tightness in the grand wizard's shoulders, the hesitation in his gaze, and the nervous fidget of his hands. He was just as nervous to meet me as I was to meet him. I might have been raised with stories of my father, but to him . . . he had essentially blinked to see his child now a grown man.

I ran my tongue over my teeth. I still had a million questions to ask, but most importantly—his description of events, his body language, his mannerisms didn't line up with Selina's descriptions. I didn't see greed or sense evil, and I'd been raised by Selina. I knew evil. Or, perhaps, he was just that good at deception.

I picked up an hourglass from the shelf on my left to give my hands something to do. "Why would Selina attack you for the stones? And if she wanted them, why give them to me with the intention to bring them back to you?"

He held his hands out. "They needed to be returned here to restore time, I assume. As for why she wanted the stones in the first place? I don't know. This poses a far more important question—what is her plan once time was restored?"

"To get back her throne? I don't care. My job here is done. She will arrive any moment to arrest you and bring you before her and the king and judge you then."

The corner of Tovan's lip tugged in a crooked grin, and for a moment I felt I was looking in a mirror. "If you think Selina is done with you, I hope you aren't shocked when she sends you on another quest. She may have raised you, but she also raised me, and I fear I know her a little more than you do."

"You knew her without her heart for, what? Three years tops? I've known her for at least sixteen years," I snapped back, balling my hands into fists. "You have no idea what she's put me through, so don't say a thing about knowing her better than me."

My *father* watched me in silence.

"Your wife is Selina's pet bird," Ismae chimed in, uninvited, and completely changing our topic of conversation.

When I scowled at her, she challenged my look with a cock of her brow.

"Conversations have giving and taking, Gerard," she added calmly. "You can't resort to shouting. Now his question is answered, you can ask one of yours."

"I know how conversations work," I grumbled.

She held her hand out toward my father and gave a gentle nudge of her head.

Relenting a breath, I faced Tovan again. I'd always dreamed of meeting the mighty wizard but never expected I would find myself lacking questions. Shifting my weight to my other foot, I stupidly asked, "What was I like as a kid?"

I didn't know why that was the first thing that came to my mind. Perhaps it was desperation that maybe, just maybe, he hadn't abandoned me. Instead, I should have asked what he did when he discovered Selina's heart had been taken. Or where Quist was. Something other than asking about me.

Tovan smiled and the tension in his shoulders relaxed a bit. "You've always been so full of life. You were always curious, wanting to know what everything was and how it worked. You took apart a coo-coo clock because you didn't understand where the little bird hid." He walked to a shelf and pulled a tray down. Although a layer of dust covered every component, it was clear the gears and screws on the tray belonged to an old clock. He lifted his gaze to mine. "The thing is, you didn't break it, nor did you use tools to dismantle it. You used magic to take the pieces apart. I still don't know how you did it, because most magic in our world is used through spoken spells unless you are in possession of a magical artifact as I'm sure you know.

You were always at my side when I practiced, but I had never pressured you to learn magic. You didn't know a single magic word."

"Maybe I just watched you a lot and picked it up."

"Perhaps." He set the tray on his desk. "I was going to have you help me fix it someday."

"So you could test my magic?" I folded my arms.

Tovan chuckled. "Can you blame me? My son showed magic at three years of age? Showing the ability to use magic that young is extremely rare. Any father would be proud."

My chest ached.

Pride radiated in his golden eyes, not envy.

I had to look away. If only he knew who I was now, *what* I was, he wouldn't be so proud of me.

"Have you found your main form of magic?" he asked.

I hesitated and glanced at Ismae, not that she could help me, but it gave me somewhere to look that wasn't my father or another dust-covered artifact.

"Go on," she urged softly, adding a nudge to my arm.

"You know what I am?" I asked. Again, stupid.

Ismae placed her hands on her hips. "How many times do I need to tell you we know each other?"

I rolled my eyes. "I'm a necromancer," I replied as I faced my father.

Tovan's face shifted into confusion. "Necromancy?" He frowned deeply and muttered, "Undoubtedly due to Selina's influence."

"First fifteen minutes and I already disappoint you."

"I never said I was disappointed," he quickly said in an attempt to recover. "Surprised, yes. Necromancy takes a lot of power."

"I summoned a wraith dragon a few months ago," I found myself saying as if I needed him to be proud of me again.

But when his eyes widened, I couldn't deny the joy I felt. "A *wraith* dragon? Remarkable! Tell me more about this wraith dragon. How did you summon it? When?" He walked around his desk and took a book from the shelf. More journals, ones I hadn't read.

He set a quill on the desk.

I told him all about how I was in a battle in Griswil and had opened a massive portal. I'd summoned undead to battle, but as the battle continued, my power built and I summoned the wraith dragon.

Of course, I left out the details that I had tricked Elisa into being my fiancée and I was attempting to steal the throne from her. I didn't tell him that I had nearly banished the fae into extinction when I burned down their cliffside city.

As I spoke, the quill wrote.

"You fought dragons?" he asked.

"Not me, the wraith dragon."

"Ah, yes." He tapped a finger on his lip. "How many dragons were in the battle? And do you know their names?"

I shrugged. "I think there were three dragons total, but only two were adults. One was Elisa. There may have been more, but that happened almost eleven months ago."

The pen relaxed on the desk and Tovan returned to his feet. "How near is the winter solstice?"

"Why is that important?"

"Sixteen years . . . exactly? I suppose a spell could have a duration." He was talking out loud now, but not to me, and pacing. "But sixteen is hardly a meaningful number, unless . . . unless it's in correlation with love. Also historically related to angels."

"Angels?" I scoffed.

Tovan straightened his robes. "And what is so silly about angels? You are a necromancer. You can summon forth demons."

"But angels must mean there's a . . ."

"Heaven?"

I frowned.

He continued. "Sixteen may have to do with wisdom too. I was never too good at numerology. Oh! But if you returned time to its proper position, I can speak with a wizard who will know." He clapped his hands and walked to his door.

However, when he opened it, castle guardsmen stood on the opposite side.

I straightened immediately and pulled Ismae behind me.

Behind the guards stood Selina, now wearing an expensive gown and royal crown. "Just where I expected you would be."

"Mother," Tovan said stiffly.

"Arrest him and bring him to the kingdom."

The men standing nearest to Tovan looked up at the wizard and then back at Selina. They didn't know why their queen wanted them to arrest their prince.

Tovan drew a deep breath, his shoulders rising as he did so. "I shall walk with you. After all, it has been some time since we've seen each other, hasn't it? Sixteen years?" He extended a hand toward me.

Selina smirked, wildness in her dark eyes. "You will be brought to the castle and finally charged for all of the wrongs your foolish magic has wrought upon our people."

He slowly shook his head in disbelief. "I will go with you willingly, but I demand a conversation with Hazel and my father."

Selina gave a short, shrill whistle, and her raven flew up from behind her to rest on her right shoulder. "She may struggle a little with answering you." She reached up and stroked the raven's breast.

Tovan's jaw flexed.

"You didn't expect to see me again?" She smirked. "Chain him and bring him to the palace."

TWO

As I walked down the street—with Selina leading the way, the group of soldiers surrounding my father, and Ismae at my side—I took the opportunity to look at Servad. The city was big, much like those in the fairy realm, but unlike those I'd visited in my quest to reclaim the magic stones. Tovan must have spoken the truth when he said he was trying to help Servad become more efficient. If a city could grow and function well at this size, I could only imagine what could have been if the other realms had also expanded.

Around me, the people stood on the street, dazed. They'd woken from a sixteen-year nap and had no clue. I wondered if they felt tired or stiff and if Selina would tell them why. Knowing her, she would and blame Tovan entirely.

"This city is amazing," Ismae said, voicing my thoughts.

"Yes, I suppose," I answered nonchalantly.

She extended her arms to a nearby building. Its main level was comprised of shops, but it had five floors above with small windows revealing them to be homes. "One building for multiple families to live in? And if they own the shops below, that is rather convenient. A brilliant idea to save space in a city."

I threw her a sideways glance, but this time I did so to take her in.

Ismae's brown eyes were aglow with excitement, never mind she was a prisoner to me. She acted like my guest. Small freckles adorned her nose and cheeks. She was, simply put, beautiful. And when I looked at her, my heart had a weird skip to it.

In the blink of an eye, I stood in a little home, knife in hand, dicing potatoes and Ismae was asking me to let her help. She told me she didn't know how, being a princess and everything. But some part of me knew that wasn't the case because I'd shown her. But I longed to be closer to her and allowed her to step between me and the cutting board.

I heard myself whisper in her ear, *"Why do you intrigue me so?"*

She turned and looked up at me with her chestnut eyes. *"Everyone needs someone, Gerard."*

Each flash of memory was like waking from a pleasant dream and struggling to remember the details. My heart knew something should be there, something had happened in that moment, but all feelings were blocked. In its place was an empty hole.

I had wanted to be close, to touch her, but . . . those memories couldn't be real.

Could they?

Ismae looked at me, concern lining her brow. "Are you okay?"

Massaging my temple, I picked up the pace. "I saw . . . nothing. It's nothing."

"Like the shadows we saw when we were first on our way through the town? I feel them still too."

"Shadows?" I shifted my attention from the brightly colored garments of the townspeople to the walls past them. I'd forgotten about the shadows that had been moving when we first arrived, despite everyone being frozen in time.

As I looked carefully at the now-awake townspeople, their shadows moved with their movements. Nothing was strange about that. I had just relaxed when I saw one. A solitary shadow moved a fraction slower than the person it belonged to.

I nearly stopped in my tracks, but that would have drawn unnecessary attention to me. I would consult with Selina. They were something that needed to be addressed. However, I stayed alert as we continued back to the palace, noting three other instances where the shadow of a townsperson shifted slightly off from what should have been.

As we walked, I found it oddly amusing that the people had no idea their lives had been disrupted. They carried on like they would have otherwise, calling out that new boots had just been made, a woman gloating about a new perfume she'd purchased, and so forth.

Overhead, though, windows opened and a couple of women shook out rugs or clothing to get rid of all the dust. Undoubtedly, that would be the talk of the city by nightfall.

If they had family outside of the city, would that family suddenly remember them? Had the entire kingdom woken to memories of Servad? I imagined a lot of conversations at dinner tables with spouses asking if they'd ever traded in a city named Servad, or if it were a dream.

My thoughts halted when we crested the small hill and I spotted the castle. It wasn't what I expected. I had anticipated something grand—a towering white building like Zelig.

Pink trees stood in a row acting as a wall on either side of the courtyard. A massive water fountain with dragons flowed into a large pond in the center of the courtyard, allowing horses and carriages to go in a circle around it. Two staircases led up to the main doors. The stairs and pillars of the castle were white and shimmered, while the exterior walls of the castle were blue, and long purple flags fluttered atop the roof. The castle and its gardens sat atop a hill overlooking the city.

This was supposed to have been my childhood home.

I should have learned to be a prince there, played with toys, or been taken to swim in the Troll River in Arington or to climb the Drakespine Mountains in Griswil. This country should have been mine. My *parents* should have been mine.

Bitterness tingled in my chest like claws being twisted inside of me.

"I bet you're overwhelmed by all of this, aren't you?" Ismae observed while everyone else continued onward. "I can't imagine how you feel seeing your home for the first time. You've wanted little more than that."

"I don't know what to think," I replied.

She stepped forward, took my hands, and lowered her voice. "You once said something to me I'll never forget. You told me you understood what it was like to pretend to be someone else, that you understood how it felt to parade around, to do what others want, just to stay alive."

I looked her up and down. "I said those words?"

"More or less." Ismae's lip tugged at a smile. "Gerard, I know Selina used her magic to make you forget me. But I am *not* letting you go so easily. You fought for me. I'll fight for you too."

"Why?" I whispered. "What good have I done for anyone?"

"You taught me to stick up for myself. You taught me that I'm important. That I'm more than just a princess to be wed off for the good of my father or kingdom."

I rolled my eyes and pulled my hands away. I couldn't have done that.

Ismae scowled and grabbed my arm, spun me around, and shocked me when she took my face and kissed my lips. My vision went white, and pain exploded behind my eyes. I shoved her away—a little too hard—and placed my hand on my head to calm the throbbing drum now echoing.

A guard approached us. "Sire, is there something I can help with?"

"Get her away from me," I hissed.

"Gerard, please!" she said desperately.

"Put her in a room near mine so I can keep an eye on her." I closed my eyes, silently willing the pain to subside.

I heard the guard mutter for Ismae to go with him, and I could almost picture Ismae's glare of defiance before she stormed off with him up the stairs. The farther away she got, the more my headache went away.

When I could open my eyes without seeing orbs of light, I studied the dragon water fountain. If Ismae wasn't important, how did she have the power to make my head ache? Why would she have kissed me if I didn't know her?

Staring at the water pouring from the open mouths of the dragons, I tried desperately to cling to the fragments of those memories I'd recalled earlier, but it was like grasping at fog. Finally giving up, I trotted up the stairs and entered the castle.

A guard standing inside gestured for me to follow him. "They are this way."

Two staircases curved upward to the same second-story balcony overhanging the main hallway. The banisters were gold, and a purple and gold rug ran the length of the stairs and floor before me.

The guard led me through the arch leading into the hallway beneath the balcony and down a hall to a surprisingly small throne room. Selina sat on the raised platform with a man—who I assumed to be her husband—at her side. The guards positioned themselves with their backs to the walls.

Tovan stood before his father and mother, head held high, shoulders squared, and hands at his sides. He looked more regal than Selina.

"Ah, Gerard, we were waiting for you," Selina said. She waved for me to join her at her side.

I exchanged a look with my father as I walked by. I couldn't read his expression, and I didn't know what he was hoping to gain from looking into my eyes—maybe he could read minds and I didn't know it.

I stepped up to Selina's side.

She took my hand, making my shoulders tense, and turned to the man. "Torian, darling, this is Gerard. He's Tovan's eldest son. You remember him, don't you?"

Torian gave me a huge grin and practically jumped to his feet. "Last I saw you, you were a wee one!" He grabbed my shoulders and pulled me into his chest for a big bear hug I hadn't anticipated. "My, you've grown!"

I didn't mean to go tense, but how could he blame me? It wasn't as if Selina ever hugged me. Yet at the same time, it felt familiar.

He pushed me back and kept his hands on my shoulders. "Selina was catching me up on things. It's a shame time got disrupted. I would have enjoyed spending time with you, young man. At least we get the rest of our days together, hmm? I imagine you would prefer to spend more time with your father, of course, but I would still like to get to know you."

Nodding, I managed to get out, "Of course, sir."

"Now, back to the matter at hand." The king, Torian, released me and turned to Tovan. "Is it true it was your spell that disrupted time and you were meddling with things you didn't understand?"

Tovan pondered before answering, "I had no other choice, Father. Mother had put a spell on the stones, what else—"

"My spell was hardly any trouble. Merely a locator spell," Selina cut in.

"Besides that, every wizard practices with things we don't understand. It is how we become better at magic as a whole," Tovan stated bluntly.

King Torian nodded and returned to his seat on the throne. "Why is he here then?"

"Because Tovan's magic went against the laws of the wizarding academy. He practiced magic without notifying anyone *and* without proper safety measures in place. The spell occurred on their grounds. I am proposing he be placed in one of their holding cells until we can properly sort out how to best . . . help him."

Torian heaved a sigh. "If the magic occurred on their grounds and went against *their* laws, why are they not addressing the punishment?"

Selina's chin lifted ever so slightly, and she sucked her cheeks in. I doubted she had considered that. "Torian, darling," she said in a low voice, somehow remembering to smile. King Torian wasn't me. "Our son ruptured time. That sort of magic is terrifyingly dangerous, don't you think? He sacrificed his family."

"You think our son has lost his mind?"

"Certainly! If he can truly impact time, who is to say he didn't set this all up? And poor Gerard was raised without a proper home, without a family because of it. Not to mention, it took me sixteen years to fix the horrid spell." She traced her fingers up and down King Torian's arm.

I rolled my eyes.

The king relented. "Have him placed at the Quinary Wizard Academy. Tell Tern Colter to place him in their strongest cell, for now."

Selina's familiar smug expression returned to her face.

Before Tovan was directed out of the room, he looked to me. "Don't forget yourself. Only you can overcome it."

I didn't answer. I had no self-identity. How could I possibly forget myself?

"Now, Gerard, why don't we get you settled?" King Torian pushed himself out of his throne. "From the way it smells in here, I would imagine the servants have prepared quite the feast." He clapped his hand on my shoulder and gave it a brief squeeze as he passed.

I shifted my attention to Selina.

"What?" she asked innocently, though she smirked.

"This is it? I join my . . . grandfather for dinner like nothing has ever happened? You and I pretend . . . what, exactly?"

With a shrug, she too stood. "Make up whatever life you want to. You've fulfilled everything I trained you to be. Now, you get to relax. Isn't that wonderful?" She cocked a brow.

I didn't miss the threat behind it. Undoubtedly, she was going to focus her claws on her husband. A fleeting thought that she was going to take his heart that night, if not as soon as possible, crossed my mind.

When she left, followed by the guards, I remained alone in the throne room. I turned in a slow circle, taking in the painted portraits of previous kings hanging on the wall opposite the windows, the gold filigree along the ceiling and throne, golden chandeliers, and two suits of armor—one for a man and the other a woman. I imagined those would be worn for ceremonial purposes, considering there wasn't a dent or scuff on them, though there was sixteen years' worth of dust layered on them and everything else in the room. The servants would be up all night cleaning and well through the next day.

Do as I wish?

I looked through the nearest window, out into the garden with a tall hedge and the fireflies now flickering as the sun began to set. I couldn't believe it was finally time for me to do what I wanted. And what I wanted, more than anything, was to go to the Quinary Academy to visit their library and speak with the Terns.

A man cleared his throat, drawing my attention to the doorway.

He bowed at the waist and didn't straighten. "Your Royal Highness, I have put the young woman in the room adjoining yours. I can show you now or after your supper."

"Take me after supper."

The guard straightened and turned to go.

"But please make sure she is fed," I blurted. "She's traveled long and must be exhausted and starving." I might have had my mind manipulated by Selina, as Ismae claimed, but I hadn't forgotten the battle just hours ago in the fairy realm where Selina had tried—and failed—to take Tavia's heart. Ismae had been there fighting alongside her friends.

The guard, not looking much older than myself, nodded his head stiffly and left the room.

I followed and, as soon as I stepped through the archway, the lights in the throne room went out. When I glanced over my shoulder, I wondered if that was something Tovan had thought up. Even if I didn't like him, it was brilliant.

I joined my grandfather and grandmother for an awkward dinner. Selina slid right back into the role of loyal wife and queen. She acted the role of a caring woman so well even I briefly forgot she was as much to blame for all of this, if not more.

King Torian started telling me stories about Tovan. "I remember when he was little and he discovered his magic for the first time. We were outside playing in the gardens, one of those rare moments where I got to slip away from busy meetings. He saw a flower and asked me what it would look like if it were a butterfly. And then, to my complete surprise, the flower turned into a butterfly!" He burst into boisterous laughter.

It wasn't hard for me to picture that. Selina had explained to me that when new wizards discovered their magic, it wasn't uncommon for them to accidentally make things happen.

The king leaned his elbows on the table. "Tell me, do you remember anything about your father?"

I shook my head. "Not particularly. I remember playing in mud with him, exploring rocks and such, but I was young."

He nodded. "That you were."

Everything in the castle was what I had dreamed of, what I had longed for my entire life. A table overflowing with food, the ability to eat as much or little as I wanted, a meal I didn't have to prepare. And that night? I would sleep in a soft bed I didn't have to make under a roof I didn't have to find. I would be warmed by thick blankets or glowing fire I didn't have to keep going all night.

And it was uncomfortable.

After eating, the guard who took Ismae to her room led me up the stairs and down a long hall I felt would never end until he turned down into a wing of the castle.

"These are the royal quarters. The king and queen are at the opposite end." He turned to nod behind us to a double door painted the same hue of purple as the rug with ornate golden handles. He extended his hand to another double door, white, but with the same golden handles. "The crown prince's room is here. You will be at the end of the hallway."

Instinctively, I reached out to open the door, but the guard beat me to it and pushed the door open. Again bowing low, he held his arm out in a gesture for me to enter.

Like the throne room, when I entered my new quarters, the sconces on the walls and the chandelier ignited with fire. "Is there a way to turn these off should I not want every one of them to light?" I turned to the guard.

The guard smiled respectfully. "Certainly, your highness. You simply speak what you want off and then the magic word. For example, chandelier, lulla."

The chandelier dimmed until the candles went out.

"Brilliant," I said aloud. "Simple enough a commoner could do it. Fireplace, lulla."

The fireplace went out, leaving only the warm glow of the sconces on either side of the enormous four-poster bed and fireplace.

"Are you familiar with the traditions of the palace?" the guard asked.

"What is the difference between a palace and castle?"

He hesitated. "I suppose . . . it might be that a palace is shorter in height?" He shrugged a shoulder.

"What is your name?"

"Sir Adam." He shifted his weight and placed his hands behind his back, eyes darting.

"You're not in trouble," I grumbled. When he visibly relaxed, I folded my arms. "To answer your question, no. I know little about palace life aside from the manners Selina taught me."

"Is it true, then . . . Forgive me, I shouldn't ask questions of you."

I rolled my eyes. "Please. I might be some sort of royalty by bloodline, but I was raised sleeping on bedrolls in tents or under the stars." To add emphasis, I gestured to my well-worn clothing from Ashwrya. "You don't need formalities with me."

Adam paused, then shook his head. "Regardless of circumstance, blood is all that matters here, I'm afraid. I only wished to inform you breakfast is always at seven thirty. A servant will come to wake you and dress you in new attire in the morning."

"Will I see you again? Did Selina assign you to babysit me?"

His brows furrowed. "Only tonight. My main assignment is to patrol Servad's borders."

I nodded and motioned for him to go. "That is good. Thank you."

"The young maiden asked to speak with you at your earliest convenience. Good evening, sire." The door clicked shut behind him.

I let out a loud sigh and ran a hand over my face, then crossed to the bathing room and washed up. My appearance was just as exhausted as I felt—stubble on my face, bags under my eyes, my hair oily, and braid falling out. Despite the time of day in Servad, I was positively exhausted. After all, I'd been awake traveling . . . traveling with who?

The dull ache in my head started again.

I had traveled somewhere with someone before arriving back at the castle of the fairies. Prior to the battle with Selina, where I attacked Ismae's brother and broke his arm. I had fought in behalf of Selina. I remembered.

Willing away the pain in my head and the exhaustion in my bones, I decided I would just go to bed. However, after shedding my jacket, vest, and boots, I found myself standing in my room staring at my door in only my sweaty and dirty undershirt, trousers, and bare feet.

I could summon a wraith dragon from the depths of the underworld but couldn't face a princess I'd taken prisoner?

With a frustrated curse at myself, I quickly left my room and walked to the door beside mine. I raised my hand and rested my knuckles on the white paint.

Why should she wish to speak with me?

We *didn't* know each other.

Given my disheveled appearance, I wouldn't want to speak with me either. I likely smelled too. Deciding I should clean up before speaking with Ismae, but feeling too tired to do so at the moment, I lowered my hand, turned away, and walked back to my room.

I could have sworn I heard her door open before I closed my own.

THREE

After spending too much time in the warm bath the next morning, I climbed out and looked at my reflection. I liked that my stubble made me look a little older, but it also made me look gruff. My eyes seemed to do that enough for me without needing to look even worse. While debating whether to shave it off, I brushed through my brown hair and tied it in a knot at the back. The sides of my head hadn't been shaved in a few months and the hair was getting long enough to reach my ears. I needed to shave them soon.

The knock on my door finally made me leave the bathroom. "You may enter!" I called.

A gangly boy around twelve years of age pushed the door open with his elbow, slipped inside, and nudged it closed with his foot. He carried a pile of clothes in his hands. He bowed like the guard had—

at the waist and keeping his eyes down. "Your Royal Highness, I am pleased to be your servant."

"You don't need to serve me. I'm sure I can manage." I strolled over and took the clothing from his outstretched arms and placed them on my bed.

I was used to leathers and inexpensive linen. This clothing was different even down to the fabrics—cotton for the undershirt and underwear, silk for the vest, and the finest linen for the trousers.

Noticing the boy hadn't left yet, nor straightened, I looked at him. "What are you waiting for?"

"You need to dismiss me, sire."

Doing my best not to roll my eyes and cause trouble for the boy, I waved him away with my hand. "You're dismissed."

"Are you certain you don't need help?" He lifted his blue eyes, a bit of a wince on his face. "It's my duty to assist you however you need."

"Does that include challenging me?" I dropped the towel and put on the undergarments and trousers first.

He flinched and looked at his feet. "No, sir. Please forgive me. Sir Adam told me you were new to the castle, and I am only trying to help. My tasks include making sure you are taken care of, and that includes making your bed, drawing your baths—"

"I already had a bath, can't you tell?"

The poor kid started fumbling for words. "Yes, of course. I could smell. You look like it too, and the towel . . . I just mean . . ."

I slid the undershirt on. It had lace sleeves around the wrist and I lifted my lip in a sneer of disgust. "Do all people here dress this way? The trousers are short and tight, the sleeves pointless . . . how does anyone work wearing this?" I held up my arms and let the sleeves fall. They were at least six inches in length.

"Only royalty and nobility wear such fine clothing," the boy replied. "Not to mention, you *are* a prince . . ."

I turned to examine his clothing. He too wore short, tight pants and a vest, but they were less finely made and there were no fluttering sleeves at his wrists.

Shaking my head, I held up my arms. "The sleeves need to go. I'll not be able to get anything done with them on my arms flapping like flags. Should I need to do something as simple as write, I will smear the ink."

The boy gulped. "C-Certainly, sire. You could also call for a scribe . . ."

"Are royal people so incompetent they have others to do everything for them?" I scowled.

Without a moment's hesitation, the boy nodded.

I rolled my eyes, balled the sleeves into my hands, and pulled my arms through the purple vest, buttoned it, and turned to face the boy. "Not too bad for doing it on my own, hmm?"

He raised a finger but hesitated to speak.

"What is it?"

"Y-Your sleeve, sire. There."

I looked to my right shoulder, which was bunched up under the vest, and fixed it. "Now?"

"Much better." He flashed a smile, opened the door, stepped back, and then bowed. "Breakfast is ready."

I drew a breath. "I'm going to visit with Princess Ismae first. You may tell Selina she can start without me." I exited the room and walked right to Ismae's door.

The door opened shortly after I knocked. Ismae stood in the middle of the room on a stool with three women garbed in simple but fine clothing surrounding her, servants helping her prepare for the day.

Ismae faced me, wearing a golden dress with far too much poof at the back and a scowl on her face. "Can you believe how they've dressed me?" she complained.

I held up my arms, showing off my fancy sleeves. "At least you don't have banners dangling from your wrists."

"*You* can sit down," she argued. "I have this . . . thing under my skirts, not to mention a corset! I only wear corsets for seasonal celebrations. I can't breathe!" She swatted at one of the servant girls who tried to step forward and fix the skirts Ismae had disrupted.

Ismae's hair had been rolled along the back of her head and hung over her right shoulder in a long, curled ponytail. The gold hues in her dress lit up her face and made her freckles pop, and the shape of the corset thinned her waist and pushed her breasts up. I hadn't ever seen her in a dress so elegant. She was absolutely radiant.

I couldn't resist a grin while my heart fluttered.

"What are you smirking at?" she grumbled.

"I'm not smirking, I'm smiling. The corset makes your . . . uh . . . *you* look good."

"All of this and the only thing you point out is my breasts?" With a glare, she tried to reach behind her back. "Take it off. I don't need it."

"Ismae . . ." I stepped forward, but she turned a glare to me.

"I would like to wear a different dress. One I'm comfortable in. One in which I can still breathe and enjoy my day."

The gown shifted of its own accord. The corset softened into a simple bodice and the plumage of the dress settled, making it a still-beautiful but far more comfortable dress.

"How did you do that?" I stared at her with my mouth hanging open.

"Magic," she replied simply as if I should have known she was capable all along. She gathered her skirts and stepped down from the stool to face me. "I wanted to speak with you last night. Did Adam not send the message?"

I glanced at the servants. "He did. You have magic?"

"Why didn't you come?" she pressed.

"I . . . wasn't ready to speak with you. I was tired." I shifted my weight to my other foot. I didn't understand why I felt so shameful about it.

Ismae looked me up and down. "Want me to use my magic to make *you* more comfortable?" She had already relaxed and a playful smile rested on her face. "You look like a glorified pirate, to be honest. I think

James would adore your sleeves." She grabbed the lace of my right sleeve and lifted my arm with it.

I frowned. "I don't think even a pirate could stand sleeves this long. It would get caught in their riggings. Besides, James is simpler than this."

She cocked her brow. "You remember James?"

"Of course." I pulled my arm away. "I was on his ship for a period of time when I collected the summer stone. Come with me to breakfast?" I held my hand to her, then remembered to put my other hand behind my back—as a prince should.

Ismae sighed. "I would like to say no but can't. I need to get out of this room," she added in a mumble, casting a glance to the woman behind her.

"Can't tolerate being waited on by servants? What kind of princess are you?" I teased.

She took my hand and left the room with me. "It's weird, isn't it?" Once in the hallway, Ismae stopped us and leaned back so she could look me up and down again. A smile slowly spread across her lips, though she tried to resist it, even placing her hand over her mouth.

"What?" I demanded, looking down at myself.

"It's just . . . not you." She giggled.

I scowled at her.

"You look silly. You wear leather vests, linen shirts, and fur. That matches your broody face much better than this . . . outfit."

"Broody face?" I opened my mouth to object, but Ismae burst out in a fit of laughter. "How can you possibly be laughing when I've taken you as my prisoner?" I demanded over her ruckus.

She giggled one last time before wiping at nonexistent tears. "Gerard, we both know I'm not your prisoner. Take me to breakfast. I'm famished." She looped her arm through mine.

Giving her a perplexed look, I shook my head and started us down the expansive hall. "How are you confident that you're not my prisoner?"

"Because somewhere in your heart or brain, you remember me. You remember what I mean to you," she replied softly. "Whatever Selina did to you, I'm going to find a way to fix it."

"Why?" I stopped us in our tracks in the light of the window.

"Because I love you, nitwit." The look in Ismae's eyes was earnest. She hadn't loosened her grip on me. "The first time we had a *real* kiss, I knew you were everything I needed. For the first time in my life, I felt at home with someone, and you deserve to feel that again. I'm not letting you go because Selina put some spell on you. I'll find a way to break it."

"You have too much confidence in yourself." I took a step, but Ismae didn't move.

"No, I have just the right amount of confidence. It's *you* who is lacking." She straightened and stepped up to my side.

I didn't have anything to say to her the rest of the way to the dining hall. I didn't know *what* to say. However, when we got to the doorway of the dining hall and I looked inside, Selina was absent. Torian would likely give us an excuse that she was running late or some other nonsense. In my heart, however, I knew something else was going on.

Nudging Ismae, I whispered, "Get seated. I'll be there in a moment."

Ismae frowned but complied.

I followed my instincts to the throne room and overheard several voices seeping into the hall. I stopped just outside the door and focused on Selina's.

"Our people are already going through enough. This must be done as silently as possible," she said.

"Your Majesty, this isn't something that can be done silently. The people will notice all of the soldiers leaving, their husbands and sons *leaving*. This isn't something that won't go unnoticed. The people will ask questions." The man's voice sounded polite, but the speaker was also clearly frustrated.

"Ashwrya is vulnerable right now and we must expand our kingdom while we have the chance. The barbarians will barely put up a fight."

There was a pause, then the man asked, "Has the king approved this?"

Selina scoffed. "Of course he has."

"I don't see a decree from him with his seal."

"I am the queen," Selina said, emphasizing each word.

The man exhaled a frustrated breath. "I know, Your Majesty, but the king is the one with the power. I cannot act without his seal or speaking with him directly."

Wrong thing to say, I thought.

Selina's silence confirmed it. I could practically see her sitting on her throne, her glare digging into the general. "I shall get the seal, then, and you will realize how foolish you've been. I will demote you and put someone else in charge." Her skirts rustled, and I bolted for the dining room.

Selina wanted to conquer Ashwrya. The "barbarians" had been good to us. I'd been practically raised in that land, and even though I never viewed it as "home," it was the closest thing I had to one.

Torian raised a questioning brow when I rushed in and took my seat as casually as possible between him and Ismae.

The food was already sitting on the table, waiting.

Selina entered shortly after and sat across from me.

"I would like to visit the wizard academy," I offered before anything else could be brought up. I lifted the glass of juice to my lips.

Selina gave a stiff smile and picked up her knife and fork. "We have a library here in the palace you can use."

I shrugged. "I want to see what the academy is like."

"Undoubtedly to see where your father spent most of his time," Torian chimed in, wagging his fork at me. He gave a warm chuckle—Selina evidently hadn't taken his heart yet. "I'm sure one of the terns will be pleased to show you around. Maybe you can even see Tovan's office. He is rather brilliant, you know, which is why this situation has me so confused."

Selina twitched her brow but refrained from saying anything.

"May I join you?" Ismae asked. I hadn't recognized how stiffly she sat until I looked at her. She wasn't touching her food, and her hands rested in her lap, squeezing her napkin tightly.

"The academy is for men only," the king stated.

Ismae returned her attention to me, raising both brows. "And what am I to do all day? Sit on my bed and daydream?"

I'd learned all of Selina's little expressions, which ones were warnings, questions, moments when I shouldn't speak. Ismae? I didn't understand her expressions yet. I had to quickly file through what little I knew about women and realized she was either pleading with me or . . . angry with me. Perhaps both.

"Um. Perhaps they'll let you enter as a guest?" I offered.

"I don't think that's a—" Selina started.

Torian cut her off. "That's a wonderful idea! Go on and spend the day together. Explore the city! It's a pity about Tovan, though," he finished in a mumble. "He would have loved to show you around."

I stabbed the sausage on my plate and watched the grease ooze out of it.

"Ismae, where are you from?" the king asked, and I was grateful for the change in conversation.

"I'm the princess of Arington, youngest child of King Patrick and Queen Gemma."

"Patrick is a good man. Last I saw of them, you were just a little one." He paused. "Did you say King and Queen?"

She gave a polite, but stiff, smile. "Yes."

"Hmm. Your father was a governor when I saw him last. The power of our throne has been dispersed between the land?" He turned to me.

"Temporarily," I answered, glancing at Selina.

The king followed my gaze to his wife.

Selina reached over and patted his hand. "I'll explain everything when we get the chance."

I nudged Ismae lightly with my elbow and whispered, "Eat up."

Her gaze darted to Selina, then her plate. "Yes, of course."

I slipped my hand under the table and placed it on her knee. She was worried about Selina, and why shouldn't she be? The last time she saw Selina . . .

Ismae collapses to the ground, smoke smoldering from her burned clothes where Selina's bolt of magic had struck her. I sprint to her side and scoop her up into my arms. Her face is already pale, her eyes distant.

"You can't leave me," I beg her, stroking her hair. "Ismae, stay with me. I n—I need you."

"Why?" Her voice is already weak. Her lips are turning blue.

Desperately, I say, "Because you're the only person I've ever trusted. You're my one."

She gives a weak smile with those blue beautiful lips. "You love me?" Her eyelids grow heavy and slide closed before I can plead with her again.

"Ismae? Please. Don't go! I . . . do. Yes, I love you. Ismae!" I shake her in desperation, trying to wake her. But I know what death looks like.

"I . . . love you too." Her body goes limp in my arms.

Her voice echoed in my head.

White light ruptured my vision, and my head ached so horribly, I thought I would vomit.

Ismae had died.

Selina had killed her that day.

And I had told Ismae I loved her.

I felt someone's hand on my back and underwater voices tried to reach out to me. Icy fingers pressed to my scalp, and the headache and memory dissipated. A blanket of darkness tried to hide Ismae, but her final words remained—*"I love you too."*

Selina stood at my side, her fingers on one side of my face, which rested on the table. Ismae stood on the opposite side of me with her warm hand on my back.

Selina's jaw flexed. "Have you been having those moments a lot?"

I shook my head and somehow lifted it from the table in spite of how heavy it felt. To make matters worse, I'd put the confounded sleeve in my breakfast, and it was soaked in gravy. "That was only the second time I've felt that and the first my head has hit a table."

"False memories, Gerard," she warned coldly.

"I know," I answered obediently. "Let me change my shirt." Not waiting to be dismissed, I left, Ismae on my heels. I closed my bedroom door before she could follow me in, but I should have known it wouldn't deter her.

Ismae let herself in and closed the door. "Are you okay? What was it?"

I ran my tongue over my teeth while I unbuttoned the vest. "I hate this. I hate these clothes and being here and feeling like everything is wrong." I balled up the purple vest and threw it to the ground, then practically ripped the shirt off in anger.

"You feel it's wrong?"

"Of course I do!" I shouted. "I saw things with *you*! Things that don't make sense. Don't match up with what I remember."

"What *do* you remember?"

I looked down at the shirt still in my hands. "I remember giving you the rose, the one I enchanted to put you under a spell. I didn't complete the spell correctly, and it bled out, putting your entire castle under the enchantment. It worked better for me because it forced you to come with me to find your ruby." There were other memories, though, shadows I couldn't grasp even with magic and didn't want to tell Ismae.

She touched my arm. I hadn't even heard her draw near and cursed myself for being so distracted. "There's more," she insisted.

"Of course there's more." I lay the shirt at the foot of my bed and marched to the closet to try and find something else to put on that wouldn't try and kill me.

Ismae gave a frustrated sigh. "Gerard, maybe if you stopped resisting those memories, you would remember how you love me."

"Stop saying that!" I wheeled around to face her.

"Stop yelling at me!" she shouted back.

I blanched and straightened, startled that she would react to me so boldly. The surprise was momentary, and I glared. "I don't love you, and you don't love me. If I ever said that to you, I must have been trying to get something."

"You tried that trick on Elisa, my best friend, remember? You pretended to be engaged to her. I threw a vase at your head when I recognized you." She twitched a brow.

The familiar metallic tang of magic floated in the air, and once again, I saw white as pain coursed through my mind, and my body struck the hard ground.

FOUR

"Oops. I'm really sorry," Ismae said.

I peeled an eye open. The room tilted back and forth like I was on a boat, and I clamped my eyes shut again with a groan to hold back the roll in my stomach making me want to vomit for the second time that morning. My left knee and shoulder ached from where I hit the floor, not to mention my head.

"What . . . happened?"

"You passed out. I tried to use my magic to get you to remember, but Selina must have strengthened the block on your memories during breakfast." She stroked my cheek.

I should have pushed her away, shunned her touch, asked her to leave. But her touch felt familiar. Soothing. I had felt her touch before, and that touch held memories I both longed to access and was afraid to. Her touch made the churning in my stomach calm down.

Slowly, I opened my eyes again to look up at Ismae.

She gave me a soft smile and started to let go.

I found myself holding her wrist and saying, "Don't stop."

Her smile couldn't have grown any bigger, and her fingers again touched my cheek. "Do you remember something?"

She was dangerous.

I finally got enough strength in myself to escape from her and sat up. "You made me pass out by using spells? But ones you didn't have to speak. You did it earlier, with your dress."

Ismae leaned back on her ankles and shrugged a shoulder. "I do have magic, orator magic. You taught me that. But I don't think it was me so much as it was the spell Selina put on you. I think she suppressed your memories of me specifically."

"She couldn't do that," I snorted.

"No, *she* couldn't. But Vivian could."

I stared at the princess.

She raised her brows at me.

"It makes sense," I conceded. "She took Vivian's heart. You think she's using Vivian's powers to control me?"

"Why else would she have taken Vivian's heart?" Ismae countered. "She regained full control over you. You were going to leave her, Gerard. You were going to take the stones and do all of this on your own, leaving her behind. You wanted to fix all of this yourself. She couldn't afford to have you do that for whatever reason."

"How do you know all this?" I wanted to shout but found myself too exhausted. My head still hurt.

Ismae tilted her head. "Ask yourself that question." She rose to her feet and dusted at her golden skirts. "Let's go check out that wizard academy. I'm excited to see it."

"No."

Her smile dropped. "No?"

I grunted as I hoisted myself to my feet with the aid of the bed. "You're staying here. This is the third time your stupid memories have caused me to see white and the second to make me pass out completely. I'm not risking that while I'm at the academy." I grabbed the first shirt I saw and ripped the frilly ends off, rolled the sleeves up to my elbows, and put it on.

When I faced Ismae, her lips were drawn tight and I thought she might punch me. "Well, then," she finally said. "I'll have to find some *other* way to keep myself occupied while I'm your prisoner."

"Yes. I tried telling you that this morning."

Her jaw flexed as she gathered her skirts. She stormed to my door. "Don't bother finding me for lunch or dinner. I don't want to speak with you for the rest of the day." She slammed the door shut behind her.

I let out a sigh and put the vest back on before I made my way down to the academy. It was a long walk, and I had plenty of time to take in the sights and smells of the city once again. Only this time, the people of Servad were setting up their wares and preparing for the day. Women were out shopping with each other, and men merrily flirted with them.

But wherever I walked, people threw sidelong glances my way.

If I truly did look like my father, I supposed it would make sense they would stare. They saw Tovan, only younger than he should have been, younger than when last they saw him, and without his sun magic.

My thoughts suddenly shifted.

If my father had sun magic, why didn't he just break out of the cell or prison he was placed in? If he controlled time, he could have gone back and fixed whatever spell Selina had put on the stones in the first place. I would have a chance to be raised with my family then.

Selfish thoughts, but true.

The academy bustled with energy when I entered through the front doors. The frozen fish in the ceiling were swimming now, and the paintings on the walls were having hushed conversations with each other. Students scrambled on their way to their next class—up the staircase or through the doorways leading away from the main room in which I stood. Teachers ushered them on.

Thinking I could blend in with the crowd of students, I slipped in and followed a group up the main staircase and broke off when I reached the library—it wasn't difficult to find, considering the wide doorway without a door.

A thin man with a gaunt face stood just inside and stuck his hand out, halting me. "You do not belong here."

"And why not?" I asked with indignation.

"You are not a student. And before you ask how I know, you wear no wizard robes."

After a quick survey of the room, I realized everyone wore a robe and immediately felt foolish for not recognizing sooner or for remembering those details from my father's journal.

"I must ask you to leave." The man held his hand down the hall. "There is a library in town on the corner of Ocean Avenue and Peak Canyon."

"Do they have books on magic there?"

He chortled. "No. Of course not. We can't have common people attempting spells."

I raised my brow and gestured to my obviously rich garments. "Do I look like common people to you?"

The old man finally looked past my clothing, and his eyes slowly narrowed. "It can't be. You can't be a Du'Prei."

"I am Prince Tovan's son," I said firmly. "Gerard Tovan Du'Prei."

He didn't appear to believe me.

I let out an annoyed sigh. "You must not have heard about the disruption with time? Servad was locked in time for sixteen years, and the surrounding kingdoms and towns promptly forgot about you. So, yes, I am Tovan's son but grew while he was stuck here with the rest of you."

He rubbed his chin and gave a glance at a student watching us from beside a bookcase.

The student quickly looked away.

"Come with me, boy."

"It's Gerard," I repeated as he walked past.

He didn't seem to care, and I rolled my eyes before following him. I expected him to lead me out the front doors and tell me to leave or to take me to the meeting with all of the Terns, but instead, he took me to an empty room with white walls, a windowed ceiling, and a tiled floor.

I stopped at the door. "You won't fool me into walking into a prison as well."

He shook his head with a chuckle. "This is no prison. Do you sense magic? This is a practice room," he continued when I remained silent. "I know Tovan is locked away here by the queen's orders. If you are truly Tern Tovan's son and want to help him, I would like to see what magic you can do."

"A trial?" I raised my brows.

The man nodded and motioned for me to enter.

I had two choices—trust the man, enter the room, show him what I could do, and impress him, or stand there and get nowhere. My intention wasn't to be accepted into the academy. I knew everything I needed to about magic. All I wanted to do was find books on how to take someone's heart and reverse those spells so I could figure out if the others were right and I had Selina's heart.

"Are you afraid you won't live up to your father's reputation?" he challenged.

I took note of the smirk. I knew he was baiting me. Relenting, I entered the stark room and stopped five paces from the wizard. "You want to see what I can do?"

He nodded eagerly. "Whatever spells you can do. Let's see them."

My head still twinged, and I wasn't in the mood, but the old man was asking me to prove my power to him. I wasn't going to disappoint.

Holding my hands out to both sides of my body, I called upon the familiar sensation magic brought—burning and tingling in my extremities. Without hesitation, the underworld answered. A pool of darkness spread from beneath my feet and out toward the wizard. I called upon the undead, deciding to show him everything I could bring forth. Skeletons and corpses crawled out of the hole, anxious for a chance at being on the earthly plane. I even summoned a low-class demon that was nothing more than an imp. A more powerful one would be gloating.

The man gasped. "Death magic. You're a death mage?"

"I prefer the term necromancer."

"Return them. What else can you do?"

A zombie hobbled toward the wizard, who took several steps away with a disgusted scowl on his face. The corpse's arm dropped to the ground, and the wizard sneered. I used the magic, like the thread of puppet strings, to pull the corpse away and back into the underworld. I kicked the arm in after him before sealing the portal.

"Lovely," the man mumbled.

"I can manipulate shadows as well," I offered.

"Show me."

So I did. I drew his shadow away from where the light made it land on the wall, lengthened the shadows in the edges of the room, and expanded the darkness to try and squelch the light.

The wizard waved his hand dismissively before I could. "You have high proficiency in the dark arts. What other magic do you know? Light magic? Show me that." He walked to the window, retrieved a pot of soil, and placed it in the middle of the room.

Seeing the pot reminded me of when I'd first discovered my necromancy powers. I was nine and Selina was trying to get me to control the earth.

"But Selina!" I whine. "It's too hot and I'm tired!"

"Too hot?" She raises her brows at me from where she sits on a lichen-covered boulder at the edge of our current town, Aberdeen.

Behind her, the wooden main house looks like a grass-covered hill. Except for the torches. And wooden walls. And windows. So it doesn't look like a hill, but the grass on the roof helps keep it warm when winter hits.

Selina wears a simple green dress with a layer of blue skirts and has a silver wolf's pelt for a coat. Her long black hair is bundled up in a tight braid.

My hair is brown, unruly, and in much need of a wash, which Selina promises I will get when I am done with my training for the day—if I ever get done with my training.

I stand in the center of a ring of short, dark, carved stones. She calls it a fairy ring, but I have never seen fairies, and I remember the stories from the sages to the south who told stories of fairy rings being made of flowers, not pieces of rock. I've heard the shaman woman call them runestones.

"Put your hands back out in front of you and try the spell again," Selina urges.

I roll my eyes and stick my hands out in front of me.

"No. Palms down! You don't want to shoot your magic into the sky. Vines don't grow in the clouds," she scolds.

I turn my hands over. My gangly nine-year-old body is outgrowing my clothes, and I notice how long the gap is between my sleeves and my wrists. "Hemsing dart—"

"Hemsung!" she snaps, emphasizing the uh.

"Hemsung dart et purd." Green light shoots from my hands and hits the ground, just as she wanted. I grin and look over at her. "I did it!"

Selina is massaging her temple. "No, you didn't. You just called to a mountain troll."

My face pales and hands go clammy. "What? How!"

"You didn't clear the spell before restarting it, and you said purd instead of purdt. You didn't emphasize the T." She rises to her feet. "Gerard, are you paying attention in our lessons at all?"

"I told you I'm tired! I've been out here all day and didn't even get to eat lunch!"

"You have to earn that."

"Haven't I?" I stomp my foot. "None of the other kids are out here in a stupid circle of rocks! They all get to go play and pretend to be warriors and go home and eat when their moms and dads say."

Selina crouches in front of me. "You don't have a mother or father. They pretend to be warriors, pretend to use magic. Gerard, you're not like the others. You have real magic. You don't need to pretend."

My stomach sinks, and I look away. "But I want to play."

"Not until you get this spell right."

"But Selina—"

"No more arguing," she says with finality, her eyes narrowing.

I bite my bottom lip and nod.

Selina straightens, then starts walking away to a safe distance.

"Aren't you going to tell the troll to not come?"

"Oh, yes." She spreads her hand out toward the ground and a spark of red magic travels away toward the distant mountains. "Try again."

I try a second time. Third time. Seventh. Tenth. Finally, out of frustration, I shout the words and a huge ball of green magic hits the ground and ignites the grass around me in green flames.

Selina quickly used her magic to douse it and then puts her hands on her hips. "Gerard Tovan Du'Prei!"

she scolds. "Get your mind focused now! You've wasted the entire day!"

I start wailing. Lifting my head to the sky, I drop to my rear and let my limbs fall to the ground. "I can't! I'm hungry and tired!"

"Enough!" Selina shouts. A crack of lightning hits the mountain and an echo of thunder rumbles toward us. "You will stop your crying, you will get to your feet, and you will cast this spell or you are not getting dinner either. Now stand up!"

I rub at my eye.

She scares me when she gets mad.

I climb off the ground, hating everything about being out there. I never get to play with the other kids, I never get to pretend to be a warrior—sometimes I don't care that I have magic. Why does Selina care so much anyway?

With a sniffle, I mumble the spell.

"Not good enough."

I groan and say it again.

"Gerard, I'm growing impatient."

Anger burns through my chest. I have been in the sun all day, not given a moment's break, been denied lunch, and haven't been given the chance to play. Now she says I am not good enough? I have been working the hardest I can!

I let the anger feed me, even though Selina has warned me about it more than once, and growl through my teeth. My hands tighten into fists, and I let out a shout of frustration as I slam my fist into the ground. An enormous black pool spreads around me, and I drop into its darkness.

It isn't water, yet I can't breathe.

I flounder around, grasping at anything but touching nothing. My feet finally settle on something, and I gasp, gulping in air. But when I open my eyes, I never imagined I'd see what stands before me.

Corpses.

Skeletons.

All kinds of dead things, all with their eyeless sockets focused on me. I don't belong there. And they know it. I look up, not sure how I can make it back out. Did I jump? Climb? Fall?

My heart starts pounding in my ears.

The dead things around me seemed to all realize at the same moment that I am unwelcome, or rather that I am still alive, and all scramble toward me. Selina has never trained me on what to do with the dead. That is far beyond any magic we have gotten to, and I know of only one thing to do.

I scream.

Skeleton fingers scratch my arms, corpses tear at my clothes, and something draws blood as it slams against the side of my head. I scream for help again, pleading for someone to save me. I don't know where I am or who would come to my aid, but I have to try.

"Stop!" I shout with everything in my small body.

All of the dead things freeze.

Startled, I slowly lift my gaze from behind my fingers. The creatures stand unmoving.

I rub my eye with my fist, clearing the tears. "Back off," I say, trying to sound stern.

Those gathered around me lower their hands and step back several paces.

I stare at them in bewildered silence. They are listening to me?

"Impressive," a voice speaks from behind.

I glance over my shoulder and see a man with his arms folded and wearing elegant black clothing with red glinting from light that didn't seem to come from anywhere in particular. "Wh-who are you?"

"You may call me Nicholas. I thought I felt a living thing, though I certainly wasn't expecting a boy." He smiles, lowering his arms, and when he reaches me, he crouches and holds his hand out to me. "May I help you to your feet?"

I accept his help. His grip is strong as he rights me. "What are you? Who are you? Why are you here? And . . . where is here?"

Nicholas holds his hands out to either side, presenting the darkness around us. "This? Why, this is the underworld. Not what you imagined it to be?"

"I . . . was taught the dead go to Valhalla. No, that is the good dead. This is . . ." I scrunch my face and tap my head, trying to remember the different places the dead of Ashwrya go. "This is Hel!" I gasp. "Are you . . . no, the goddess Hel is a woman, and you are not."

Nicholas's thin lips tug at the corner in a wry smile. "I am not, nor have I ever been a woman. I'm certain you want to go back to the surface world?"

"How do I get out?" I look up.

"You didn't fall through the ceiling. You walked through a door." He extends his hand to the left.

I follow his gaze and see a massive black door with golden hinges and a handle. "Oh. I don't remember opening it."

"I'll help you open it if you help me."

"How can I help you? You're dead," I point out.

Nicholas laughs, an unnatural sound amongst the dead—who are still watching us. "No, I'm not. I am no corpse. But I have a feeling I will see you again, especially since you show such strength with the undead. Tell your teacher you're a necromancer."

"What's that?"

"She'll understand." He gives me a wink and walks to the door. "I didn't get your name?"

"Gerard." I grab the handle, pull the door open, and step into the thick murkiness I had felt when I fell through the puddle I'd made. I somehow know to pull the door closed behind me, and when the lock clicks, the feeling of suffocation disappears.

When I open my eyes, I am standing in the middle of the fading pool of darkness, facing Selina.

She stands at the edge of the rune stones, her eyes wide, face pale, and mouth agape. "Gerard," she says breathlessly. The instant the black pool is gone, she is holding my hands, prodding my shoulders, and turning my face. "What happened?"

I gasp. "I'm a necromancer."

FIVE

The wizard patted my back when I completed my last spell. "You are a very impressive young wizard. Tovan will be proud to hear of all you can do."

"I feel a 'but' coming," I said through pants of breath. I was exhausted and starving. What time was it?

"But I don't think you've realized your full potential." He lowered his hand and lifted his shoulders. "I can sense you're holding back. You use necromancy because it is familiar, but necromancy is so much more than summoning forth dead things to battle." He relaxed and exited the room, expecting me to follow as he continued to speak. "I would like to present you to the Council of Terns and have you placed in one of the branches here to train your magic further."

"Uh . . ." I dragged out, then rushed after him. "I don't think that's—I mean, I didn't come here seeking an apprenticeship or anything like that. I only need access to your library."

"And as a student, you will have that access granted."

"But I don't need to learn anything else."

"Don't you?" He looked over his shoulder, pausing on the staircase. "Every wizard has something more to learn. You admitted your enchantments bled, you can't utilize light magic to save your life, and even your earth magic is shoddy. The only thing you're confident in is your control of the undead."

I frowned. "How is that bad?"

"Because wizards must have an understanding of all of the elements. Not mastery, but each wizard must have a balance. If you were to meet another necromancer, they could pull that power away from you, and then to what will you resort? Or a powerful light wizard who could squelch your darkness?"

"I suppose I never thought of that," I admitted. It wasn't exactly like Selina cared. She'd just wanted me to find whatever I was powerful at and strengthen it.

"Good. It is settled. Come to me tomorrow and we will take you to the council."

We stood in the foyer, and only then did I see the darkness coming through the windows. "I hadn't realized it was so late," I admitted.

"They say time passes quickly when one is having a delightful time." He chuckled.

"Wait," I said when he turned to retire. I sucked in a breath, suddenly not as confident as I had been.

"What sort of power does it take to steal one's heart without killing them?"

The man's face grew grim and he stepped close. "Do not *ever* attempt such magic. Do not even read books on it."

I shook my head. "I'm not interested in it myself. I ran into a sorceress who . . ."

He stared me down, trying to see if I was lying or perhaps trying to work figure out if he knew her.

"She took the heart of another sorceress named Vivian who lives in the Weeping Woods on the edge of Arington." The words tumbled from my mouth before I realized I'd spoken. "She can use the magic from that heart to channel Vivian's magic over minds. And I'm afraid I may have been subject to that magic."

"Hmm." He straightened, and the vice on my tongue loosened. "Interesting." He stroked his chin and slowly turned. "Come to me tomorrow. I will speak with you then."

Knowing I would get nothing else out of the man that night, and too tired and hungry to try, I left the academy and made my way back to the castle. All I wanted to do was have a big meal and fall asleep in my bed.

Luckily for me, Torian was still at the dinner table when I arrived. Selina's plate was gone, and he explained she'd already eaten and that Ismae had been brought dinner since she refused to leave her room to join them.

I'd completely forgotten I'd upset her that morning. As I took my seat, I asked, "Where is Selina then?"

"She had a matter to attend to. Some guests arrived for her."

"Guests?" I set my fork back down after having barely picked it up.

Fearing the worst, I didn't even excuse myself from the table before leaving the dining room and rushing down the hall to the throne room. The day before, she had made plans to send soldiers to attack Ashwrya. When I entered, I was startled to see the guests had familiar faces.

Prince Ulrich and Princess Odette from Terricina stood with their wrists bound in front of them and Captain James Hook between them.

Selina sat on her throne, smirking proudly. "Ah, Gerard! I trust you remember your friends."

Odette and Ulrich turned simultaneously, both with matching scowls of betrayal etched on their faces.

"What are you doing?" I asked, shifting my attention from them to Selina. Realizing the error of my wording before she could, I quickly corrected myself. "I mean, what are they doing here?"

"James is helping me to fulfill my plans." Selina walked down from the throne and patted James on the cheek.

When James turned as Selina walked past him to me, I saw the vacant expression on his face and remembered something I'd long forgotten. Selina had James's hand. She could control him.

"You seem surprised," Selina said, sliding her arm around my shoulders.

"I . . . am. I don't see why you need these two."

"I need them all," she replied casually. "James will help me to collect Princess Elisa next, and *you* shall bring Prince Mathias and Princess Tavia to me in the meantime." She lowered her arm and stepped in front of me. "Won't you."

Hesitating could mean punishment, so I nodded. "Certainly, Selina."

"Good boy." She patted my cheek.

I hated when she did that.

She turned back to James. "Bring them here as soon as you can, but make sure Elisa doesn't suspect. Stifling the magic of a dragon is difficult. We'll need her to bring Quist to us."

"You're just going to stand there?" Ulrich snapped at me.

I shifted my gaze to him, keeping my face unreadable. I didn't know Selina's plan. She hadn't included me in any of this. I didn't understand why she needed to gather all of the princes and princesses, unless . . . unless it was for some kind of horrific revenge.

"Why don't you send them a letter instead of raising suspicions by capturing them?" I offered, turning back to Selina.

Selina stopped speaking with James and looked over her shoulder at me.

I rounded my shoulders. "If you abduct them, their parents will know. If you sent a royal decree, say . . . to a celebration, that would draw them all here anyway. Wouldn't it?"

"I . . . hadn't considered that," Selina muttered with a frown.

I nodded. "I am going to go eat dinner and go to bed."

"Where were you today?"

I lingered by the door. "I walked around the city and went to the academy. You told me I could."

"What did you do at the academy?"

I shook my head and put my fists on my hips. "They kicked me out. I'm not a student, therefore I'm not allowed to be in there. Some old man that very nearly looked like a corpse was the one who told me I couldn't even see Tovan's office."

"Ah, Tern Colter. Brilliant man. Too bad he didn't want you there." She turned her back to James.

I hesitated. "Do you *want* me to learn there?"

"What else could you possibly learn that I haven't already taught you?" Her air of arrogance on the verge of laughter made my skin crawl.

"Anything? Perhaps light magic? You know I'm horrible at it."

Her eyes narrowed. "To what end?"

I shrugged. "Learning something new?"

She took me in with a suspicious gaze but nodded. It was as close to a *yes* I was going to get. "You're dismissed."

Ulrich glowered at me as I passed. After all, I had spent time with him on James's ship. He was exploring magic and was rather good at it, but I helped him perfect a few things. He always worked on spells that caused mischief. We might have even been considered friends had it not been for me constantly betraying them all.

Confused and overwhelmed with information, I sat and ate my dinner in silence, even when Torian attempted to make conversation. Eventually, he folded and left.

What would Ismae do when I told her about her friends?

I finished dinner and walked to my room, but found myself standing outside of Ismae's door like I had the night before. She had told me not to bother her the rest of the day, that she hadn't wanted to see me, but . . . I couldn't talk to anyone else.

Pushing aside my pride, I straightened and knocked loudly on her door.

"Who is it?"

"Gerard."

Inside the room, a chair scooted across the floor, and then the sound of footsteps drew closer before the door opened and Ismae stood before me.

She wore a long white nightgown and her brown hair had been brushed. She looked both relieved and annoyed to see me. "What do you want?" she demanded, keeping her hand on the door.

"I wanted to speak with you."

"Come to apologize?"

I paused. "For what?"

She rolled her eyes and tried to shut the door, but I put my foot in the way.

"You left me alone all day today!" she shouted in a whisper.

"You told me to!"

"Only *after* you said you would abandon me and not take me with you to the academy." She tried slamming the door again. "Move your foot!"

Placing my hand on the door, I leaned forward. "Ismae, I *need* to talk to you. It's important, and I have no one else to go to."

With a huff, she stepped back, then stormed over to the chair beside the glowing fire. I found the fire rather unnecessary, considering how warm it was outside.

"What is it? Tell me so you can go." She refused to look at me.

After closing the door, I used my magic to try and sense any magic lingering in the walls or floor—just to make sure Selina was preoccupied and not listening in. I even made sure to check for mirrors, but the only mirror in the room was over the vanity and didn't give off any magical energy.

Certain we were safe and alone, I walked to Ismae and sat on the rug in front of her. "Please don't be mad."

"I have every reason to be mad," she answered stubbornly.

"Ismae . . . Odette and Ulrich are here."

"What?" She gasped and jumped to her feet.

I reached out and grabbed her nightgown, tugging it to keep her down. "Sit. Please, sit."

"Let go." She kicked at my hand. "I'm going to go see them! Where are they?"

"Will you *please* listen to me? For crying out loud, I shouldn't have to shout to get through to you!"

Ismae clamped her mouth shut but didn't sit.

I shifted to my knees. "A while ago, Selina took James's hand. It's complicated, but she took it as an act of payment. With magic, if you possess a part of someone, be it blood or hair or—"

"Hand."

I nodded. "You can control that person."

Ismae finally lowered back down into her chair. "She is controlling James. She used James to bring Odette and Ulrich here."

"Exactly."

"Why tell me this?" she whispered.

"Because I don't know what to do," I admitted. "No matter how desperately I would love to just fall into the role of a prince, I'm not cut out for fancy clothes and sitting on my . . . rear all day." I took note of my near slip of a cuss word and stopped myself from saying it in front of Ismae. She was a lady.

Ismae's lip tugged in a small smile. "Told you it wasn't you."

I lifted my lip in a half-smile back at her and her smile grew.

"I love it when you smile like that," she said softly, only to blush and look away.

I rubbed the back of my neck. "Yeah. Um. There's more, though."

"What do you mean?"

"More than Selina just taking them. She wants the others too. She's asked me to fetch Mathias and Tavia."

Ismae balked. "What? Why?"

Shaking my head, I held up my hands in a gesture of defeat. "I don't know, but I didn't try and get it out of her either. She seemed to be on edge, but I suggested she send invitations to a made-up celebration instead of capturing them. Things get worse. She's sending an army to Ashwrya."

"Gerard . . ."

"I don't know what to do," I said firmly. "This isn't my fight. I did what she wanted me to do, I set time back to normal, I'm . . . I'm here. I'm home. I should be spending my time learning more magic or . . . something." I leaned back and turned my attention to the flames.

Ismae slid out of the chair and onto her knees before me. She cupped my face. "Gerard . . . You're right. Your fight is here." She placed her hand on my chest. "As long as you bear the weight of Selina's heart, you will never be able to be at peace. You must find a way to return it to Selina. If you do that, she will return to herself and stop all of this madness."

"Where do I even start?" I whispered, my throat feeling tight. "I don't know who to trust. What if the wizards are under Selina's command too? If I go to them, they could warn her."

"I happen to know a wizard who isn't."

"Besides me." I frowned.

She laughed. "Besides you. Your father. You need to speak with Tovan."

I stared at her like she had two heads. "He's in prison for a reason."

"Yes, for standing up against Selina." Ismae rested her hands in her lap. "Gerard, if you had evil plans to take over the world, why would you lock away one of the most powerful wizards? What has she been doing to you all of these years? Control."

Shaking my head, I got to my feet so I could pace. "I don't want to get involved in this."

"You're already involved in it."

"But . . ." I looked to the window, to the lights of the city below. "I went to the academy today. That's where they're keeping my father. Because they have prison cells that are magical and apparently have the strength to confine his magic."

Ismae was soon behind me and slid her arms around my waist. "You're so much stronger—"

I pulled away. "Stop. Whatever magic you're using, stop. It makes my head want to explode."

Ismae looked helpless when I faced her. "I just want you to remember me!"

"Well, I don't want to! It hurts!" I shouted back.

"You're always so stubborn." She folded her arms and glared hard. "Grow a pair and go see your dad."

"I've already spoken to him once."

"Yes, for like ten minutes. You got no helpful information about returning Selina's heart and ending all of this!"

Half frustrated, half annoyed, and maybe a lot angry at myself, I groaned and ran my hand over my face.

Ismae didn't add anything else. What else could she *possibly* have to say anyway?

Eventually, I faced her. "Okay, you're right. The reason I went to the academy today was to go to the library and see what I could find about getting rid of her heart. There was an old wizard who met me and told me I wasn't allowed to touch books on that kind of magic, so I have a feeling they are restricted."

She raised her brows. "Gerard."

"Fine! Fine, I'll . . ." I drew a steadying breath. "I will speak with my father first thing. I promise."

She smiled softly and nodded, then roamed over to the chair and picked at the blanket laying across the back of it. "I guess I should wish you a good night's sleep."

I crossed the room and looked at her when I set my hand on the door's handle. "Ismae, for whatever reason . . . I mean, I shouldn't have . . . What I'm trying to say is I'm sorry for leaving you alone today. I don't have . . . friends. I don't know how to do this."

Ismae's eyes softened. "I know."

"Um. I guess thank you for being patient?"

"You do know you aren't leaving me here when you go on whatever quest you need to go on in order to return Selina's heart. Right?"

I frowned. "Why would you want to go?"

She rolled her eyes. "Because I don't want to stay here alone with her."

"Ah." I nodded. After a brief moment of silence, pondering how miserable she must have been locked up all day, I looked over at her again. "Would you like to go see the gardens?"

Ismae's eyes lit up, and she grabbed her robe without even a second thought. She pulled her arms through the sleeves, stepped into her slippers, then hurried back to my side while tying the robe closed.

"You're excited about this, aren't you?"

"Are you kidding? This is the palace in the capital of our country! It's been frozen for sixteen years, and I can't wait to see what flowers and plants they have." She unexpectedly looped her arm through mine, and the heat of a blush crept onto my cheeks.

I hadn't been to the gardens yet myself, and judging by the way it looked on the outside, the palace appeared to have more than one garden. Princess Ismae and I went down the nearest staircase and through a series of doors until we finally made it outside.

Her smile was worth it.

"You know, when this is all over, I would love to sleep out under the stars with you again," she said.

"You have fond memories?"

She nodded and turned her gaze to me. Her eyes reflected the starlight. "I mean, not all of it was good. You and I hated each other at first."

"Oh?"

She grimaced. "Yes. But before you ask why, I'm going to say it doesn't matter. Because we got over it and we were happy."

I felt myself smiling. "So am I allowed to ask why?"

"Nope." She rested her head on my shoulder, and my heart pounded against my ribs. "Do you think you'll ever remember me?"

I was overwhelmed by a flurry of thoughts. On one hand, if it was true, yes. On the other hand, if she was lying, no. The familiar ache from trying to remember her began to wash over my mind, and I shook my head. "It's too bad it's so late at night and you can't see anything out here."

"I don't care."

"You don't? Isn't that the point of coming outside?"

"Not if I get to spend time with you."

I rubbed the back of my neck again, grateful for the disguise of darkness to hide my blush. To our right, fireflies danced around a flower with multiple stems. The petals had a blue glow almost like bioluminescence and yet, at the same time, looked like the moonlight was hitting them just right.

A shiver ran through Ismae and then another.

"Should we go in now?" I asked softly.

"I suppose." She straightened and pulled her hair over one shoulder. "Thank you. You'll have to take me when the sun is out and we can look at everything under proper light."

I took her inside and back to her room, but she lingered at the door.

So did I.

"Tomorrow, we will figure out how to help them, Ulrich and Odette." She looked up into my eyes. "And when we have them free, they will help us with your heart."

"Let's see how tomorrow plays out first. Sleep well, Princess Ismae." I gave a polite nod.

She bit her lip, and I read in that look that she wanted me to stay or at least leave her with a goodnight kiss. She reluctantly closed the door, though, and I turned away to stroll to my room to clear my head and worry about the next day instead.

I would get to speak with my father.

SIX

Breakfast was tense. Torian said little and seemed to be distracted. I suspected Selina had taken his heart in order to keep him in line. No one would be okay with their son being locked away in prison, and Torian hadn't brought up Tovan at all that morning.

Ismae had no desire to be any closer to Selina than she needed to and remained surprisingly quiet during the meal.

Selina slid a small stack of papers to her husband with a wooden box holding thin bricks of purple-colored wax, a deep metal spoon, and a thick, wide candle. "I need you to put your seal on these documents. I'm sending an official decree out to our people asking for them to gather this evening so we can explain what happened with time. I'm certain by now some of them may have caught on, especially if they've traveled anywhere outside of Servad in the last day or so."

"Ah, certainly." The king removed his signet ring and broke a few pieces of the purple wax into the spoon while Selina rose to light the candle from one of the wall sconces.

She set it on the table in front of King Torian. He held the spoon over the flame and we all watched silently as the wax began to melt. It didn't take much time, and Torian poured a pool of wax at the bottom of the first document, but his ring lingered over it. His brows pinched as if he were struggling to remember what he was doing or perhaps arguing with himself not to.

"Go on, dear," Selina urged.

Torian pressed his ring into the cooling wax without reading the parchment.

Selina played with the hair on the back of his neck. Judging by the proud expression on Selina's face, I knew she'd slipped in the papers to declare war on Ashwrya. I drew a breath, ready to warn him, but Selina gave me a look from the corner of her eyes that made me finish my meal quickly and leave the dining hall.

She knew I knew.

Ismae, having finished her meal, scurried after me. "Are you certain I can't come to the academy? I'll even stay in a sitting room if I must." She caught my arm. "Please don't leave me with her. Who knows what she'll do when you leave? I'll try and search the castle for Ulrich and Odette and likely get in trouble, which will then get you in trouble, and—"

"Yes."

She blinked and took a gasp of breath. “Really?”

I opened the front door of the palace, ignoring the guard who tried to reach and open it for me. “I’m beginning to realize you struggle with remaining in one place. How do you keep yourself entertained at home?”

“I devour books.” She hurried down the palace stairs at my side. “I could read all day and be satisfied. You promised to send me books on magic to help me with oration, so maybe the wizards wouldn’t mind letting me borrow a book or two.”

I gave her a sideways glance.

“It was before you left me to get the stones from Selina and ended up not returning. Besides, how else am I to learn how to control my magic?” she countered before I could utter a word.

A few people looked at us and whispered behind their hands as we passed. An old man lifted the canopy of a wagon outside a bakery and returned with warm trays of rolls smelling of cardamom and sprinkled with sugar.

Ismae stopped. “What are these called?”

“Vetebröd. Want to try some?” The man smiled and held one out.

“We haven’t any money with us,” Ismae replied.

He waved his hand as if it didn’t matter. “If you like it, you will come back. Maybe even purchase a lot for the palace.” He looked at me.

Ismae accepted the roll, tore a piece off, and handed it to me. She tore a second piece and put it in her mouth. I watched her eyes widen before I ate the piece she'd given me. It was warm, close to a cinnamon roll but less sweet.

"This is very good," I admitted.

The man's wrinkled eyes scrunched in pride when he smiled. "Thank you. Enjoy your day."

Walking to the academy was unusually comfortable. Ismae continued to share her treat while she pointed out pieces of architecture I hadn't noticed on the buildings—how the under part of the roofs were held up by carved pieces of wood on each corner of the buildings, or how one building looked like two had been stacked on top of each other because nothing lined up, or the windows of another building that had thick glass with bubbles in it.

"How do you think it happens?" I asked.

She shrugged. "I just know old windows are like that. The academy is absolutely beautiful. This whole city is! I could walk the streets all day."

I entered the academy first, and Tern Colter was there waiting.

He arched a brow at Ismae. "You brought a lady friend?"

"She wanted to get out of the castle. I don't know if anyone could help, but she has oration magic and no one to teach her." I stepped to the side, presenting Ismae. "This is Princess Ismae from Arington."

"How do you do?" She gave a princessly curtsy and delicate smile.

"We don't train women here. This is a wizard academy. What you need is the sorceress academy, and that—"

"As I said, she doesn't have anyone to teach her." I hinted with my brows.

Tern Colter folded his arms. "Perhaps . . . maybe we can find someone. For now, is there something you would like to do? Gerard will be busy most of the day."

"Can I see your library?" She grinned.

"She has a thing for books," I mumbled.

He chuckled. "A lady after my own heart. Come this way!" He led us to the library.

It was nothing as I dreamed it could have been, and not the one I'd seen the first time I'd snuck my way into the academy. With the use of magic, no doubt, the wizards had placed an enormous library into a closet. Literally. Tern Colter opened the door to what should have been a closet, yet it opened to a three-floor library with thousands of books organized on floor-to-ceiling shelves. Chairs and desks were positioned in the center of the room and end of each shelf, creating places for readers to spend their time, and many of them were occupied by students.

Ismae hadn't even stepped into the room yet and her mouth hung agape.

Tern Colter chuckled. "I have a feeling you may be able to spend your time in here. Is there anything else you may need?"

She blinked as she came to. "Perhaps a parchment and quill so I can take notes?"

"Certainly. The wizards at the center desks will help you. The only warning I must give is that you cannot open the doors along the outer walls. Enjoy your day." He bowed his head.

She turned to me with a childish grin. "In the underworld, when I died, I woke up in a room with a library very similar to this."

"That was your heaven?" I chuckled.

"And I left it to get back to you," she pointed out. "Now let's see what I can find to help you." She gathered her skirts and eagerly rushed to the main desk.

"She has a lot of spunk."

"You have no idea." I faced the tern. "I had hoped . . . I wondered if I may speak with my father before we practice anything."

Tern Colter gave a knowing smile and waved his hand for me to follow once again. He directed me up several staircases, through hallways that made no sense, and finally ended at a metal door that took up an entire wall. I wouldn't be able to find my way back on my own.

A dragon lay curled up in front of it and lifted its head when we drew near.

"Tern Colter and—"

"Gerard. Eldest son of Tern Tovan Torian Du'Prei, necromancer, lost soul." The dragon's white eyes saw right through me. The dragon was about the size of a horse and had bird feathers on its wings. "I am the guardian of the prison. You wish to visit with your father to gain help with . . . a problem."

I swallowed nervously. "Yes. I don't know who else would know other than him, and . . . it's sort of important."

The dragon's gaze darted to Tern Colter.

"I'll leave you be. Redeshka, let me know when Gerard is finished so I can guide him back to his lessons." The tern left us alone.

The dragon, Redeshka, didn't budge. Those knowing eyes tore into me, and I couldn't look away. "Your heart is not your own."

"It is why I need to speak with my father," I answered softly. "Things are happening, and I fear I may be the only one able to stop them. But I have to get this out first." I tapped my fingers on my chest.

"You are safe here. Prying eyes cannot see, nor prying ears hear. He cannot use magic, nor will you be able to while you are inside." She finally took her gaze away, and I felt like I could breathe again. "You may enter."

I stepped up to the metal door. "Doesn't it need to open?"

"It is."

Giving the dragon a distrusting look, I reached out to touch the metal, but my hand went through it. *Of course. Magic.* I stepped through the mirage of the door and into a room built in the shape of a hexagon with high blank brick walls. The ground had various symbols etched into the stone—wards to suppress magic.

To my right was a bed, to my left was a desk, chair, shelf with books, and a sitting chair.

My father sat in the chair and set his book down when I entered. "Gerard. I am surprised to see you. Please, have a seat." He gestured to the desk chair. "To what do I owe the pleasure?"

"You're mighty calm for a man in a magical cell." I lowered myself into the seat.

He glanced at the cover of the book he held. "I pondered fighting Selina, but I was weak and chose inaction instead. Perhaps it was a foolish choice on my part." He lifted his gaze back to me. "Or perhaps I recognized that the path of helping Selina lies in the hands of my son."

I clenched my teeth.

"What questions do you have?"

"I need to know about Selina's magic. How she takes hearts and uses that power herself. How is that done?"

Tovan shook his head, his golden hair lay over his shoulders and glistened in the dim candlelight. "I'm afraid I can only tell you it is treacherous magic."

"Fath . . . Tovan." I cleared my throat and shifted in my seat. "Selina placed her heart *inside* of me. She hid it *in* me. I need to get it out so I can return it to her. How am I to do that if I don't know what magic she uses?"

"And who relayed this information to you?" He looked me up and down.

"A wizard named Merlin."

He leaned back and stroked his chin. "It is possible he would know. He is Selina's brother, after all. As for freeing her heart . . ." He lifted his shoulders. "I'm afraid I don't know how."

I looked down at my boots. "I was foolish to ask."

"Have you spoken with Selina about it?"

I laughed. "Are you blind? Could you imagine me going up to Selina? 'Pardon me, but your heart is hidden in my chest, and I would like you to remove it.' Please." I scoffed and shook my head. "She would lock me away with you or . . . retrain my mind . . ."

A flash of light blinded me, and my head ached like it had a few times before.

I am bound to a chair with Selina standing before me. Her eyes are black and she is shouting at me, furious. "Tell me everything about her!"

My head pounds. Somehow, I know Selina had been at this for hours, but I can't recall what she was doing. Against my will, yet unable to stop myself, I begin speaking through clenched teeth, "I met Ismae in Arington after I enchanted the castle."

"How did you fall in love with her?"

"I didn't mean to." Pain racks through my mind like nails through mud, and flickers of Ismae's face come and go—sitting by a fire, her bleeding, her laughter, worry, tears, joy, even a kiss.

A nearby chair scooted as someone rose to their feet, and I lifted my gaze to see my father standing in front of me. "She has done more than hide her heart in you."

I massaged the memory from my temples.

"I said I didn't know that magic. However, my familiar was lucky enough to be on a different plane when time froze. I have a feeling he will be able to help you and guide you in how to return Selina's heart to her."

"Quist," I stated.

He smiled sadly once again. "It is a shame that you only got to know me through my journals. I doubt Selina even gave them all to you.

I shook my head. "They ended shortly after you'd first enchanted the stones."

"There is much you missed out on, then. Like how much I loved you. All of the silly things we did. You adored Quist." He chuckled. "He was a kitten under your touch."

I tightened my lips. I wanted to believe it desperately. It was the only thing I had wanted in my entire life—a home and a family. But it seemed too good to be true.

"Forgive me. I remember things much differently than you, it appears." He placed his hand on my shoulder. "I feel robbed, not getting to raise my own children. Are Mathias and Tavia alive and well?"

I nodded.

He squeezed my shoulder and walked to the center of the room to stand with his hands behind his back. "I never meant for any of this to happen."

"If you're a wizard of time, why don't you go back and fix it?" I rose to my feet. "You can go back to you enchanting the stones and choose not to. Or go back and stop Selina's curse on them. Any of it!"

"It isn't that simple. To go back in time, anything I do can alter the future."

"That's sort of the point," I argued.

"Yes, but who is to say what future I could accidentally create? What if it were me and not Selina who became desperate and prideful? And raised you children to be that way too? You wouldn't know the people you know now, and what if they didn't know each other?"

I hadn't considered any of that.

Tovan studied me with apathy. "Time is fickle and dangerous. I may have some power over it, but I am far from being an expert. No wizard who has ever touched time has come away whole. Back then I had only just discovered it if you recall. It would take my lifetime to learn about the magic of time."

I shook my head. "But we could have been a family," I whispered.

"We still can be." He placed his hand on my shoulder again. "Go release your mother from Selina's claws. Hazel will help you find Quist. He was practically as in love with her as I was. Oh, and that young woman you brought with you. Ismae?" He smiled. "The four of you can surely stop Selina."

"Or at least get you out of here and then we can all work together." I felt myself smiling, and for the first time in a long time, I allowed myself to feel the warmth of hope.

Tovan pulled me into a hug.

In spite of all the confusion with how I should react, I allowed myself a moment and wrapped my arms around him. I could get used to hugs.

SEVEN

I sat with my father and told stories about the time I accidentally set an entire meadow on fire when I was learning how to pull the energy of fire from a torch and the time I took a lizard and made him as big as a dog so I could ride him up a mountain. Selina had been furious with me.

Tovan, my father, was impressed.

He laughed.

I felt warmth inside of me I didn't recognize.

He told his own story. "When I was a student, I once thought it was very practical to create something to make my bed for me every morning. I took a toad and used a gargantuan spell, just like you did with the lizard, and tried to give it intelligence enough to make my bed. When I came back from my lessons, my bed was made, but there was a slimy residue on *everything* and the entire room was in disarray. It turned out I had chosen a toad with poisonous mucus. The more advanced students had to catch him and dispel him while I was treated in the hospital wing." He chuckled.

"We're more alike than I thought," I said.

He nodded. "We are. Which is why I know you can do this. Magic that comes from love is far more powerful than any other form of magic. You pull your necromancy powers from fear and pain. Imagine how powerful you could be with love."

I shook my head. "Using that kind of magic means I would have to feel love."

He raised his brows.

I bit my lip. I knew he loved me, he kept saying as much. I knew Ismae loved me too. But that sort of magic was something I had to *feel*. "I've never felt it before. The idea of love scares me," I admitted.

My father nodded. "I can understand why. I hope we have a lot of time to fix that."

"We *could*, you know." I gave a teasing grin.

He winked. "I've got to get out of here first."

"Right." I slowly exhaled and rose to my feet. "I enjoyed spending time with you."

"I look forward to the next time we speak." Father gave me a smile that warmed me to my core and made me long for more.

That warmth must have been love.

I left and was in a sort of daze while Tern Colter made our way back to the main areas of the wizarding towers. I came to my senses when we entered the library and cast him a confused look.

"I thought you were going to bring me to the council?"

"The queen has sent a notice throughout the city," he explained. "All must gather at the castle in a few hours. You need to get back to prepare for whatever announcement she makes."

"I'm not ready to go back. I just got here."

"It's past lunchtime." He smiled. "I believe you enjoyed spending time with your father."

I blinked. "So it seems." I entered the library and made my way through rows of bookshelves until I found Ismae sitting at a table in a far corner with books and parchment spread around. She hadn't noticed me yet, so I stopped and just looked at her.

Ismae was beautiful, and it wasn't the first time I'd had that impression. But more than that, she was intelligent, bright, and challenged my attitude when I needed it. If I had once loved her . . . I wouldn't mind falling in love with her again.

I made my way over, catching her attention.

She looked up with a big smile. "Gerard, you wouldn't believe the books they have here! I've found a book all about oration. I had no idea I needed to be so careful with it." She held up a blue leatherbound book, then a second book with an orange-red cover. "And this one is more about *how* the magic happens and where it comes from. I also got this . . . what?" She paused.

I lifted my brows. "Hmm?"

"What are you smiling at?" A blush swept across her face.

"You're cute when you're excited. That's all."

"Cute?"

It was my turn to blush. "I spoke with my father." Absently, I pulled a parchment with notes on it toward me. Her handwriting was pristine.

She slid the pages all together, including the one I was fiddling with, and stacked them. "You can tell me all about it over lunch. I think we should ask to eat on the back patio of the castle. The gardens, I hear, are impeccable in daylight." Setting the paper on top of the books, she gathered it all up into her arms.

"Selina is making an announcement."

"Oh." Ismae grimaced. "Any idea what it's about?"

I shook my head. "I think she's going to tell them they've been stuck here for sixteen years. She'll blame it on my father, try and get the people upset, and . . . whatever she has planned with those pages she had Torian put his seal on."

"Of course she will," Ismae said under her breath. She stopped by the desk and asked if she could take the books with us back to the castle.

The wizard took note of the books, wrote them down, and handed her a small slip of paper. "Bring them back in two weeks. We have students here who will need to use those books too."

"Thank you!" She beamed and practically skipped out of the academy and down the streets, which were already crowded with people.

The crowd only got worse the nearer we got to the castle. Already, the people were gathered and speculating about what the queen and king would announce. I had to take the books from Ismae and grab her hand to guide her through the throng as I pushed my way to the castle steps. The guards nodded as we passed and opened the door for us before I could reach them.

Once in the safety of the palace walls, I finally took a breath. "Maybe cities aren't for me," I said, giving Ismae a nervous laugh.

She tucked her hair behind her ear. "It's different than traveling around in farmland, isn't it?"

"Definitely."

Selina cleared her throat, and I turned to see her in an elegant black gown with her crown upon her head.

Torian stood at her side appearing just as regal. He clapped his hands at me. "Gerard! Hurry, get dressed!"

"And put your *pet* in her room," Selina ordered.

I tightened my lips.

Ismae, gratefully, kept her mouth shut and hurried ahead of me and back to her room.

I followed. "I'm sorry," I said once we made it into her room. I handed her the books.

Ismae shook her head. "It's not your fault she hates everyone. And if you're worried about me not hearing anything, I know exactly which bedroom to go to, to open the window so I can hear whatever she announces." She grinned.

I opened my mouth, about to point out she couldn't have known where to go unless she was sneaking around the palace at night and that doing so would be dangerous, but the young servant boy burst out of my room. "Sire, there you are! Hurry, hurry. I've been searching the entire castle for you." He ran around and pushed against my back, forcing me to my room.

"I'll speak with you after!" I called over my shoulder to Ismae before my door was slammed shut.

The boy was in such a state, I had to tell him to calm down. We had plenty of time to put on the stupid royal clothing.

"I had them change your wardrobe. I recognized how uncomfortable the traditional clothing made you feel and asked them to make something similar to what you wore when you arrived." The boy handed me a pair of trousers.

Proper trousers. Even though they were made out of fine black material, they were still far more comfortable than what I had worn the day before. They reached my ankles, as pants should. The shirt didn't have frilly, dangling sleeves either—they ended at the wrist. The purple vest and black jacket with gold buttons completed the outfit.

The boy stepped back. "Perfect!"

"I never asked your name," I said as I looked at myself in the mirror.

"Oh. My name is Collin, sire."

"Collin, you did well. Thank you for finding me more comfortable clothing." I gave him an approving nod of the head.

Collin beamed and gave a flourishing bow when he opened my door.

Now I just had to face Selina. Or I could use the distraction to get to Hazel . . . I lingered just inside the door and glanced back down the hallway.

"Sire, they are waiting," a guard called.

"Coming." I would have to find another time when Selina was busy.

I ran down the stairs and sucked in a breath before stepping out in front of the city full of people. My stomach jumped into my throat and I nervously tried to clear it away.

King Torian glanced at me and lifted his arms in the air, calming the noise of the crowd. "Thank you for waiting patiently! First and foremost, I would like to present to you my grandson, Gerard Tovan Du'Prei, eldest son of Tovan." His voice echoed down the road as if carried on the wind.

The crowd politely applauded.

Torian nudged me forward to awkwardly wave in response before I retreated behind him and Selina.

"Some of you may remember Gerard from when he was a young child and may be confused why he is now grown. I shall explain. Our son Tovan, your crown prince, cast a spell sixteen years ago that trapped the entire city of Servad in time. The world around us moved on while we remained stagnant. Two days ago, Gerard counteracted that spell and restored time to its proper order. However, we will all still feel the effects of it, meaning any family you had outside of Servad has aged by sixteen years."

Murmurs spread through the crowd.

Selina was making the king give the news, further manipulating him and the people.

"I know this is upsetting information. For now, Tovan has been imprisoned. Unfortunately, Queen

Selina and I have concluded there is only one way to answer for a crime as horrific as this. Tovan has been sentenced to execution."

All breath went out of my lungs.

The crowd gasped collectively.

I stared at the back of Selina's head.

Selina was going to kill Tovan. My father.

The crowd started shouting, erupting in noise and chaos. King Torian tried to silence them by raising his hands, but they only grew louder.

The people were protesting.

I realized for the first time that the people loved my father, and *that* is what showed me the truth of my father's character. Selina had lied to me my entire life about him, and I had foolishly believed her. The people weren't afraid, they weren't angry at *him*. They were shouting, saying that Tovan *didn't* deserve to die, there must be a mistake, something else must have happened, someone else must have been responsible.

Torian was unable to quiet their anger.

Selina stood shocked. She stepped forward then, after basking in their shouts for several moments. "My people! My people! Please know and understand this decision was not made lightly!"

The people began to quiet.

There was no way I could stay out there and pretend I was in on it. I wouldn't show the people during my first time being seen as prince that I supported the murder of my father. I stormed back into the castle and skipped steps as I ran up, more determined than before to do something.

I didn't care if Selina saw me either.

I burst into the royal chambers. A birdcage stood in the corner of the room with Hazel snuggled up and her beak buried in her feathers. I marched over, popped the cage open, and stepped back.

"I know you're my mother. I was foolish for ignoring you, and I need your help. Father needs your help."

The raven turned its head around, searching for Selina, then spread its wings and landed in front of me in the form of a woman with golden hair long enough it touched the ground and a bright smile. "Gerard . . ."

"I know." I clenched my hands into fists.

She reached out and touched my cheek. "I've tried so hard to get your attention all these years but wasn't able to."

I shook my head, causing her to lower her hand. "I'm blind. Please help me. Selina is going to kill Tovan."

She gasped. "She can't! Torian would never . . . She took Torian's heart, didn't she?" Her shoulders fell and her arms dropped down to her sides in defeat.

"I believe so."

"Tell me what to do."

I licked my lips. "I spoke with him today. Tovan, I mean. And he told me to find Quist, that you would know where to look. I'll pack a bag and provisions and we will leave this evening under the cover of darkness."

"We could use a mirror or go through the underworld," she suggested.

I shook my head. "Where would Quist even be?"

She hesitated. "If time is restored . . . perhaps he is back with the dragons? He loved being with them. It would be safe there too."

I nodded. "I'll get you as soon as I have a chance." I turned to go, but my mother caught me by the arm and pulled me into a hug.

She took a deep breath and just . . . held me.

I closed my eyes. "I'm sorry for everything. You've seen all I've done. I must disappoint you."

"No." She released me and rested her hand on my cheek. "I am not disappointed in you one bit. I've been watching you grow up. I've seen the amazing things you've done. I *am* proud of you, and I know your father is too." She kissed my forehead.

Warmth spread into my body and made my chest ache. The heart that wasn't mine twisted. "I'll return once I have everything in order," I repeated. After giving her a brief hug, nothing too intimate, I departed and made my way to Ismae's room. I slipped inside without knocking.

She rushed in after me and took my hands. "She set the execution date for the day of the winter solstice."

"That only gives us a week." I tore my hands out of Ismae's and ran them through my hair. "A week. A week to figure out how to get Selina's heart back to her. You're coming with me. I'm taking Hazel—my mother—and we're going to the Drakespine Mountains to find Quist. Father said he would know how to help. I pray that we find him quickly . . ."

There was a knock, and when I ripped the door open, Sir Adam said, "Selina wishes to speak with you."

With a sigh of frustration, I nodded.

He bowed and left.

"I'll begin packing," Ismae said softly. She had already dragged a bag out from a back corner of her closet. "But you must find me trousers. I learned my lesson trying to travel in dresses. They are not conducive to adventures."

"For what it's worth . . . I'm glad I abducted you." I half-grinned.

She looked up. "Well, for what it's worth, I'm glad you did too." She waved me off. "Go. Go on."

When I entered the throne room, Selina paced the purple rug. The room was empty, save us two. I braced myself before approaching her. She stopped when she spotted me and lifted her chin, staring at me in silence.

I folded my arms. "You're upset I left."

"Yes, I'm upset you left!" she snapped. "The people need to see you!"

"And they did."

"Are you on my side, Gerard?" She leaned close, and the familiar sensation of her trying to read my thoughts pricked across my mind.

"Who else's side would I be on?" I challenged, throwing up a mental wall.

She heaved a sigh, and the pressure on my mind subsided. "I sent James this afternoon to Griswil to collect Elisa for me. He should, hopefully, arrive sometime tomorrow afternoon." She fiddled with a bracelet on her arm. "I have prepared a mirror for you to cross through to gather Mathias and Tavia. I believe they would appreciate seeing their father executed, don't you?" She lifted her dark eyes, looking at me from beneath her perfectly shaped brows.

"I told you it would be better to send invitations. You're going to anger every kingdom." With a shake of my head, I lowered my arms. "Don't you see it? You're making enemies out of the kingdoms when they should be your allies."

"There is only *one* kingdom, and it is *mine*," she growled, seething with anger. "This. Fidsa. This is my kingdom. The *regions* have been disobedient!"

"The spell made them forget."

She took a sharp breath. "Gerard, are you taking their side?"

I gave a start. "No! Selina, it was you who always said keep your enemies close. If you start taking all of the princes and princesses, the leaders of those lands are going to instantly become upset and may even revolt. They've been without a governing king or queen for *sixteen years*. They have soldiers of their own. If you make enough enemies . . ." I raised my brows.

"Hmm, good point. I must show them power. I should send the soldiers to collect the princess, not James." She began pacing again.

"No. That's . . . that's not what I'm saying."

"I don't want you returning to the wizarding academy. I don't like the thoughts you're beginning to have."

With every ounce of self-restraint, I managed not to roll my eyes at her. She was getting worse. This was insanity.

She threw her hands up. "Everything is so near! So close! I can't have you forgetting that."

"You told me I was done."

She laughed maniacally, then composed herself. "With your power, you'll never be done."

I clenched my teeth, then drew a breath in through my nose. I had known better. I let the breath out. "Selina, I want to go to the academy so I can learn new skills and hone those I have. Tern Colter said I have strengths, but if I can refine my other skills, could you imagine how much more powerful I could be? You and I, taking the world together? Isn't that what you want?"

Selina calmed, her placid smirk returned to her face, and she pretended to think a moment before replying, "I suppose it is good for you to get out of the castle and learn from the wizards. You becoming more powerful *will* aid us." She eyed me up and down. "As long as you truly are with me."

"Especially when you send an army to conquer the southern isles." I gave a grin, playing on the idea that she wanted world domination, knowing she had plans to attack Ashwrya already in motion.

"You want to lead that march?"

"Certainly. Even if you don't pass for another one hundred years, I will take the throne eventually, and why wouldn't I want more power?"

Selina's eyes lit up with a rare moment of pride. "Good. Yes, in that case, yes. But do not tell a soul."

I shook my head adamantly. "No, this is only between you and me. Though, I imagine they will want me to spend lots of time at the academy like they did with Tovan when he was a student. He lived there, didn't he?"

"Yes, but you have a prisoner here."

I shrugged. "She can manage without me. She has so far."

"Let's see how things go. I am proud of you, Gerard." She rested her hands on my shoulders.

I looked into her eyes.

And I didn't believe her.

EIGHT

I had Selina convinced I was going to be at the academy the entirety of the next day. However, that night I packed my necessary clothing—the familiar weight of my pack comfortable over my shoulder—and snuck into the kitchen to steal a loaf of freshly made bread, some dried meat, and whatever provisions I could think of for a week's trip.

With everything prepared for our departure, I only had one final thing to do, and that was to retrieve my mother.

Without Selina knowing.

I'd planned everything else but that.

Standing outside of Selina's door, I couldn't come up with a way to convince her my mother was still in the cage unless I replaced her with another raven. I hadn't learned how to summon animals from the air—

if that was even a power—and had no idea where to find and catch one in the middle of the night.

Ismae found me standing in the hallway and held her hands up in a silent "What?" She had packed all of her things and left a note on her door requesting no servants bother her, that she was quite capable of dressing herself.

"I don't know how to take Hazel without Selina knowing," I whispered.

"You told her you were planning this, right?"

"Yes."

She shrugged and gestured an open hand to the door beside the main side of the bedroom. "If you had told me you were going to save me and I were a bird, I would create a lot of noise and chaos until she was so annoyed, she would put me in the other room."

"Even if she is in there, wouldn't Selina know something was up if she walked in tomorrow and her bird was gone?" I countered.

Ismae grinned proudly and tapped the tip of her nose with her index finger.

I had no idea what that was supposed to mean.

She silently opened the door, waved for me to follow, and slipped inside.

The room was a private study with an entire wall covered in books, a fireplace opposite—which was shared with the royal chambers—and comfortable couches and chairs. Ismae had somehow been right. Hazel sat in her cage, which rested on a table near the door.

She fluffed her feathers when she saw us but remained silent.

Ismae didn't wait for me to take action, she unlocked the cage and reached a hand in for my mother to hop onto. Then the princess straightened, looked directly at Hazel, and said, "A duplicate raven will appear in your cage now to mimic your habits and movements until the day of the Winter Solstice. Then, the raven will disappear as if it never existed."

The feathers resting at the bottom of Hazel's cage lifted into the air, multiplied, and swirled around until a raven sat in her place.

Ismae closed the cage and faced me. "What?" she asked with a proud, but innocent grin.

I gave an impressed frown and nod of the head. "You've already learned more with your magic."

"It's amazing how helpful books can be, isn't it?"

Hazel fluttered to the floor and transformed. "Enough lingering, let us go."

Ismae smiled and gave a curtsy, which looked a little silly with her wearing pants. "I am honored to meet you officially."

"And I, you, but we will have plenty of time for greetings later. Come." She snatched my hand and dragged me to the door.

Together, the three of us darted down the hallway and finally out into the cover of night. We ran with me leading the way. We had to get into the woods, away from accidental attention, so I could get us to Elisa's land through the underworld before James made it. It wasn't the ideal way to get there, but I couldn't risk wasting time finding a mirror to get me there, nor could we waste time traveling on horseback.

Seven days wasn't enough time.

"You're not going to like this," I muttered when we finally made it so deep into the woods we could barely see. I stopped and touched my fingertips to the ground and summoned magic to open a portal to the underworld. Ismae sucked in a breath, and I looked at her. "I told you that you wouldn't like this."

"I will be fine. Just tell me what to do."

"When we get in there, I can use my magic to keep the undead back. It's the demons you've got to watch out for," I explained. "They can appear as anyone and anything, making promises or threats. Unfortunately, controlling demons is extremely difficult. Most of the time, I'm able to pass through without much interference, but it's only because Nicholas has a claim on me."

Ismae scowled. "I remember him."

"You . . . met him?"

She waved her hand dismissively. "Selina tried to use him to possess you, remember? Instead, he possessed me because I stepped in the way. And then when I died, he tried to convince me staying there was a better option." She shrugged. "I'm fine. Stop looking at me with such worry."

I relaxed my face and held my hand out to Hazel, the other out to Ismae. "Stay together. We may need to hold on to each other if we have to."

They took my hands, and I embraced the darkness as we were dropped down into the plane of death and decay. When our feet settled on the ground, Hazel leaned heavily against my side and Ismae groaned.

"I forgot to warn you about the drop," I apologized.

Ismae took a little breath and straightened. "How does this portal thing work?" She rubbed her stomach.

"Well, I created a portal in Griswil at the beginning of the year. When portals are created on the surface world, I can tap into that residual energy and create a new portal fairly easily."

"Even this far away?" Hazel asked.

I nodded. "It's taken a lot of practice, but yes. Ideally, it works better if I'm closer to that location from this side, but we can't waste time running around down here."

Ismae stepped closer, and I turned to see a corpse with its head dangling standing nearby.

"Don't worry, he doesn't know you're here," I comforted.

"I can still see him."

"Then don't look."

She cast a glare at me.

I shook my arms and shoulders and stretched my hand upward. The most recent portal in Arington was easy to feel. At least that part of Ismae had been true. I stretched my attention beyond that portal and felt the energy from the far older portal in Griswil. Its energy had nearly faded. Reopening it was going to take a significant amount of power. If I wasn't careful, I ran the risk of exhausting myself to the point of passing out.

Reaching my fingers out to the edges of the portal I'd once created, I sought out the fear I'd grown comfortable with, worry that Selina would find us before we could get to Quist, worry that I wouldn't live up to my potential and return Selina's heart, that my parents would despise me once they learned the horrible things I'd done, and even the fear of returning to Griswil. After all, Elisa had told me if I ever set foot there again, she would kill me.

All of that fear stitched the faded edges of the portal together and I pushed my energy into it once again to force it open. My brows furrowed and sweat beaded my brow. It felt like there was opposing magic trying to keep it sealed, like a door that had been locked.

The fae, no doubt.

It would make sense they would guard the land with their own magic—magic of light. Unfortunately for me, their charms and enchantments were powerful, and I needed more strength.

I broke the barrier that had been keeping the undead from seeing us and poured energy into the portal in Griswil. Finally, the door took shape before us. The portal had opened.

Ismae let out a squeal and clung to my side, and I knew the corpse had seen her.

Hazel clutched me too, and I summoned what bit of energy I had left for the shadows to hide us. Opening the necessary door, it felt as if the world tilted sideways like we were walking up a wall. I pushed Ismae through first and then Hazel before

I dug at the edge of the portal with my fingers. My strength was waning. The portal was closing. I barely managed to haul myself from its depths while the familiar sensation of hands grabbed at me.

I rolled onto my back, gasping for air, and the portal snapped shut.

A sword tip touched my throat.

I tilted my head back to see one of the fae soldiers standing over me.

"You were given strict warning never to return. I must take you to the castle."

"Lovely." I groaned and rolled to my hands and knees. "Let Elisa know danger is headed her way."

"Or rather, that it's already here?" the soldier snarked.

I gave him an unamused scowl. In spite of getting through the portal and ending up with a sword to my throat, at least we hadn't run into a demon.

Ismae shoved the man. "Let him get to his feet. I am here with him, so that should account for something. Gerard speaks the truth. Selina has sent danger to your borders, and we need to speak with Elisa immediately." As soon as the guard left, Ismae crouched back at my side. "Can you stand?"

"I didn't know it would take so much energy," I admitted. "Give . . . give me just a moment to catch my bearings." I closed my eyes. My whole body trembled like I was sick with fever.

I wasn't given much time to recover.

There was a rush of footsteps on wooden floors, and I realized for the first time I had pulled us through the portal and into the foyer of the newly built castle. Soldiers, both fae and human, gathered around me.

I couldn't exactly blame them.

Last time I was there, I had manipulated Elisa into believing I was her fiancé, deceived the people of Griswil, attacked their castle, tried to take her throne, and killed her sister.

Hazel stood protectively at my side. "What did you do?" she whispered.

"This greeting is going to be typical in every kingdom I step foot in," I replied. With a grunt, I forced myself to stand on my wobbling legs.

Ismae wrapped her arms around my waist to steady me.

Elisa appeared at the top of the stairs, and she stopped halfway down them. She was far more confident than I'd seen her before. Her blue eyes bore into me with justifiable anger. "I thought I made it clear I never wanted to see you again."

I swallowed nervously.

Ismae spoke up, "Elisa, hear him out."

"I know you care for him," Elisa said before Ismae could add anything else. "But he was banished from our land and broke that."

"For good reason," Ismae replied. "He came to warn you."

"Warn? Speak!"

"Yes. I, um." I glanced at my mother. "This is Hazel, by the way. Hazel is my . . . well, uh, she's my mother." I shook my head, cursed myself, then straightened. "Look, the short of it is Selina is planning something big. She wants to capture each prince and princess who stood against her so you can't interfere with her plans."

"And what plans are those?" Elisa placed her hands on her hips, distrust dripping from her voice.

I shrugged. "What else do bad guys in stories want? Power. She is sending an army to Ashwrya as we speak to invade and conquer them. Once she has each of you, she will take away the royal power each family in Griswil, Arington, Zelig, and Terricina has been given. She is the queen and will not tolerate anyone acting against her. I wouldn't be surprised if she orders your executions too."

Elisa looked to Ismae. "You heard this with your own ears?"

"No, but—"

"I do not trust you, Gerard."

My mother stepped forward. "I was Selina's raven the past sixteen years, trapped in a form I couldn't control until Gerard taught me to shift." She looked over her shoulder at me and smiled. "You were only a boy."

"I . . . thought that was a dream. Selina said it never happened," I said, stunned.

Hazel smiled sadly and looked back at the princess of the land. "You're aware Captain Hook has no hand?"

"Of course I am," Elisa said stiffly.

"Then you would also be aware that someone with magic can manipulate another with any part of their body?"

"What are you saying?" Elisa's eyes narrowed.

I growled. "She's saying I saw Selina and James in the throne room. He had brought Odette and Ulrich to her. He has no choice. He's on his way now to collect you. I know you don't want to trust me, and I'm not really asking you to, but you've got to at least trust this information for the sake of your kingdom."

"Not to mention, we sort of need you to get us to the dragons," Ismae added with a pleading grimace.

Her eyes widened. "Excuse me? No! You must be—"

"We have to find Quist!" Ismae shouted over her. "I'm tired of you acting so self-righteous when there is very real danger coming!"

Elisa exhaled in a big burst of air and her shoulders relaxed. "He told me someone would come to see him. I didn't imagine it would be you." She looked at me.

"There's a lot that's happened," I explained. "When I restored the stones and fixed time, Selina had my father locked away. She announced tonight that she will execute him on the winter solstice at the biggest celebration the country has seen because everything's been stuck for sixteen years."

"She's . . . executing your father?" Elisa asked softly.

I nodded.

"For what?"

I shook my head. "Made up charges. She's blaming him for everything. The only way I can help, the only way I can stop her, is to give her heart back to her. *That* is why I need Quist. My father said Quist would know what to do or could at least steer me down the right path."

"A week isn't much time," Elisa added.

"No, it's not," Ismae chimed in. "Especially since we still have to get into the mirror realm to warn Mathias and Tavia too."

Elisa chewed her bottom lip.

Hazel reached out and gripped my hand.

I wasn't worried she would say no, Ismae had done a fine job pleading our case, and maybe she could throw in a little apathy for me. "Look, if it makes you feel any better, you can bring me back here once we speak with Quist. And if killing me ends Selina's reign of terror, because you'll destroy her heart that way, then do it."

"Gerard!" Ismae exclaimed.

"I'm not going to kill you," Elisa said softly. She grabbed the skirt of her nightgown and finished walking down the stairs, through the gap in the soldiers, and stopped in front of me. "Dahlia wouldn't want that. I'll take you to the dragons. Hopefully Quist is there. When we are done, I *will* bring you back here and we will talk."

I nodded immediately.

The soldiers backed off, and we followed Elisa outside. It had been months since I'd seen her . . . no. I'd seen her only recently. Where? The fairy realm. She'd fought in her dragon form in the fairy realm against Selina.

My head was aching again, but this time it was different. I could recall a moment in the fairy castle when I was trying to help Tavia get back into the fairy castle. Selina's voice had penetrated my mind and . . .

"What is it?" Ismae whispered.

I looked up from the ground and realized I'd stopped in the middle of the path. "I just remembered some part of the battle with Selina and the fairies. It's nothing. Let's go." I walked to Elisa's side, too embarrassed to admit I remembered that Selina had manipulated me.

That's what that memory had to be. The phrase Selina had spoken had to have been a spell. Of course, manipulating me wasn't a surprise, she'd used me my entire life. But to make me forget something as simple as the fight in the castle made me wonder if my supposed relationship with Ismae was actually true. And what harm would that memory do?

None too eager to climb onto Elisa's back, I was the last one up, and with a few beats of her mighty wings, we were in the air. I remained silent as the bitter wind cut through us the higher into the sky we climbed. I sat in front of Ismae, acting as a shield, and felt her draw nearer to me for added warmth. Hazel flew at our side.

After several agonizing minutes, we made it to the top of the mountains. The dragon nest was silent when we landed, and then Elisa let out an earth-trembling roar.

I jumped down first, then helped Ismae off Elisa's back even though my weak arms trembled. Mother landed and returned to her human form. The ground rumbled as dragons appeared around us. I was getting tired of being surrounded, even if I did deserve it.

I'd never seen so many dragons. In fact, aside from the dragon at the academy, and the few who had fought the night I summoned the wraith dragon, Elisa was the only other one I'd seen and was certainly the only dragon I could say I knew.

"Has Quist arrived?" Elisa asked.

Dragons larger than her stepped forward and shook their massive heads. "No, he has not."

I looked at Hazel, who appeared as dejected as I felt.

She gave me a worried look and helplessly held her hands out.

"Had you heard he would be here?" Ismae asked Elisa.

"I only heard him in my mind and heart that he would come." She transformed into her human self. "Perhaps he is farther away than we think. Maybe we all need some rest and we can look in the morning."

"James may arrive in your land before noon," I explained to her.

She nodded. "Don't worry, they are already fortifying the border, and everyone will be on the lookout for James."

"I've always wanted to see the dragons!" Ismae said with giddy eagerness.

"We're supposed to sit and wait?" I reiterated impatiently.

My mother put her hand on my back. "Sometimes, things take time. You used a lot of energy opening the portal. I believe Elisa can see you can barely stand. Rest will be good for you."

"And some tea," I muttered under my breath. "And can we maybe talk a little? You and I?"

She smiled. "I would like that very much."

I reluctantly followed them into the caves as Elisa explained the rooms down the hallway to the left were enormous rooms for the dragons. She guided us to human-sized rooms to the right. Mine was nearest to the side with the dragons. I wouldn't have put it past her to set a guard outside my door either.

I didn't care at that point.

Upon entering the room, I set my bag down and looked around the small chamber. The light from a single candle by a homely bed was all that gave light. I inhaled deeply and exhaled all of the stress building in my body. In spite of my fears, I was relieved to be out doing things instead of sitting around in a palace where I didn't belong.

I sat down in one of the two armchairs in front of the fire.

"Are you sure you can be alone with him?"

I tried not to turn my head and watched from the corner of my eye as Elisa stood in front of my mother, questioning her safety.

My mother was barely taller than Elisa. She offered the princess a smile, whispered she was fine, and closed the door behind her as she entered. She didn't say anything until she sat opposite me. "What is it you wanted to talk about?"

I lifted my shoulders and leaned back, listening to the fire crackle a moment. "Everything has been so . . .

overwhelming, you and I haven't actually talked." I gave her a sideways glance.

She offered me a small smile and reached her hand across the space between us to set it on my knee. "We don't have to catch up on everything right now. You look like you may fall asleep at any moment."

I shook my head. "I can keep myself awake long enough to talk with you. I just want to know about you and . . . Tovan."

"It's hard for you to call him your father."

My brows pinched, and I took her hand. It was so small compared to mine, but not as small as Ismae's. "My entire life, Selina made me believe he's a horrible person. But the times I got to speak with him, I see a man with regret. He's not . . . not like her."

"No, he isn't. He's a lot like you, honestly. Or, rather, you are like him."

I lifted my gaze to see her tender smile. "You think so?"

"Oh, the two of you were inseparable. He would take you with him to the academy and show you all of the neat things. You were obsessed with the fish in the ceiling as a baby, and I could just imagine you were trying to figure out how they got them in there." She laughed lightly.

I found myself smiling. After squeezing her hand, I let go to rub my hands over my knees. "I wish I could remember those things. When I was a kid, I would tell Selina about my memories, and she told me they were only dreams, that my father would never do such things with me. I guess now I can't remember what happened and what didn't."

"Perhaps he can help you with that when we get home."

My lip tugged. *Home?* That word sounded so foreign to me. It was the biggest dream I'd ever had.

"How did you meet him?" I asked.

"He walked into my shop one day to get his wizard's robes adjusted. It seemed his sleeves were too long to accomplish daily tasks." Her green eyes, so much like mine, lit up with the fond memory.

I couldn't hold back a little chuckle myself. I too had been the victim of long sleeves. If Father had troubles with them back then, why hadn't he changed the fashion?

"Oh, he was dashing. He knew it too." She smiled fondly.

I grinned. I'd read Father's journals, but I always wondered what the story would be like from my mother's perspective. I didn't have any of her journals if she even kept any.

"He stared at me with his mouth hanging open."

"He wasn't subtle at all that he found you attractive, hmm?"

She laughed again. "I had to practically close his mouth for him. Though, I have to admit I was a bit distracted because it was the first time I'd met a wizard. I didn't even know he was the prince until I'd taken his robes from him." A blush crept across her cheeks. "After we met, he kept finding excuses to see me."

"What sorts of things did he do for you to let you know he was interested?"

Mother folded one leg over the other. "We spent a lot of time together. That's what I remember most. We would go on walks through town and just talk. He knew I had a fondness for plants and found a rare one for me. That meant a lot too. If I made a comment about a dress I found flattering, he would buy it, or even a hairclip. He was into showering me with gifts."

I pursed my lips to the side. "Is that what I should be doing for Ismae? I think I like her. She seems to like me, at least."

She shook her head. "You and Ismae have a different relationship. She already loves you for you. Is there something that sticks in your mind that she might like?"

I rubbed my chin. "I remember, when I was traveling with her through her land, there was a little glass shop. She thought their artwork was beautiful."

Pain twinged in the middle of my forehead sharp enough I had to squeeze my eyes shut and lean forward.

Mother set her hand on my back. "Watching the artisans blow the glass be fascinating indeed."

"Thank you." A half-grin slid to my face as I suppressed my memories once more. "I'll keep that tucked away in the back of my mind."

She chuckled and rose to her feet. "I would love to tell you more stories about you and your siblings as well, but you truly do need sleep until Quist arrives." She stepped in front of me, leaned down, and kissed my head. Her hands lingered on the sides of my face. "You have no idea how heartbreaking it was to watch you be raised by Selina. To be forced to silently observe all you went through. I'm sorry I couldn't help."

I reached up and wrapped my arms around her, and she held me close. "It wasn't your fault. None of this was. But before you go, can you tell me what happened when you and I were taken by Selina?"

Mother pulled back, her green eyes full of sadness. "I couldn't fight her. She took you, and I was so afraid she would kill you. She snatched you up into her arms and jumped through the mirror, and I had no choice but to follow after her."

"You went willingly?"

She nodded. "I was going to take you and bring you back, but . . . that's not what happened." She placed her hand on my cheek. "Selina saw an opportunity in you. When I refused to willingly follow her insanity, she turned me into a raven."

I climbed to my feet. "Thank you for trying. I can't imagine what it would have been like from your side of things."

She drew a deep breath through her nose, then wiped at her tears. "I'm just happy to have you back. Get some sleep, son." She smiled.

I watched her leave before I climbed into the bed and stared at the ceiling, exhausted but unable to sleep.

What if I couldn't fix this? What if Selina won?

What if I never got my family? My home I'd always wanted?

No.
I had to try.
If not for me, then for my mother.

NINE

I didn't remember falling asleep but must have because I woke to a knock on my door. Without waiting to fully wake, I stood and stumbled while trying to tuck in my undershirt. When I opened the door, I froze.

A handsome man taller than my father stood in the hall, radiating with light.

He didn't need to say his name.

It was Quist.

"I thought you were a dragon . . ."

He smiled, showing perfect teeth. His amber eyes sparkled. "I am, but in my time away, I learned to transform. You and I need to have an important conversation alone. Come with me." He headed down the hallway.

I considered grabbing my boots, but it didn't look like Quist was waiting, so I rushed out after him barefoot. My toes touched the dewy grass, and a shiver trickled up my spine.

We walked across a large meadow, the same in which Elisa had landed a few hours earlier. It was the wee hours of the morning when the world is surrounded in complete silence, the moment before even the day creatures know it is time to wake and the creatures of night have just sought refuge. The sky was an eager grayish-blue shade, anticipating dawn.

Quist sat at the edge of the pool beneath the roaring waterfall, and I stopped several paces away.

"I knew when you were born that you had a good heart. You were bright and radiant," he said.

I rolled my eyes. "I'm sort of tired of everyone saying how wonderful of a child I was." I folded my arms. The air was a bit nippy. "Look, I only came to you to find out how to get rid of this heart inside of me. You know. Selina's heart."

Quist's knowing smile grated on my nerves. "I've seen a lot more than you know. When time froze, I entered a plane between existence. I don't rightly know how to explain it. Alive, but not. Existing, but not. I decided to act as a guardian, but as you grew more powerful with dark magic, I was less able to come to your dreams. So I sought other ways to help. I spoke with Elisa shortly before she confronted you."

"Oh?" I scoffed.

"I told her someone needed to show you the light."

I recalled that moment. Kneeling in blood-soaked dirt, bound, at the mercy of the fae and Elisa, she—the missing dragon child—tore the sword from Dormir's hand. In an instant, I saw the flash of torchlight across the silver of the blade and knew she would behead me.

"You killed my sister!" she had shouted.

It was my fate. Elisa would not believe I never intended to kill Dahlia. If it hadn't been for the wandering skeleton . . . no, if it hadn't been for my ineptitude with keeping track of and controlling the undead, it never would have happened.

I had resigned myself to death.

Necromancer or not, Selina's puppet or not, Elisa was acting within her right.

A life for a life.

But the final blow never came.

She removed my gag. Elisa, covered in the blood of her now-dead sister, covered in her own blood from the battle with the wraith dragon I'd summoned, knelt before me with pity in her eyes.

She met my gaze, challenged it with her newfound courage. "What good is another death? You've caused so much heartache." Her eyes had searched mine for an answer.

One I could never give.

Her eyes held such pain—agony I would never understand because I'd never felt love for anyone and no one had ever loved me.

But then she freed me.

I recalled looking at Elisa with confusion. I'd murdered her sister and she had let me go? I had demanded to know why, and Elisa stunned me when she closed the gap between us.

For a moment, I had thought she'd changed her mind and would drive the blade through my chest after all. Instead, she said, "Because you were raised in darkness. And someone needs to show you the light."

Darkness. If only she knew how much.

That night, the world I knew was destroyed.

Elisa should have killed me for murdering Dahlia. But she'd shown mercy and let me go.

"Gerard," Quist said, pulling me out of the memory. "You have more power than you could ever imagine. But you must find it for yourself. Your memories of Ismae *are* accessible to you. You've always had the power to look inside yourself."

A part of me knew that. I chewed my lip. "I'm afraid of what will happen if I do."

Quist patted the rock beside him.

I shuffled over and sat. "What if my feelings aren't my own? I have Selina's heart. How is it possible I can . . . *love* when it's not my heart?"

The wise dragon nodded softly. "I can understand your confusion. But Selina doesn't have your heart."

My breath hitched. "That can't be."

"You have an affinity for dark magic because of Selina's heart, combined with your own magic. It is why you are an incredible necromancer." He paused, then chuckled. "Judging by the paleness of your face, I suppose I should back up and explain what it means to steal someone's heart. It isn't the physical heart, but the power from it." He rose to his feet and walked to a nearby tree. "Come take a look at this tree."

I felt weakness in my legs and tried to argue with myself that it was due to the use of my powers earlier that night when I opened the portal and not because I was afraid. I looked closely at the bark of the tree. "What about it?"

"It appears normal, yes? There are still pine needles, still bark."

After I looked it over, I shrugged. "I suppose."

He lifted a finger to get my attention, then reached out and broke a brittle piece of bark off, exposing the pale flesh of the trunk behind it. Veins spiraled around the bark. "This tree is infested with beetles that burrow into the center of this tree and devour it from the inside out. It still lives, but it will not be able to grow." He faced me. "Selina's victims are like this tree. They have life, they can still serve a purpose, but without their metaphorical heart, they can't grow. They'll never feel love again, they'll never enjoy the things they did prior to their essence being taken from them. They become stagnant."

"Like a walking corpse," I added, comparing it to what I knew.

Quist nodded and handed me the piece of bark he'd broken from the tree.

"Like what she's done with Torian. He should be upset his only son is about to be executed. I don't understand, though. If I have Selina's . . . power, essence, why is she still so powerful?"

"Because she can use the power from others. She collected enough hearts now, enough power, that she's forgotten what it feels like to have her own."

I lifted my gaze to the tall dragon. "She wants to capture you and use you against my father. She's set his execution for the winter solstice."

For the first time, Quist's expression dipped into sadness. "I knew she would have dark plans for him, but execution?" He looked up at the night sky.

Following his gaze, I found myself sucking in a breath of the cool morning air. Quist said I had the ability, the power, the strength to see what memories Selina had suppressed with her spell.

I slowly inhaled another breath and closed my eyes, calling to me memories of Ismae.

I recalled breaking my leg crossing a bridge.

I remembered traveling with Ismae to a small house, seeing the breach on the border of the Weeping Woods, and protecting the family that lived in the house.

And then I remembered the first time I opened up to her.

"My responsibility as the princess is to wed whoever will bring the best for our country. My father has always believed that to be Mathias. I believe I only wanted Ulrich to thwart my father's wishes." Ismae watches me wipe healing ointment over my broken leg. "You can't possibly understand what this is like."

My head exploded with pain and whiteness clouded my vision as it did every time I tried to remember something with Ismae. But I clung to the image of her from that night. She wore a dress covered in dirt, dirt smeared across her cheek, and she had ram's horns on her head. The pain blinded me again.

"I do know what it's like to have someone hold daunting expectations over you." I look at her, my heart racing. She is like me. Not exactly, she was raised in a castle, but she still hates the expectations of her parents. "You asked me to be honest?"

She gives a small nod of her head.

I run my tongue over my teeth and lie down on the small bed to look at the ceiling. I've never spoken a word to anyone about Selina. But Ismae is comfortable, so I speak. "When my grandmother discovered I could use magic, it was as if nothing else mattered. She trained me all hours every day. As far as fulfilling expectations, she has no desire to see me married off. In fact, that would only thwart her plans."

"What about Elisa?" Ismae asks, but there is no anger behind it.

I still flinch and don't want to look at her. "I had to pretend in order to get the stone, and it was the only way I could do it without harming anyone." I feel Ismae's silent glower and turn my gaze to her.

She has her brows raised.

"I know. It all sort of fell apart." I roll my eyes and then draw a breath to try and calm my beating heart. "Selina was furious and punished me severely for it."

"H-how?" Ismae stammers.

For the first time in my life . . . I feel I can trust someone. "She made me spend three days and nights in the shadow realm. I ran for my life all three days and nights. I mean it when I say it's a horrible place. My powers have . . . little effect in a place like that."

The pain in my mind made me feel like my entire head might explode. I had fallen to the ground, but I wasn't going to give in to the pain, and I wasn't going to forget this night, this moment with Ismae. It was the first time in my life I'd opened even a part of myself.

Then, as instantly as the pain came, it washed away.

I remembered Ismae smiling at me, holding my hand. I remembered how beautiful she looked. I had told her a very fragile piece of me, a personal part of how Selina raised me, and she didn't push me away. She knew what I'd done, but that night stayed with me.

My heart, *my* heart, swelled as I remembered everything else. I remembered the fluttering in my stomach every time Ismae's skin brushed against mine, the sound of her laughter, the way she flirtatiously said something meaning something else, the peace of being with her. Even in the palace, when I didn't want to try and remember my emotions, she stayed by my side, insisting there was a way to help.

She loved me.

And I loved her.

Under the stars, in the mountains with the dragons, my heart swelled. My throat tightened, hands going clammy. If that was what love felt like . . . I wanted to live on it forever.

Forgetting Quist, I rushed down the small hill and into the dragon's cave. Ismae had been assigned the room next to mine, and I forgot to even knock before entering. She lay in her bed, sound asleep, her brown hair spread over the pillow like a halo.

I leaned down and kissed her cheek.

The warmth of her skin on my lips, the smell of autumn leaves in her hair, all rushed back to me with familiarity.

She groaned and pushed my face away. "Keltin, get off. It's too early," she mumbled.

"It's me. Gerard," I whispered.

Her eyes snapped open, and she fumbled around in the darkness.

"Allul," I spoke and the candles lit.

She sat up. "You . . . hi." She smiled with a shy blush. I could tell she wanted to ask questions, but having just woken, she didn't know which to start with.

I reached out and tucked her hair behind her ear. "I remember you."

Tears swelled in her eyes. "And?" she pressed.

Cupping her face in my hands, I leaned forward and pressed my lips to hers. I kissed her with every ounce of romance I could. She wrapped her arms around my neck, and I pulled her supple body against mine.

"Gerard," she whispered against my lips.

I didn't want to pull away.

But she leaned her head back. "How?"

I licked my lips. "Quist helped me. Sort of. He told me I had the strength inside myself to basically break Selina's spell. And I did."

She laughed and touched her forehead to mine. "And Selina's heart?"

I hesitated. "I never got that question answered. I was excited to remember you . . . I sort of forgot."

Ismae leaned forward and captured my lips again. "Hmm, I think you should probably do that."

"Do you want to come with me?" I asked, sliding my hand down her back.

"And meet this mighty dragon? Absolutely!" She scrambled out of the bed to pull on a robe and slipped on her shoes. "Are you coming?" she asked at the door.

In honesty, I had gotten lost in her movements. The Ismae I had first met, the one who acted like a beast, never would have run out so early in the morning wearing only a nightgown and robe to meet a regal dragon. How could I have forgotten my love for her? To have magic strong enough to make me forget love?

When I reached Ismae's side, I took her hand, and we walked together back into the meadow with the waterfall. The sky was finally giving way to color as the sun began to wake it. I saw myself in that sunrise. It was the dawn of a new day, a new chance for me.

For us.

When we reached Quist, he chuckled. "I feared you wouldn't return."

"Forgive me for being rude and leaving so abruptly."

He shook his head. "Not to worry. Hello, Princess Ismae."

"You know my name?" Her eyes widened.

He gestured to me.

"Oh. Of course." She smiled and stuck out her hand. "Pleased to meet you."

Quist accepted it and kissed the back. "And I, you. Now, this issue with you getting rid of Selina's heart. I've thought about it a long while, and there is only one solution I can come up with. You don't have the power to give her heart to her. You know nothing of that form of magic. I believe what you need to do is find the key to true happiness for her. Visit the giants in the sky. They have something I feel will help you."

I raised my brow and looked up at the watercolor sky. "Giants. In the sky? How?"

He chuckled. "It is only accessed through a portal. You must climb up to it."

I shook my head and waved my arms. "How am I supposed to find something tall enough to get up there?"

He reached out and set his hand on my shoulder. "There is a way through a magic seed, but first there is some anger you need to qualm. You need forgiveness from not only Elisa but her family."

The hair on the back of my neck prickled, and I sucked in my cheeks before turning to look at the cave. Elisa would never forgive me. I'd given my word to return with her after I'd spoken with Quist and delivered my warning to the dragons. Now that was done, would she have me executed?

Quist patted my shoulder and stretched with a groan. "I don't know about you, but I'm exhausted."

I watched him walk down the hill and enter the cave. "Get forgiveness from her family?" I whispered.

Ismae took my hand. "She said she already forgave you."

I nodded solemnly. "But has she really? Quist is right. I need to sit with her and her family. I will ask her to return us to the castle and go into a private meeting. It's time I face the consequences for what I've done. If she has me executed for it, perhaps it will end Selina's reign."

Ismae squeezed my hand.

I kissed her cheek and we meandered down to a large stone and sat on it to watch the morning sun peel back the blanket of night. Ismae rested her head on my shoulder. It felt right having her at my side.

After a few moments, she whispered, "Do you feel like you're sitting on the edge of something wonderful? Like the calm before the storm, anticipating the dark clouds, the lightning, and thunder. Do you feel that?"

I nodded. "I've felt that way for a long time, but this is a different sort of anticipation to me. For the first time in my life, I am standing up to Selina. I'm terrified."

"But this time you're not doing it on your own."

I rested my chin on top of Ismae's head. "If you say so."

"I mean it." She sat up and turned to face me. "You're not alone, Gerard. I love you. Elisa will fight at your side, and so will her people. Once you warn Tavia and Mathias—"

"You assume a lot," I cut in. "They aren't loyal to me. They aren't friends of mine. All of you faced Selina once because Tavia led the fight. Do you truly think they would aid me? They all think I'm on her side. I haven't done anything to show them otherwise."

"You won't know if you don't ask." She raised her dark brows at me.

"True," I relented and looked back up at the sky. "One thing is certain. Selina's actions impact not only us but the world. It would be wrong of me to sit aside without acting, even if I have to pay for it later."

"Stop being so dramatic." Ismae got to her feet and dragged me to stand and then walk the small distance to the mountain. "Let's go get a few more minutes of sleep before breakfast is ready. It does you no good to sit here and brood over something you can't act on yet."

"I'm not brooding. I'm thinking."

"What's the difference?" She cast me a sideways glance.

"One implies gloom."

She stopped and put her hand on my cheek. "I'll stop calling you broody."

I leaned forward and kissed her once again. "Thank you," I murmured against her sweet lips.

I felt her lips slide into a smile before she wrapped her arms around my neck again. A rush of sensations filled me—cold sweat, heat in my chest and extremities, clamminess, and the tremble of adrenaline. Doubts still lingered on the edges of my mind even as she ran her hand up my chest, her fingertips caressing the muscles of my abdomen and sending my heart in such a rushed frenzy I could hear it pounding in my ears.

I pressed Ismae up against the stone of the mountain and slid a hand around her waist, enjoying the feeling of her hips against mine.

Lost in Ismae, I barely heard the rustle of skirts and feet skid to a stop on rocks. Elisa gasped. "I see you two have made up."

Feeling flushed, I straightened just enough to face her.

Ismae was bright red at having been caught by her friend and gently pushed my hands away. "Elisa, you're up! Gerard wanted a word with you. I'll go see about breakfast." She held on to my hand as long as she could as she walked away from me until only our fingertips clung to each other, and then she let go and disappeared.

I cleared my throat and straightened my ruffled shirt. "I didn't mean for you to walk out and see that."

Elisa folded her hands in front of her. "What did you need to speak about?"

"I . . . have done a lot wrong in my life." I lowered my gaze. "I remember Ismae now. Quist helped me find it. I remember everything . . ." I shook my head, ashamed to face Elisa, but forcing myself to look at her. "I remember *everything*, Elisa. I remember that night with you." I shifted uncomfortably.

"Would you like to go somewhere private and talk?" She had already turned toward the hallway from which she exited.

I nodded. "Yes, please."

TEN

Elisa led the way down the wide corridor and opened a door to a sitting room with tables, chairs, and two fireplaces to light the space. She walked in and took a seat on a chair, gesturing with her hand for me to take the other.

I closed the door and followed her direction. "I feel the need to give you some information about myself that you likely don't know. I don't want to make excuses for myself, that's not my intention at all, but I feel it necessary to let you know. *Especially* you."

Elisa's expression remained stoic.

"My father cast a spell that froze time in Servad. Selina, even then, didn't have her heart." I absently lifted a book from the coffee table and rubbed the corner of the pages between my thumb and index finger. "I was three years old when Selina took me from my parents. She raised me to be what I am through means of darkness."

Elisa frowned. She had to have known I wasn't there to meet with her about my parents.

When Elisa and I had been engaged, almost a year ago, I had accidentally found her on her quest to find the fae. She had been searching for a cure for a nonexistent curse that would turn her into a dragon, completely unaware at the time she was, in fact, a full-blooded dragon and her adoptive parents had lied to her during her childhood.

I looked down at the leather book in my hands. "When I came to Griswil at her side, my only intention was to get the stone and get out. You . . ." I licked my bottom lip as I thought of how to word the next sentence, then lifted my gaze to meet her blue eyes. "At first, you were just a princess. Someone I could manipulate to accomplish what Selina needed me to. We were engaged, albeit in a fake engagement. The night in the tent when I took things a little too far . . . I lost myself. You're the first person I've ever kissed." I heaved a sigh. "It's not an excuse. I should have held my emotions in check. I should have paid attention when you said you wanted to stop. I knew better."

"How far would you have taken it if I didn't use my dragon power to push you off?" she asked, her voice steady and cool.

I rubbed the back of my neck and leaned back in the seat. "I would like to think I would have stopped. I would like to believe I wasn't so far gone I would have stooped so low." I swallowed as my stomach rolled.

I'd replayed that night in my head more than once. "Still . . . I've done horrible things, and I know it now. Everything Selina taught me is a lie."

Elisa shook her head. "No matter who you are or if Ismae, my best friend, loves you, I don't trust you."

"Yes, I know. Starting the fae city on fire, leaving you in prison to die—all of it was wrong. And then your sister . . ." I closed my eyes, her scream echoing around me. "She was the biggest mistake of all." I opened my eyes but lacked the courage to face Elisa's again. "Because of my pride, I lost control of the skeletons during that battle. I foolishly thought I could take your kingdom from you, even knowing Selina still had plans for me. If I had been stronger, if I had paid more attention . . . if I hadn't summoned the dragon or any of the monsters . . . It's my fault. Dahlia's death is my fault. I know I can't fix it. I can't change what happened, but please . . . please know how sorry I am for what I did to you and your people."

Elisa remained silent.

Tears stung my eyes, and my throat slowly began to tighten. This wasn't the first time I'd apologized for my actions, but it was the first time I meant it. To be honest, at that moment, I would have been satisfied with an execution. And as I suspected, Elisa hadn't forgiven me.

With a heavy clearing of my throat, I placed the book I was holding down on the table where I'd grabbed it and stood. "Right. So. I, um, need to find a magic seed or something to get me through a portal, so . . . when we're done with breakfast . . ." I put my hand on the back of my seat, my back to Elisa. "When you take us back to your kingdom, I would like to apologize to your family."

"Why are you doing this?"

"Pardon me?" I looked at her.

"Why are you suddenly apologizing?" Her eyes burned with anger, and she rose to her feet. "Because Ismae told you to? Because she threatened to leave you? Or was it Quist that told you to apologize?"

"I already apologized to you in your castle. It has nothing with being told to do so, because I wasn't," I replied. "And even if you don't forgive me—which I can't imagine why you would—at least I'll know I apologized. Maybe then Dahlia will stop haunting me."

"Haunting?"

"I'm a necromancer, remember?" I mumbled. With a shake of my head and nothing more to say, I left Elisa behind.

Shoving my hands in my pockets, I found myself soon back in my bedroom, suddenly not so hungry anymore, and not wanting to be with anyone. I sat in front of the fireplace and rubbed the bridge of my nose before closing my eyes. I knew she wouldn't have ever forgiven me. I don't know why it hurts that she didn't.

My chest ached, and I hated it.

I'd always been good at pushing the guilt aside because it only made me hate myself more.

But Ismae wouldn't let me sulk.

She burst into the room and practically dragged me down to the dining hall, which was filled with dragons and shifted people alike. I had no desire to face the dragons—who looked down their scaled noses at me like everyone else did—but like with Elisa, I had no choice if I was going to get their help in the future.

I should have reveled in my time with the dragons, like Ismae and my mother had. Instead, Ismae filled the awkward silence between us by diverting the conversation to Elisa's birth parents, whom I hadn't met until that morning.

Elisa, however, remained nowhere to be seen.

Hazel reached out her hand to me. "Are you okay?"

I shook my head. It was true. I felt awful.

"Can I help?" she whispered and took my hand.

Again, I declined.

She gave my hand an empathetic squeeze and kissed my cheek before she resumed eating.

Elisa's parents, Misla and Nicholia, sat across from Ismae and me on a long table with other dragons packed around us. They were telling Ismae stories about Elisa, how she'd been taken from them during a battle I'd never heard of. In honesty, I was grateful to Ismae. She must have been able to see or feel my anxiety and discouragement. My heart swelled when I thought about that. She cared enough about me to create ways to divert uncomfortable questions.

I didn't deserve it.

"Elisa is waiting for you outside," a dragon said as he approached. "She is ready to leave."

"Thank you, we'll leave immediately," Hazel replied.

I held my breath while we walked outside.

"Are you ready? Quist mentioned you have a long road ahead of you." Elisa stated. She didn't even wait for my response before she transformed.

I cast Quist a glance.

In return, he gave me a comforting nod.

Sucking air between my teeth, I marched up to Elisa and helped Ismae climb on but noted my mother was nowhere to be seen. She had been right at my side at breakfast, yet she had disappeared.

The ride back to Griswil was just as tense as the ride there and breakfast that morning.

"I always wonder how it would feel to be the one flying," Ismae commented as we descended over the valley.

"I could give you a shove and you could find out," I teased.

Ismae scowled over her shoulder at me.

I flinched. "Sorry."

"I take it your conversation with Elisa didn't go so well," she said, lowering her voice.

I shook my head, unsure if Elisa could hear us over the wind or not. I hadn't anticipated her forgiveness, but I also hadn't expected her to remain so cold toward me or the pain that would linger in my chest. Not that I didn't deserve it, but I predicted something like that from Tavia, not Elisa.

Elisa landed a little harder than the night before, and my teeth snapped together from the sudden jolt, making my jaw ache.

Ismae jumped off and I followed before Elisa transformed. We turned to see Elisa's youngest sister,

Marigold. Behind her stood the former king and queen of Griswil.

My breath immediately caught. The little girl was the spitting image of Dahlia. They had the same long black hair and deep-brown eyes.

The girl held her head high, and she approached me without fear. "My name is Princess Marigold. I remember you."

"And I remember you," I replied carefully, still holding my breath. Meeting with her family was a terrible idea.

"He wishes to speak with us in private," Elisa said as she sauntered past me and her family, back into the castle.

Ismae gave me a nudge with her shoulder and whispered that it would be okay.

I remained on guard, however, as I followed the royal family to a small room with a table in the center and chairs surrounding it. Elisa sat at the head with her parents on one side and Marigold on the other. I sat opposite her, placing my hands in my lap. There was a painting behind her head of a battle, and I did my best not to imagine that battle had been one I was involved in.

"Gerard has something he would like to say to all of us," Elisa began.

Shame made my stomach churn, but I straightened my spine and lifted my chin. "I came to apologize for murdering Dahlia," I stated bluntly. "My inability to control my magic, my . . . lack of attention caused me to lose control and that slip of attention resulted in her death. Had I not lost that control, more importantly if I hadn't summoned the creatures in the first place, Dahlia would still be here. It is because of me she is not. I take full responsibility. I know by your law, and what Elisa ordered me before I left, you are within your rights to have me executed. I only ask for a stay in your hand until I can stop Selina's plan."

"You said killing you would stop her," Elisa said flatly.

My jaw tightened and I stared her down. "Yes," I finally answered.

"You're not actually going to kill him," Marigold blurted.

Elisa heaved a sigh and reached out to take Marigold's hand. "No, I'm not. There is something I request, however, before we make any sort of decision toward complete forgiveness."

My mouth went dry.

Elisa locked her gaze on me. "I wish to speak to Dahlia."

"You can't. She's dead," Marigold whispered loudly.

"I'm a necromancer. I can summon forth the dead and speak with them," I replied without looking at the girl and leaned back in the chair. I should have seen something like this coming.

Marigold gasped. "You can bring her back from the dead?"

I grimaced. "Technically, I could, but she's been gone for several months, not to mention I would have to find her soul in the underworld."

"But you *could*," Marigold insisted.

"It's not that easy, I'm afraid. I can summon her forth easily for a conversation, but if she is at peace where she is, if she is happy, and I pull her away from that to force her back into her body . . . she won't be the same person you remembered."

"How do you know this?" Elisa's mother demanded.

I turned my head slightly, shifting my attention onto her. "Selina raised me. She's ruthless in her training and wanted to see just what I could do. She had me visit a graveyard in Ashwrya and resurrect every person in it. Not one of them came back normal. Yes, they were alive. A few remembered families, things they enjoyed, but . . . they weren't right. And nothing I tried helped them. Most killed themselves to return to the afterlife within the first year, and the rest followed shortly after. Those two who didn't . . . well, last I heard, one wanders from village to village and the other is now an angry drunk."

The queen looked to her daughters.

Elisa licked her lips, disappointment evident on her beautiful face. Clearly, she'd been hoping I could do such a thing. "But you brought back Ismae," she finally stated, anger burning the edges of her word and sharpening her diction.

"She was dead only minutes, and she was the one to come out to me." I rested my arms on the table. "Elisa, I can't bring Dahlia back forever. Even summoning her forth for a conversation is difficult and—"

"Do it. Now."

As I studied her face, I knew Elisa wouldn't cave, nor would her family. I rarely summoned forth the dead for conversation anymore. I had done well as a child. It was an easy way to earn money while Selina and I traveled, but it still felt gross dragging a dead soul forth to weep with their family for an hour.

"I'll need to prepare some things before I can summon her. And you have to know that she may not hear me. It may take several efforts, and if I can't bring her forth before tonight . . . I'm afraid I must leave. Sad to say, the fate of the world right now is more important."

Elisa's lips tightened, but the family seemed to understand.

I rose to my feet. "This will work best if I have access to her body or at least can stand near it."

"We can go to her tree!" Marigold said with excitement and scooted the chair back. She jumped to her feet. "Follow me!" she shouted before darting out the door.

I only briefly glanced at Elisa, then followed the little girl out the castle doors and down a dirt path into the noisy forest. Squirrels shouted at each other and birds called at them to quiet down. I hoped I still had my necromancy book in my pack somewhere. I'd created it as I discovered my powers, writing down everything that worked or what I tried and didn't work. Just in case something were to happen and I did something wrong.

Marigold stopped in a beautiful meadow where the flowers were aging and giving way to summer. I realized that this was the first time the spring season had changed in Griswil for sixteen years. Absently, I wondered if the snow was melting in Zelig.

"This is where she is buried." Marigold knelt before a sapling.

Politely, I knelt a little bit to her left. "What kind of tree is it?"

"It's a mimosa!" She beamed at me, her eyes scrunching up with the little baby fat remaining in her cheeks. "They grow into big, beautiful trees perfect for climbing and they blossom these feathery pink tuft flowers. Hummingbirds love them. We got the baby tree from Ismae when she visited after the funeral."

My lips tugged. Of course Ismae would do something like that.

"Will this help you?" she asked softly.

"Do *you* want me to bring her?" I asked.

She pursed her lips to the side of her face and looked at the little tree with folded leaves. Upon closer inspection, the leaves appeared to be tiny palm leaves, like the trees in Terricina. "I just want to know that she's happy," she finally said. "I want to know that she's okay."

Nodding, I rose onto my knees. The others approached, but I didn't acknowledge them. Grasping a stick on the ground, I used it to drag a wide circle in the dirt around myself and the sapling. Carefully, I drew in the four symbols like a compass, then added a small circle around the tree. I stood to assess it all, bent down to fix the circle a little, then walked around it, pacing out how wide I had made it.

"Fourteen. A little off, but not bad," I muttered to myself. "I need Ismae, or at least I just need her to bring my bag."

Elisa held it up. "I figured you would need something, so I asked for it before we followed you."

I accepted it and dug inside my pack for the necessary supplies. First, a white candle, which I lit and then dripped the wax into the symbols I'd made in the dirt until the symbols were clear and precise. I used the wax from a blue candle to melt into the circle around the tree, then stepped back and assessed my work one final time.

Hopefully, Dahlia would want to converse with her family and make this easier on me.

Stretching my neck side to side, then front to back, I rolled my shoulders and held my hands out toward the summoning circle.

Spirit of Dahlia, I summon thee
To come forth and speak with thy family.
Pass through the door now open
And hear these words now spoken.
Come forth to me.

Nothing happened. No smoke, no trembling of earth, not even the leaves of the sapling shifted. I knew I'd spoken the correct words. I knew I'd set up the symbols the right way, but Dahlia, it appeared, wasn't eager to visit. At least, that was my hope. I lowered my hands, still tasting the magic seeping into the outer ring from the spell and down into the earth surrounding the sapling.

"How long will it take before we're supposed to see something?" Elisa's father asked.

I shook my head. "It varies. Eager spirits, it's nearly instantaneous."

"You're saying she doesn't want to see us?" her mother snapped.

I leaned my back on a nearby tree, folded my arms across my chest, and placed my index finger to my chin. "I warned you it may not work."

"Unless this was all a lie in the first place," her father added.

I rolled my eyes and stopped on him. "And what purpose would that be?"

He snorted. "I don't pretend to know how your filthy mind works."

"I am doing this for you," I said, suddenly angry. I shrugged off the tree. "My negative energy isn't going to help here. Stay as long as you want. Let me know if she shows up." I stormed off. I shouldn't have been angry, those kinds of spells struggled around anger and bitterness, but I was furious. I was doing this for them, for their comfort, for their peace.

I stopped some distance away, alone, and sunk onto a stump.

I felt like I was being suffocated by the pressure of everything. There was too much responsibility, and I was nearing my breaking point.

The grass rustled, and I looked up, expecting to see Ismae or even Marigold but was startled when it was Elisa who entered the meadow. I straightened, sucking in a breath.

She walked to my side and stopped. "You have a heavy weight on your shoulders."

"In what way?"

She continued to stare straight ahead until her shoulders fell and the sternness of her face relaxed. She looked sideways at me. "Ismae told me your grandmother beat you."

My lips tightened at the same time my hands balled into fists.

"She told me Selina punished you severely, that your body is marked with punishments. Judging by the cold expression on your face, it is true?"

"I told you Selina wasn't really one for affection." I pushed myself to my feet.

"No, stay sitting," Elisa tried to object, but I was already standing. She sighed again. "Gerard, I can't imagine what growing up was like for you being raised under those circumstances. When you attacked my kingdom, even I thought how horrible it must have been as a child to be raised among the dead."

Not sure how else to respond, I shrugged a shoulder. "It is what it is."

She wrapped her arms around herself and faced me fully. "I can't blame you entirely for what happened the past several months. It seems you weren't raised to understand right from wrong."

I nodded when she paused.

Elisa closed the gap between us and looked up at me. "I so desperately wanted to continue hating you last night and this morning. I wanted to cling on to the anger I felt for the death of my sister. But you brought the fae and my people together. You helped Odette and Ulrich find their way. Ismae . . . she's everything I remembered her being as a child. She's happy again." Elisa smiled. "And even Tavia and Mathias have changed because of you. You set things in motion that have needed to change for sixteen years. Quist reminded me this morning about our last encounter, that you have light inside of you. I see it, Gerard, in your eyes now more than ever. You have to find it for yourself."

I shook my head. "I don't have light magic at all. I'm terrible at it."

She gave a wry smile. "I think there's more to you than you realize. Selina's beaten you down so severely you lack confidence in yourself. You need to do more than prove Selina is wrong about her direction for the kingdom. She's wrong about you too. In spite of what you've done wrong, there's so much more you can do right." Elisa set her hands on my biceps. "I don't even know your full name."

"Gerard Tovan Du'Prei."

She smiled a bit wider, the light in her eyes now gleaming. "Gerard Tovan Du'Prei, I grant you amnesty. I forgive you. We all do."

Warmth washed over me from head to toe.

Forgiveness.

I couldn't speak. Tears blinded me.

Elisa wrapped her arms around me, and I squeezed her in return.

"I don't know what to say," I whispered, my voice cracking.

"A thank you will suffice." She pulled away, radiating light.

I quirked a grin. "Thank you."

"Elisa, Gerard, come quick!" Marigold shouted.

ELEVEN

I felt the magic before we reached the royal family and meadow—the summoning had worked. Dahlia stood in front of the sapling giggling with Marigold while her parents held each other.

Elisa gasped and ran over.

I stopped a good distance away, able to hear, but not wanting to get close and intrude on their private time as a family.

"Are you safe? Are you happy?" Marigold demanded first.

"Yes to both questions. It's beautiful. I met our grandparents and uncles and aunts. There are so many family members waiting," Dahlia answered. She looked up at her older sister and gasped. "Elisa! You're radiant!"

Elisa blushed and gave a little shrug—a hint of the shyness she once possessed. "We just wanted to speak with you a few moments."

Dahlia shook her head, dark locks bouncing. "I cannot stay long. You don't need me here."

"We don't have any closure," Elisa argued.

Dahlia grinned. "Of course you do, silly. You followed the ceremony of burial, and I've been given this beautiful tree to help grow for others to enjoy. Thank you so much, Marigold, for choosing a mimosa, by the way."

Marigold lifted her chin proudly.

"We miss you," their mother said.

"I know." Dahlia looked at each member of her family. "You have each other, and we will see one another again soon enough. But there is one person I *must* speak to." She turned her head to me.

I straightened and dropped my folded arms. "Me?"

She nodded. "My death wasn't your fault, Gerard. It was a moment in your life, and you need to forgive yourself for what happened."

"Well . . . maybe." I shoved my hands in my pockets.

Dahlia leaned her head forward. "Marigold, do you still have my acorn collection?"

Marigold nodded.

Dahlia motioned her near and whispered in her ear.

Marigold scrunched up her face but straightened. "Okay, if you insist."

Dahlia looked at each member of her family. "You have everything you need here. I'll be waiting for you when you arrive. Mother, Father, I'm at peace. You should be too." She blew them each a kiss and faded into light. "I love you all."

Elisa placed her hand on her heart, tears lingering in her eyes. "Thank you, Gerard," she said through a tight voice.

I gave a nod.

Marigold grasped my hand, much to my surprise, and started dragging me back to the castle.

"What is it?" I asked.

"Dahlia told me she had something special for you."

I exchanged a confused glance with Elisa, who shrugged.

Marigold took me through the castle and all the way to her bedroom. I lingered at the door while she lifted the lid of a cedar box on her vanity. I was near enough to see a collection of little painted acorns. Marigold plucked one, examined it, shook her head, and set it back into the pile. She followed this routine three times before she finally settled on one.

"Marigold, what are you doing?" Elisa asked for me.

The little girl marched over and held out a cupped hand. "Dahlia told me to find her favorite acorn and give it to you. She said it would help you to keep us all safe."

Realization dawned on me. I stepped forward and extended my hand to accept the acorn. It was ordinary, other than the pink paint with white flowers all over it.

"That's precious," Elisa commented.

I shook my head and looked at her. "It's the answer to Quist's request. He told me to find a magic seed that would get us to the giants in the sky. This . . . this is that seed."

Elisa's brow furrowed with skepticism. "It's hardly magical."

"Not all magic is tangible. Sometimes it requires a little bit of faith." I gave a wry grin and crouched to look Marigold in the eye. "Thank you."

She surprised me yet again when she threw her arms around my neck. "Thank you for bringing Dahlia back even though it was just a few minutes."

"You're welcome." I patted her back.

She released me and walked to Elisa to hug her arm.

Elisa smiled softly while I rose to my feet. "I think Dahlia's right, Gerard. It's time for you to forgive yourself. We all do things we regret, but we can't move on without forgiveness. There's only one person left to forgive you and that's yourself."

I nodded and ran my thumb over the bumpy hat on the top of the acorn. "Thank you for your help. I need to plant this. I don't know what spell or energy or power it will take to make it grow, but I've got to try. I also don't know how long it will take for the tree to grow, so . . ." I rubbed the back of my neck. "Ismae can stay here. I'll set up camp in the forest nearby."

"Gerard. You're welcome to stay in the castle," Elisa said.

I could barely face Elisa's gaze, and she wanted me to stay in the castle? No. I shook my head and made my way through the halls and exited out the front doors so I could find somewhere to plant the acorn.

"Gerard, where are you going?" Ismae called, scurrying to catch up to me.

"Dahlia gave me an acorn." I held it out so Ismae could see. "It's the seed that will take me to the giants."

She gasped. "Oh wow!"

The forest was warm, and the scent of hot pine sap, dust, and flowers filled the air. My stomach growled, and I glanced at the sky to see the sun at high noon. Without the weight of worry, I realized I was famished.

I found a spot in the woods far enough from the castle for the tree to grow to whatever height it needed to be, got on my knees, and tore into the soil with my fingers. "I don't know what it will take, but I know it will work," I said to the little acorn before plunging it into the dirt and covering it back up.

A raven's deep caw warbled down to us, and I instantly flinched.

"We left your mother with the dragons!" Ismae exclaimed. "Oh my goodness, how could we forget?"

"I'm not exactly used to having a mother, so . . ." I straightened. "I noticed she wasn't with us when we left."

The raven landed. Hazel's hands were on her hips when she finished transforming, but an enormous smile was on her face. "I haven't had so much fun in ages!" She threw her hands up in the air. "I'd forgotten how much I adore Quist. Thank you for carrying on without me so I could have a few moments alone with him."

"We didn't—"

I elbowed Ismae. “I’m glad you got to spend valuable time with him.”

Noting the dirt on my hands and the freshly dug earth near my feet, Mother walked over to my side. “You found a magic seed, then.”

I nodded. “I believe so. For Dahlia to give me one of her acorns, it must be real.”

“You know what they say, a watched pot never boils.” Mother put her hand on my back. “Why don’t we go get some lunch?”

“I’m starving,” Ismae added.

I cast another glance at the soil, urging it with all my heart to grow because each day that passed was another day nearer to Tovan’s execution.

Unfortunately, the day dragged on.

Hazel fell into easy conversation with Elisa’s parents, catching up on everything that had occurred in the kingdom. They’d known each other years ago apparently. Dormir and his mother joined us. He cast me an intense look, but Elisa explained what happened that day.

I was content watching everyone speak.

After lunch, I checked on the acorn and ended up standing there in the peace of the woods for several minutes until Ismae came out to me.

“I think you should get some rest,” she stated, draping her arm around my waist.

“Why is that?”

“You’re out here staring at the ground.” She raised her brows. “And how much did you sleep last night?”

I shrugged. “I don’t sleep much.”

"I know. You told me that once." She stepped in front of me.

I blinked and focused on her.

"See? You need sleep. Besides, I have a feeling that little acorn may feel a little bit of pressure right now." Giving me a wink, Ismae took my hand and directed me back to the castle. "Elisa gave us rooms next to each other."

"I told her she didn't need to do that. I have a bedroll."

"Mm-hmm." She took me inside and showed me the room I would be staying in.

I didn't want to admit how tired I was or how grateful I felt to be able to keep sleeping on real beds. I could get used to that. "You could nap with me," I said from where I stood beside the bed.

Ismae's lips spread in a sly smile. "I could."

I faced her and kicked off my boots, then removed my outer layers until I was down to my undershirt. "You don't have to. You probably aren't even tired."

She stepped into the room and closed the door behind her. "You know, it's been fascinating to watch you change."

I raised a brow.

"Even when you claimed you didn't love me, you were always respectful toward me. Gerard from a year ago wouldn't have done that." She sat down on my bed. "You're showing kindness because you want to. You didn't *have* to summon Dahlia to speak with her family, but you did so to give them closure. Because you could. Her gift of the acorn was gratitude for that."

"And if I hadn't done so, I wouldn't have found the acorn."

She shrugged. "Or another opportunity a different way would have presented itself. You just don't know."

Sitting by her side, I took her hand. "I feel so overwhelmed by everything, yet time seems to be standing still."

She lifted my hand to her lips and kissed the back. "Maybe you need to let go of some of that burden or distribute it. Elisa can hunt down a mirror to get into the fairy realm while you and I are with the giants."

"Do you want to travel with me to keep an eye on me?" I tilted my head dramatically, giving her a playful skeptical look.

"How did you know?" Ismae laughed. "No, silly. Because I want to show you that you aren't alone."

I shook my head. "I don't deserve you. But I'm grateful for you. You make me feel things I've never felt. And I'm sorry if I'm awkward. Sometimes I just look at you and wonder how it is you evoke these emotions in me."

She rested her head on my shoulder. "I just have a knack for it, I guess."

I kissed her hair.

"You look tired, Gerard. You should sleep until dinnertime."

My eyelids instantly felt heavy, and I pulled back to look at her.

Ismae smiled victoriously and her eyes sparkled.

"You cheat."

She helped me lie down, covered me with a blanket, then climbed onto the bed at my side. She snuggled close to me and reached up to play with my hair. She didn't say anything. She didn't need to.

I relished in her comfort and stopped fighting the exhaustion she had caused to sweep over me. I closed my eyes, and within moments, sleep embraced me.

TWELVE

As Ismae's spell promised, I didn't wake until dinnertime. She was gone when I got up, but I found her chatting with her friends in the castle's sitting room. All eyes were on me when I entered the room, but for some reason, I didn't feel the added stress of judgment behind those gazes that was usually there.

"Hazel wants us to have an unconventional dinner outside on the veranda," Queen Rachel said. "It's a beautiful evening, and the servants have just come by to tell us all is prepared. You've arrived just in time."

Everyone started standing.

"And it looks like a full moon tonight," Marigold commented. "I can already see the moon in the sky."

I looked out the window. "I noticed the season seems to be changing. The sunlight is lasting longer."

"That doesn't make me any less hungry." Marigold jumped to her feet and ran out the door.

I followed them outside and joined them at a table overlooking the forest in which I'd planted the seed. All of the treetops were at the same height. Not one stood out as a portal to a giant world in the clouds.

My stomach—and hope—dropped.

"Gerard, why don't you fill us in on everything that happened with how you got the summer stone?" the king asked. For the first time since we'd arrived, he didn't have bags under his eyes or look sickly.

I looked at Elisa. "I'm certain Odette told you."

"Odette barely remembers your being there, other than you helped get them to Zelig," she answered. "Apparently, you took a very different approach with her."

I lifted a shoulder in a shrug. "I didn't want to draw as much attention to myself, so I stayed in the background. I hired James's ship to take me to Delphi, which was easier than traveling directly there myself especially with everything that happened . . . here. There wasn't anything exciting, aside from rescuing Odette along the way and Delphi being at the bottom of the ocean when we arrived. I did give Ulrich some advice with his magic, though."

"Oh, *that's* why he's improved," Elisa commented.

"What is your favorite country you've been to?" Marigold asked.

I scratched my jaw. "I'm not certain. Ashwrya is beautiful, and it's the closest I had to a home, so the land will always be close to me. Each country in Fidsa is beautiful in its own way. The mountains in Zelig are unmatched, but I love the rolling forests here. I can imagine they will look breathtaking when autumn catches up."

"You sound like you prefer cool climates," the king said with a chuckle.

"I don't know about that." I shook my head. "All I've truly wanted is to finally have one place that is my home. A place where I feel comfortable. Where I feel like I belong and don't have to put on a mask. I want to find things I enjoy doing because I want to do them, not because I have to. Quite frankly, I don't care if that place ends up being as dry as the deserts of Sheblom." I wasn't sure if I had made any sense as my thoughts jumbled together.

"Where is Sheblom?" Marigold asked.

"The southern isles, dear," her mother responded.

Marigold studied me with a quizzical expression. "You don't know what you like to do for fun?"

Although I tried not to glance down the table, I failed and noticed the king and queen shift and Elisa sucked in her lips.

Awkwardly, I cleared my throat. "I haven't had time for fun. Though, I did enjoy sailing with Odette and James." I smiled, doing my best to try and shift the conversation. "I'd never been on the sea and would do that again. I also saw some children in Zelig sliding down hills in the snow. That looked fun. Maybe I can try those things when all of this is over."

Marigold scrunched up her eyes and leaned across the table. "I know just what to do." She stood so quickly, her chair flipped and crashed to the floor.

"Marigold!" her mother scolded.

The child was already running around the table to me, completely disregarding her mother. She seized me by the hand and hoisted me to my feet.

I gave a worried glance to Hazel and Ismae, but my mother had a hand to her lips to stifle a giggle and Ismae urged me to go. With my meal only half-eaten, I was hauled away by Marigold and out into the meadow in front of the castle. The full moon overhead bathed everything in a dim glow.

Marigold stopped, dropped my hand, and got to her knees. "Dormir has been teaching me to use fae magic. You want to know what's neat about fae magic?" She placed her palm on the grass and looked up at me. "It all comes from your heart and everything around you." When she pulled her hand back, a small green stem with tiny leaves had grown beneath her palm.

"I know," I replied. "I'm a wizard."

She leaned back on her ankles, her hand still outstretched toward the plant. "Yes, but when was the last time you created something beautiful?"

The stem began to grow until it stood nearly a foot tall with several branches of stems breaking off of the main one. Buds formed along the smaller stems, and I watched in fascination as Marigold expertly controlled her power. The buds fattened and spread open, swelling into dozens of wide black petals with pointed tips.

"I made this for you. It reminds me of you."

A dahlia flower.

Bitterness spread across my tongue, and my lips tightened.

"Hold your horses," Marigold scolded at my expression as she stepped up to my side. "Take a closer look." She clasped her hands behind her back and swayed up and down on toe to heel, looking like she may explode from excitement.

Reluctantly, I crouched and peered more carefully at the flowers—black as my soul. But upon closer inspection, the very edges of each petal had the tiniest line of silver that made the flower glow. It was then I realized the moonlight was energizing the flower, and the edges soon sucked up the moonlight, transforming the petals from black to a breathtaking white.

"Everyone sees you as something to be feared," Marigold said, suddenly kneeling beside me. "But you're not. You're beautiful, and I can see in your eyes that you glow. You should see the way you look at Ismae."

I looked at the small girl with more knowledge in her young mind than I had. "I don't think anyone has ever done something so kind," I whispered. "It's . . . it's beautiful, Marigold."

She beamed. "Now do me! Make a flower for me!"

"You want a flower for you. Hmm." I rubbed my chin in thought, glanced once more at the flower she'd made for me, and moved away a bit so I could have some space.

Creating a marigold flower would be too expected. When I thought of Marigold, I thought of energy, light, warmth, and honesty. At first, I was nervous to try this magic—it was light magic. But I could create a flower, especially for someone like her.

I brushed my fingers against the sticky blades of grass until my fingertips touched the earth. Light magic needed a different type of focus than I was used to. Like meditation, I needed to open my mind's eye and concentrate on things outside of my body, to feel the energy from life around me.

When I opened my focus, I could smell the night and the bitterness of winter on the edges of the wind. I could feel the warmth of the soil seeping through my fingers and into my arms and shoulders. I tasted the grass.

With the energy concentrated in my hands, I pushed the magic into the earth. I thought of what I wanted and slowly lifted my hands to allow the flower to grow. In just a few short moments, a plant rose from the ground with fat leaves like lily pads. The flowers were small, delicate, and my heart expanded as I watched my vision come to life.

The petals of the flowers were translucent, like glass, with blue in the center and yellow where the petals attached to the stem. The middle of the flower glowed in the night, like the fireflies at the castle in Servad.

Marigold gasped.

I leaned back, resting my hands on my lap. The warmth of the magic and earth filled me and made me smile drunkenly.

"Gerard, those are so . . . so . . . wow!" Marigold crouched and leaned in as close as possible. "Glass petals."

"In Ashwrya, there is a meadow of Skeleton Flowers. When it rains, their white petals become clear. I think you are very much like that. You speak your mind, let people know how you feel and you don't hide. You also glow." I gave her a wink.

Marigold grinned up at me. "That was fun, wasn't it?"

I nodded. "That was a lot of fun. I never got to do anything like this."

She patted my arm. "Selina sounds like a horrible person for raising you the way you were raised."

"But she's still my grandmother. And she raised me nonetheless." I looked sideways at Marigold. "What would you do if the only way to save the world was to get rid of your grandmother?"

"I would do whatever it took to get her heart back to her. If that proved to be impossible . . ." She pointed a finger in the air. "I would make a whole army of good guys. I would have Arington and Zelig and Terricina join with me and stand up to her. If I was friends with people in Aswhrya, I would even ask them! And the dragons and sirens and fae." She paused, tapping her chin, then finally nodded. "But you know her best. You know how to help."

I found myself smiling. Friend or not, everyone else in the country had the same goal as I did. "Thank you."

"No problem." She winked and took off running inside. "Elisa, come look!"

I reached out and touched one of the petals of Marigold's flower. The glass-like appearance didn't make them glass. They were still flowers, still tender.

I shifted my attention back to the flower she'd made for me.

I have light in me. Quist said that. Even Marigold sees it. Maybe they're all right . . . Maybe I really do have it inside. I touched the glowing petal.

Elisa rounded the side of the castle, followed by Ismae and the king and queen, and then my mother. Everyone was impressed with the flower Marigold had created for me. Ismae was stunned to silence, and I could have sworn I saw a tear in my mother's eye.

After Marigold showed Elisa the flower I had made for her, Elisa gave me a soft smile. "I think Marigold might just have woken something inside of you."

Shoving my hands in my pockets, I shrugged. "It is a different sort of feeling. One I think I could get used to." I withdrew one hand and put it on my chest. "It almost hurts."

"Appreciation. Warmth. Love." Elisa gave me a knowing smile.

"Love?" I glanced at Ismae. "I love Ismae. It's not . . . quite the same as that."

"There are different forms of love," Elisa explained. "I love Dormir romantically, but I love Marigold as my family. I love flying. It brings me happiness and peace."

"Then . . . I love using magic?"

"Perhaps using that magic to do good for someone else?" she hinted.

Ismae slid her arm around my waist. "Or love for Marigold and appreciation for what she's taught you tonight. I love Ulrich, but it's platonic now, which is how you feel for Marigold. Friendship is a form of love."

Love meant so many more things than I thought it did, and I *felt* it differently too.

I thought of my love for Ismae, how just thinking about her made my tongue go numb and my hands go clammy. I crouched and reached my fingers into the dirt. I remembered the rose I'd given her, the one that had pricked her finger and turned her into a beast. But Ismae was so much more than that.

From the dirt rose a single flower—a rose as big as a sunflower, with enormous vibrant orange petals. I straightened and tilted my head. "I'll need to work on it a little, I think."

"What is that?" Marigold asked.

"It was supposed to be a flower for Ismae."

"Are you kidding? I love it!" Ismae crouched and took a big breath. "I love the smell. Like autumn leaves." She looked up at me.

"I remembered how you intentionally walked through the fallen leaves when we traveled. You could have avoided them, but you never did. Just crunching them brought you joy."

She grinned.

I winked.

Dormir cleared his throat. "I don't mean to interrupt this moment, but Gerard, you may want to come see this." He stood at the edge of the forest, leaning forward as if he'd halted mid-run. He beckoned me with his hand.

I didn't hesitate to follow him, plunging into the sudden darkness of the trees. "What is it?"

"The acorn you planted—it grew."

The trail widened to what should have been the meadow in which I planted the seed. I stared in bewilderment. In the spot where I planted the acorn now stood an oak tree whose trunk reached up into the night sky far beyond my line of sight. Adding to the wonder, the trunk and branches were pink, just like Dahlia had painted the acorn.

"How did you see this?" I asked, breathless, and rested my hand on the trunk. It was brimming with energy.

"I felt it. It must have been around the time you and Marigold were making the flowers. Perhaps your magic seeped out and helped it to grow."

I turned to Dormir. "I should collect my things."

Dormir caught my arm, stopping me. "We haven't gotten the chance to talk yet. I wanted you to know I forgive you too."

I barely had a chance to brace myself before he surprised me with his forgiveness. I gave a short nod. It was all that needed to be done, all that needed to be said. I'd meant to speak with the fae, after all, I'd destroyed their home, but Dormir took the opportunity for them and that was all.

"We also stand by your side, should you need our assistance," Dormir added, giving me space. "My people are protecting our borders now, and I sent some scouts to follow Selina's army."

"Ah. That's where you've been."

He nodded.

"Thank you. Again."

Everyone finally made it into the meadow, and Marigold gasped out loud. I left them to absorb the excitement, feeling rejuvenated on my mission to return Selina's heart to her. We had the means to get to the giants.

Ismae met me at the bottom of the stairs after I collected my pack. "Dormir has things in order here and will catch us up when we return."

My mother walked out from the kitchen with a handful of food. "Elisa insisted we take these fresh provisions, even though I told her we just packed yesterday."

I dropped my pack on the floor and opened it to put in the fresh meat and other things. "Are you coming with us as well, Mother?" I glanced up at her.

She wavered. "I want to. I really do. But I'm concerned about your father and his mental health."

"I'm worried about Selina realizing the truth," I added. "Undoubtedly, she will realize tonight when I don't return for a meal or tomorrow morning if she hasn't noticed already. If you go to Tovan alone, I'm worried she will know to expect you there and capture you again." I straightened and wrapped my arms around her. "But I understand."

She let out a bottled-up breath and embraced me tightly. "I worry about him."

"He looked well when I saw him, just lonely. He's strong, though, and seems to know something about all of this." I kissed the top of her head.

Ismae hoisted the pack onto her back. "I still need one of these magic packs. It's incredible how light it is even though it's bursting with supplies!"

Hazel stepped out of my hug and then pulled her cloak around her shoulders. "You're right. Besides, I need to keep an eye on my son, don't I?" Worry still lingered in her eyes, but her jaw was no longer tight.

"You never know what injury he might get," Ismae added, nodding her head vigorously.

"If you hadn't used your magic to make the bridge weak, I wouldn't have fallen through and broken my leg in the first place," I argued.

Ismae laughed and nudged her head to the door. "Let's get out of here, shall we?"

She didn't need to ask me twice. We walked together, and this time I could see the enormous tree towering over the forest and casting a black shadow against the clear sky, shrouding the moon and billions of stars.

The bottom branch was easy enough to get on to. I didn't even need to provide Hazel or Ismae a boost. I considered leading the way, but if one of the women slipped, I could at least attempt a levitation spell to catch them before they got injured or, worse, fell all the way to the ground below.

Mother, after hauling herself up three branches, stopped to pant. "I'll fly a few branches ahead. It's faster, and I can warn you if any danger nears."

"I never did ask you what spell Selina used to make you a raven." I grunted as I pulled myself across a particularly wide gap between boughs.

Ismae acted like she'd climbed trees her entire life and was easily eight or nine boughs above me.

Mother shook her head. "I'm not a magic wielder myself. I'm afraid I know very little about magic, and certainly not enough to remember the spell."

"I suppose it's a good thing I didn't attempt to dispel it, then." I clambered up to the branch beside her and smiled.

She laughed. "I don't know that I would be climbing this tree with you otherwise. I wouldn't be able to do this." She tilted her head back to look up into the darkness above.

Ascending the tree at night was proving difficult to gauge the distances between branches. Ismae squeaked when she reached to grasp one but missed and tumbled forward. Luckily, she caught herself by wrapping her arm around the trunk and gripping the bark with her nails.

She gave me a wide-eyed look and frozen smile. "That was close."

I dragged myself up to her side. The unforgiving bark bit into my palms. I knew they were bleeding. Pointing behind us, I said, "I think you should try this direction. We can step over to this branch and hopefully reach that one."

"It's so dark, I can't tell how far away that is."

"You should be okay."

She ran her tongue over her lips and turned her back to me. "Can I have some water?"

I dug into the pack for our water pouches, gave one to her, and looked out across the forest. I'd been trying not to look down because it felt like we'd already been climbing the tree for hours and I didn't want to be disappointed by seeing we'd barely reached the tops of the trees in the forest. However, as I looked over the sleeping land, we had made it well over the treetops.

The cool water soothed my aching lungs and throat. Man or not, strong or not, pulling myself up a tree was wearing on my shoulders and arms. I imagined Ismae felt the same exhaustion I did, whether or not she was an expert climber with better skills than I had.

"We used to climb to the tops of the trees," Ismae commented, drying her bottom lip with the back of her hand. "All of us, including Keltin, Ulrich, Mathias, and Tavia. We would have races to see who could get to the top first." She grinned at the memory. "One time, Tavia beat us all. We had no idea she could climb so fast! We challenged her again, but this time Ulrich hid behind the tree where Tavia climbed. He told us she wasn't climbing at all but was transforming into a phoenix and flying up there." She laughed. "Of course, I never believed it until Mathias showed himself as a phoenix when he saved me because I jumped out the window of my castle . . ."

I swallowed another mouthful of water and looked up at the branches. "That sounds like something she would do. This tree doesn't look like it's ending soon. We shouldn't waste any more time."

She groaned. "Don't your arms hurt? Or hands?" She looked down at her outstretched hand. "I feel like I don't have a palm left."

"Yes, they hurt, but we still have to keep going."

Ismae sealed her water pouch, I sealed mine and then placed both back into the pack.

"Maybe I could call a star down to offer us light while we climb?" she offered.

"Hmm. Or I could summon an orb of light instead." It took me a moment, but I finally remembered the spell, and an orb of light appeared between us, casting light all around.

"Oh, much better!" Ismae said proudly.

Satisfied, we resumed climbing.

And climbing.

And climbing.

THIRTEEN

Sunrise washed across the blanket of clouds like a rainbow being smeared across a pile of cotton. Every part of my body felt like it would fall apart if I climbed another forsaken branch when I heard Ismae gasp.

My stomach jumped into my throat.

"What is it?" I scrambled up the last two branches only to stumble to a stop.

We'd reached the giant's land. I didn't understand how the portal worked, nor how the giants could have such a sprawling land up in the clouds. The top of the tree protruded from a flowerbed in front of a stone cottage looking just like a bush. There were no signs that we were in the clouds other than a rolling morning fog filled with dewdrops.

We stepped out into the flowerbed. It was well tended, lacking weeds and growing with lush green plants and flowers.

The cottage that stood before us had a door at least twelve feet high. It had a low-hanging roof over a stone porch with a well-worn rocking chair on it.

"Did Quist hint at where to look?" my mother asked.

I shook my head. "He just mentioned finding something that would bring Selina joy."

"That's not helpful," Mother muttered.

Ismae opened her palms in front of her and released a groan. "My hands are torn to bits."

I leaned over her shoulder and saw how cut up her palms were. I looked down at my own, and they were equally as bad.

"I think it would be a good idea to rest," she stated, taking a seat on the dirt and leaning her back on a stone. "I'm tired and would like to take care of my hands, not to mention eat some breakfast. Are you all right with that?" She looked up at me, still holding her hands out before her.

I sat at her side and leaned my back and head against the rock as well. "Not a bad idea. I don't have any more of that healing potion. I should have thought to replace it before we left. But I do have the ingredients to make—"

She gasped. "The salve! The one you used on your broken leg!"

I gave a half-grin. "Yes, that one." I straightened. "Hand me the bag and you can find some breakfast while I make the medicine."

"You're bleeding too."

I shrugged. "It was bound to happen."

"I suppose we should have asked Elisa for gloves," Ismae mumbled.

"I should have thought of that too. Now we know for next time." I chuckled and gave Ismae a playful wink before starting to assemble the ingredients to make a salve.

She and my mother cut up some fresh apples and oranges, tossed some blueberries and raspberries into the bowl with them, and added some nuggets of oats that had been roasted into granola with nuts.

By the time I finished the salve, they had a small breakfast ready.

As we ate, we heard the residents of the cottage wake. A woman's voice hummed a joyful tune while pots bashed together. In just a few moments, the smell of frying meat filled the air.

Interestingly, there were other cottages relatively nearby—perhaps it would have looked a lot closer from the perspective of a giant. The house across was at least twenty feet tall, one level, and long. Behind it, I could see a wooden fence tied together with rope. Beyond the fence was a fat, enormous goat munching happily on a line of laundry that likely had been hung to dry the night before.

A window opened in the house to our left, releasing the sound of children grumbling and the smell of a burned breakfast.

I couldn't help but ponder how monotonous their lives might have felt. They woke every morning to do chores—milk the goat or cow perhaps, pluck berries, ensure the chickens weren't eaten during the night, do the wash, sweep the house, or go off to work to chop down trees or mine rocks in quarries. I wondered how many teenage giants whined for another five minutes of rest or fought with their parents because they had plans to go spend the day with friends.

I'd seen enough of that behavior in towns Selina and I had passed through.

I always wondered how they would feel to be pulled into a chaotic life.

A life like mine.

"What are you thinking about?" Mother asked. "You don't speak out loud much. You never have with Selina."

"She doesn't care what I have to say."

She nodded. "I know. So tell me, what are you thinking?"

"I'm thinking . . . this town is lovely. I wonder if they have any technology or if they're behind our ways. Mostly, I wonder if any of them realize how good they have it. I often dream of what life would be like with mundane chores to accomplish."

"You'll never know that," Ismae chimed in. "Not even when this is done. You're a prince, the next king in line for the throne. You'll never know what it's like to only have chores to do."

Mother chuckled. "You lived your life doing chores for Selina anyway. I am excited to see what you're going to do with your life when you get the chance."

I frowned. "True."

"When everything calms down again, I would like to ask the wizards to send me to someone who can help train me with my magic," Ismae said, popping a blueberry between her teeth. "I want to help people who are going through difficult times. Maybe I can speak words of comfort to them, help calm their troubled minds. Like Queen Grimhilde."

"Mathias and Tavia's temporary mother?" I asked.

She nodded. "She's still at war with her mind. Imagine how much good I could do if I could calm that."

Mother licked her thumb and wiped her hand on the apron of her dress, a content smile on her face. "When this is done, I can't wait to just be human again."

I swallowed the last of my food, drank another mouthful of water, and pulled some bandages from the pack. I rubbed the salve into Ismae's hands first, then wrapped them with the torn rags.

She did the same to me.

We jumped to our feet when the door of the cottage behind us slammed open.

"Have a lovely day at school!" a woman's voice called from somewhere inside.

"I will, Mum!" Boots and the hem of a lovely dress hopped down the stone steps, then took off down the dirt road. The little girl's blond pigtails bounced as she went.

"If Quist means an item, we are going to have a very difficult time finding that item," Ismae said when it seemed we were safe. "Maybe we need to find a wizard or someone like that. Shaman, perhaps? Sorcerer?"

"You read too many books," I teased.

"No such thing." She leaned around a flower. "Or maybe we could meet with the leader. I bet they live in that enormous house down the road."

I peeked around both her and the flower and spotted the two-story house practically the size of a small mountain. "I think I should go in first. That way, one of us can flee if anything happens."

"Sounds good to me," Mother said.

Ismae frowned. "You don't have to do everything alone, you know."

"But I would feel a lot less guilty if I got caught instead of you." I raised my brows at her, daring her to argue.

She pouted but nodded.

"If you want to worry about such things . . ." Mother transformed into a raven before she finished the sentence and I knew what she was doing.

"Mother, you are tiny compared to their birds," I tried to argue, but she was already flying up into the sky—a tiny pinprick against the enormous land around us.

"I know where you get your stubbornness."

I cocked a brow at Ismae.

"I always assumed it was your dad." Her eyes were focused down the road, to another house that released three children.

The one girl wore a dress with lace around the edges, like the girl from the cottage behind us had, and the two boys wore pants with straps over the shoulders that buttoned to the front of the pants—a pocket on the chest. Peculiar clothing, in my opinion. What was even more interesting was the giants looked just like humans. At least, this clan did. The only difference was the yellow hue of their skin.

"Let's start walking for that big house." Ismae dusted off her pants before she glanced left and right and darted across—what the giants likely considered—a path to the other side.

I followed, nearly jumping out of my skin when the door to the house on our left burst open. I leapt and rolled under the bush near Ismae.

She shook her head at me with a playful smile. "Tad dramatic, don't you think?"

"I don't want to risk them catching me. I don't know what they would do. I've never met a giant," I grumbled while dusting my shoulders.

We continued down the side of the path, keeping as much to the safety of weeds, flowers, or bushes as possible. We were passed a couple more times by children running to go to school, and as we walked, I observed the trunks of trees on the opposite side of the road were stripped of branches and had a thick wire dangling on each one. The wires then branched off to each house.

"What do you keep staring at? You look like you're trying to solve the world's most difficult problem."

"I don't know what those are for." I pointed upward.

Ismae shrugged. "Perhaps they are barriers to prevent man-eating beasts from devouring the giants." She burst out into laughter.

I chuckled. "Not entirely ridiculous."

Unfortunately, walking to the two-story house took longer than either of us anticipated. I grew more concerned with each passing moment because Mother hadn't returned yet. When we did arrive, we faced four stone steps which should have felt easy enough to conquer, considering they were only a couple of feet tall. However, we'd spent all night scaling an enormous tree. Getting up the stairs meant using the same movements we had used with the branches.

I realized after the first step that it wasn't only my hands that were hurt, but my knees and shins as well. I pushed down on my tender palms and dragged my body up and over the lip, then reached behind to help lift Ismae by her armpits.

She grimaced. "I would normally object—"

"Yes, you would."

She frowned, while I grinned. "Hey."

I chuckled and then repeated this movement for each step until we finally reached the top, where we sat next to a pillar to catch our breath—hoping we were hidden enough. The door to the house was even taller than that of the cottage next to the portal.

"This giant is going to be bigger than the others," I commented, gesturing to the door. Maybe that's how they decide who is in charge."

"Holy smokes! That door has to be, what, eighteen feet tall? No wonder this house is so large." Ismae patted my thigh and then hauled herself to her feet, gave me a weary smile, and held her hand out to me. "Let me help you up."

"Normally, I would object . . ." I teased, stealing her line. I accepted her hand and let her assist me.

She pulled me right into her arms. "I love seeing you relaxing a bit. You're rather funny, you know." She let go and tapped my nose.

"I don't have to pretend with you."

"Good." She turned and then walked right up to the door and knocked.

My eyes widened. "Ismae, what was the point of hiding the whole way here if you're just going to knock on the door?" I grabbed her wrist and tried to drag her to the side.

"This is their leader, right?" She pulled away from me. "We can't sneak around here for the next five days hoping to find something that jumps out and tells us to take it to Selina. Without help, we'll never make it back to your father in time."

I held my breath, anticipating a giant squashing us like we were vermin and using our bones to make their bread.

Heavy footsteps matched the thumping in my chest and the wooden door groaned open. A woman wearing trousers and a button-up shirt looked out over her veranda, sniffed the air, and muttered, "I smell a . . ." Her gaze dropped to where I stood with one arm across Ismae, ready to act however I needed. "Human."

"We came to you for aid," I declare. "We were sent to your land by a dragon named Quist."

Her face brightened. "The wise young dragon, yes, I remember him fondly! Come in, come in. I just pulled out a fresh loaf of bread. You can have some of that and honey while we speak."

"Did a raven, perhaps, show up here? She would be tiny by your standards?" I asked.

The giant gestured to the table. Mother sat on the very top and waved down to us. "I was going to fly back and tell you, but . . . wasn't given the chance." She smiled tightly and glanced at the giant.

Remaining on guard, I followed the giant into her home. She was about twelve feet tall with long red hair and freckles across her nose and cheeks. Her eyes wrinkled in the corners. The light in the home came from a chandelier hanging overhead with torches aglow inside of circular lanterns.

"Your torches," I commented while she pulled out a stool for us to use to climb up to the table.

"You mean the light bulbs? Those are electric. We use wind and water to harness our electricity and make light." She set out a plate. "Do your people not have such things?"

I shook my head, mesmerized by the electric light. "We use magic. The only form of *electricity* I know of comes from lightning."

"Hmm, we do not have magic here."

I tore my gaze away from the brightness of the light, which left a white spot in my vision. "No magic? If not magic, then what?"

"Science." She laughed and set a plate on the table. "Here is a piece of bread, if you can just make your way up."

Ismae twitched her brows at me and climbed up the step ladder that had been placed against the table. One more thing to climb. I followed behind and we took our seats on top of the table. I raised my brows to my mother, asking if we were going to be okay with this giant.

She gave a meager shrug in response.

"What is it you needed help with, my boy?" The woman sat down in the chair across from us and dug her knife into the butter.

"Simply put, there is a magical woman who had her . . . powers stolen." I didn't want to try and explain the whole "heart-taking" thing to someone who didn't understand magic. "Quist sent us here to find something from our world to help restore it."

The woman's lips pursed in thought.

The smell of the fresh bread permeated the air and, even though I'd had a decent breakfast, I couldn't resist the warmth of the bread with a smear of honey.

"I wonder what Quist could have meant," she finally muttered. "He's not direct, that one."

"Perhaps more detail would help?" Mother hinted.

I sighed. "It's very complicated. It's more than her power, it's her . . ." I tapped my fingers on my peck, searching for the right word.

"Her heart, the source of her power, is trapped inside of Gerard," Ismae cut in. "Someone took it from her and put it inside of him. Now, she's become a vindictive woman who steals other people's hearts—or essence—in retaliation and uses their powers to do whatever she wants. She's on the verge of sacrificing her own son because she blames him for something that happened in our kingdom."

I blinked.

She raised her eyebrows in response. "You weren't saying anything."

"That makes a lot more sense." The woman nodded, brow still lined with thought. "A few years ago, we had some trouble with creatures and things from the other world showing up in ours."

"Things like . . .?" I prodded.

"Monsters. They snuck under our children's beds. Then Quist showed up. Oh, and this silly stick in our garden." She stood and plucked a stick from a flowerpot sitting on the window's ledge. "We would have left it there, were it not so odd looking." She set it on the table in front of me.

The "stick" took my breath away, for it was no stick at all, but a wizard's staff. True, it was made of wood, but the wood was black with a streak of green through one of the folds. The way the wood had been warped made it bunch together like folds of a curtain, and they twisted from the narrow end to the wider top. And resting on top of the staff was an emerald.

"I don't know what it is, but whenever we put it in the garden, it somehow helps us get a bigger harvest or it helps our ailing plants." She reached out to grab it, but I snatched it away. "Pardon me?"

I traced my fingers over the smooth surface. "This is from our world." I looked up at the giant. "This isn't a stick. It is a wizard's staff. The reason it helps your gardens is because it is radiating magic."

She scoffed. "Magic? I told you, we don't have—"

"How do you think my friends and I got here to you?" I argued. "And Quist for that matter. Or any of the things you say *showed up* from our world. Besides, this could be the very thing in which Quist referred to!" My heart jumped with excitement.

"Hmph! That doesn't give you any right to take it." She snatched the staff from my hands and stabbed it back into the dirt of the flowerpot.

I was about to argue, in spite of Ismae tugging on my sleeve, but the table trembled beneath our feet, and I turned to see an even taller giant sauntering down the hallway. The man was at least four feet taller than his wife, and I was stuck blinking up at him in shock.

The man wore a blue tunic and a white and gold vest tucked into a light-brown pair of pants with a large brass buckle that had a book pressed into it. "Well, hello humans! I am Andre. I am the keeper of books. This is my wife, Folly. To what do we owe the pleasure of your visit?" He slid into the seat nearest me.

My mother stepped forward. "Thank you for welcoming us into your home. My name is Hazel. This is my son, Gerard, and his girlfriend, Ismae."

I glanced at Ismae. We hadn't exactly *established* ourselves as such, but she didn't look over to share the glance with me, so we must have been okay.

Mother continued, "We came seeking your help. The dragon, Quist, sent us here. Your lovely wife, Folly, has given us food and drink and welcomed us into your beautiful home."

The giant gave an adoring smile to his wife.

She, in turn, wrapped her arm around his shoulders and leaned against his side.

"And why should Quist send you up to the land of giants? No doubt to collect something of great importance."

"It's . . . complicated." Mother turned to me and motioned me forward.

After again explaining the very *vague* idea of an item that would help bring happiness—although I avoided saying her name just in case they had heard of her—I stood beside my mother, cringing on the inside. With so little time to save my father, I was beginning to lose hope something of the sort existed. I finished by explaining I'd felt a bit of hope with the staff, perhaps that could be what we were looking for, but that Folly already said she wouldn't part with it.

The giant man slowly nodded. "I think I have an idea of what he means. Quist came to us with a dear friend of his, Zuri, and we told her she could hide here in our land."

"Zuri?" I looked at Mother as if she knew the answer.

She shook her head. "I never knew a dragon by that name, but your father was the one who spent all of the time with dragons."

"Ah, she is not a dragon," Andre clarified. "She is a fox, and you can likely find her in the hills nearby. If anyone might know what Quist means, it will be her." He sipped from the mug Folly had set before him.

"I don't suppose you have any tips on how to find her?" I asked.

"None, I'm afraid. I haven't seen her since that day."

I ran my hand over my face. One more quest, one more thing to do, chiseling time away from my father's life. "I suppose it's off to the meadows. Any way we can travel faster? We are small and any journey will take time I'm afraid we don't have."

"Oh, you can ride the chickens!" Folly exclaimed. She didn't wait to hear our response before she left out the back door in the kitchen.

"Yes, I think she's right," Andre said, stroking his beard. "They'll be the perfect size for you to ride. Our children learned to ride them at a young age, so they are perfectly tame for you."

Ismae stared at the giant with her brows pinched. "Did . . . did you just say we are going to be riding chickens?"

FOURTEEN

I wasn't sure I'd heard correctly either and exchanged a wary glance with my mother and . . . girlfriend. Even if the chickens were giant sized, how could they be strong enough to carry us? More importantly—how in the underworld were we supposed to ride them?

Andre tilted his head back with a belly laugh and rose to his feet. "Come along."

Mother transformed and alighted on the floor to transform again and walk out after the giant.

I inclined my head, shrugged my shoulders, and held my open hands out to Ismae. "I guess we're riding chickens?"

"Depending on how this goes, we may agree to leave this part out when we tell everyone the story of what happened up here," Ismae said.

"Agreed." I climbed down first, then reached up to help Ismae and immediately remembered she didn't need any help, so I stepped back and let her descend on her own.

I, however, kept my attention on the "stick" sitting on the windowsill. I didn't know how to explain it, but I felt as if it were reaching out to me, begging me to take it away from this place. I knew better—pieces of wood can't talk. At the same time, this was no ordinary piece of wood, and I felt a desperate pull in my chest.

Ismae stepped up beside me, then gasped. "Don't even think about it, Gerard!"

"They don't need it," I argued, frowning at her when she put her hand on my arm.

"And what do you think will happen when they discover it's gone missing? They'll know we took it!" Her brown eyes darted to the back door, which still stood open, as if one of the giants would walk in at any moment.

She was right. It would be foolish of me to do something so blatant. So, I went to follow her but felt the magic beckoning to me again. The staff called to me in a way I couldn't explain.

"Gerard," Ismae warned again.

I shrugged her off and held my hand up. "The nice thing is, I have a magic pack to hide it, remember?" I gave her a confident wink, then whispered the words to a summoning spell. The staff didn't even fight me. It flew through the air and landed in my palm with a slap. "Could have been a little less forceful with that," I muttered, shifting the staff to my other hand so I could flick the pain away.

Ismae shook her head while I shoved the staff into my pack, then she turned and walked out onto the porch.

They had an enormous yard, and on one side of that yard was a pen. The "chickens" were much bigger than I anticipated, and not like the chickens we knew. Overall, they were leaner, with longer legs and necks than our chickens down below. Their tail plumes were short, beaks curved and wide like a hawk's, and not even their feathers were colored like the chickens we knew. Instead, their feathers were white from their head to their chest, but their bodies were blue-green.

"No wonder they say we can ride them," I muttered.

"The kids used to race them," Andre grinned proudly, thumbs looped into his belt.

His wife already had little riding saddles and harnesses on them.

Ismae walked right over.

I, however, was full of apprehension and followed behind at a greater distance. Ismae was able to start petting the chicken she'd approached. She was talking to it like it could understand her, telling the chicken how amazing it was, and all sorts of silly things.

Mother was already on the back of her chicken, stroking the feathers on its neck. "This is going to be an exciting adventure." She beamed at me.

I cleared my throat a bit nervously and held my hand out to the chicken that had been selected for me.

Its eyes blinked, and it cocked its head from one side to the other, then jerked its beak down to my hand. Thinking it was about to take a bite out of me, I pulled my hand away. That only made the chicken scream at me and ruffle its feathers.

"Easy," Folly said, crouching to pat the chicken roughly on the head. "He's just going to ride you. You don't have to like him."

That sentence didn't feel necessary to me. How was it supposed to let me ride if it didn't like me? I glanced over to Ismae, who already had her foot in the stirrup, and watched as she hoisted herself onto her chicken.

I licked my lips and tried to follow suit.

My chicken wouldn't have it and ruffled its wings to block me from gripping on to the saddle, then sauntered side to side to prevent me from putting my foot in the stirrup.

"This is impossible!" I shouted. "I'll just walk." I turned to storm off.

Folly sighed. "Chester, dear, you've gone and upset the small one."

I turned to scold the woman, but Ismae interrupted me. "Chester? Isn't that a wonderful name, Gerard?" She widened her eyes at me, hinting.

"Yes," I said shortly.

She nudged her head toward the chicken.

I really hoped these chickens weren't—I almost slapped myself in the forehead. The chickens were different because they weren't chickens at all, but most likely related to hippogriffs or griffins, which meant they were extremely prideful.

"My apologies for offending you," I said to the chicken, approaching it again. "You intimidated me with your beauty."

Chester bobbed his head and straightened a bit taller.

I chuckled. "You are remarkable. I've never met a chicken I could ride, and you seem to be the strongest and fastest of the lot."

The other chickens clucked at me, but Chester remained still.

Finally, I was able to climb onto his back and rubbed his head. "This is going to be fun."

Folly straightened. "They'll find their way home should you get separated. Take good care of them. They like to eat worms, so let them have their fill when they need."

"Thank you for your generosity," Mother said while she finished tying her long blond hair back. She turned to us. "Are you two ready?"

"Ready as I can be," Ismae replied with an excited grin. "Let's do this." With a gentle push of her feet, the chicken shot forward in a sprint. She let out a squeal that turned into an excited laugh.

Mother followed.

And then it was my turn. I smiled and leaned forward. "Chester, let's show those ladies how it's done." I gave a nudge, and the chicken sprinted across the ground, through the long grass, and out onto the main road.

Within moments, we surpassed the women and headed up into the hills overflowing with wildflowers.

Ismae wanted to leave this part out of the story? There was no way. I was riding a chicken through a field of pink and purple wildflowers.

We breached the first hill, and I caught a glimpse into the distance of several more hills rolling into the horizon. I didn't know how we were supposed to find a fox out here, so hopefully it would find us.

Chester suddenly lurched, and I glanced over my shoulder to see Ismae gaining on us. With a playful grin, I nudged Chester to run faster. "We aren't going to let them catch up, are we?"

He balked at the idea and leaned forward, lunging in bursts that propelled us down one hill and up the second.

Ismae's chicken remained just over my right shoulder, and I heard Ismae let out a giggle. "Okay! Okay! You win!"

I pulled Chester to a stop and tilted my head back to laugh long and hard. I couldn't remember laughing like this with anyone but Ismae. She made me feel so . . . light.

Ismae reached across the space between us and took my hand. "I could get used to that sound."

I gave her hand a squeeze, my cheeks hurting from smiling so big. "I could get used to laughing. How do you think we should find this fox?" I looked out over the fields.

"Start shouting her name?" Ismae shrugged.

Mother and her chicken pulled up on Ismae's other side. "Your father would never believe we are riding chickens in a giant world." Her gaze was distant.

"Well, considering he got to ride dragons and go on adventures with them, I say he can stand being left out of this one. I say we start calling for—what was her name?"

"Zuri," Ismae replied. "And I think we should stay within earshot of one another, just so we don't get lost."

I pulled her hand, making the chicken step sideways, and I kissed the back of it.

She blushed. "Oh, stop it."

I winked and let go.

We spread out across the hills with me flanking Ismae's left side. Memories of the mountain troll I'd nearly summoned as a child flickered through my head, and I had half a thought that we shouldn't be yelling so loudly.

As I crested a second hill, the flowers changed from open meadow wildflowers to vibrant warning shades of violet, red, and orange. They bordered a forest of enormous trees overgrown with tendrils of thick gray moss reaching down to paint at the ground.

A swamp.

"Zuri!" Ismae's voice floated in the background.

As I turned to look over my shoulder and redirect Chester away from the swamp, a blur of white flashed in the corner of my vision. I wheeled back around and faced the trees. I scanned beyond the moss, through the thicket of bushes, into the shadows and splotches of light stealing their way through the branches.

I spotted it—the head of a white fox peering at me with as much caution as I gazed at it. "Zuri?"

The fox didn't move.

It was almost as if the face I'd seen was nothing more than a knot in the tree's trunk, but I knew better. The creature had put on a mirage spell.

I nudged the chicken with my heels and clicked my tongue as I would a horse—which only made Chester cluck back at me merrily. "So much for being discreet," I mumbled.

When we drew near enough, I slid off the chicken's back, and my boots squelched in the thick mud I hadn't noticed leeching out into the meadow. I scowled down at it, but heaved a sigh and looked for an easier path that wouldn't get me stuck forever, and spotted a row of rocks a bit to my right.

Luckily, the sticky mud couldn't hold my feet, and I picked my way through the dryer sections to the stones.

I looked in the direction I'd seen the fox, and the knot on the tree's trunk was gone. Thinking I'd lost her, I spat a curse and then ran as quickly and carefully as I could across the rock path and into the canopy of moss. "Zuri!" I shouted.

The moss muted my call, as if I stood in a library surrounded by books and couches.

I suddenly became very aware of the silence.

"Zuri?" I called a bit softer, all my senses heightening in the unfamiliar space.

I'd been in strange places. I'd traveled alone. I knew magic when I felt it prickle the hairs on my arms and back of my neck. And I knew danger.

Unfortunately, I felt the danger far too late and reacted even later.

The moss had spread out behind me from branch to branch, creating an impenetrable net and preventing me from returning in the direction I'd come.

Not knowing which direction the magic originated from, I remained as still as possible. "Zuri, if you can hear me, I need your help. Quist sent me to find you. He said you can help me."

The branches creaked, and my gaze shot upward just before the net of moss slammed against my body. The weight dropped me to my knees.

"Alluhura!" I shouted.

The moss should have caught up in flames, but it smoldered instead.

"Wizard!" a voice announced.

The branches groaned and leaves rustled with the sounds of multiple people scrambling about while I struggled to pull against the weakened portions of the net. "Salund!" I uttered, and the moss went brittle and scattered into the wind. My breath hitched.

I was surrounded by a group of men with fierce orange paint, deep-tan skin, and piercing lavender eyes. Their headdresses were made of branches, and they had spears made of stone. They stood shorter than the giants, but still at least two feet taller than me.

They seemed primitive.

A man with black smeared around his forehead stepped forth and jabbed his spearhead at my chest. "You desecrate our land!"

"I haven't even—" I stopped myself, realizing rather quickly they weren't looking for excuses. I drew a big breath. "I entered the swamp because I am looking for Zuri, the fox."

"Zuri?" The men and . . . women? I couldn't tell if there were women amongst their ranks. They bowed their heads while repeating her name three times.

Okay, so they worship her.

I let my shoulders relax and placed my palm on my chest. "She is a friend of mine. I came from the other world." I pointed down.

The man with the spear bumping my chest suddenly stomped the end on the ground. "Ah, a middle earther!"

"Middle earth?" I muttered.

"Yes. Our earth is the top of the world. Because you come from the world below us, you're from the layer of middle, which means you are a middle earther. Of course, the lowest layer is the dark world."

"We call it the underworld." I looked the man up and down. He was far more articulate than I anticipated.

"Merely because you are a middle earther does not mean you are friend."

I raised my brow. "I am not foe. I rode a chicken here."

He frowned. "This means you spent time with the giants. Bind him!"

I rolled my eyes. "I'm a wizard, remember? I'll just break your bindings. Not only that, but me visiting the giants and stealing their riding chickens doesn't mean I am friends with them any more than it means I am a threat to you."

Still, the men stepped forward and grabbed on to my arms.

"I only wish to speak with Zuri," I said firmly. "I don't have time for this!" I struggled against the men.

One of them pinched my shoulder at the neck while the other placed his ring finger and thumb to my forehead. My vision exploded into a burst of colors, and my body collapsed under me.

FIFTEEN

The smell of incense wafted around me, and my tongue tingled with heat. Trying to open my eyes was like trying to wake after only being asleep a short time. My heavy eyelids protested, but a salty smell mixed with rose made my eyes snap open.

A man leaned over me. When I looked past him, I realized I was in a small room lit by a chandelier of candles, not electrical like the giants had. The mattress on which I lay was on the floor in the middle of a circular rug, and the walls were blank, save a mirror on each side of the window.

I swallowed and sat up. If one of those mirrors was a Windforn mirror . . .

"Forgive us for using the chakra on you, but we had no choice." The man's light voice drew my attention to him.

"Had no choice? I would have walked with you." I frowned at him.

"Then you would have known where we've hidden ourselves." The bottoms of his orange robes came to a rest on the floor as he stood. His long black hair was tied into a ponytail at the top of his head and dangled straight down his back. Unlike the others I'd seen, he had no face paint on him, and as he walked to the door, he tucked his hands into his sleeves.

I got to my feet. "How long have I been gone? I was with friends."

The man turned away. "Zuri has summoned for you. She rarely appears to anyone, let alone a stranger." He looked over his shoulder at me, took me in, and continued out the door.

I was used to being sized up, and used to the disappointed look after, but his gaze seemed to pierce right through me. Whatever *chakra* was, maybe he was doing some of it then.

He led me down a long corridor passing several closed doors along the way. The walls were painted with a deeper shade of orange than what the man's robes were, almost brown, and the doors were made of dark wood. At the end of the hall, there was a set of double doors and to the right was a staircase going up. He took me out the doors and into the most stunning garden I'd ever seen in my life.

Massive statues of ancient beings covered in dulled paint stood in deliberate spots. The swamp water had been directed down deep ditches that made the shape of a circle inside of a triangle. The statues stood on the edge of the outer circle. In the center, enormous goldfish kissed the surface of a large pond.

A gentle breeze brought with it the smell of the murky waters, and the humidity in the air stuck my clothes to me, but in the shade, the heat was tolerable.

"Wait here," the man directed, gesturing to the space around the pond. "Zuri will show herself when she is ready." He bowed at the waist and, when he straightened, gave a knowing smile before leaving me alone in the garden.

I turned to look at the nearest statue, wondering what he'd done to be so immortalized. He probably didn't burn down a castle, attack princesses, kill innocents, or help evil prevail.

The scent of grapefruit surrounded me, and I turned in a circle, trying to identify where it came from.

A woman stood on the opposite side of the pond from me, but in a blink of an eye, it was a fox. A long, enormous, white fox with black ears and toes. It was far bigger than any fox in our world. In fact, it reminded me of when Ismae had been trapped as a huge wolf. She was at least the size of a horse.

She sat straight, and her blue eyes studied me from afar. Her nose twitched.

I didn't know why, but I felt the urge to kneel, and so I did. "You must be Zuri."

She didn't reply.

"Do you know of Selina? And Quist?" I asked.

Her ears perked.

My heart jumped, no it *pulled* toward her. My heart—Selina's heart—knew her. I lifted my chin a bit. "You are Selina's familiar?" My voice was low.

Her ears slowly pulled back.

I knew a familiar could only speak with their companion sorceress or wizard unless they grew powerful enough to do otherwise. Even though I felt power radiating off Zuri, it seemed she chose to not speak with me. Her eyes, however, begged for answers to questions she wouldn't ask.

"If you're wondering how she's doing . . ." I reached out a bandaged hand toward her. "She's not well."

The fox's ears drooped. She stood and walked around the pond to me.

When I got to my feet, I kept my hand out toward her, and she allowed me to rest my hand on her snout.

She closed her eyes, and I felt the sadness in her.

"I know. I had hoped you could help right things. Her heart has been trapped within me. I can feel it pulling toward you, and I need to get it back to her. Quist believed you could help. Please . . . please help us."

She opened her eyes and looked at me.

I wished I knew what she was thinking or that she would at least speak with me. Not knowing what to do in the awkward silence, I realized I'd never introduced myself. "I am Gerard. I'm Selina's grandson, and I travel with my mother, Hazel, wife of Selina's son, Tovan."

Zuri's tail swayed behind her, and she began walking toward the building. She paused when she saw I didn't follow, and I got the silent cue that I was supposed to do so. She resumed walking again only after I started behind her.

She led me around the back of the building and sat.

The building was beautiful, with a deep sloped black roof, green pillars supporting it and the second-floor balcony, and red paint framing the windows.

The man who had taken me to the pond stepped out of the house and bowed to Zuri. "It seems you found your spirit mage."

My brows pinched.

The man straightened and looked at Zuri. "Yes, they are ready and waiting. I will take them out the front, and they can wait for you there." Again, he bowed.

Zuri nodded her head to me and disappeared like vapor.

The man in orange motioned for me to follow, but I was already walking after him.

"You called me a spirit mage," I pointed out. "I haven't gone through any challenge to find my powers yet."

"You don't need a formal test with other wizards to know where your strengths lie. You must test only yourself and you will know."

I glanced at the simple carpet on the floor.

The stranger suddenly stopped. "Two sides rage inside of you. Two very powerful opponents. Many will try and give you direction on how to proceed. You will receive information, some good and some bad. You must remember one thing and one thing only—only you know what is best for you." He placed his hand on my shoulder and smiled. "Only you can discover yourself."

"You never told me your name."

He smiled. "I go by Chiso."

I bowed to him. "Thank you, Chiso, for your advice." I didn't know if I believed him, but at least he had something positive to say.

He chuckled and continued to the front door.

When I stepped outside after him, I was shocked to see the three chickens standing to one side, happily eating from buckets of grain while my mother and Ismae stood with a small group of men chatting. Ismae, animated as always, had them all engaged with a story.

I didn't care about the story. Watching her movements, her smile . . . my heart burned with love for her.

Zuri entered the clearing from the far end.

The men in robes dropped to their knees, all but Chiso, who smiled at Zuri. "They are ready for you to take them back. Hazel, Ismae, this is Zuri. She's been eagerly awaiting your arrival. All of you." He turned to me.

I approached my mother and Ismae, then took Ismae's hand. "How long have we been here?" I whispered.

"A few hours. Why do you insist on wandering off on your own?" Her tone was filled with both relief and anger.

"It wasn't intentional. I spotted Zuri at the border of the swamp, and at the time, I could still hear you calling for her."

Zuri reached my mother and sniffed her hand. Her eyes brightened, and she leaned her head forward to nuzzle her.

My mother smiled and wrapped her arms around Zuri's neck. "I remember you now. I don't know if I ever knew your name. You loved to watch over Tavia and Mathias when I laid them out in the sun."

Zuri's tail wagged happily.

I led Ismae over. "This is Ismae."

Zuri leaned over and licked Ismae's cheek.

Ismae blushed. "I think that means you like me?" Her blush deepened, and she looked at me, squeezing my hand.

Zuri must have said something to her, and I felt a pang of jealousy that Zuri wouldn't speak with me but brushed it aside when she nudged her head toward the chickens.

"She wants us to get on them and follow her," Mother instructed.

Zuri nodded and shifted her tail.

"Do you think you'll get a familiar large enough you can ride?" Ismae asked me before climbing onto her chicken.

"Knowing my luck, my familiar will be a poisonous salamander small enough to fit in a pocket." I climbed onto Chester, who started shouting at me—likely for leaving him all alone at the edge of the swamp.

"Why do you think that?" Ismae asked with a frown. "Why shouldn't you get a big one?"

I raised a brow. "Have you seen my luck?"

"Okay . . . maybe you are a bit cursed." She shrugged.

"Perhaps there's some unknown prophecy about me destroying the world after all, huh?" I twitched my brow and gave her a half smile.

I didn't anticipate my mother reaching over to smack me on the back of the head.

"Enough of that. You are *not* cursed."

"I was joking." I smiled, brushing the hair from my face.

Mother gave me a stern look. "You have definitely gone through some terrible things, but I'll not allow you to speak of yourself in such a way any longer. You're strong and brave. Now, let's get Zuri back to Selina and prove to everyone there is good in you."

I raised my brows at Ismae after Mother had directed her chicken away.

Ismae giggled behind her hand.

"I'm not used to having a mother."

I felt the warmth, the familial love Elisa had mentioned. I loved my mother as much as I loved Ismae, just in a different way. I would die in battle for both of them, but Ismae knew parts of me that my mother never would, and the same went for my mother knowing things about me Ismae never would. After all, she'd been forced to be a silent observer most of my life.

We followed Zuri through the swamp and back out into the meadow, over the hills, and back to the giant city so we could travel back through the portal.

"The portal was at the end of this road," Ismae said, even pointing. "Just under that bush way down there."

"The giants seem agitated," Mother mentioned.

As we drew near, we could see a cluster of giants, one of them being Andre, and by the way they moved their arms, I could tell they were upset.

"We've searched all over the meadows nearby and haven't seen a trace of them."

"We looked all over town too," another added.

"But where are the chickens?" Andre countered. "They have to still be in our land because the chickens haven't returned home."

Chester heard Andre's voice and ruffled his feathers and started to cluck at him.

Andre's eyes darted to me. His face went stern. "There they are! We demand you stop! You've stolen something from us, and we want it back."

"Stolen?" Mother turned and looked at me. "Gerard?"

"Why are you accusing me?" I snapped back.

Ismae huffed in exasperation. "Because you stole the staff! I told you not to, and now they're mad!"

"I'm aware." When she gave me a wide-eyed look, I sighed. "Ismae, it's not even from their world. Not to mention, I can feel its power. Maybe it will help us defeat Selina. I couldn't leave it behind."

The giants started running for us, shouting for us to stop.

I nudged Chester. "Let's run! See how fast you can go!"

He was confused at first, wanting to run to Andre, but with another nudge and a prompt from Zuri running, he took off.

"I still can't believe you stole it," Ismae called to me as she tried to catch up.

"You *do* know me . . ."

I heard her huff and envisioned the scowl that was likely on her face.

"Did you think I'd changed entirely?"

"Yes," she replied shortly.

Zuri slid under the bush and crouched in wait.

Chester was the first to arrive, but after I jumped off, I didn't start climbing, not until Ismae leapt off her chicken, followed by Mother. She gave me a stern look, to which I rolled my eyes.

Zuri disappeared down the branches, looking rather like a snake sliding from one level of branches to the next. Mother transformed into a raven and flew down, while Ismae scrambled as quickly as she could.

With one final glance to see the giants closing in, I jumped down the branches and through the portal into our world.

"Do you think they'll try and follow us?" Ismae called from somewhere below.

"I don't know how they could possibly fit. The portal is barely big enough for Zuri. Besides, I don't see why they would chase after a stick."

"They must have really loved that stick."

I glanced down. The sunlight was no different between the two worlds, albeit a little less bright, but we were still too high to see details of the ground below. My ribs rested on my current branch and I reached down to the next branch with my feet when the entire tree tilted. I fell, striking ribs, knees, my face, and seemingly every other part of my body on branches until I managed to grasp one and stop my descent.

With my right ear ringing, I looked up and saw a giant hand gripping onto the top of the tree and then a foot trying to balance on the smallest branches several feet below.

I gasped. "Impossible!"

Ismae dropped down at my side, breathing hard. "Are you all right? Your head has a cut." She reached out to wipe at it with the bottom of her shirt, but I pushed her away.

"We need to keep going."

"Too bad we can't fly," she said. But then her eyes lit up. "Gerard, I'm a genius, and you can thank me when we get to the bottom." She placed a palm against the main trunk of the tree. "Use your branches like hands to get us back to the ground safely."

It was frightening, almost, how easily Ismae had adopted her oratorial magic.

The branch I clung to wrapped around me and bent down to another, handing me off from branch to branch. "You should have done this to get us up the tree," I called to Ismae.

She laughed.

Climbing the tree had been an all-night excursion, but with the aid of magic, we got down in only a few minutes. The lowest branches settled us on our feet before they stretched and stiffened.

I peered up the tree. "We can't leave this portal to the giant world open. We need to cut down the—ah!" A root from the tree wrapped around my ankles and began to pull me down toward the ground.

Ismae cried out. She too had been seized by the tree's roots. "What's happening?" she squeaked, fighting against the roots to try and scramble away.

"What is it exactly you said? You said to get us back to what?"

"Back to the ground, but—"

"The tree must have thought you meant *into* the ground." I groaned in pain as the roots dragged me through the rough soil until I was covered to my knees.

Zuri barked at Ismae.

Mother grabbed on to Ismae's hands but couldn't stop the tree from dragging her toward its base.

"Ismae, use your magic and tell it to release us," I ordered.

With fear in her eyes, she wet her lips. "Tree, stop!"

The roots went rigid.

She took a few gulps of breath. "Release us. Shrivel up your roots. All of them."

"Ismae, if you do that—"

"The tree will fall." She met my eyes again. "And the portal will be closed."

I nodded. "Far more efficient than chopping it down, I admit. But I still wonder if that giant fit through that portal." I lifted my gaze upward as the tree's roots released us. "If he did . . ."

There was no sign of the giant, no awkward swaying of the tree.

I crawled to Ismae, then dragged her several feet away, crawling through the overturned earth on my knees. Once I knew she was safe, I scrambled to my feet, my ribs screaming in protest. I was getting really tired of breaking things.

Ismae sat up and watched as the tree groaned and began to sway. She gasped and used the nearby tree to get up. "I should have directed it which way to fall."

"Yes. It would be a shame if it went through the roof of Elisa's pretty new castle," I commented sarcastically.

She elbowed me in the ribs, and my breath escaped with a grunt of pain.

I clutched my side.

"Oh my gosh, I'm so sorry! I didn't really mean to hurt you!"

I winced, focusing too much on gasping for breath to reply.

"You're back already?" Elisa called while running toward us.

"Hold on!" I shouted back, only to double over while holding my side. "The tree." I pointed just as the tree finally gave up and tilted in Elisa's direction.

Elisa gave a warning shout and dove into a nearby bush.

The tree hit the ground with a thunderous *boom*, and the branches of the enormous oak tree gave final whispers before everything calmed. The leaves rustled, and Elisa climbed out from under the branches with scratches to her cheek. It was only then I realized the leaves of the tree had changed from vibrant spring green to autumn yellows, oranges, and reds.

"Sorry about that. We had to get the portal closed," Ismae apologized. She looked up at the morning sky one last time.

"Did you find what you were looking for?" Elisa wiped a leaf from her shoulder.

Zuri trotted forward and bowed before Elisa.

"You're beautiful." Elisa smiled and gave a curtsy. "Welcome. You went up there and found a fox?" She looked at me with narrowed eyes.

I nodded and hummed in pain. "Yes. I think . . . Zuri is Selina's animal familiar. We just need to get her back to Servad, and that should do it."

Elisa remained silent.

Still holding my side and leaning awkwardly, I frowned. "What is it?"

"It's just that, well, Dormir just received word from the scouts he sent. Selina's already conquered Ashwrya."

My eyes widened. "Already? How long were we gone?"

"Just a night."

"Autumn happened overnight?" Mother asked, looking at the trees surrounding us, which had indeed changed color.

Elisa nodded. "There's also information from the scouts that Selina's searching the land for you using spies of some kind."

My mind went instantly to the shadows Ismae had spotted in Servad, the ones I hadn't been able to control. If Selina was using shadows, I could be followed anywhere. "Wonderful," I muttered. "I suppose it doesn't matter if she catches me now. I have Zuri, so if she captures me, she will inadvertently be giving herself her heart back."

Elisa cleared her throat.

"There's more?" I groaned.

"She's preparing an army for the southern isles."

With labored breath, I stood and thought. My ribs were killing me, but my head hurt more trying to sort out what our next play should be.

Ismae pursed her lips. "Elisa, get the dragons. Keep Quist safe and send someone to warn the southern isles about the coming attack. Selina has Odette and Ulrich, so Gerard and I *have* to get to Tavia and Mathias before she does."

"You really think she would waste her energy getting back at Tavia and Mathias?" Elisa asked skeptically.

I shook my head. "I heard her myself. I know you want to get Tavia and Mathias, but *I* have to get Zuri back to Selina. That was our entire purpose for coming here in the first place. *Not* to go after Tavia and Mathias."

Ismae turned to me. "They are your brother and sister, Gerard."

"Yes, and if Selina wanted them, she would have done something by now."

"And you think she won't? She told you she wanted each of us!"

"I only have five days, four if you don't count today, to get back to Servad and save my father from her claws. If we go into the mirror realm, we risk time passing too quickly, and I can't risk wasting my time with fairies when I could be saving him!"

"So you're going to let Selina capture them?"

I shrugged. "Again, if she captures them and we return with Zuri, her heart returns and everything will be fine anyway."

"And what if Zuri isn't the key?"

I stared at Ismae. "She has to be. That's what Quist said."

"Quist was speculating," Mother stepped in. "Quist doesn't know everything. He makes calculated decisions based on experience. He knew Zuri was in the realm of the giants and led you there to get her to help *if* she can. Ismae has a point. We need to get the others to safety before we face Selina."

I frowned. "This has nothing to do with you wanting to see your other children?"

She smiled with a guilty slant to it. "Perhaps."

I rolled my eyes and looked at Elisa. "What would you do?"

"Honestly?" She licked her lips. "I'd take Zuri to Selina."

I held my hand out toward Elisa. "See? Even Elisa agrees with me for once."

Ismae scowled. "Fine. You take her to Selina, and I will go through the mirrors myself. It's not like I've never been. Besides, someone has to get there before James does." She spun on her heel and started walking deeper into the woods.

"Ismae, I can't chase you," I called. My ribs clashed against each other, and I sucked in a breath. Softer, I confirmed, "Mmm, I really can't."

"Did I hear someone say my name?"

I spun around, hand over my ribs, and faced James as he stepped over one of the fallen oak's branches. My jaw flexed, and I glanced at my mother.

She slipped carefully behind me without James noticing. His attention was locked on Zuri.

This was bad.

"Where is Ismae going?" James asked.

"To find a mirror! If you're not coming, there's no reason we shouldn't split up," she called back, too far away to realize it was James who asked.

"Except the whole keeping you safe thing!" I shouted at her, ignoring my agonizing pain. "She's going the wrong direction," I stepped in. "She fell getting out of the tree and it cut her face. She doesn't realize *she's going the wrong way!*" I finished in a shout trying to warn Ismae, only to double over again. I ran a hand over my face and silently asked Elisa what to do.

Elisa reached out toward me, then retracted her hand and stepped aside. "James, help me get him to the castle to get his ribs taken care of. Hopefully, they're just bruised."

I knew better than that. I'd had enough broken bones in my life to know my ribs weren't bruised. I looked in the direction Ismae had gone and licked my lip, tasting the iron of blood on my tongue. Apparently, I had a split lip too.

James hoisted my arm around his shoulders. I wished I knew the counterspell to Selina's hold on him, but there was no more powerful magic than owning the flesh of another. I noticed a raven perched at the top of a tree. My mother was smart enough to hide her presence from James—unless he already knew at this point. Zuri was nowhere to be seen.

I tried not to lean too heavily on the pirate captain while he assisted me into the castle and sat me down in the nearest chair just inside the sitting room.

"What were you doing that got you so injured?" His dark eyes studied mine in a way that made me wonder if Selina was looking through them, and I prayed to whatever god existed that she hadn't seen Zuri.

"Practicing some magic with Ismae. Her powers are still unpredictable." I grimaced as big as I could, hoping to prompt him to shut up.

Elisa returned with a couple of fae who deemed my ribs were, in fact, broken. They gave me some healing potion, which I swallowed in one gulp, one eye closed, and wrinkled my nose at the taste. I shifted my gaze to Elisa.

"James, thank you for helping us get Gerard into the castle. Why are you here without Odette?" Elisa took a seat and folded her hands in her lap.

"I came to speak with you." He focused his attention on her. His tone had grown flat. "With the capital of Servad restored, the king and queen are hosting a celebration. They would like to invite you to join them. Odette and Ulrich are already there."

Something in my gut wrenched. If James was here and Selina had shadow spies, Ismae was in danger. I needed to have Hazel fly off and stop Ismae, or Zuri run ahead. I needed to get a message to them without looking suspicious to James.

When I shifted, his eyes snapped to me.

Selina's eyes.

SIXTEEN

My body froze.

James's large lips pulled into a smirk that didn't match his dark face. "Having supper with Elisa, are we?"

I straightened my spine, biting the inside of my cheek to prevent myself from grimacing at the aching pain searing into my lungs with each breath. I couldn't let her know I was injured. She would become suspicious. "What are you doing here?"

"You don't look surprised to see me."

"At this point, nothing surprises me anymore," I replied.

James laughed, but Selina's shrill voice echoed behind it. "Not much gets past you, does it, Gerard? Except, perhaps, a certain little princess who has put all of these thoughts in your mind to leave me. She nearly ruined you once. I can't let her ruin you again, now, can I?"

My breath caught.

"Ah. Yes, there's the fear. Don't worry. I'll take good care of her."

I jumped to my feet and slammed my fist into James's cheek, making him stagger, trip over a side table, and then fall to the ground hard enough his head cracked on the wood floor.

"Gerard!" Elisa exclaimed.

Not waiting to apologize, I ran out the castle doors, shouting behind me, "Arrest him before he takes you back to Selina!" I tore the wizard's staff from my pack and felt the magic inside vibrating beneath my hand. I'd never used a staff to enhance my magic, but if I ever needed to do so, it would be this moment.

I used the pain to fuel my footsteps as I ran through the unfamiliar woods. With each gasp of breath, each jarring shock through my body, I was drawing nearer to Ismae. I could feel it. The shadows of the nearby trees pulled to me, accelerating my footsteps. I accepted the darkness to me, let it propel me over fallen logs, through bushes, and over small streams. I had never run so fast in my life. The thought of losing Ismae . . .

I broke into a shallow meadow and spotted Ismae about to step out of the sunlight. "Wait!" I held my hand out. The shadows around me snapped to Ismae, caught hold of her, and yanked her back into the sunlight before it banished them.

"What was that?" She whipped around to face me. The momentary anger melted, her eyes widened in fear, and she stepped away. "S-Stay back."

Zuri ran past me, a blur of whiteness, and circled behind Ismae to keep her in the light.

Mother transformed at Ismae's side and faced me.

Zuri flashed her teeth.

Confused, I stopped approaching and explained, "Selina sent spies to find us. I fear they lie beyond the light of the sun and in the shadows of the forest surrounding us."

"Or inside of you," Ismae stated, distrust still evident in her eyes.

I frowned and looked down at myself. The familiar smokiness of shadows lingered on my skin, battling to hold me in spite of the sun glowing overhead. The familiar sensation of darkness tingled through my veins, and for a moment, I relished in its power.

I shook my head, letting go of my fear and banishing the darkness to the light. "Better?"

"I didn't know you could use shadow like that," Ismae whispered.

"Shadow magic is almost second nature to me. Dark magic comes easily, remember?" With the shadows gone, I collapsed to my knee, leaning heavily on the staff, and grimaced before I touched my hand to the ground. Already weakened by my injuries, I would have to expend a lot of energy to draw the portal from the castle to me, but it wouldn't be impossible.

"Gerard, what are you doing?" Ismae demanded.

Zuri was no longer growling, but the three women still stood cautiously distant.

"I'm opening the portal to the underworld so we can get Zuri to Servad. I had to come and chase you down because Selina is coming for you, and I can't let that happen. I only hope Elisa can handle James and get him trapped before he arrests her and takes her back to Selina." I lifted my accusatory gaze to her.

Ismae glared back. "Oh, don't you dare try and pin anything on me. You should have come with me in the first place."

"When I open the portal, Zuri, you just step into it, and we'll drop into the underworld. Luckily, I opened the portal in Servad and we can get back rather quickly, days before my father is to be executed. Good timing, if you ask me."

Zuri snorted and turned around, strutting away with her tail swaying behind.

My brows pinched. "Where are you going? This will get us to the Servad before nightfall. If we walk, it will take us a few days. *Wasted* days."

"I think she wants to go with Ismae," Mother commented. With her hand on Ismae's back, they turned to follow the giant fox.

I ran my hand through my hair. "I thought you were on my side," I said to Zuri.

She didn't acknowledge me.

I gave a frustrated groan. "Do you even know where a mirror is to get to the fairy realm?"

"I know there are some in Terricina and obviously Zelig, but there must be one in Griswil somewhere, right? Or even Arington?" Ismae stopped walking.

"You don't even know? You're wandering a forest in hopes one will fall from a tree?"

Ismae tightened her hands into fists and stormed over to me. "I don't know what I did to make you so mad at me, but you need to stop being so . . . so . . . *stubborn*! Not all of us find it easy to leave people we care about behind when they could be saved." She stormed off.

I looked at my mother. "What did I say?"

She shook her head. "We'll need to work on your conversational skills. For now, let's get to a mirror."

I rubbed my hand over my side. "You know, I can open a portal and take us to Zelig and use one of the mirrors there. That's how Tavia got back through into the fairy realm."

Ismae stopped but didn't turn to me.

Zuri looked over but seemed to be frowning.

"Look, I don't know what in the underworld I'm doing, okay? You fell in love with me without really knowing who I am. I'm not a good person, Ismae. I've said that over and over and you still cling to some fairy-tale idea that I can be saved. Well, maybe I can't! I don't know how to stop Selina except to get Zuri back, and by the gods, that's what I'm going to do, and you aren't going to stop me."

My mother placed her hand on my back, and the warmth of her touch seeped into my spine.

Ismae, however, gritted her teeth, and tears glistened in her beautiful brown eyes when she looked at me.

"Each minute we waste—"

"Is another minute closer to your dad's death. I get it," Ismae interrupted me.

I threw my hands out to the sides in frustration. "This whole thing is pointless. All of this. You taking off into the trees without a plan, us chasing after. I can literally open a portal to the underworld and take us where we need to go, and you want to go off and spend even more time to get Mathias and Tavia when they aren't even in real danger!" I winced and sucked in a breath.

"Zuri refuses to go into the underworld!" Ismae shouted back at me. "Don't you get it, mister mighty powerful wizard? If you are so powerful, why can't you feel that she won't step into the darkness with you? That she refuses to speak to you?"

Anger blinded me. "Oh, all of a sudden you know everything. Don't you, *princess*?" I countered with a sneer. "She refuses to speak with me because of the darkness within me. You of all people should know about the darkness inside of me."

Ismae stepped forward, her stance challenging my own. "She's a Fylgja Fox, Gerard. A creature of light. A mythical creature from Ashwrya. I would think *you,* of all people, would know that." She had her hands in fists and leaned toward my face. Even though she was nearly a whole head shorter than me, the fervor behind her made me take a breath and look beyond her to Zuri.

The Fylgjur were guardians. I'd heard a little about them as a child, recalling a couple of instances when I saw a charm or engraving of the fox and someone explained to me that a Fylgja would be a companion spirit for generations—as long as the individual didn't become wicked.

No wonder Zuri had left Selina.

Zuri was a creature of light, and Selina had turned to darkness.

I relaxed my stance. "I didn't know you wouldn't enter the portal. I'm afraid I know little about light magic," I conceded, keeping my focus on the beautiful fox.

She bowed her head, both telling me she understood and appearing sad for it. I wondered what Selina must have been like before to have earned a Fylgjur companion—something so pure—and what she must have done to lose it.

I noticed my mother exchange a worried glance with Zuri.

The fox approached and gently nudged Ismae aside. Zuri touched her nose to my chest. *The pain of betrayal you feel does not come from you, but the burden of the heart you bear.*

Breathtaking joy wrapped around me.

In the blink of an eye, Zuri stood in the meadow before me as a woman in a white gown with long, flowing white hair. Fog surrounded her—no. Not fog. Light. The weight in my chest felt heavier than ever, and her brightness was so blinding I had to turn my gaze away.

"Your soul is being consumed by darkness." Zuri's voice floated around me and scratched at the icy shell of my heart. "Selina's heart is poisoning you more every day. She feeds it darkness, and you add more and more with each dark spell you cast, with each dark thought you have."

I rubbed my chest as if I could banish the pain. "I know nothing different."

"For that, I am sorry."

"If Selina trapped her heart within me, there must be some way to get it out. Please. I'm begging you to help me." I tried to face Zuri but had to keep my gaze on her feet because she was too bright.

"The only way to help her is to let the light in." She drew nearer.

"It hurts." My skin felt like it was burning, and I staggered backward. I gasped and clutched my chest. "I can't. It hurts. I . . . can't."

"How long have you been her host?"

I shook my head, gasping for breath, but not because of my broken ribs. Zuri backed off, and the pain in my body subsided. "I . . . don't exactly know. Perhaps the entire sixteen years she's had me? More? Less?" I finally answered.

Zuri remained silent.

I lifted my gaze to her, the light coming off her still nearly blinding, but tolerable.

"You must pierce the darkness. You *have* to let the light in. You've started opening up with Ismae, you're allowing yourself to feel love, but you must cling to those around you. It is the only way to heal her heart. You turn to darkness and fear because it's all you've known. Selina has harmed you in ways no one will understand. But not all of us are like that. Ismae loves you with every part of her heart. Instead of reacting in anger, think."

"But how do I get Selina's heart back to her? Loving Ismae won't help Selina's heart. How do I end this?"

Zuri shook her head, blue eyes sad. "The easiest way is for her to take it back willingly. But if you can help her heart heal . . . perhaps she will feel the need to take it back without you pushing. Dark magic is powerful and can be terrifying in strength, but light . . . that will always banish darkness. If Selina feels how powerful a heart full of love and light is compared to how heavy a heart of darkness is, she'll want that back. You'll feel it as well."

I turned my face away from the light. Sixteen years tortured and trapped in darkness, and this Fylgja wanted me to simply learn to love? To allow light in? "Is it possible I could reject her heart?" I whispered.

"Through an act of self-sacrifice, possibly. But, Gerard, if you do that, it will destroy you too. Hold on to your own heart. Don't lose it to her darkness." She reached out and placed her palm against my chest.

Agony burned through me, and I realized the scream tearing through my throat wasn't only my voice but Selina's too. The white-hot power of light magic shocked the nerves in my body, feeling like electricity.

Selina's heart wrapped around mine like a parasite. It pulsed and clung to me tighter, refusing to release.

For the first time in my life, I felt the difference between her and me.

I was aware of the second heart dragging mine into the darkness Selina had embraced all those years ago. Somehow, she was still impacting her heart through her actions. I saw beyond myself, beyond us, into light and worlds I couldn't explain if I had the words. I caught a glimpse of what my life could be like with joy in it. I knew what it would be with darkness.

And for the first time, I tasted what peace could be.

SEVENTEEN

For the second time that day, I found myself lying on my back staring up. The crystal sky felt endless. The warmth in my heart tingled all the way to my extremities. A shadow fell over me, and my gaze shifted to Ismae sitting on her knees at my side.

She smiled and brushed a tear from my cheek. "You're back." Ismae, my stubborn, stronger other half. Not willing to give up on me. She barely knew me, and yet it felt like she was the only one who knew me at all.

I blinked a few times, took a breath, and found my tongue too numb to speak.

"Zuri said she carried you away in a vision. It may take you a moment to recover." Her cool fingers brushed my forehead, nearly lulling me back into rest.

I let my eyes close. “I’ve never felt this before,” I whispered, tongue still tingling. “I want this feeling to stay.”

“Then hold on to it.” Ismae leaned down and kissed me.

Her light clashed into my darkness, and I took her shoulders and pulled her close as if I could feed on the goodness inside of her. Her lips moved with mine, and I dug my fingers into her hair.

“Breathe,” she chuckled against my lips and then pulled back.

Far too soon, the sensation began to fade.

I looked up at her. “Why?”

“Why what?”

I touched her cheek and ran a thumb over her freckles. “Why do you care about me? I treat you so harshly.”

“You push me away because no one else has shown you kindness, and that frightens you. But I’m not going to stay forever,” she warned. “You need to change your actions. I can’t keep having you change on a whim all the time. I can’t deal with you yelling at me.”

I nodded and kissed her again. “I’m sorry. I shouldn’t have yelled at you, and I’m going to do my best to be better, but . . . it won’t happen overnight. It’s taken me months just to get to this point.”

“I understand. If we get Tavia and Mathias, they can help. Two phoenixes added to our side would make us that much closer to being unstoppable.”

I pushed myself to my feet, grabbing the staff I'd dropped. The pain in my ribs and knot on my head were gone. In fact, my hands didn't hurt either. Zuri must have healed me. I gave her a grateful smile and thanked her.

She bowed her head.

I held my palms out to the ground in front of us. "Andurn sür tradur."

Shadows pulled away from trees and swarmed together in a tight and angry ball of energy, then faded away like smoke, revealing one of the Windforn mirrors.

"Next time you do a spell like that, try using the light instead of darkness," Mother commented.

I glanced over at her and gave a sheepish shrug. "Sorry. It's second nature."

Ismae gave my back a shove. "Time changes differently in the mirror realm, and we're going to lose at least a day, possibly two, so we better hurry up and get in there."

I crouched at the mirror and studied the edges. I'd chosen the correct mirror. "This mirror is the one that opens into the throne room of the fairy castle. It doesn't look like they've destroyed it on their side."

"How do you know?" Mother asked.

"It's still intact." I propped it up on a nearby tree and crouched. "Mirror, mirror on the wall, open and let us through." I felt Ismae's skeptical look before I turned and saw it.

"You think that's going to open the mirror?" she asked.

"For some reason, I can't recall if this mirror is the one that uses the spell or has a button."

Ismae groaned and sat on a nearby rock. "You don't even know how to open it?"

"I summoned it, didn't I?" I caught myself, the anger at the edge of my tongue. I took a steadying breath. "I'm trying to remember the phrase. You don't understand, each of the mirrors has an individual way. I've got to recall the right one, that's all. It's not a sentient being. It's an enchanted object, and enchanted objects need a particular phrase spoken in a certain way to get it to open." I touched the surface of the mirror and let out a frustrated sigh. "The mirror I used with Tavia was different. This one was the one Selina dragged me through after she sewed my mouth shut. I'm trying to remember what she said."

As we sat in silence, I went back to that day. Selina had bound me with magic and dragged me to the mirror. It hung next to a white tapestry with purple words on it saying something about sacrifices. And then I suddenly remembered how to open it.

"Mirror, mirror on the wall, calm and peace before the fall," I spoke.

The familiar crack of the mirror opening echoed around the forest.

Ismae laughed. "I can't believe that was it!"

I looked around, making a mental note of where we would exit after retrieving the prince and princess who were my long-lost siblings. I stepped through the mirror and entered a dusty room in the back of a tavern—based on the smell of alcohol, stale food, and body odor. It was *not* the throne room.

I heard Ismae and my mother step through behind me, and then Zuri before the mirror crackled shut.

"This isn't the throne room," Ismae observed aloud.

I looked over my shoulder. "You don't say?"

"I'd rather have you sarcastic." She smiled and took my hand. "I can't say I blame them for taking the mirror out of the castle, all things considered, but it does complicate things."

I ran my fingers through my hair, decided it was annoyingly long, and pulled it back into a knot. The concern then became getting us all to the castle floating thousands of feet overhead. We couldn't get anywhere by standing in an empty room, so I crossed to the nearest door and opened it at the same time someone on the other side pushed it open.

We locked surprised gazes only a moment.

Bernard Andrew the Devourer.

I'd met him once before with Tavia at my side. He'd given Tavia the key that would open Selina's Vault of Hearts locked away in the fairy castle. He'd known more about me than I had him in that meeting. I didn't know where he'd gathered his information, but he seemed to recognize me as well.

The hairy man lunged at me. I expected him to draw a weapon, but he unexpectedly laid into me with his fists, landing two blows to my poor ribs before sending me staggering with a left hook to my jaw.

Ismae's voice came from somewhere, and when I managed to get my eyes to focus again, the empty chairs were stomping around Bernard, grabbing at his arms and kicking him in the shins with their wooden legs. More people poured into the room.

"Stomp me on the ground and say *Ondur!*"

I turned in a circle to see who spoke.

"I'm in your hand! Stomp me on the ground and say *Ondur*," the voice repeated.

My attention landed on the wizard's staff I'd taken from the giants. The *talking* wizard's staff.

"Don't stand there like a nincompoop! Unless I've chosen the wrong wizard . . ."

Not fully understanding why I was obeying an inanimate object, I stomped the staff on the wooden planks under our feet and shouted, "Ondur!" A bust of magic rippled away from me and toward the men. The unexpected shift in the floorboards made them stumble and fall into each other.

The power from the staff seeped into my palm and into my core, where it echoed like the shock of bumping an elbow. I'd felt the same sensation when I chased after Ismae in the forest.

Feeling only the need to use the powerful staff again, I pointed it toward the group of men and bellowed, "Valdor!" A ball of energy from the staff slammed into the nearest man and hurtled him into the four men behind him. I was about to utter another spell when the staff was suddenly snatched from me. I wheeled around to glare at Zuri. "Give that back! You can't use it, and I need it."

She growled, digging her blue eyes into me. *Magical artifacts are dangerous.*

I held both hands out toward the frightened men now staggering toward the door. "It's helping me with them. Besides, my father has enchanted items his entire life."

Yes, and look where he is now and the damage four enchanted gemstones have done. This isn't an enchanted piece of wood, Gerard, it's pure magic. An actual item forged from powerful magic, and I believe the reason why darkness is clinging to you again right now.

I looked at myself, at the shadows clinging to my skin like it had earlier with the argument with Ismae.

"He's arguing with a giant fox," a nearby man mumbled.

It was only then I realized that from their view, the argument was one-sided. I cast them a glance.

"Can we stop arguing about the stick and focus on warning the castle?" Ismae asked, pointing her thumb to the door.

"Warn the castle? Why do you need to warn them?" Bernard demanded, his claws extended and ready to pounce.

"Because Selina's going to try and take Princess Tavia and Prince Mathias," I answered, giving my cheek a little stroke to see how bad the swelling was from his blow. Not too bad.

Bernard scoffed. "I heard Selina took you and left. *And* you took the girl."

I nodded. "Yes. Look, it's complicated, and I don't have to tell you."

Ismae shook her head. "What he means is we would rather only tell the story once, so get us to the castle."

The man sighed. "Sorry, we were given strict orders to stop anyone who came through that mirror. I'm assuming they specifically meant you."

"Do you two . . . know each other?" Ismae questioned, looking between us.

"It seems he knows me better than I know him," I replied.

"Bernard." The wolf held his hand out to her.

Ismae tilted her head. "Bernard The Devourer? Tavia mentioned you when we were discussing how to get to the castle to stop Selina the first time. She said you called yourself BAD wolf." She grinned.

The wolf's toothy grin looked predatory, and I stepped between him and Ismae. He chuckled at my defensiveness. "Relax, little wizard, I'm not going to eat her. But if you're friends with Tavia . . . that means you're the girl that was taken by Selina's pet." His eyes settled on me.

I didn't try and hide my anger and annoyance with him.

He met my gaze with an intensity of his own.

"That is true," Ismae confirmed and grabbed my arm to push me aside. "But I am quite all right. I went willingly."

"No, you didn't," I mumbled.

She elbowed me and widened her eyes.

"Oh. Yeah, no she came with me because she wanted to."

Bernard wasn't convinced.

Ismae sighed. "He was under a spell. Selina has the heart of a sorceress who can manipulate minds. I met that sorceress a few months ago and was even subjected to her powers. Her name was Vivian."

Bernard's smug look melted.

"Yes, *Queen* Vivian, the queen of the fairies," Mother added. "Selina took her heart and used that magic to manipulate Gerard's mind. At the uttering of a phrase, he was under her control, just like Florian was in that final battle. He had no choice and neither did Gerard."

"Please let us pass," Ismae added.

Bernard rubbed the back of his neck. "I'm not supposed to. By order of the king and queen, I'm afraid."

Zuri huffed and pushed past us. The men, not knowing what to do against an oversized fox, stepped out of the way and looked to Bernard for instructions. The familiar wasn't going to stand and wait any longer. I was growing to like her more and more, even if she had taken the staff I needed.

I shrugged at Bernard and followed Zuri, taking Ismae's hand and dragging her with me as we went.

Bernard scowled and followed. "You can't simply walk up to the castle. It's impossible. You need someone to take you up there."

Out on the street, Zuri drew a lot of attention. She wasn't bothered in the slightest and lay on her belly. *Get on and I will carry you there.*

I glanced over my shoulder and saw the outside of the tavern—the Choking Cyclops.

"Makes sense why they're so one-*sight*ed." I grinned to Ismae, pleased with my joke.

She gave me a confused look, and I pointed to the sign. She rolled her eyes at my bad pun but grinned nevertheless.

I looked at my mother. "You can fly up. Zuri wants Ismae and me to ride on her back."

"She can fly?" Mother asked.

"Apparently. She's magical, remember?"

Mother nodded and transformed to fly ahead.

Ismae climbed onto Zuri's back and I followed. I smirked at Bernard. "Guess you'll have some explaining to do. You didn't try very hard to stop us."

Bernard scowled, lifted his hand, and motioned forward.

All of the men who had been standing back ran toward us. Zuri jumped, but two sets of hands grabbed me by my shirt and arms and yanked me off the back of the magic fox.

"Gerard, why can't you keep your mouth shut?" Ismae shouted back.

The mercenaries rolled me onto my stomach and bound my wrists behind me. I pinched the end of the rope between two fingers and said, "Alluhura!" The rope caught fire, which also burned my wrist as it started melting. It was how the spell was *supposed* to go, though.

Bernard put out the fire quickly and dragged me to my feet. "You're not going to the king and queen without me. I won't be the reason the royal family is harmed. Ismae can carry your message, and you can wait here like a good little bad guy."

"Wouldn't that make me a bad little bad guy, then?"

Bernard's eyes narrowed, and he punched me in the gut, stealing my breath and making me double over.

I lifted my eyes and saw Zuri running through the air as if it were ground, up and toward the castle.

My heart twisted. I was always appreciated when convenient but always left behind when things became difficult. No one trusted me. Just as well, I never trusted them. This sort of thing happened everywhere—I was the one who got them the mirror and into the mirror realm and protected them from the mercenaries until—

Who was I kidding?

Zuri was the one who pushed her way through the men.

All I did was make a snide comment and got myself arrested for it. I'd tried to help Ismae and her kingdom and confronted Selina when I should have just stayed behind. No one had come to save me in Alahl Lu'ehn a few days ago. They had come to the fairy castle to save Mathias. I just got picked up along the way because they conveniently stepped into the tower in which I was trapped and ended up needing my help to get back.

With a flex of my jaw, I turned my gaze away and allowed the men to drag me down the road. I could only hope Ismae would eventually come back for me. They needed me to get Selina's heart back, after all.

Didn't they?

"Not putting up much of a fight now," the man at my left elbow snarked.

I raised a brow. "Anta eshte bün."

The man's feet turned to stone mid-step, and he fell forward, smashing his face on the stone street.

"*Tsk*. Watch out for the rocks there," I said, shaking my head with a smug grin.

Zuri landed in front of us, Ismae still on her back, and glared hard at Bernard.

Bernard stopped, halting his men. "Why didn't you just go to the castle?"

"Because, you numbskull, my *boyfriend* needs to be with me. And you're welcome to come explain yourself to the royal family."

"Even Tavia said he was bad! He's done horrible things!"

"Everyone makes mistakes. It's part of being alive. Now, let him go or I'll use a spell and make the stones in the street trap you in a prison."

Ismae had come back from me. More than that, she wasn't afraid to stand up for herself against a man nearly three heads taller than she was. He'd seen her magic. He knew she could do what she wanted.

Bernard heaved a sigh and ran his hand down the scruff on his face. "Not everyone murders people. If you want to be responsible for him, fine. Just let them know it isn't my fault if he all of a sudden goes evil again and kills the entire royal family." He yanked me forward and cut through my bindings with his dagger. "I swear if anything happens to the royal family, I will gut you."

I jerked my arm away and mumbled a curse under my breath before climbing onto Zuri's back behind Ismae. I slid my arms around her small waist, pulling her close. "I thought you'd left me," I whispered in her ear.

Zuri turned around.

"Are you kidding?" Ismae rested an arm across mine. "I'm never leaving you alone again, remember? Let alone to be subjected to whatever stupid punishment they felt was justified."

I kissed her neck. "How did you get Zuri to come back?"

I was never planning on leaving you. The men just needed to believe we were. She winked at me, then took a giant leap into the air and ran forward and upward like I'd seen her do earlier.

"You're not alone anymore, Gerard," Ismae reminded me.

I was beginning to see she might be right.

EIGHTEEN

When we landed on the hexagon-shaped bailey, we were greeted by the castle guard with weapons drawn. Mother exited the castle with the king and queen at her side, princes behind, and some other people I couldn't see until Zuri landed.

Florian and Ferdinand stepped up to their parents' sides, both dressed in royal garb, but Florian wore a sash across his chest and had a bigger crown on his head than Ferdinand, not to mention a scowl that clashed with his fancy attire. Judging by the number of people gathered, it appeared we had interrupted the coronation of Prince Florian.

Ferdinand's jaw was tight, his lack of wings a harsh reminder that I'd sliced them off during the battle. Tavia stepped up to his side, her hair now red, orange, and yellow like flames, and her orange eyes locked on me with anger and hatred. She glanced at Ismae, then back at me.

Everyone was on edge.

One wrong move and I would ignite another battle. Maybe I should have stayed with Bernard . . .

I slid off Zuri's back, careful to keep my hands away from anything.

The fox trotted over and set the staff at the feet of the king so she could bow.

I flexed my hands, itching to call the staff back to me. If I was attacked, I wanted to have a way to defend myself. I was far too aware, however, of the increasingly large crowd pressing up against the new windows of the throne room trying to see what was happening. More squeezed together behind the soldiers.

The tension was palpable enough to be sliced with a sword.

Ismae broke the tension as soon as her feet hit the stone. She sprinted to Tavia and threw her arms around her. "You're beautiful!"

Tavia pulled her away, behind the soldiers, and whispered to her quickly in a fervent tone that told me she was likely demanding to know if I'd harmed her.

Ferdinand held his sword down by his side, his gaze never leaving me, but it was unsheathed nonetheless.

I held his glare, trying to decide whether or not to intimidate him or if it would only ruin things in the end. I decided Ismae would be upset if I prodded a sleeping dragon and turned my attention to my mother.

Hazel cleared her throat softly. "As I mentioned, Gerard has important information about Selina."

"Speak, boy," the king demanded. "You have five minutes, and then my men will arrest you."

"That's not much incentive to—" I caught Ismae's wide eyes over the king's shoulder and changed course. "I'm not certain if you know, but Mathias and Tavia are my brother and sister. Hazel is their mother." I held my hand out to Hazel.

Mathias and Tavia didn't react, and I realized they knew.

I suddenly felt awkward and shifted my weight to the opposite foot. "Okay, so maybe being family doesn't matter, but Selina wants revenge for you standing up against her. She's got James's hand, remember? She's controlling him, and he just attempted to capture Elisa. She already had him bring her Odette and Ulrich. She wants you brought back to her as well."

"And we should just believe you?" Tavia snarked.

"No. I'm not asking you to believe me, but it's true. It's better than choosing a heartless prince as the next king, isn't it?"

Tavia's eyes narrowed dangerously. "Oh, he has his heart back. As does Vivian. Because *we* figured out how to fix it, no thanks to you." She gestured between herself and Ferdinand. "You kidnapped one of my dearest friends and left us behind to pick up the pieces."

I scoffed. "Yeah? And how do you restore someone's heart?" In disbelief, I was unable to hide my condescending tone.

Tavia folded her arms. Her eyes were practically burning. "And why should I tell you?"

I rolled my eyes. "Thought as much. Look, Ismae came with me to warn you, and now we've done that, I must take Selina's familiar back to her, and hopefully I can figure out how to restore Selina's heart and end this since you won't share with me how you did it to save me some time." I bravely turned my back to the swords and arrows pointed at me and climbed onto Zuri's back.

"I'm going with him," Ismae insisted and tried to step around Tavia.

"No, you aren't," Tavia said firmly, grabbing her by the arm.

Mathias closed the gap between them and said in a low voice, "Ismae, you've just been returned to us. You've been missing—"

"What, a *day* your time? Or a few hours? I know you don't trust him, but he was under Selina's spell. Selina used Vivian's powers to manipulate him, control him. Even Elisa has forgiven Gerard. He needs our help. He can't do this on his own!"

"Do what, exactly?" Mathias asked.

"Face Selina! He needs as much help as he can get! Surely, you understand that having joined him once to face her." Ismae's eyes pleaded with them, and it took everything within me to remain silent.

Mathias glared over his shoulder at me. "Then maybe he shouldn't have burned so many bridges."

I set my jaw. They wouldn't allow Ismae to return with me.

My mother caught my gaze before I looked away. "Perhaps you would trust me echoing Ismae's thoughts?" she said quickly.

"You were her pet bird. How do we know you aren't on Selina's side as well?" Tavia snapped.

"After everything I've done to help you?" Mother replied, echoing the edge in Tavia's voice.

"All you did was tell me Gerard needed help. I helped get him out. In return, he nearly killed Keltin *and* he kidnapped Ismae."

"Keltin?" Ismae's voice squeaked. "Where is he? Can I see him?"

"I'll take you to him," Tavia said, redirecting her toward the castle.

I tightened my hands in Zuri's fur on the back of her neck. "We should go. We're wasting time. I delivered my message."

Is there nothing else you'd like to say?

"Like what? That I'm sorry?" I shouted. "I'm sorry I was raised by an evil sorceress who only taught me dark magic? I'm sorry that I wasn't raised in gilded walls with meals brought to me by servants three times a day? That I worked day and night to perfect my skill? Or perhaps that I wasn't raised by loving parents who kissed my owies better? No. I'm not apologizing for a damn thing to these spoiled little brats. If they don't want to help, that's their problem. I'll face Selina alone. I've always been alone, and that is the best way. I can't trust anyone." I held my hand out to the staff still at the fairy king's feet, and without a summoning word, it flew to my hand.

Gerard—

"Go! Now!" I commanded.

Mother ran to me. "You aren't leaving. You can't! You aren't strong enough to face her alone!"

I glared at my mother, feeling the darkness rise with my anger. "Zuri was wrong about healing Selina's heart. It's not possible. And tell Ismae to marry Mathias. She'll be safer that way and taken care of if I die." I pushed my mother back and yanked on Zuri's fur to get her to run, leap, and get us back to the mirror.

The fox turned and stepped to the edge.

Mother turned a pleading look to the king and queen, to the princes, to her children. She had tears in her eyes. "Will none of you help?"

Zuri wouldn't leap. She teetered on the edge, watching to see what would happen, if even one person would take a chance.

I wouldn't wait for any further rejection. My soul was being torn apart. I cursed Ismae and Zuri for giving me false hope, for making me think there was even an ounce of goodness in me.

There wasn't.

I was evil.

Raised by evil.

Trained by evil.

Shaped by darkness.

Darkness was a part of me, decaying everything inside and filling it with an empty void I clung to instead of feeling the pain of loneliness and betrayal. I jumped off Zuri's back when she refused to budge and stormed to the edge to jump, but Zuri shoved me back with her nose at the last moment.

I snarled. "Back off."

She growled and stomped her foot.

I went flying back with an unseen force, hit the ground on my back, and slid several feet. I realized I was merely steps away from the royal family. Clutching the staff tightly in my hands, I rolled back to my feet, anticipating the soldiers attacking.

Mathias stepped forward before anyone could react. My younger brother. He looked a lot like Mother but had Father's jaw. He stared at me.

I stood poised in a fighting stance, adrenaline making my hands tremble.

Finally, Mathias sighed and shook his head. "I've thought a lot about you lately. Everyone has caught me up on what you've done the past year. But . . . I was the only one that saw what Selina did to you."

I flexed my jaw.

Mathias glanced down. "I saw how she punished you when you attacked Griswil and failed. I turned a blind eye to your screams coming from beyond the black door because I felt you deserved it." He shook his head again and met my gaze, but this time his expression was that of pity. "I suspect you faced more darkness and horrors behind closed doors but didn't see it until you saved me from Selina. I watched her stitch your lips sealed with magic so you wouldn't be able to say a spell. You got me out of there. And who knows what did she do to you while you were trapped here in this castle?"

Florian stepped forward. "She tortured him here. I was a witness to that."

Everyone suddenly seemed very uncomfortable and refused to meet my gaze or shifted their stance, rubbed their necks, or had an itch on their arm or hand.

"I don't think it's you who has betrayed us," Mathias said. "I believe everyone has always failed *you*. How many others saw the nightmare Selina put you through and refused to help? How many people heard your cries and never once stopped her?" He stepped even closer.

I backed up, anticipating a dagger ready to gut me, but stopped when I looked down and saw he had his hand outstretched. "You would ally yourself with me?" I asked softly.

He nodded. "Ismae is right."

The anger ebbed and my throat tightened. "You will fight by my side?"

"Yes. This isn't your burden alone. It belongs to each of us. We will take part in the aftermath, why shouldn't we help fight for it?"

I extended my hand and accepted the handshake. The surprise must have been evident on my face.

Mathias gave me a half-smile. "All right. Let's get our things and we shall return with you to our land. And by the way, the way Tavia gave their hearts back was simple. All they had to do was accept it."

"I know how to get more help," Tavia offered.

We turned our attention to her.

"If you can help us with our mother . . ." Tavia hesitated and glanced at Hazel. "I suppose I mean our adoptive mother. She may be able to help. She was a very powerful sorceress before all of this happened. I don't know if Selina took her heart or not, but she's been suffering with illness for several years."

My brows furrowed. "I hadn't considered asking for help from other sorceresses."

Mathias pinched his lips. "Hmm. You know, that is a good idea. If she could return to her full power, she might be able to convince Queen Athena to help too—Odette and Ulrich's mother."

I blinked. "Adding a couple of sorceresses to face her, should we need to, is actually brilliant."

"*If* she can convince her," Ismae added. "We don't know if Athena is on our side after what she did as the sea witch."

"True." Mathias shrugged.

Tavia cocked a brow at me. "See what happens when other people help too?" She gave me the smallest hint of a smile, and I knew it was the only way she would express her forgiveness.

I wasn't ready to admit that I didn't know exactly how to help their mother, but I needed them on my side.

While Mathias and Tavia went into the castle, bringing Ismae with them, Ferdinand cleared his throat. "Any way you can heal my wings?"

I grimaced. "Sorry about that. It wasn't . . . I mean, I didn't exactly mean to. And no, I don't know how to heal. I don't do that. I thought fairies could?"

Ferdinand didn't answer. Clearly, they had already tried.

"So. Florian is king?" I glanced at the younger of the brothers. "Why not you?"

Ferdinand shook his head. "Tavia and I want to travel and see worlds. We can't do that if either of us is stuck on a throne. It was a mutual decision for me to step down. Besides, Florian will be an impeccable ruler."

I grunted. "Hmm. Will you be joining us?"

"Of course. I don't trust you around Tavia."

I arched a brow. "I've never done anything to Tavia."

"There's a first time for everything. Mathias might fall for your sob story, but I don't." He shrugged.

"Ah. A sob story. I suppose you could call my life as much. You don't see me sobbing, though, do you?" I tightened my grip on the staff and left him behind so I could stand beside Zuri to wait for the others to return.

Zuri reached out and took the staff from me again.

I rolled my eyes and folded my arms.

Mother stepped up to my side and wrapped her arm around me in a side-hug. "I'm proud of you."

"For what?" I mumbled.

"For staying and seeing this through. You could have run."

I looked down at her. "I tried to. I would have jumped had Zuri not pulled me away from the edge."

She took my hand. "What you've gone through—"

"Isn't an excuse for what I've done."

"I was going to say, I think you can use it to your strength. You know how you've felt going through pain and suffering and you don't want others to endure that. It will make you a better king."

"I'm not going to be king for many years. Tovan has been trapped in time and he doesn't appear to have even aged. You do know that makes him only six years older than me?"

She laughed. "Now, *that* is odd to consider, especially if his age doesn't catch up to him. You can still be in a leadership role without being king. People will relate to you more."

"If they don't see how much of a mess I am," I grumbled.

Ismae was the first back at my side and she wrapped me in a hug. "Keltin is fine. His broken arm is healing and he's ready to come home," she said as if I were worried.

Still, I nodded and said, "Good."

Keltin offered me the same stoic scowl Ferdinand had plastered on his face.

Mathias, Tavia, and Ferdinand approached Keltin from behind, and we were one happy little group of friends ready to take on the sorceress.

"We'll use the Windforn mirror to get us back to Servad," Tavia said.

"We'll need to take that mirror with us." I looked from her to Ferdinand when he gave me a confused look. "If you want me to go help Grimhilde, the only way for me to do that is to walk through a mirror in her castle. The mirror that was in the tower will take us to Servad, the one in the tavern will take us to

Griswil, and I don't know where the third mirror will take us if you even have that mirror."

Ismae fiddled with the sleeve of her shirt. "The safest way to get back is to go through the mirror in Griswil and then . . . use a portal to the underworld to get us to Zelig's castle?"

I looked at Tavia. "I know that thought doesn't appeal to you."

"If I recall correctly, that was Odette," Tavia said.

"It's settled then." I climbed onto Zuri's back and scooted so Ismae could sit in front of me. "Since neither Keltin nor Ferdinand can fly, Zuri will have to return to get you and bring you down."

"Then we shall wait," Ferdinand replied.

Mathias and Tavia flew down in their gorgeous phoenix forms. I had to admit, I was a tad envious of how easily they rode on the wind. I didn't have any ability to shapeshift. Perhaps that would be a skill I could teach myself at the academy—whenever I got to attend as a student.

Zuri let us off and we waited outside of the tavern while she ran to collect Ferdinand and Keltin.

"I really am sorry about his wings," I said absently, not looking at Tavia. "If I knew a way to heal them, I would offer."

She nodded silently.

Ismae took my hand, offering a comforting smile.

Once everyone was gathered, we returned to the back room of the Choking Cyclops, walking past Bernard and his men, who gave apologetic glances to both Tavia and Ferdinand. We opened the mirror and stepped through.

NINETEEN

I blinked against the dim light and found myself standing in a cave with only my mother at my side. It definitely wasn't where I had left the Windforn mirror. Each stalactite dangling from the roof of the cave glowed orange while the stalagmites jutting upward glowed green. The strange glow cast light at odd angles throughout the room, and more than once I thought I saw something move at the corner of my vision. The hair on my arms prickled, and I knew something was very wrong.

"It worked!" a voice exclaimed in excitement.

I snatched my mother and yanked her behind me as I wheeled around to face the source of the voice. A man was running toward us. I couldn't see much about him other than he was at least as tall as me.

"Stand back!" I commanded, holding my hand out.

He skidded to a halt and looked from my hand to my eyes. He was close enough now I caught some details of his face. He had a short, narrow chin and high cheekbones. He reminded me of the fae in Griswil, were it not for the two stubby horns on each side of his forehead. His eyes had a faint yellow glow to them.

Mother placed her hand on my arm and stepped up to my side. "Flynn? Is that you?" her voice was full of disbelief.

His gaze flickered to her, and the yellow glow faded. "Yes, Hazel."

She smiled, pushed past me, and ran to him, meeting him halfway to embrace him.

I had to struggle through my memories. How did my mother know him? The name, Flynn . . . I thought I might have read about him in one of Father's journals, but all I could recall was that my mother knew him from before she knew my father.

"It has been far too long. What are you doing here?" She pulled back and looked up at the stranger.

I didn't like the feeling coming off him and reached out and pulled her back. Having worked with demons in the past, I wasn't going to give him an inch.

"Gerard, relax," Mother said, smiling brightly. "This is Flynn. He practically raised me. He is the one who saved me from the tower and got me to Servad. He's the whole reason I met your father."

I would have to ask her later for some further explanation.

I kept my eyes locked on *Flynn*. "Has he always been a demon?"

He ran his tongue over his teeth and frowned.

Mother's brows furrowed, and she turned to him with an accusatory look as she ran her gaze over him.

Flynn rolled his eyes and mumbled, "*Half* demon. And no, I wasn't one at the time Hazel knew me. I was half orc then. Being partially demon is the reason, however, I am here and now you are too."

"Explain yourself." Mother's green eyes narrowed.

He sighed and his shoulders dropped. "It is a long story, I'm afraid. Basically, I made a deal with a sorceress. She wanted out, and that's not the way I work. My contracts, as you know, are binding, and not because of my own will. She didn't like that even though I explained there was nothing I could do to get her out. So she thought she could turn me into a demon so she could control me and get rid of the deal. However, she was interrupted, so the spell didn't take hold in its entirety. Still, the demon resides near enough to influence me."

"What was the deal and who was the sorceress?" I interjected.

Flynn's gaze slowly drifted to me, telling me silently that I had interrupted and wasn't invited to this conversation. However, he tapped the tip of his nose. "Why do you think I summoned you both here?"

"Selina," Mother blurted after a gasp, catching on.

He nodded.

"How long have you *been* here?" Mother reached out to touch Flynn's shoulder.

He shook his head. "It's hard to say when I have no way of knowing the time."

"So why summon us here?" I asked, gesturing to the empty cave. "And where are my friends?"

"Friends?" Flynn lifted the corner of his lip in a questioning grimace and tilted his head to the side. "A bit of a generous term, don't you think?" he asked in a loud whisper.

I narrowed my eyes at him. "Answer my question or I'm leaving."

"You can't, I'm afraid. Not without my permission." A sly grin appeared on his face, revealing the demonic half of him.

Mother lowered her hands to her side, scrunched her eyes in a glare, then placed her hands on her hips. "Flynn, why have you summoned us here?"

His lips tightened briefly before he walked to the center of the cave and snapped his fingers. The green and orange light in the stalactites and stalagmites turned white and brightened the room, revealing hundreds of mirrors surrounding the cave. And revealing his features as well. His skin was green, his long hair black, and his bottom jaw jutted forward just enough two fangs jutted up over his top lip. His horns were ivory.

"I have a simple deal for you," he said and sauntered over to a large chair that looked almost like a throne sitting at the side of the cave. I hadn't noticed it before. He flopped down on it and draped one leg over the arm of the chair.

"Flynn—" Mother's voice held a warning tone.

He lifted a finger. "Wait. I let you go, and you break the largest Windforn mirror, the original. That is it."

Mother eyed him skeptically.

I took in all the mirrors. "Why don't you just choose one and walk through?"

"I can't. They're mirages, simply cruel reflections for me to watch the world outside pass on by without me." His attention was drawn suddenly to a young girl in a peasant dress and he walked over to the mirror.

The girl set her bonnet on the bed and faced the mirror. She was covered in smudges of dirt from whatever hard work she'd been forced to do that day. Her face lit up with a smile and she held her hands out to her sides, then moved them up over her head like a ballerina. She spun around with grace that didn't fit the state she was in.

Flynn's face saddened, and he reached out like he might try and touch her, but his hand dropped.

I was about to ask how he knew her, but Mother walked over and slid her arm around his waist. "You can't save her," she whispered. "She's already gone."

"That's what hurts the most," he replied, his voice strained. "I need out of here, Hazel."

I rubbed my chin. "If you can't exit through the mirrors, if they are only mirages, how did you get us through one?"

Flynn's gaze snapped to me, annoyed and eyes glowing yellow . "You are wise, young man. You know just the questions to ask." He grinned, the demon inside of him shining through once more.

"And?" I pressed.

He lifted his shoulders to his ears. "I had a bit of help."

I sensed the darkness around the room heighten before Nicholas appeared at the side of the room, confirming to me we no longer resided on the mortal plane. I ran to my mother to protect her, summoning forth the shadows as I went. I knew they had told me to use light magic, but I couldn't feel any tree or living thing I could try and get energy from.

Nicholas appeared near where I had just been standing and cocked a brow. "Relax, Gerard. I'm not here to harm you." The demon's sharp teeth teased the bottom of his lip as he grinned. His black hair was down behind his back, a posture I knew meant he was in a particularly good mood, and he wore his favorite red-flecked black tunic.

My gaze darted to Flynn. "You made a deal with *him*?"

"Yes. He provided me with some of your blood a little while ago . . ." He pulled a vial from the pocket in his vest and held it up. "In exchange, I taught him how to give darkness physical touch."

My mind immediately flashed to the times I'd been locked alone with Nicholas as punishment, how darkness had scratched, then clawed, and finally bit into my flesh. "You practiced blood magic on me," I voiced aloud, turning an accusatory sneer to Nicholas.

He smirked. "Guilty. I sense your anger. You *do* know my being a creature of darkness as well, you can't harm me with those shadows? I've had *years* of practice controlling them. Longer than you've been alive."

"Remember your light," Mother urged from behind me.

"You helped him!" I shouted at Flynn, ignoring my mother.

He grimaced. "I didn't know."

"You know how he got my blood you now hold? He bled it from me. While he was torturing me!" Selina's heart ignited in anger, and the edges of my vision began to turn red. "And I don't care if you're a creature of darkness or not. You deserve to go through the same pain I have." I flung the shadows at Nicholas.

He held a hand up with his first two fingers raised, and the shadows parted around him and returned to where they should have been in the room. "You cannot kill me here. I am more powerful than you in the underworld."

My lip twitched. The anger inside of me mounted, and I sent a flurry of attacks at Nicholas.

His laughter only made my hatred grow.

"Gerard, stop this!" Mother's voice rang over the blood pounding in my ears.

The tremble in my hands ran all the way into my shoulders, down my spine, and through my legs.

Mother grasped my arm, standing behind me, and said in my ear, "You're better than this. You can control the darkness, remember?"

I let out a growl and tightened my grip, but didn't attack again.

"You should go, Nicholas," Flynn said. "You aren't helping."

He rolled his eyes. "We'll see each other again, Gerard." His eyes blackened with promise before he gave a snide bow and faded away.

Tense silence lingered in the cave.

My blood calmed, though the pain in my chest didn't. Selina's heart fueled my hatred for Nicholas and the pain he had caused me. I *wanted* to feel that. Even more, I wanted to harm him in the way he'd harmed me.

Mother tugged on my arm. "Let it go."

I exhaled and lifted my chin to the ceiling, releasing a heavy breath and the darkness with it.

"I truly didn't know," Flynn said after a moment.

I glowered at him.

Mother shook her head. "I cannot say what you've been through or if there's any part of you that is still the Flynn I know. But you must answer my only question—why should we help you?"

The half demon's eyes saddened. "I can't get rid of this demon inside of me trapped here, and it is the Windform mirror that keeps me in prison. I must learn the demon's name and release him back to the underworld." He looked down at me. "I am sorry for what Nicholas did to you, but you must know I had no other choice. I had to time the spell just right and only had one shot at it. If I messed it up . . ."

I watched him look at the vial of my blood before tossing it to me. "An act of faith," he said.

I caught it and ran my thumb over the glass.

Mother turned to me and asked with her eyes what we should do.

I looked down at the vial. "Where is this original mirror?"

"In a country called Sheblom."

"The Southern Isles . . ." Mother took in a breath. "We can't possibly get there until we're done with Selina."

Lifting my gaze to Flynn, I saw the honest look in his eyes. He was holding his breath. Another soul ruined by Selina. I empathized with the demon-orc.

Finally, I nodded. "Okay. I'll get to the Southern Isles and break the original mirror."

Relief washed over Flynn's face. "Thank you. Oh, I should add that you do not need to perform this task immediately. However, you must fulfill your end of our bargain within the year or you'll be imprisoned here with me."

I twitched my brows. "Always a catch, huh?"

Flynn shrugged innocently and walked to me with a parchment of paper and an old black-feather quill. "Sign here."

Without looking at my mother, or thinking on it further, I signed the paper.

He smiled. "I'll see you on the other side."

Mother closed the gap between them. He went to hug her, but she placed her hand on his chest. "You listen here, demon. You best let go of Flynn before he gets out of the mirror because he *will* find a way to get you out, and he *will* destroy you."

His eyes went yellow, and the sly grin appeared once more. He leaned so his face was inches from hers. "I have no intention of letting him go, my lady.

He shall never learn my name. I can't wait to see the surface world and grow until I overcome him entirely."

"We'll see about that." She pushed him back and faced me. "Can you banish him?"

I blanched at the sudden request. "What? Um . . . I must confess, I've never tried to pull a demon out of someone being possessed. I risk harming the real Flynn if I mess up. I could even kill him. Besides, it takes dark magic to control a demon."

The demon laughed and winked. "I can't wait to see you again."

"It will only be if we run into each other in the underworld," I said firmly.

He blew me a kiss.

Mother's eyes saddened. "I'm so sorry, darling."

Flynn sucked in a breath, his eyes returning to normal. "I wait anxiously." He snapped his fingers and gestured to a mirror on the other side of the cave. The face of the mirror was blue, showing it was ready for us to exit through.

Mother gave his hand one final squeeze and followed me over to the mirror.

"You first," I directed.

She took a breath, glanced over one more time, and finally stepped through.

"Gerard," Flynn said before I could follow. "I know you have been affected by Selina."

I looked at him but gave him no response.

He nodded knowingly. "I could sense it. I don't know how to help you. I have seen some of what you're going through." He gestured to the mirrors for explanation. "I've seen some of what she's done. Your mother . . . she is a wonderful person. I've loved her as a brother for a long time. I was there when she married your father, and it brought me peace knowing she was finally with someone that loved her. She deserved it after the life she was put through. Whatever you do, keep her safe." He flashed a smile.

I nodded. "I will protect her with my life."

"I know you will."

TWENTY

I stepped out on the other side of the mirror in the middle of everyone demanding answers from my mother about where we'd been and what had happened. I'd barely set my feet in the grass when Ismae slammed against my side and wrapped her arms tight around me.

I pulled my arms out so I could return her embrace, and her warmth washed over me. I closed my eyes and held onto her.

"Now what, mighty wizard?" Ferdinand asked sarcastically.

"Obviously, we need a quick way to get everyone to my mother's," Tavia reminded. "While you were flirting with demons, we discussed that Mathias and I will fly and you will use that spell you did getting everyone into the castle when we were in Diova."

"I tried to tell them we could just ride on Zuri," Ismae said, "But not all of us non-fliers can fit."

I opened my eyes and looked at Tavia with a cold stare. "I was *not* flirting with demons. And that spell requires an item I can bind us all to."

Tavia removed the necklace from around her neck and tossed it to me.

Ferdinand reached out to stop her but was too late. He scowled. "I gave that to you," he whispered to her.

"I know, and we'll get it back. When we had to get back to the castle, before I faced Selina in the battle and became a real phoenix, Gerard used a spell to bind us all to the key to the Vault of Hearts. With a phrase, we can be summoned."

"I don't like the sound of that."

I arched my brow. "Well, the other option is always a portal through the underworld, but my mother isn't fond of me using dark magic right now, and I don't know that taking you through the underworld is a good idea either."

"Yeah? And why is that?" Ferdinand snapped.

I smirked. "You're a creature of light. Demons would be clawing over each other to get their nails and teeth into you. Fairy blood strengthens their powers."

Ferdinand's lips tightened.

"Stop teasing him," Ismae said, jabbing me in the chest with her finger.

I looked down at her and felt Selina's heart calming again. Of course the heart had fueled everything once again. I was growing concerned that her heart had come to life and was doing whatever it could to drag me away from the light I was attempting to cling to.

"Judging by the sky, we've lost another day," Mother said.

I looked up. It was evening. We'd lost the entire day, indeed. As exhausted as I was, we couldn't stop now. We still had to get to Zelig and help Grimhilde if we were going to get her on our side. The thought of wasting more time made me clench my teeth. Did we really *need* Grimhilde on our side if we had the dragons? I wasn't convinced.

I believe you need some rest, Zuri said to me. *You need to recover some of your strength if you are to use your magic to help Grimhilde.*

I looked over at the enormous fox sitting at the side of the group watching everyone and nodded. "Zuri is right. I need some time to rest and eat."

"This whole time you've been pressed for time and *now* you want a break?" Tavia said.

"Well, you've been in a different time stream, remember?" Ismae said kindly. "We just got back from running from giants and Gerard has used a lot of magic to help us so far. We can spend a couple of hours to rest." She looked up at me. "I can help find firewood. You sit."

"I can help—"

She placed her hand on my chest and raised her brows. "Sit."

"Okay." I begrudgingly agreed, not wanting the others to look at me like I couldn't help, and took a seat on the ground near the mirror.

Noticing the reflection of the trees on the mirror's surface, I turned to look at them. The leaves had already fallen into big piles on the forest floor, and winter teased at the bare branches with an icy wind that cut through the air.

I looked down at the necklace Tavia had tossed to me. It was a golden apple. I didn't understand the reference, but it must have had some kind of significance between them. It meant something to Ferdinand that Tavia had given it to me so freely. If I were to give Ismae anything . . . it would be a library.

The corner of my lip tugged in a smile. I would go see the palace library when all of this was over and make sure it was up to my standards for her. I would make sure there was at least an entire bookshelf filled with books about oration magic, and I would send a letter to the sorceress academy—wherever it was—and ask about Ismae having lessons.

"What's got you smiling?"

I lifted my gaze to Keltin, whose broken arm was against his chest in a sling. The others had gathered wood and were already in the process of starting a fire. "None of your business," I muttered.

"You don't need to be so sensitive, you know. We all have things going on." He paused. "How is Ulrich?"

"My question is why wasn't he there with you in Alahl Lu'ehn?" I threw back.

"He wanted to go home with Odette. She mentioned something about James asking them all to go back. She said he was acting weird, and Ulrich wanted to go with her to make sure things were okay. I guess I know why James was acting strangely." Keltin's jaw flexed, and he looked over at the fire.

I felt Zuri's eyes on me. "I . . . know what that's like. Having someone you care about taken from you."

Keltin shifted his gaze back to me. "I thought you'd done something horrible to Ismae. I'm glad to see she's still her same self." He smiled softly. "I thought you were going to take her heart and make her one of Selina's slaves."

"Nah, I'm fighting to get away from Selina." I looked down at the necklace again. "Fidgety, floppity, release them from the necklace." The necklace grew warm in my hand and the white light around it faded.

Mathias walked over, brow raised. "That's it? That's the spell?"

I stood and handed the necklace over. "Yes. You repeat that phrase and it will, essentially, transport us all to you in Zelig."

He shrugged and gave the necklace to Tavia.

She draped the golden chain around her neck.

"We can fly on ahead. We'll summon you all forth in a few hours. That should be sufficient for rest?" He turned once more to me.

I nodded. "Yes, that should be sufficient."

Mathias's lips slid into a smile, and I saw a bit of mother behind it. He faced Mother and held his hand out to her. "I know you are our birth mother. I hope we shall have enough time soon to properly catch up."

She extended her hand to take his, but Mathias shook his head and then wrapped his arm around her shoulders to pull her into a hug. She closed her eyes, and a tear ran down her cheek.

"Let's go, Tavia." He transformed into a phoenix.

Tavia kissed Ferdinand on the lips. "We'll see each other soon. Don't kill him, please?" She raised her brows at Ferdinand as if she were being serious—as if *Ferdinand* could actually kill me.

The wingless fairy rolled his eyes. "I promise." He kissed her forehead one last time and watched with the rest of us while she transformed and flew off after Mathias.

Mother and Zuri followed, and I let out a heavy breath.

Ismae stood at my side and rubbed her arms. "It's cold, isn't it? Strange for Griswil."

I rummaged through my pack and produced a fur cloak and draped it over her shoulders, then began walking back and forth. "Winter is finally catching up. The solstice is just a few days away. I'm thinking we only have four days left . . . so tomorrow must be the third day before the Winter Solstice." Even though I told Ismae, I spoke myself and tried to work out the timeline.

"Will you stop pacing? You're making me nervous," Ferdinand demanded sharply.

I hadn't even realized I was, but when I stopped and turned, I found myself several feet away from them.

"What's so important about the Winter Solstice?" Keltin asked.

Ferdinand crouched at my pack to search through its contents and pulled out another cloak.

"My father will be executed."

Keltin's eyes darted to me. "You have a father?"

I clenched my teeth. "And a mother too. Hazel. I wasn't born from the darkness, you know."

"Could have fooled me." Ferdinand stood and tossed Keltin one of the cloaks he'd pulled from my pack, then placed the third—and final—around himself.

Ismae approached me and wrapped her arms around my waist, pulling her body closer to mine and giving us both warmth. I adjusted the cloak around her so it wouldn't fall off her shoulders. I didn't understand how her touch alone could calm me. It didn't make sense, and it wasn't the first time I'd had the thought.

I puffed out a hot breath and returned her warm hug.

Keltin and Ferdinand exchanged a glance, but I didn't acknowledge either of the princes.

"Maybe we can sleep in Elisa's castle until they summon us to them? It will be warmer there," Keltin suggested.

"How far away are we from that castle?" Ferdinand asked.

I shook my head. "We can't go back, I'm afraid. Selina has spies we may run into, and I don't want to risk it. I have bedding in my pack we can lay out, and we can get a couple more fires started if you'd like."

"You cause a lot of problems, don't you?" Ferdinand stated. He crouched to gather more sticks and twigs.

"It would seem so," I replied stiffly.

Ismae heaved a sigh. "Ferdinand, please. Let's not start arguing again. Gerard is doing the best he knows how, and he's doing very good at it." She looked up at me.

Her gaze relaxed my building frustration. I placed my forehead against hers and stiffened when a gust of cold air struck my back.

"You can wrap the cloak around us both," she whispered. "Or you could put it around you and just hold me."

I chuckled. "I *am* holding you."

She tilted her chin up and kissed me. Once again, I tasted her light—like summer apples and bright winter days. The coldness around us melted, and her brother and Ferdinand disappeared. It was just Ismae and me in the winter forest.

I drew her as close as she could get, her soft body pressed to mine, and took another breath of her. I dug my fingers in her hair, and Ismae tempted me by sliding her tongue into my mouth.

"I don't know how she can want him like that," Ferdinand mumbled to Keltin, but I caught it, causing me to pull back.

Ismae let go of my shoulders to grab my face and keep my attention on her. "You ignore them. I don't want anyone else, remember? I just want you. I love you for you, Gerard."

"I love you too." I kissed her again and then settled my forehead against hers. "Selina's heart is raging inside of me," I confessed softly, ensuring the other two couldn't hear me.

Ismae's gaze filled with concern. She tucked her brown hair behind her ear, the wind still catching and trying to tug it away. "What do you mean?"

"Zuri . . . when she pulled me into the vision, I think she aggravated Selina's heart. It feels . . . different. There's an intense burning of constant anger." I rubbed my hand over my chest.

Ismae placed her hand over mine. "I noticed you've been a bit more short-tempered, but I thought it was because you are nervous being around everyone again. Why didn't you say something earlier?"

I scoffed. "The others think I'm an angry person already. That I'm dangerous, even born from darkness. If they found out Selina's heart was dragging me toward that darkness or attacking my heart or . . . or whatever is going on . . ." I shook my head.

Ismae pressed as close as she could get to me. "Don't you dare let go of yourself, Gerard. Don't even think about that darkness. If you start to feel it, tell me. Please."

"You have no idea how much I need your light." I felt like an idiot for saying it. Vulnerable. Uncomfortable. But it was true, and Ismae deserved to know how much I needed her. How desperate I was for her. I kissed her ear. "I love you, Ismae."

She smiled up at me, her perfect teeth brightening even the darkness, and she kissed me again.

Behind her, Ferdinand had a second fire started, and he and Keltin sat close together while he tossed another stick on the flames.

I reluctantly released Ismae's warmth and guided her to the flames. When I sat, she sat at my side and snuggled against my arm, but pulled the cloak around my shoulders, too, so we were sharing the cloak.

I kept my gaze on the shadows beyond us. Any time the flames flickered against the shadows behind Keltin or Ferdinand, my heart jumped into my throat only to calm when they didn't move. Selina's shadows must have moved on.

"I thought you were supposed to be resting?" Ferdinand snarked.

"Wizards can sleep with their eyes open," I lied.

He looked me up and down and glowered at Keltin when he chuckled.

I did, however, close my eyes and rest my head on top of Ismae's. Even just an hour of rest would help.

Before I knew it, the taste of metal filled the air—I was familiar with the scent because of the forges in Ashwrya where blacksmiths worked with iron and copper to forge axes, swords, and even jewelry.

It was also the scent of magic.

I snatched the bag in my hand, pulled Ismae closer, and gasped a breath before an unsettling sensation of being dragged forward, upward, and then dropped from a high point filled the pit of my belly.

Keltin fell to his knees when we appeared just outside the doors of Zelig's castle.

Ferdinand turned and wretched into the nearby bushes.

I steadied Ismae, who blinked a few times. "That was . . . an exhilarating sensation," she said.

Ferdinand wiped his mouth off on the back of his hand. "That's not the word I would use." He drew a steadying breath and scowled an accusatory glare at me.

I shrugged. "Everyone reacts differently, and I didn't have time to warn you."

Mother stood with her hand on the door with Zuri sitting by her side, her fur catching the falling snow. "Tavia and Mathias entered already," she explained.

I spat a curse, and nearly shoved Mother off the stairs as I pushed the door open and sprinted inside. I knew Queen Grimhilde was unstable, but more importantly, she was once on Selina's side. If they made one wrong move or if the shadows were in there, we were done for.

"They only went to get Queen Grimhilde!" Mother called.

Zuri follows behind.

The others rushed after me, down the cold corridor and up the spiral staircase to the next level. I'd lived in the castle for several months and knew where Grimhilde's room was. The fact Selina's agents could be in every corner of the practically pitch-black castle only willed me faster.

"Allul!" I commanded, and all of the sconces, candles, and fireplaces in the castle ignited.

To my left, a shadow ran alongside me against the wall until the light banished it.

They were already inside, now fleeing for whatever darkness was left.

I extended my hand behind me and summoned the wizard staff from Zuri. I was a little surprised when I felt it hit my hand. I thought she would refuse to let it go.

My boots slipped on the smooth stone floor as I rounded a corner, causing me to slam into a nearby table and send all of the contents crashing to the ground. I wedged the staff against the gap between stones and propelled myself to my feet and forward to the golden door of the queen's quarters. I didn't bother knocking before bursting in.

Tavia stood with her back to Mathias, fire in her hands. Mathias's gaze flickered from the ceiling to me and I saw the darkness gathering in the top corners of the ceiling. All of the artificial light possible was offered in the bedroom.

The queen stood, perplexed, by her bedside and near the children she'd raised, wearing only a floor-length nightgown and midnight-blue robe.

I held the door open and motioned the others inside, keeping my attention on the lights being stifled behind them by the incoming shadows. Selina had somehow gathered a whole army of them.

"Why are we all coming in here? Why are you running?" Keltin demanded when he caught up.

"Look behind you," I replied.

He stopped just outside the door and turned as the last of the candles in the hallway went out. His eyes widened, and he jumped across the threshold.

Knowing it was futile to lock it, but feeling necessary to do so anyway, I turned the key in the lock and hurried to the side of my siblings. "These are Selina's agents," I explained. "Her spies. They will send word we are here and she will come to collect us. We must leave immediately."

"We're stuck here until daylight, at least," Tavia said.

"Unless we get back through a mirror," Ismae offered. "Queen Grimhilde, where does the mirror above your mantle lead?"

The confused woman shook her head. "Nowhere. It isn't a Windforn."

"We'd have to go back out there," Mathias mumbled. "You *did* promise to help our mother. We can't just leave her here with them."

Grimhilde turned to me, and then her gaze fell on my mother. "Oh Hazel . . ." Shame washed over her face and she lowered her gaze. She fell to her knees in front of my mother's feet, surprising all of us.

"Grimhilde, you do not need to kneel." Mother crouched.

"I didn't raise your children the best I should have. You begged me to keep them safe, and I didn't. I should have sent them to a better family." She broke into tears.

Mother wrapped her arms around the woman and held her.

I flicked my gaze to Mathias and Tavia, both looking at their mothers embrace each other. I kept an eye on the shadows behind them. Their numbers were growing by the second, and each corner of the room grew darker and darker. I knew they would press forward and then down. We needed someone with powerful light magic.

I turned to Zuri. "I know you are an entity of light. If you could keep the shadows at bay, I can see if I can help Grimhilde."

She nodded. *And Gerard, remember what I said about the light.*

"Yes, light is more powerful than darkness, which is why I'm asking you to—"

In more ways than that, Gerard. Light can also help a troubled mind. Had she brows, she would have lifted them at me.

I got what she was hinting at. She wanted me to tap into light magic to help Grimhilde. I gulped. I wasn't ready to experiment with light magic at that scale, especially on the queen. I wasn't brave enough to try it on Flynn!

Dark magic came easily. I could focus on all of the pain in my life, all of the heartache, fear, and nightmares, and use that to propel the darkness I felt. Light magic . . . that came from somewhere else entirely. From a place I'd never been able to reach—my heart. Light magic came from love. From joy.

I glanced at Ismae, and she gave me a brave smile.

Too wrapped up in what to do, I didn't return it.

But I knelt at my mother's side and reached my hands out to Grimhilde's head. Mother let go of the queen, allowing me to draw nearer.

Love? I wondered.

What was it I loved? I loved Ismae. I loved the way she smiled, how peaceful she made me feel. I loved my mother—even though I didn't know her well.

I nervously rubbed my lips together and closed my eyes.

I loved sunrises and the smell of rain.

I loved using magic, even if I did screw up sometimes.

I loved music.

I loved knowing I had a place.

I loved the family I never had, the family I longed for, and the family I *could* have if only things were different.

Selina's heart, the familiar darkness, begged for me to use it.

But my heart . . . my *real* heart pulsed.

I exhaled, clearing away the fear and worry of the shadows around us. Zuri's light warmed my skin, and I knew she was keeping the darkness at bay. Ismae's smile lingered behind my eyelids, and the memories of her touch warmed me from the top of my head to my toes.

Despite my inadequacies, my mother loved me. Ismae loved me. Quist trusted me. Even Zuri saw hope in me. And it was my father who had sent me on this journey with confidence I would know what to do.

I took a slow breath inward.

Everything around me muted. My hands warmed. I focused my energy and power on my heart—mine.

Something happened that had never taken place before. Something ignited through my core, my soul, and through all of my extremities. The hair on my arms and legs stood on end, and I gasped for breath as it was taken from me.

Before I could use the magic to help Grimhilde, I had to pull away.

It was consuming me.

"Open your eyes!" Zuri ordered.

I could hear her voice as she spoke, no longer in my head.

"Gerard, now! Open your eyes!"

Magic vibrated through the air, and I forced my eyes open. White filled the room. My body trembled as if it might explode, tear apart into a billion pieces, and the magic inside of me made my every part of my body ache.

"Good. Focus on me. Now control it." Zuri knelt, as a woman, behind Grimhilde, whose eyes were wide with fear. "Grab on to it. Hold it. You're about to lose control. Don't let go."

"It's . . . volatile." I groaned as power surged inside of me, searching for any way to escape. I slammed my eyes shut and let out a cry.

"It's consuming him!" Mother shouted.

I felt someone touch my arm at the same time Zuri shouted, "Don't touch him!"

She screamed, and I opened my eyes. Mother held her hand out before her, the palm and fingers red with a burn.

"He can do this. Let him do this," Zuri insisted. I felt her hand on my knee. "Take a breath." She was using her light to try and help me balance mine.

"It hurts! Oh gods, it hurts."

The darkness inside screamed.

The light fought against it.

I clawed at my chest. If I could let out Selina's heart, rip it from my body, I would be all right. I could control the light. But the light and the dark inside of were fighting, and I was going to lose control of both soon if I didn't do as Zuri said and take control.

But I had no idea how.

As I tried to grip on to the light side, on to the warmth in my chest, it slipped out like I was trying to grasp on to the rays of the sun.

No matter how much magic I knew, how well Selina had trained me, I didn't know how to control two different types of magic on opposing ends of the spectrum—I'd never heard of a wizard who had.

Voices swelled around me, and I was aware of myself, then everyone in the room, and suddenly people beyond. Voices from the shadows filled my mind—hungry. They were starving, waiting to snatch me as soon as my light magic failed. Their raspy voices faded, and I could *hear* the trees of Zelig humming while snow gathered on their branches just outside the castle.

The power of my heart surged, but Selina's heart screamed.

I gripped my chest again and let out a scream of pain 0f my own.

Her heart raged and engulfed the light with darkness, smothering it. The light within me snapped like a leather whip down my spine, and I couldn't get a sound out. In agony, my body imploded, and I fell to the ground, writhing in pain as billions of needles of darkness pricked through my veins where love and light had been only seconds before.

"Selina's heart is far stronger than I thought," Zuri whispered.

"Shh. I've got you." Mother held my head in her lap. She stroked my damp hair until my body stopped seizing.

Mathias dropped to his knees and held my head to the side so my foaming saliva spilled to the rug.

Finally, with two final jerks of my limbs, my body relaxed.

The darkness had won.

I was utterly spent. I couldn't lift my arms to touch Ismae when she knelt at my side. I shifted my eyes to look at her and found I couldn't smile. I couldn't move. A fog washed over my mind like it had before the final battle in the fairy realm, and I struggled to push it away. Selina couldn't take me again! Not now!

"Sleep," Zuri's voice soothed. "It is me. You need to rest. Shh."

My heavy eyelids fell over my eyes, but I didn't fall asleep, more like a state of meditation where I could still hear everything.

Ismae gripped my hand hard, and she sniffled. "H-he tried so hard."

"What was that?" Mathias murmured.

"That was a conflict between light and dark," Zuri explained, heaving a sigh. "Selina's heart has held him so long in darkness that it is nearly impossible for him to use light magic. Light is a part of him, yet he can't reach it."

"Why not?" Tavia asked. "I thought light was more powerful."

"It would be if he had something to cling to. Light comes from love."

"But I love him," Ismae said.

There was an uncomfortable silence before my mother added, "Yes, you do, sweetheart. I know he feels that. But I know what it's like to live half a life thinking no one else on earth loves you."

"Wow," Keltin said from somewhere far away. "I guess I never thought about that. About not ever feeling love. I can't . . . I can't even imagine that."

"I suppose it makes sense why he would do the things he does," Ferdinand added, his voice low. "I should have listened to you, Ismae. We all should have. He needed our help, our compassion, and support."

"He just told me Selina's heart was fighting inside of him. I didn't know how bad it was," Ismae whispered and stroked her fingers over my cheek like she was tracing the veins in my skin.

They pitied me. I didn't have the strength to care.

"So he can't help our mother," Tavia said, her tone dejected.

"He can't, but I can," Zuri replied.

Warm lips touched my forehead. I didn't know if it was a kiss from my mother or Ismae, but the comfort behind it dragged me over the edge into sleep.

TWENTY-ONE

The first thought that entered my mind when I came to was failure. I had tried to use my magic for good, to finally reach into the light, and I had failed. The thought lingered in my mind as I opened my eyes and stared at the fabric canopy of the four-poster bed. Judging by the amount of light sneaking its way through gaps at the top, bottom, and edges of the curtain on the windows, it was daylight outside.

With a groan, I sat up but had to close my left eye against a wave of pain that radiated from my forehead to the back of my skull. But it was nothing compared to the tearing sensation in my chest and the anger at myself.

When the pain subdued, I realized I was in my old room or, at least, the room I had lived in while Selina claimed residency there. I got up and shuffled to the bathroom. Catching my reflection in the mirror, I froze. I had one green eye and one dark-brown eye—almost black. On the same side of my face with my new brown eye were black veins.

That must have been what Ismae traced when I'd fallen unconscious.

I turned my head. The veins stretched from above my right ear to the corner of my eye and down my jaw. I reached up and rubbed at it, but the marks didn't fade.

Whatever had happened with my magic had changed me.

And I didn't believe it was for the better.

"Gerard?" a sweet voice called.

I dumped the chamber pot out the window and exited the bathroom to find Ismae standing at the foot of my bed.

Her eyes searched my face, seemingly trying not to focus on my newly changed eye. She appeared nervous, but not afraid.

"What happened?" I asked when I reached her. "What is this?"

"I didn't know your eye was affected too." Ismae traced her fingertip down the branches of darkness now taking physical claim on my features. "Zuri said your light magic and dark magic are conflicting with each other. She said it's imperative you get rid of Selina's heart as soon as possible."

I rolled my eyes. "What does she think I've been doing this entire time? Dancing?"

Ismae's lips quirked into a weak smile. "If you've been dancing, I'm a bit jealous you didn't ask me to be your partner."

We both laughed.

"I'm worried about you." She dropped her hand, but I took it and looked down at her palm.

"When I was trying to tap into my magic, the light . . . I saw you. I focused on how you love me and that my mother loves me."

"Did you focus on your love for anyone else?"

I lifted my gaze.

Her eyes saddened, and she turned her face away, but she didn't take her hand from mine.

"Ismae, I love you. You are the only person, and I mean the *only* one, I can say I love." I turned her face to look at me. "I mention love and I see Keltin roll his eyes or hear Ferdinand scoff as if I'm not capable of it. And I *feel* that. Me? A murderer? Liar? Pawn of Selina? I'm not capable of love. To think I could love . . ." The words faded, my chest ached, and I looked at Ismae's hand in shame.

"And why shouldn't you love?" She touched my chin and lifted my face.

I peered into her eyes. "I want to reciprocate it, but . . . why should I get to have love when I've harmed so many others?"

"Because you aren't the same person you were a year ago. Time changes people."

"And Selina has already killed you once. If she harms you because I love you—"

"You need to stop thinking that way." She cupped my face in her hands. "You're not alone, remember? And if she attacks me, so what? I have some pretty powerful friends. Not to mention, a mighty brave, powerful, and loving wizard boyfriend."

I didn't try and resist the smile that slid onto my face. "How do you do it?"

"Hmm?"

"Make me feel so at ease."

She winked. "One of my many talents."

I chuckled and kissed her.

A knock drew my attention to the open door where Mathias stood. "You're awake." He eyed me up and down.

"It's late in the afternoon," Ismae explained. "Zuri is ready to travel to Selina to see if she can help draw her heart back. Do you feel well enough to travel?"

I drew a big breath, focusing on the ache in my chest where just a few hours ago a raging battle had taken place and felt like it burned my insides. I nodded in spite of the dull throb in my temples.

Mathias lingered a moment, then walked away.

Ismae walked with me down to the dining hall. Grimhilde and my mother were chatting like best friends, catching up on everything, and I could tell by her eyes that Grimhilde was healed. Grimhilde was telling Mother how when Tavia was little, she always took care of Mathias and wanted to participate in all of the sword fighting lessons, refusing to take on the typical—and expected—role of a princess.

Tavia watched the conversation with a mute expression with Ferdinand at her side.

They all turned their attention to me when I entered the room, and the conversation stopped.

"Where is Zuri?" I asked.

"Undoubtedly pacing a hole in the sitting room," Grimhilde answered. "Come and eat and we can be on our way. I've already used one of the Windforn mirrors to send a message to Queen Athena. She's very concerned about Odette and Ulrich—"

"James took them," I cut in. "It's complicated. I can eat along the way if you'd like. I'm not all that hungry." It was true. With my pounding head, I was afraid I would vomit if I ate.

"You need your energy," Mother said, pushing a full plate a few inches in my direction.

"We haven't the time. The shadows may have recovered, Selina could be on her way now," I observed.

"Gerard." Mother raised her brows.

She was probably right. Eating could help settle the nerves in my stomach, especially if the uncomfortable rolling sensation was that of hunger and not anxiety. I obediently slid into the seat and silently ate. Everyone's eyes remained on me, on the new mark of darkness on my face.

Ismae spoke up. "Everything is packed up?"

"I've even got the mirror selected. I've lost track of where some of the mirrors lead and the phrases to open them, but there is one that will take you to a lovely little flower shop near the palace," Grimhilde responded.

I pushed my half-empty plate of food away. "Let's go." I dabbed the napkin to my lips and stood.

"Go where?" a smooth, steely voice asked.

My blood ran cold. How had Selina gotten to us first? I turned slowly. Standing in the doorway, she looked more regal—and powerful—than ever. Her long black hair cascaded over the shoulders of her blood-red dress and she wore the silver crown of the queen.

The shadows undoubtedly told her where we were. Selina was just as familiar with the mirrors as Grimhilde, and if there was one in the palace . . .

"Gerard . . . your eyes are rather beautiful. I like your new . . . tattoo." She smirked, pupils dilating and making her eyes entirely black.

Her heart gripped mine like a vice in response to her powers.

I dropped my hand to the table and gulped a breath.

"Interesting," Selina murmured.

Everyone else in the room remained frozen at the table.

"I left to find something for you," I explained, trying to get her to see maybe perhaps I was still a little bit evil, or at least to try and convince her I was foolishly still on her side.

The icy cock of her brow showed me I was on thin ice. "And what could you possibly find for me that wouldn't disrupt my plans?"

"Zuri."

Selina's pupils returned to normal, and she spun around to see the white Fylgja standing behind her, elegant and powerful. "Zuri?" she whispered. She smiled and crouched. "Is it truly you, old friend?"

You've lost your way, Zuri said, keeping a safe distance. *Gerard found me and begged me to return. I've come to help him with your heart.*

Selina's window of joy clouded. "Why would I do such a thing as take my heart back? I'm more powerful now than ever!"

You had a chance once to take it back, but you were hurt. Look at all of the harm you have caused. You've pulled your own family apart, forcing your grandchildren to be raised without their parents. Gerard's most powerful magic is light, and you intentionally stifled it.

Selina turned to look at us. "Gerard handles dark magic far better than light. He could never grasp it."

Look at your grandson, Selina. He is being torn apart in a battle between light and dark. It will kill him if you don't intervene.

Selina, my grandmother, rose to her feet. She looked me up and down, then beyond me to those in the dining room.

I could linger and hope she would choose the right thing. Instead, I stepped forward, facing her. "Selina, *please* take your heart back," I pleaded. "There is so much good you can do. You're powerful and smart. You could raise this kingdom to be more than it's ever been."

She reached out and placed her hand on my chest. "Yes. I could."

My heart began to slam against my ribs. "Please take it back. It's time, don't you think?"

She tilted her head in silence.

I held my breath.

"I *can* raise this kingdom. I am right now. And the first step is to execute your father." Her eyes hardened, and her lips tightened. She grabbed a fistful of my shirt and placed the palm of her other hand to my forehead.

No! Zuri shouted. She jumped against Selina's side, disrupting the spell and knocking her to the ground.

Selina gave a frustrated shout, her hair in disarray and her crown lying on the floor beside her. "Do not make me kill you, old friend!" she snarled.

Your soul of darkness will never win against the light. You know it! Zuri countered.

"You can't say I know it in my heart because I don't have one!" Selina lunged forward, the flash of a blade in her hand flickering from the torchlight.

I uttered a spell to brighten all the lights in the castle—I'd done it before with Ismae in the hut in the middle of nowhere when Selina breached the barrier of the Weeping Woods. I then turned, snatched a goblet from the table, and then flung it with all my strength at the stunning stained-glass window with a burst of magic behind it.

The window shattered, and the afternoon sun filled the room and touched Selina, making her wail in agony and scramble out from the reach of the sun against the wall opposite Zuri.

I scooted closer to Zuri. "Selina, you know this is futile. You must know you can't always live like this," I begged.

"Your father dies this night," she snarled at me. "It's a shame you won't be present to stop me! Alakma al bourd!"

Zuri leapt in front of me. Her voice rang in my head, *An act of sacrifice is an act of pure love.*

Selina's death spell struck Zuri, and a black blob slammed into her side. The darkness spread like a splotch of ink spilled across white parchment and changed the color of Zuri's fur.

Zuri hit the stone floor with a *thud.*

Selina screamed.

I dropped to my knees at Zuri's side, instinctively reaching for my powers of darkness and necromancy, but Zuri reached out and leaned her paw against my knee.

I looked at her.

She panted, the darkness spreading too quickly for me to stop it. *Remember what I said. I give myself willingly to help the greater good. Your light, Gerard . . . You* are *pure light.* Her head rested on the stone.

Zuri was dead.

Selina's nails tore into the ground, cracking the stone.

She felt pain.

She'd killed her friend, her familiar, and even without her heart, she felt the pain and guilt of doing something so horrible.

"You can stop this," I said quickly and scooted closer to her. "Take your heart!"

"Never!" She let out an ear-ringing scream and spiraled into a ball of darkness and retreated.

Silence filled the castle.

I stared at Zuri's form, feeling helpless.

Mother was the first to move and hurried to me. "We need to get to Servad immediately. We only have a few hours to save your father now."

Mathias grabbed my arm to drag me to my feet, but I refused. I stared at the once-white fur covering Zuri. She always said light was more powerful than darkness. How could the spell kill her? Unless . . .

The sun warmed my side, spilling in from the broken window.

"She can't be dead," I murmured.

"Gerard, she's gone. Look at her," Mathias said in a calm but slightly annoyed tone.

I shook my head and looked up at him. "She is light. She is a Fylgja Fox, a literal spirit of light, and light *can't* be killed by darkness. Only subdued by it."

He lifted his brows, and his lips parted in surprise. "You think she's still alive."

"The last thing she said to me was that I am light. I think she knew what was happening, I think she was telling me I can fix this." My heart began to pound.

"Do you think that's such a good idea?" Keltin voiced. "I mean, with what happened last night. And your whole . . ." He shifted nervously.

"Failure?" I said flatly.

Tavia shook her head and stepped forward. "Gerard, what if we combined our magic?"

I stared at her, my eyes widening. "Yes. You, me, and Mathias. We're all born from the sun, yes? Because Father is the sun wizard, and the sun is pure light, so if we all use our powers together . . . we should be able to help her. Brilliant!" I smiled and placed my hand on Zuri's side.

Mathias knelt to my right and Tavia knelt to my left.

"How do we do this?" Mathias asked.

I shook my head. "I've never worked in tandem with anyone to cast a spell."

Grimhilde cleared her throat softly. "I happen to know."

All of us looked at her.

She smiled. "Typically, this is done with a known spell. Gerard, what is the spell you use when you dispel darkness?"

I pursed my lips to the side of my face in thought, then got it. "Ferd â myrkr. Basically, fade the darkness. I think that would be the best spell to use in this situation. If it were *njól*, that would be night, so . . . yes. Ferd â myrkr."

I couldn't quite tell how to read the expression on Mathias's and Tavia's faces, but I could have sworn they were impressed.

"Once each of you places your hands on Zuri, repeat this phrase together," Grimhilde explained. It must be together perfectly for it to work."

"I think we should practice a few times," Tavia said. "I'm afraid that word, *myrkr*, is tricky for me."

"Me-r-kyur," I said slowly.

After practicing the phrasing a couple of times, Mathias was the one who said, "I think we're ready. Let's do this."

We placed our hands on Zuri's side.

I drew a big breath and nodded.

Together, the three of us uttered the phrase, "Ferd â myrkr," with strength behind our words. We were one, the three of us. Three siblings of the same parents. Three kids with messed up lives. Each of us had been impacted in different ways by Selina's greed and pain, and yet at that moment, we were one against her.

Light filled my chest and stung my heart, but I gritted my teeth against it and willed the light into my hands. Our palms glowed, and that light spread into Zuri. It left us and penetrated the black fur, spreading whiteness like sunlight breaking storm clouds.

"We did it!" Tavia said with excitement and a big grin.

Mathias smiled just as widely and met my eyes. "We did it together."

I felt the corner of my lip lift in a smile as disbelief filled me. I leaned back on my ankles and watched as the goodness of light magic banished the darkness suffocating Zuri.

Her blue eyes flew open, and she gulped a breath of air and then another.

"You did it!" Ferdinand exclaimed. He laughed and set his hands on Tavia's shoulders.

She smiled at me.

I nodded to her, still smiling stupidly.

Zuri sat up and leaned forward to place her forehead to mine. *I am proud of you, Gerard Tovan. You have done something few can. As you continue to let that light glow, it will aid you.*

I wrapped my arms around her neck. "I am honored."

"I think it's time to get through that mirror, don't you?" Mother said, radiating pride.

I turned to Zuri. "You will still help us, won't you?"

Of course! I can take Grimhilde and we will go to Quist and the dragons. We will see you all in Servad. She nuzzled my head and rose to her feet. *Oh, and one more thing. Keltin, dear?*

Keltin stepped forward.

A symbol glowed in blue on Zuri's forehead, and she leaned her nose down and touched Keltin's broken and bandaged arm.

He gasped and, moments later, unwrapped the bandages to reveal she'd completely healed his arm. "Thank you. Thank you so much."

Mathias got to his feet, then pulled me to mine. "All right, big brother. Let's face this sorceress one last time."

TWENTY-TWO

We stepped into the little plant shop, as Grimhilde had promised. Tavia walked straight to the window and peeked through the plants resting there to get a look outside. There was just enough light for us to see a table with four chairs, a wall with various vases or buckets for plants, and buckets of flowers on the opposite side of the room.

"Many people are closing their shops now. We seem to be at least a few blocks from the palace," Tavia reported.

"What's the plan?" Keltin asked.

"Maybe we can get to King Torian," I suggested. "Selina surely took his heart to get him to comply with the execution of his son, but if Tavia is right, we can get his heart back and maybe he can stop Selina."

Tavia nodded. "I will offer to go and do that. I can fly into an upper room and make my way through. Any suggestions on where she would keep his heart?"

I twitched my brow. "Knowing her, probably on the mantle in their room. It's on the back side of the palace, east side. I don't know what it looks like from the outside, but there is a window to the hallway and their doors are purple."

Tavia nodded.

"I will go with her," Keltin offered quickly. "I want to go help get Odette and Ulrich out of whatever prison they might be in."

I shook my head. "I'm not sure there's a prison in the palace, but you're welcome to look. Look for Sir Adam or the servant boy, Michael. and they should be able to help you. Just tell them I sent you."

Mathias placed his hands in his pockets. "I think it may not be a bad idea if we split up. If any of us have an opportunity to stop Selina from killing Gerard's father—my father too, I suppose—we step in and take it without hesitation. If I must, I will distract her to provide an opening. I don't think we need any plans beyond that. Do you?" He looked at me.

They all did.

What sort of leader was I?

I slowly nodded. "Selina's got shadows on her side. I can try and put a glamour over you, but the shadows will likely see through it. And I'm still not well versed in that sort of magic." I glanced at the door.

"I can help with that," Ferdinand offered. "Being a fairy and all that. Just don't forget what we all look like, yeah?" One by one he used his fairy magic to cast glamours over each of us.

Keltin was given the appearance of a chubby man with a brown beard and glasses. Ismae became a woman wearing ragged clothing with a flour-dusted apron, I was given a long black beard and tall hat, and Mathias now looked much younger than he was. Ferdinand let his red hair grow longer, and he aged himself by about twenty years. Lastly, he made my mother a man but kept her same blond hair.

"That should do it." Tavia nodded curtly, likely unaware she now appeared to be a tall, thin wizard.

Ismae took my hand and whispered, "Are you all right? You look . . . overwhelmed."

"I am," I admitted. "I'm confused and uncertain, and feel like I've already failed." Shaking my head, I walked to the store's door and then hauled it open. "Be careful, everyone."

"People are going to love hearing the story of how a bunch of royal children saved them from the terrible sorceress," Keltin said with a grin as he passed.

"Ulrich won't be able to keep his hands off of you looking like that," Tavia teased with a smirk.

He huffed. "You should be one to talk."

She looked down at herself. "What's that supposed to mean?"

"Nothing. You look lovely," Ferdinand comforted. "I'll see you when you return."

Tavia muttered something under her breath before she followed Keltin out the door.

The rest of us followed, stepping out into the street. The sun was higher in the sky than I'd thought, but still, townspeople up and down the street were closing up their shops, joining their families, and walking down the street to the palace located to our right. We were in a different part of town than the wizard's academy. I couldn't even see it from where we were, and it looked like the palace was downhill from us. We were walking westward.

Together, we journeyed with the clusters of people headed down to the palace. My mother walked on my left side. Ismae, on my right, held my hand tightly, for which I was grateful. She knew how much she meant to me, that I needed her by my side, and I couldn't be more comfortable that she'd stayed with me instead of wanting to go with one of the others.

A gate appeared ahead, and our small group exchanged glances at each other. I wasn't the only one who'd spotted the soldiers at the gate. Anyone with a hat or cowl was being asked to remove them, and I knew they had to be looking for us.

"I'm glad you put the glamour over us," Keltin voiced aloud.

Ferdinand nodded silently.

The people clumped together at the gate, slowed down by the inspection. When it was our turn, Keltin stepped forward to the men on the right, nodded, and passed by. I stepped up with Ismae, and a guard behind the gate reached out and grabbed Keltin by his arm.

"Wait," he commanded.

"All of them," another soldier said, meeting my gaze.

Behind him stood a shadow, and I felt my jaw tighten. We were in trouble and had to act fast.

"We've been spotted," I said quickly.

Mathias stepped forward without hesitation and landed a surprise punch across the soldier's face, grabbed Keltin by the arm, and took off running down the street. I heard him command Keltin to go a different direction, likely so he could catch up with Tavia.

Ferdinand followed suit by giving the second soldier a big shove backward and into a flower pot behind him. "Go!"

I reached out and took my mother's hand, then ran with both women down the street and into the crowd. We had a block to go before we could turn right and go to the front of the palace.

"Keltin and Tavia just took off along the back of the palace," Ismae reported.

"We're drawing too much attention," I replied. "We need to hide until they pass before we join the crowd again."

"I agree," Mother confirmed. She pulled her hand out of mine to run a little bit faster and headed for the space between two awkwardly shaped buildings. It was a tight squeeze and definitely a gap no one would think we'd get fit through if they passed by.

I pushed Ismae in after Mother, then squeezed in last. I had a disadvantage due to my size—my broad shoulders prevented me from being able to walk in and I had to turn sideways, and even then my chest touched the brick wall to the point I had to exhale to fit.

Ismae stood in a similar position at my side but didn't have to change her breathing.

As expected, the guards ran past.

"If we dispel the way we look, would that help?" Ismae whispered.

I started creeping out. "I don't think so, but at this point, it doesn't matter. Either way, the soldiers will be looking for us in this form or ours." I finally made it back onto the street, turned left and right to ensure everything was safe, and then waved for them to come out.

A woman and her husband eyed me as they passed and the man gave me a disapproving shake of his head.

I gave a friendly smile in return.

Ismae stepped up behind me, followed by my mother.

"If they tell Selina we've been spotted—" Mother started.

I cut her off, "It won't change anything. She knew we would try. I only hope Tavia finds the heart and gets it back to Torian so he can stop this. And then . . . then we only have to worry about how to get Selina's heart back to her, especially if she won't take it willingly."

Ismae took my hand again. "You'll figure it out. You always do."

I kissed her forehead, and we casually walked around the opposite corner of the building and onto the main street, which was packed with people the whole way across. Pressing my way through the crowd, I heard people speculating what my father must have done to earn such a thing as execution.

We received a few grunts or words of protest when I bumped shoulders or gave a nudge that caused a person to bump into another, but I ignored them. They were coming for a show, for entertainment. I hadn't even had an opportunity to get to know my father, but they would cheer at his death.

I stopped several rows back from the front and watched the doors of the palace open. The crowd surprised me, however, when they remained silent. Two men led my father down the steps to the lower landing and not a single person around me made a sound of approval.

My sharp intake of breath was audible. Mother squeezed my hand, and a lump grew in my throat.

No one was cheering.

In spite of being locked away for a week, Tovan appeared to be in decent health, but I didn't understand why he hadn't used magic to break free between the wizard's prison or the palace. What was he waiting for?

Selina appeared at the top of the steps wearing a mockingly white gown. She'd tied her hair back and up into her crown and *appeared* to be the regal queen they all wanted. The people of Servad lowered their heads respectfully as she descended the steps until she stood in front of Tern Tovan, one of the most powerful wizards to ever exist. And a man willing to die for nothing.

"My people! Thank you for joining me this evening on the night of a rare occasion—the first execution our land has seen in many ages. As a traitor, the man who once claimed to be your prince and friend will face death through me, your queen."

My stomach churned.

Selina carried on with her speech, but her words became a murmur in the back of my mind when my father's gaze locked onto mine.

Zuria's words came to me: *An act of sacrifice is an act of pure love.*

I understood what my father was doing.

He was allowing himself to be sacrificed because he loved his mother. He loved me. He loved his people. I'd been so focused on stopping the execution I hadn't stopped to consider if that was my father's plan all along.

His gaze flicked behind me, then back.

With pinched brows, I looked over my shoulder, then returned a confused look to him.

Again, he looked away but focused longer on something in the distance.

This time, when I turned, I realized he must have been hinting to the Quinary Academy, for there was nothing else in the distance. But I didn't understand what my father wanted from me.

And where were Quist and Zuri? Why hadn't Elisa brought her dragon army yet?

Mother tugged on my arm. "She's going to kill him! Stop her!"

The soldier behind my father with his sword poised for the blow, and Selina was speaking a spell, but I blinked, frozen in panic.

"Stop!" a voice commanded.

Selina turned her glare to the top of the palace steps.

The disheveled King Torian was running down them. "I command you all to stand down." When he reached Selina, he grabbed her by the arms.

I couldn't hear what they said, we were too far away, but I knew, by the fervent look in his eyes and body language, that Tavia had succeeded. Torian had his heart back and he would convince Selina to stand down.

However, Selina's anger was building.

Torian lowered his arms and stepped around her to address the crowd. "I am afraid there has been a bit of a misunderstanding—"

"Because there are multiple traitors in our midst," Selina threw in. "Another wizard by the name of Gerard has infiltrated the palace walls and has poisoned the mind of the king. As you can tell by his ragged clothing and unkempt appearance, the king has been unwell for some time."

King Torian turned to face her in absolute bewilderment.

Selina looked to the soldiers standing nearest her. "You should take him back to his room and lock the door until we can get his medicine." She raised her brows.

The soldiers hesitated and glanced at the king.

"Selina, my love, it is *you* who must be arrested. Tovan is our son. The only crime he committed was loving his people too much."

Selina's lip twitched.

The soldiers finally moved, but everyone in the crowd waited with bated breath to know who the soldiers would arrest.

Selina didn't wait for them to decide. She ripped the sword out of the executioner's hand and jabbed it forward, plunging it through my father's chest.

I lurched forward.

Mother screamed in horror.

Ismae clamped her hands over her mouth.

Blood poured down the front of my father's white and gold wizard robes. He looked down at the sword in his body with surprise and lifted his gaze to look directly at his wife with no hesitation or searching of the crowd.

And then he collapsed.

TWENTY-THREE

The shrill cry of a phoenix sounded and a ball of fire slammed into the ground next to Selina, making her stumble sideways. Mathias dove at her, then swooped the opposite direction to avoid an attack.

Finally coming to my senses, I stomped my staff and shouted, "Ondur!" The people blocking my path fell.

Selina heard me and turned to face me. Her face split into a dark smirk as she uttered the spell, "Taltan turrod."

I had heard the spell only once before—when she'd sewn my mouth shut after telling her I would never help her get the stones, that I didn't want to be on her side any longer. Just as before, the magic needle pierced the skin of my lips, but I managed to say, "Sál skógar!" before my lips sealed.

The trees lining the palace steps came to life and reached out to grab the sorceress. She had to come up with a counterspell while I planned my next attack. Just because my lips were sewn shut didn't mean I was completely helpless. I dropped to my knees and placed my hand on the earth. I'd used the portal summoning spell so many times I didn't need words to open it and draw forth the undead, and I didn't have time to rely on light magic. I could use dark for good, and that was exactly what I did.

Mathias flew around a second time just as Selina released a bolt of lightning toward me. I ducked, and the bolt hit the tree to the left of me, igniting it. Mathias reached out to Selina with his talons, aiming for her shoulders, but she moved at the last moment.

Still, his dagger-like talons struck Selina's back, tearing open her back and the beautiful white dress, streaking it with her blood. She screamed in agony, then wheeled around and summoned a ball of water into her hands. She flung it at Mathias. It struck him, and he landed somewhere in the gardens.

Then she turned her attention—and anger—back on me. "Adjul tan goud!"

But I had the upper hand. I'd already summoned an army of undead and they were clawing their way out of the portal.

The people in the crowd had begun to scatter, tripping over each other in a desperate attempt to flee the area.

Selina's spell darted around the skeletons and hit me in the chest, sending me spiraling into a group of people behind me. Tentacles of darkness wrapped around my arms and legs, pinning them together.

Hands grappled at me from the shadows while I growled and pulled on the ropes while I was dragged past my portal and small army of skeletons.

I lifted my gaze in time to see my mother fly at Selina.

Selina held her hand out and shouted, "Slackta!"

Lightning pulsed from her hand and hit my mother in the chest.

I gave a muffled shout in shock and dismay.

My mother hit the ground beside her husband, now in the shape of a beautiful woman, holding her hand to her chest.

"I told you that you would never win," Selina sneered, looming over her. "You never should have given Gerard hope for anything different than I wanted. You ruined Tovan. I won't let you ruin Gerard too." Selina stepped over my dying mother's body. She slapped her palms together, then threw her hands apart.

All of the corpses and skeletons I had summoned stopped and slowly dissipated into smoky darkness before my portal closed.

She grabbed me by the arm and pulled me up to her side. "James!"

I struggled against my bindings, trying to get back to my mother. She was gasping. I couldn't let her die! But the poison in the vines holding me seeped into my skin, burning away at the light I'd managed to touch.

Selina shoved me into James's arms when the pirate captain arrived at her side. "Take him to the academy." She grabbed my jaw in her hand. "You know I can't kill you because you host my heart. That doesn't mean I will let you be free ever again. You could have been at my side, Gerard. You could have been something powerful! Now you will remain locked in a prison until I see it fit to provide you with the mercy of death or until you decide being at my side is better than rotting away." She slapped me across the face.

I searched the crowd for Ismae. Somehow, I'd lost her in the chaos, and now I couldn't see her anywhere.

Ferdinand was fighting a soldier with a sword. Out of nowhere, an army poured in from the north side of the city. They weren't royal soldiers. They were dressed in traditional Ashwryan garb of furs and war paint.

My heart beat faster as I searched the skies for the dragons. Surely Zuri had arrived to get their help!

Mathias must have been injured from his fall because he wasn't in the sky either.

Tavia and Keltin were likely still looking for Ulrich and Odette and completely oblivious to the battle outside that was about to erupt into a war. If we ever got help. If not, the princes and princesses would fall to Selina. Just like she wanted all along.

I looked over my shoulder, and my heart stopped.

Mother was dead.

Selina crouched and grabbed the staff I'd been using. She looked it up and down, then handed it to James. "Take that with him and have Tern Colter lock it up."

As James dragged me down the street toward the academy, I tried to think of any spell I didn't have to orally summon instead of my parents' bodies sprawled on the palace steps. Only, every time I tried to recall a spell, it slipped away. Selina must have layered on another spell.

"Clean up these bodies," Selina commanded from behind us. "Tovan was prince and should be respected in death for his people."

My heart ached and my stomach churned, making bile rise in the back of my throat. I'd put up a fight yet found myself to be pathetic and weak. I had used my magic and the staff, but I'd been easily silenced with a stupid spell to sew my mouth shut.

Once again, I'd failed.

Selina had been right all along. I would never be half the wizard my father was.

James didn't knock on the door to the academy and instead pushed it open and walked into the familiar foyer.

Ten terns—masters of wizardry—stood inside with solemn expressions.

James pushed me to my knees. "Selina demands he be placed in the magic prison."

"Until when?" one of the eldest men demanded.

"Forever."

I glared at James, knowing full well he had no choice in the matter and not truly mad at him but at the world. At the woman who was supposed to be my grandmother and family. Everything had happened so quickly . . . and as I had predicted, it all went wrong.

My heart felt like it was being squeezed again, and I closed my eyes.

My mother had been murdered.

My father executed.

Everything had happened too quickly for Zuri and Quist to arrive. Surely, by now, Ferdinand and Keltin had been arrested.

The only person left alive who loved me was Ismae, and who knew if Selina's shadows hadn't killed her too? Tears filled my eyes. Real tears. Tears of abandonment, anger, everything humanly possible spilled over. But mostly, heartbreak—the longing for a life I would never have the opportunity to have.

Failure seemed to be my curse.

The terns reached down and hoisted me back to my feet. I didn't look over my shoulder nor did I lift my gaze from watching my dirty boots shuffle along the pristine carpet.

I should have been angry with Selina. I should have wanted nothing but revenge.

Instead, I pitied her.

She'd raised me and put me through literal hell and back. She had a family, a son who loved her, the throne, power, and all of that faded away because I had her heart. And it wasn't even my fault.

The bindings tightened around me.

Selina's heart suffocated me.

"You may enter the room," one of the wizards said.

I stepped over the threshold of my own accord, feeling the soothing sensation of water washing over me without getting wet, melting away the shadow binding my arms and the stitching sealing my mouth shut.

"Gerard, we must be loyal to the throne."

I lifted my gaze with tears streaming down my cheeks.

Tern Colter raised his brows to me. "You understand what I say. The wizards are bound in loyalty to the queen or *king* of Fidsa." His gaze flicked to the desk against the wall, then to me before he bowed and left.

I sat down on the edge of my father's bed, my face in my hands, and allowed grief to wash over me. My father was a time wizard, and he was so afraid of using the magic incorrectly that he wouldn't use it to save himself. I didn't care how fickle or dangerous time magic could be, why hadn't he tried? Or perhaps he had, and this reality was the only ending that came about—his death.

I drew a shuddered breath.

But my mother . . . seeing her blond hair spilled across the steps alongside his blood, watching her gasp for her last breaths, while I was helpless against Selina . . .

I pressed the palms of my hands to my eyes and rubbed furiously.

All of this was because I was too weak to give Selina's heart to her.

Rising to my feet, I looked up at the towering ceiling. The light pouring down cast a mysterious purple hue across the room as the last of the sun's light began to set. Selina's shadows would reign, and whatever battle I had started would end because I'd failed the people who foolishly trusted me. There would be no tales of victory, no pride in the young royals of Fidsa who had stood up to Selina.

Gritting my teeth while I circled the room, I let my fingers trail across the smooth surface of the walls as if I might find some secret passage my father couldn't. I attempted to summon any sort of magic to feel for magical artifacts or entities or anything of that matter, but it was like touching the cool surface of a lake without being unable to penetrate the water.

I stopped at my father's desk. It was organized with a single book resting in the center. I sat where he'd sat and whispered, "Allul."

The yellow candle to my right didn't budge.

I rolled my eyes and opened the drawers until I found a matchbox and struck it to light the wick, then pulled the candle nearer so I could see whatever my father had written. The hard spine of the book crackled softly as I opened it.

My dear son, Gerard,

I have struggled for some time to know what to write to you. I haven't been able to find the words to express my emotions. In reality, there are no words to properly portray the grief of a father knowing his child was taken from him. Not just taken, but taken and abused by someone who should have loved you.

If you are reading this, the final steps have been taken to end my life. Undoubtedly, you wonder "why?" Why didn't I stop her? Why didn't I go back in time? Why didn't I fix this and save you?

I answer this question with one statement: turn the page. Rub your thumb across the surface when you know it is time.

One last thing—I love you. I always have and always will. Love is the most powerful form of magic in history and you can access. Love is light. Love is going fishing with your 'Papa,' picking flowers for your mother, playing with your baby brother and sister. Love is telling stories with candlelight, healing a bird, and wanting just one more kiss before bed. Gerard, you are love.

Your father,
Tovan

I stared at my father's handwriting and felt tears once again in my eyes. As I read each part over and over, I remembered it. I saw myself snuggled up in bed with my mom reading me a book with hand-drawn images and begging my daddy for another story or one more kiss before he blew out the candle. And each time, he gave me that *one more* time. I remembered my baby brother and sister and how I made silly faces at them or sang songs to make them squeal.

I felt the same rush of warmth that always accompanied light.

It was love.

I turned the page. The rest of the pages were hollowed out in the center, and a diamond about the length of my thumb rested inside. I ran my finger over the smooth glass. Bursts of purple, green, red, and blue rippled like light fracturing, though there was no source to make it reflect. I pulled my hand away, and the diamond returned to normal.

My breath caught.

I touched the diamond again, and as before, the color reacted to my touch.

My light.

From how it looked, and knowing my father, he had somehow managed to combine the four stones into one, creating an enchanted diamond now placed before me. He wanted me to use this magic "when I sensed its power"—whatever that was supposed to mean. I was in a room that quite literally had no ability for magic to penetrate.

My hand went to my chest.

I felt my heartbeat. Not two, not Selina's, but mine. The room had stifled her heart, stilled it somehow. I took a big breath and smiled.

Whatever my father knew, I needed to fulfill.

I took the diamond from the book and rose to my feet. In the dim light of the room, I played with the diamond and watched the rainbows of light refract and dance across the walls.

I'd never been very patient, but somehow, I felt at peace. Even with the knowledge my father and mother were dead, I had something to give me a stepping stone to change the future.

The door suddenly opened, and the dragon who guarded it entered. She smiled and nodded. "Come."

Without hesitation, I stood and exited the room.

Tern Colter motioned for me silently, and I followed him through the academy, up into the tower in which I'd first met my father. He closed the door and faced me. "You've got it?"

I held up the diamond.

He smiled and walked to the corner of the room. "I put the staff in here." He turned around, holding the staff I'd stolen from the giants.

I reached out to take it.

"This is Merlin's staff. You've heard of him?"

I nodded. "He was a wizard in Aswhrya. He was a jokester and caused a lot of problems but would always fix them. If I recall, he is the one who stole Selina's heart?"

Tern Colter nodded and held the staff out but didn't let go. "It will amplify your power, so *choose your magic carefully*." He emphasized each word, looking me straight in the eye.

I set my hand on the staff and placed the diamond at the top, setting it above the emerald. "You will allow me to use my light magic and strengthen me through that," I commanded Merlin's staff.

"Someone is bossy," it replied.

"Well, you weren't exactly helpful the last little while, were you?" I snapped back. "You could have helped me at any point to save my parents, and you sat there like a worthless stick. You aren't a stick, are you?"

"Of course not!"

Tern Colter's eyes widened. "Remarkable."

The wood from the staff embraced the diamond and then groaned as the wood became smooth, losing its wrinkles, and changed to a shade of light gray. The top of the staff grew little branches like fingers to hold the stone.

I ran my hand up and down the wood, letting my skin get used to the feel. "I didn't think wizards used staffs," I commented.

Tern Colter shook his head. "Very few do. As I mentioned, the use of a staff amplifies your powers, but a staff usually only chooses one wizard to embrace until the wizard dies. To find a staff willing to bend to you . . ."

"I must be pretty important," I finished for him. "I've been getting that a lot."

"Do you believe it yet?"

I looked away from the staff to the wise wizard before me. "I think maybe I do."

TWENTY-FOUR

Tern Colter smiled and motioned for the door. "The battle still rages outside. The dragons appeared only moments ago. I recommend you get to the castle before any further destruction occurs. And do right by your people."

I turned to him just before he opened the door. "How can I thank you?"

"Thank me by improving things in the kingdom. Remember what I said about our obligation to the throne." I sensed he wanted to add more but didn't dare. I believed he was telling me if I usurped the throne, the wizards would fight behind me.

I shook his hand and stepped out into the night.

In the past, I embraced the coolness of the shadows and the feeling of the inky darkness across my skin. As I walked down the streets, I focused on one thing and one thing only—getting to Selina. She had ruined my life for the last time.

A dragon roared overhead, drawing my attention, and it dove toward the ground, igniting a trail of fire as it went. The fire clung to the rows of trees lining the front of the palace.

Pity they had to be destroyed, but I knew the dragon was creating a barrier. I hoped everyone was still safe, but the light from the flames revealed silhouettes of people fighting.

I took off running toward the palace, and moments later, a bell at the top of the highest tower peeled. An explosion of blue flame lit the fire basin at the top.

I reached the top of the hill and was surprised to find Zuri fighting against soldiers. In the distance, a horn blew—a sound I recognized as soldiers from Ashwyra when they left for a hunt or launched a raid. They were regrouping to launch another attack.

A soldier turned to dodge a blow from a dragon's tail and met my gaze. His eyes widened in shock, and I slammed the bottom of the staff against his face, catching him off guard and sending him to the ground, unconscious.

Ferdinand stood behind him, relaxed his attack stance, and gave me a relieved smile. "Took you long enough. Odette, Ulrich, and everyone else just returned. We could use your aid."

"I see that. Is Mathias okay? I haven't seen him since Selina hit him with the water spell."

Ferdinand nodded. "Lightly injured but still fighting. He's trying to keep the border guard from entering the inner part of the city." He pointed behind him.

I scanned the battlefield. "Where is Ismae?"

"She was hiding up in a tree, shouting at rocks to fly and such, but she must be somewhere—"

A soldier ran at us, yelling as loud as he could, and swung his blade in an arc downward at Ferdinand. The wingless fairy turned his sword sideways, blocking the strike, and I shouted a spell to send the soldier flying several feet away.

"What about Selina?" I demanded.

"Held up in the palace. Be careful, Gerard. She's . . . not human." Ferdinand's brows pinched.

"Can I leave you? Can you handle this?"

He scoffed. "I've survived so far without you."

I chuckled and then made my way across the battlefield. I heard the shouts from the Ashwryan warriors as they trampled down the hill and into the streets for another rally. Our numbers were minute compared to the army Selina had conjured up. To my astonishment, they were met by pirates. The pirates were fighting on *our* side.

Gathering all the courage and what little self-confidence I had, and without wasting another moment more, I pushed my way through the crowd. I couldn't fight the soldiers. I had far more important responsibilities.

As I walked up the first two steps to get to the palace doors, I jolted to a stop. My foot hovered over the third step. Blood still pooled on it and a part connected with the step's edge and ran down. My father's blood. My heart wrenched, reminding me of my pain, and Selina's heart clung to that pain. But I could still make him proud.

Through everything that had happened, my eyes had been opened to the truth. It wasn't my father's fault his mother lost her mind or, rather, her heart. Nor was it his fault time fractured and he didn't get a chance to raise me.

I set my foot beside his blood, vowing to myself that I would give my parents the justice they deserved.

A gargoyle touched down on the middle landing between me and the last of the palace guards. I'd forgotten Selina had freed a few of them from the Weeping Woods when I'd gone to help Ismae rescue Keltin months ago. The force of the stone creature hitting the stone cracked the perfectly laid granite steps. I had seconds to filter through various types of spells, finally choosing one that might work against him, but it was based in dark magic.

I set the new staff before me and whispered to it. "Some help would be nice."

"I know just the thing! The opposite of earth is air."

I arched a brow. "You want me to cast an air spell at him?"

The gargoyle jumped forward—propelled by his wings—snapped his teeth at me, and swung a fist.

I ducked and foolishly spun and swung the staff against the gargoyle's ribs. The wood made a cracking sound so loud I thought it had broken in two, but I'd caused no injury. The stone creature roared in my face.

He snatched my wrist and began to crush it, his fangs mere inches from piercing the flesh of my cheek while I desperately leaned away.

"Or you can hit him with me. That *was* rather impressive, wasn't it?" the staff jeered.

With a growl, I ducked under the gargoyle's arm, twisting my wrist free, and whipped around to face it again, but this time held the staff above my head and swung it in a circle.

"Flindalin!" I beckoned.

A tornado of wind gathered at the end of my staff and I flung it forward. The wind gathered up the gargoyle, spun him around, and lifted him into the air. The longer it spun, the more it picked up speed, and the gargoyle suddenly shot off through the dark sky.

"Well, that wasn't quite the spell I would have used, but it worked."

I scowled at the staff. "Why don't you tell me what to do instead of chastising me for not doing it the way *you* would have?" I faced the palace guard.

Eleven men stood in a V formation. The man in front wore a gold and silver helmet which hid every part of his face, save a slit for his eyes.

I stepped up to him, trying to appear as nonthreatening as possible. "Selina executed the crown prince, her own son, and his wife. You know it was wrong."

"We must act under the command of the king and queen," he answered. "No matter what."

"Hmm, and what do we do if the king and queen are unable to perform their duties to the best of their abilities? If they are ill or unstable? I am Gerard Tovan Du'Prei, son of Crown Prince Tovan and heir to the throne. I demand Selina be removed from power."

The general pulled his shoulders back and tightened his grip on his sword. For a moment, I wondered if he would truly stand down. Instead, he bent his knees in a crouch and poised his sword before him. "I swore to protect the royal family."

I frowned at him. "You did an underworld of a job, considering the queen murdered my parents on the very steps of the palace this night and you did nothing to stop her. You can open the doors and let me in, or I can kill you and still get in. Your choice." I poised in a fighting stance, as well, both hands gripping the staff.

The general stared at me. His men didn't move. His leather gloves groaned as they tightened on the hilt of his sword as he clearly weighed his options. Unfortunately, he jumped forward and swung his sword down.

His blow didn't land.

The sword he wielded suddenly lurched to the left, toward one of his own men. The general gave a startled shout, and the other soldier had to divert his attention and momentum from me to his leader. The sword dragged him toward another soldier getting close to me, and then back to the first when he stepped forward to swing his weapon.

I quirked a grin and looked around, finally spotting Ismae standing on top of a nearby balcony. Relief flooded over me. She was alive. She was safe.

She met my joy and waved. "Well, what are you waiting for? Get in here!"

Using the distraction of the soldiers, and their magic-induced internal fighting, I ran to the doors and pulled. The doors were secured from the inside, likely barred and locked with whatever mechanism or magic Selina had used. I took a step back and used a fireball to explode the door, sending wood and metal shrapnel all over the beautiful palace entrance.

I didn't bother stopping to assess the damage, but my boots crunched on the sizzling pieces of wood sprayed across the once-pristine purple rug. I found Selina just where I thought she would be—sitting upon the throne with her silver crown atop her head.

Torian, my grandfather and the king, sat at her side with a blank expression.

"Did you use the same spell to control him that you used on me?" I asked, stopping a few feet away.

She sneered. "Vivian's heart was returned to her, so no. I had to use the same spell, but my own power instead. I am, however, surprised to see *you*. I expected one of the worthless princes or princesses to try and face me again."

Ferdinand was right. She wasn't human anymore. Her eyes were completely black, and she sat with her shoulders hunched forward—like an old witch. On the wall behind her, the shadows clinging to hers, dozens of them poised in pointed shapes like a ridge of swords. Her soulless eyes studied me.

"You sound surprised." I held the staff in my left hand and leaned against it while I placed my right hand on my hip. "You had to know you couldn't keep me in there."

"I suspected you would find *some* way out, though I thought I had more time." Her thin, pale fingers stretched out from under the sleeves of her coal-black dress and clutched the armrests of her throne, looking like those of a skeleton.

I relaxed my stance but held the staff closer to me. "Selina, it's time you take your heart back." I placed my palm against my chest, feeling the beating of my heart with the small skip of hers hidden deep inside. "You've been able to feel the light growing inside of me. I know it because I can feel your heart writhing."

She tilted her chin down.

I braved one step and then another, closing the gap between us. "Please, Selina. You know it is yours to take. You know it will help you. You can end all of this now, fix all of it by one simple act."

She sucked her cheeks in, making her face look gaunter in the dim light. She closed her eyes and rose to her feet. "Take back my heart . . ." She stepped down and locked her gaze on me—her eyes a beautiful shade of blue.

I smiled. "Yes." I reached out and took her hand.

"Oh, Gerard. When will you ever learn?" She slammed the base of her hand against my forehead, using magic to fling me backward while her other hand snatched the staff.

I stumbled, but my staff clung to my hand and stuck to the ground, becoming immovable while simultaneously holding me upright. I wasn't the only one who gave it a surprised stare.

Selina grasped it with both hands and pulled while yelling, her hands starting to turn the staff black.

"I've never met anyone who literally seeped blackness from their soul."

With a gasp, she let go and fell back. "It speaks! What is this magic?"

"You should know. You made me when you splintered me," he said.

"Merlin?" The space between her brows shifted, battling between anger and confusion but finally settling on anger. "You . . . you are the one who did this to me! You deserve to be stuck in a magic stick! And you"—her anger turned to me—"you will join your father in death!" She threw back her hands, and the shadows teetering on the edge of the throne lunged forward.

I'd been in the shadows before. Selina had punished me more than once by locking me in the black room and allowing Nicholas and his evil to torture me.

Whispers of scratches sliced across exposed flesh—my arms, hands, cheeks, ears—like shards of glass exploding around me. I'd done that once—exploded an entire case of potion vials when I had been practicing a spell in the house (strictly forbidden by Selina), and I learned that day why. I'd been using small bursts of energy and trying to recall it to see if I could defend myself against someone else's magic. Instead, I sent the energy at the case full of unicorn tears, goblin blood, and other ingredients. And when

I tried to call the spell back to me, the glass tore across my face. Even after cleaning up the glass, I couldn't hide what I'd done because of the cuts on my face.

Selina wasn't going to win today.

Not after killing my family.

Not after putting me through *sixteen* years of hell.

I slapped my hands together, around the staff, and let out a shout that tore from my lungs, igniting the light in my chest. Just like I had done when I'd tried to help Grimhilde, I grasped on to the light. Only this time, I didn't try and stifle it or control it. The light exploded from me, burning through every shadow in the room and shattering the glass windows and crystal chandeliers.

When I opened my eyes, I found myself on my knees, gasping, all my energy drained from me in that one act of magic.

Selina lay in a heap at the base of her throne, and King Torian was in a heap behind his knocked-over chair. Selina lifted her head, her black hair in front of her face and tangled around her crown as she looked at me with genuine fear. Then a slow smile slid across her face. A smile that read she knew something I didn't.

"Oh, dear Gerard. Dear, dear boy. Look what you've done."

Steadying myself with the staff, I turned to see where Selina was looking, over my shoulder, to the doorway.

Where Ismae stood.

Ismae touched her hand to her stomach and blood dripped from her mouth.

It took far too long for me to register that she was injured, and I scrambled to my wobbling feet to run to her.

She collapsed and I crashed to the ground to catch her, dropping the staff on the ground with a large clatter.

"Ismae." My voice cracked as I pulled her body to me. Tiny holes pierced her body. The crystal from the chandeliers had ripped through her. Realization dawned on me, and I felt sick.

She couldn't speak. Blood bubbled from her lips, and her eyes were filled with fear and desperation as gripped my shirt and arm in her fists.

"No! No, please! Oh gods, no!" I held her as close as I could and placed my hand on her chest. There had to be a way for me to get the crystals out.

What are crystals made of? Rock. Rock put under pressure, like how glass was made of sand. If I can make the crystals hot enough, they could dissolve into sand and maybe the sand will plug up the wounds and stop them from bleeding.

Even as my mind raced, I searched her eyes. A single tear escaped at the same time her body went limp. The light I'd clung to for so long faded.

"No!" I wailed.

I had killed Ismae.

TWENTY-FIVE

For the second time in the few months I'd known her, Ismae was dead. Only, this time it was my fault. How had I not sensed her there? She had entered the room at the wrong time. And now she was dead.

Because of me.

A commotion in the hallway caught Selina's attention. Dusting herself off, she got to her feet and walked to me, scattering the glass with her skirt as she did so. She placed her hand on my head in an almost affectionate gesture. "It's better this way, Gerard. There is no one now to hold you back from your true potential." She leaned down and kissed the top of my head.

I cringed.

I should have grabbed the staff and attacked, but Selina was gone before I could lift my head.

Alone, surrounded by shards of glass, I held Ismae's lifeless body, sobbing into her hair. She smelled of autumn leaves. Getting her back from the underworld this time would be foolish to attempt. The last time, it worked because *she* had come to me. Now . . .

Like my parents, my future with her had been robbed from me.

"It's about time Selina left. Pick me up and let's get this over with."

I lifted my gaze to the staff and growled, kicking it away.

"I could have started this conversation differently. Let me try again." The staff cleared his throat. "You forgot about your father's stone."

"How can I give a thought to that stone when the only person who has ever loved me is lying dead in my arms?" I shouted.

"She isn't the *only* one to have ever loved you, but you're missing the biggest key to all of this," the voice sang at me.

I wiped at my tears. "Yes. You're right. I've brought her back from the dead once, I should try and do it again." Tenderly, I laid her down on the floor and slid her eyelids closed with my fingertips.

"No. Gerard, listen to me." The staff was growing annoyed. "The diamond your father gave you . . . what kind of wizard was he?"

"A sun wizard." I looked over at the staff, wondering what this Merlin looked like in person.

"I'll help you out here. He was a wizard of . . ."

"Time," a voice echoed.

I jumped to my feet, snatching the staff into my hand. I couldn't identify where the voice came from.

It hadn't been the staff. "Who is there?" I demanded. Had it been my father? Quist?

I ran out into the hallway, poised to attack, and heard a noise in a room across the hall. Knowing it could be a trap, someone or something luring me, I approached the door carefully. When I stepped across the threshold of the room, the diamond at the top of the staff caught and splintered light like it had when I first touched it.

Stopping in the middle of the small storeroom with shelves packed with various items, I placed my hand over the diamond. It vibrated—a sensation I hadn't felt from it before.

"Father's letter said the stone would tell me when it was time . . . Of course! He was a time wizard! I can go back in time!"

"Bingo!" the staff cheered.

I reached my fingers through the gaps in the wood holding the diamond on top of the staff and touched the surface, then rubbed it, recalling the instructions from the letter.

My breath rushed from my lungs as if I'd been punched in the chest.

I was running backward, being dragged through time. Ismae got up and left the room, I was back at the academy, then my father and mother were suddenly alive. Light sprinkled down around me.

I found myself standing in my father's office.

He smiled at me. "It worked."

I stared at my father with wide eyes. "How are you—" I didn't even let myself finish the sentence. I ran to my father and wrapped my arms around him.

Tovan embraced me, saying nothing.

I pulled back after I squeezed to make sure he was alive and not an illusion. "You died. I watched you."

His golden hair was tied back in braids, and he tossed them over his shoulders before leaning his hip against his desk. "Tell me more about it. How did I die?"

"Selina stabbed you with a sword, but . . . wait, what time is it?" I ran to the window and flung it open. The sun sat in the sky several hours earlier than it had just a moment ago. "Selina will be here for you any minute." I faced him. "You must come with me now or you'll die."

"Gerard, time doesn't work like that. Things have to fall in place the same way they did before or you mess up what happens. You've already been in this stream, yes? If you alter what happened, you alter the future, which means this won't occur the same way."

I frowned and looked at the staff. "You're saying you take the diamond back. You have to put it in the book in your cell and the staff has to stay here, right?"

"If you haven't already acquired them at this point in your timeline, yes."

I tilted the staff and held my hand out for the diamond to fall in.

"Are you confident this will work?" the staff asked.

"If you mean to ask if I'm confident I will have enough power without the stone, yes." I turned and put the stone in my father's hand.

His long fingers closed around it. His hands were like mine—worn from work. With him being a prince raised in a castle his whole life, I didn't expect that. But I should have known better. His work ethic described in his journals told me as much.

"Now, you come with me." I walked to the door, but Father didn't follow.

"In your timeline before, I died."

"Yes, but you gave me that stone and allowed me to come back and save you, didn't you? What are you doing?"

He lifted his golden eyes to me and smiled sadly. "You have to let me go, and it's vital you don't meet your past self. There is a way to save my life—you just have to come up with how."

I placed my hand on the door and scrunched my forehead. "You gave me an enchanted artifact to save you so I *couldn't* save you? That makes no sense. I'll be altering the timeline anyway."

"I'm saying, you have to be clever. My death brought you here. Figure out a way to stop it from happening while making you believe it did happen. Not only this, but if you create a situation where your past self would react differently to events, then it prevents this timeline from happening at all, and you will be pulled back. Who knows if you'll end up with the staff and diamond then? This is what I meant about time magic being dangerous." His attention darted to the door, and he closed the gap between us. "I'll go with Selina. You can save me there." He placed his hand on my shoulder and looked me in the eye. "I have confidence in you. If you believe nothing else, believe that, and my love for you." He smiled, then opened the door and left. "What is it, Tern Colter?"

I ran my hand over my face. I looked over at the staff. "Any words of advice for this part?"

"Just make sure you come back and get me when your timeline is finished. You're exciting to travel with." I imagined the staff grinning at me with a playful glint in his nonexistent eyes.

I shook my head. This was going to be difficult, and I needed a plan as soon as possible. My father stood right outside the door, and I *should* have dragged him away with me. Instead, I stood inside waiting for him to be taken away and executed. I didn't like it.

I crossed to the window again and chewed my bottom lip.

Soldiers were posting announcements on boards and people gathered around to read them.

In just a few hours, my father would be dead.

I would be stepping through the mirror with Ismae any moment now. Ismae . . . I had to warn her. Father hadn't said anything about speaking with anyone from my past, just myself.

I heard the rhythmic footsteps of Selina's soldiers before I saw them marching down the street in two columns. Their armor caught the last of the sun, and I could have sworn I saw a shadow on the wall opposite me.

I ground my teeth together and stepped to the side so none of the soldiers—or shadows—would catch sight of me in the window. A few minutes later, they turned their formation in the opposite direction, but this time my father walked between the two men at the front.

Tern Tovan, the Sun Wizard, willingly walked toward his death.

And he was relying on *me* to save him.

I let my hair down, ran my fingers through it, and then braided it in the traditional way I'd been taught in the Geat clan in Ashwrya. I glanced at the fireplace. If my hair was going to look like I was ready for battle, so would the rest of me. I crouched and dipped my first two fingers into the black ashes, then smeared it across the top of my eyelids and out to my hairline. I finished the look with a trail of black down the middle of my chin. With the added black veins on my face and mismatched eyes, I looked terrifying.

And I loved it.

I gave one last look to the staff. "You find your way back to me and I'll do my part to help return you to your natural state when this is all done."

"I would appreciate that, young wizard."

Drawing a breath through my nose and blowing it out with puffed cheeks, I grabbed the handle to the door and wrenched it open.

As discreetly as I could, I trotted down the steps, pressing my back to the wall, only stopping when a small group of wizard students walked by. They said something about preparing for a battle and recalled the moment Selina sent the alarm and lit the flame. They must have known what was about to happen.

The door of the room to my right was cracked, and I spotted a cloak hanging on the wall. Nudging the door a bit with my foot, I listened for sounds on the inside. Anyone who had a door open on its own would notice and be curious about it, but since there was no response, the room had to be vacant. I slipped in, grabbed the cloak, and threw it over my shoulders. The gray material shimmered with a glow, like the dancing of ice fire that burns without a flame but leaves a trail of light where the bluest flame should be. With a flip of the hood over my face, I was completely hidden.

I made my way down the final staircase and stepped out onto the empty streets. My stomach knotted, and I swallowed it. I didn't have time to worry. But I had only one shot at this. If I messed up, I could damage time just like my father had.

I jogged toward the crowd and stopped at the back. The people of Servad were packed as close to the palace as they could get, and this time, I heard their murmured words.

"Isn't anyone going to stop her? She's gone mad, you know."

"I heard it runs in the family."

Five women, all elderly with gray hair half pinned back or down, huddled around each other like hens.

"You're right," the one with the wide nose nodded. "Her brother had the madness, and now she's got it."

"I'll be surprised if Tovan doesn't get it," the one in the purple dress stated.

The woman with a hat scoffed. "If he lives that long."

My attention drifted to the palace. I had to think beyond myself. Who in the palace would be on my side?

I grinned to myself and made my way around the edge of the crowd, trying to keep a pace between a jog and a run so as to not draw attention.

I hopped the four-foot stone wall surrounding the palace grounds and slipped through the bushes and flowers until I reached the palace gardens. In a few hours, they would be on fire. There was a wide, open expanse of grass with flat stones placed in a row for a walkway. Benches sat around the four sides of a trickling fountain.

A group of soldiers stood outside the garden door receiving instruction before they dispersed and spread out to their posts. Slipping along the edge of the garden, allowing the tender blades to soften my footsteps, I made my way to the back door of the palace. Rather pleased with myself for not raising any alarms, I ran down the hallway heading for the main entrance of the palace, but voices floated to me. I heard Selina and my father, and knew if I tried to go that way, I would definitely screw up time. Selina had to get him outside first.

Down a hall to my left, I spotted a servant staircase. I carefully approached the blind corner where the steps went up and let out a breath I'd been holding when no one was descending the stairs. I ran up them and pressed my back to the wall to peer down the hallway. The stairs let me out behind the room Ismae had stayed in. I spotted my room, and then beyond it the royal chambers.

With a nervous lick of my lips, I slid out from my hiding place, keeping my eyes locked on the adjoining hallway. I sensed there was someone else nearby but couldn't pinpoint where. By now, hopefully Tavia and Keltin had made it into the palace and retrieved King Torian's heart.

When I finally had to run across the hallway opening, I saw two soldiers standing at the window.

If my father was already on the steps. I had very little time.

I ran across the gap and to the door beside the royal chambers. It sat open and I headed for it, only to jolt to a stop when I spotted Keltin and Tavia still inside.

Keltin grabbed the box with Torian's heart and turned. "That was easy."

I pressed my back to the wall beside the door, my heart thundering against my ribs, hoping he hadn't seen me.

"Good," Tavia said. "I can find King Torian. You search the main level for some kind of prison or entrance to a dungeon."

"Got it. See you on the main floor," Keltin replied.

I ran to a nearby pillar and managed to slide behind it just before the two of them exited the room.

I held my breath while waiting for their footsteps to fade, then gulped in a breath and put my head back against the pillar. *That was close.* I poked my head around the pillar to make sure I was alone, then slipped inside the room. My gaze darted across the objects inside—the dead raven in mother's old cage, a stack of father's journals on the coffee table, and finally what I was looking for. I ran over and grabbed the hand from the mantle.

"How did you get in here?"

I spun around, and my racing heart finally relaxed when I saw James Hook standing in the doorway, his sword drawn and dark eyes narrowed at me. I grinned at him. "Just my luck. I was hoping to see you."

"I'll repeat myself—how did you get in here?"

"I think you should ask *why*." I held his hand up in mine. "Want it back?"

James's big lips sucked in, and his gaze shifted from his hand to my face and back. "In exchange for what?"

I approached him with small, cautious footsteps. "You follow whatever orders Selina has given you. You'll see me outside and when Selina tells you to take me to the wizard tower, do so. But don't return to her. Get the pirates. We will need them to fight against the soldiers." I stopped in front of him and held out his hand.

"That's it?" He studied me with a distrusting glint.

I rolled my eyes. "I know I've caused a lot of problems. I get it. I'm trying to right things, okay? Take your hand."

James shoved his sword back in its scabbard and removed the hook prosthetic from his wrist. "I just touch it?"

I nodded.

James reached out and touched the stub where his hand had once been to the hand sitting in my palm. As soon as he did, it faded and regrew on the stump. The skin tone matched the same dark skin, there was no scar at the attachment site, and his fingers moved as he wiggled them.

He lifted his gaze to me. "Why do this?"

"Because I'm going to return Selina's heart to her whether she likes it or not. Oh, and Keltin is looking for Odette and Ulrich, so maybe you could help him find them." I gave him a firm nod and slipped past him and out the door.

"Gerard."

I stopped and looked at him.

He nodded. "Thank you."

"We can talk more later." I waved dismissively, then ran back out the way I came.

With that taken care of, I had to get to the steps and come up with a way to let my father and mother die while simultaneously saving them.

Easy.

I ran out the same door I'd entered, and when I made it back outside, I cut through the garden, sucking in a breath when I nearly ran into the back of a soldier I hadn't seen hidden behind a tree.

He turned and gave me a nod of acknowledgment. I tried to read in his eyes what he was thinking, but he made no move to sound an alarm or prepare to attack me. He turned away.

If he knew I was who I was . . . would he have let me go so readily?

My fingers brushed across the hem of the cloak. Perhaps the cloak had magical properties I hadn't realized. I couldn't linger to find out what it might be. The crowd had grown significantly since I'd first arrived, and I dropped from the wall to try and peer over the sea of heads, searching the crowd until I spotted myself with Ismae at my side clutching my arm.

My father's eyes met mine. Not my past self, but my current self. He then looked at my past self, and it dawned on me. He'd seen this moment before. Two of me. And when I'd turned back then, I had thought he was hinting at the wizard academy, not at a cloaked figure in the back of the crowd who was, in fact, me.

No sooner did I have that thought than past me turned to look at what my father stared at. Considering I had the weight of the world on my shoulders, even I had to admit I was rather handsome. I could see through the glamour Ferdinand had used. I also realized how much I looked like my father, except for the one black eye and weird veins of darkness across my cheek.

I reached up and touched it.

Selina strolled down the steps of the palace, and I remembered I only had a few minutes to act. I moved carefully to avoid bumping into anyone. I inhaled sharply when a man suddenly reached back to stretch and nearly struck my shoulder. After a groan, he scratched his rear, and I rolled my eyes.

I climbed gingerly atop the stone wall again and waited for the right moment.

From the corner of my eye, I saw myself frozen while the executioner stood poised behind my father with his sword at the ready, waiting for the command.

With a nervous lick of my lips, my mind raced to come up with a way to save my father. Being familiar with the dead, I knew I could create a portal to the underworld and wait for his soul to drop, but the chances of me *seeing* his soul enter the underworld were next to none, and if I missed it or wasted any time, I would miss my mother's soul too.

I tried to recall every word Quist and Zuri had spoken. A breeze from nowhere gushed through the trees, carrying on it the scent of oranges and burnt wood.

"Quist, if that's you, I could use a bit of help here," I whispered, keeping my eyes on my father while I walked closer.

The wind caressed my face. *You know what to do.*

But it was my own voice. No one was telling me what to do.

I had to trust in myself.

I stopped close enough I could leap upon the steps if I so wanted. I was close enough I could almost reach out and touch my father's arm.

I knew what to do?

My heart thumped in my chest.

A second beat underneath it echoed.

And then an idea came to me . . . I placed my hand over my heart. Everyone around me claimed light magic and dark magic were separate entities entirely. Light magic was good while dark magic was bad. But had anyone tried to combine the two? I was living proof darkness and light could coexist, otherwise, my soul and body would have been torn apart.

But I was very much alive.

As I watched Selina giving her speech, reaching the point in which my father would die, an idea settled on my mind: my father didn't have to die. But I could make it *look* like he did.

King Torian ran out the doors of the palace and down the steps, "I command you all to stand down!"

I leaned back and waited on bated breath.

"Selina, my love, look at what you're about to do. Execute our own son? This is madness."

"He's destroyed so much. We can't allow people to step out of line like this!"

"He's our son."

Selina's shoulders raised, and she pulled away from him.

King Torian, my grandfather, stood before his people. "I am afraid there has been a bit of a misunderstanding—"

Selina interrupted him as she had before, stating he was crazy and arguing he needed to be arrested.

"Selina, my love, it is *you* who must be arrested. Tovan is our son. The only crime he committed was loving his people too much."

I held my hand out to my father. I might not be able to get into the underworld and catch him, but maybe that old monk, Chiso, was right. Maybe I had a type of magic no one had seen.

I reached my fingers out, but so did the power of the light and darkness that made up my soul. Almost as tangible as grasping an apple off a tree, I felt what I wanted.

Sál slite, I echoed in my mind.

There was a flash of light at the same instant Selina drove the sword through my father's chest. His body collapsed and fell to the stone steps of the palace, and my father's soul glowed in my hand.

TWENTY-SIX

His soul crackled in my hand. It pulsed like a heart. No, more like a star high in the night sky. Selina's heart-ripping magic must have been similar, and I felt deep down that what I'd just done was not only wrong but incredibly dangerous. I tore my gaze away from the orb of white light in my fist and followed the path of Mathias's flight overhead. He released a fireball from his breath like a dragon would, and it distracted Selina, but too late.

The old me snapped to and attacked.

My father's soul caused my hand to ache, but I couldn't act. Not yet. I had to sit aside and watch as a small army of undead climbed out to attack Selina while the people of Servad fled for their lives until my mother transformed into a raven.

I held my hand out, ready and waiting until Selina screamed, "Slackta!" and a lightning bolt struck the raven.

I gritted my teeth as I watched—and allowed—my mother's body to tumble from the sky and strike the stone stairs. My lungs burned, reminding me I hadn't taken a breath yet.

Selina towered over my dying mother's body, her teeth flashing like a wolf about to devour its kill. "I told you that you would never win. You never should have given Gerard hope."

Hope.

It was Elisa who first gave me hope, Ismae who taught me what love was, and my mother helped me learn forgiveness. Selina didn't realize how many strong women had reshaped my future, or that she could have been one of them.

My mother reached out and took her husband's hand, fear and sadness spilling over into tears from her green eyes. My eyes were the same shade, or at least my good one was.

Biting back tears of my own, I held out my free hand and spoke the same spell, this time feeling far more confident, "Sál slite!"

In other words, *soul rip*.

I was literally tearing their souls from their bodies.

I staggered when my mother's soul slammed into my hand, and my shoulder hit the nearby tree. The balls of energy in my hands sent waves of pain through my arms. They were growing hotter, begging for freedom, but I couldn't allow them to reach the underworld. Hopefully, it didn't hurt them being separated like this, but I had no idea what I was doing and had no one to lean on but myself.

The combination of my light and dark magic had allowed me to do this. The dark magic, my strength in necromancy, allowed me to touch their souls while the light magic helped me hold them without absorbing their energy and without releasing them.

Selina needed to move up the stairs and get out of the way so I could release my mother and father's souls before something happened.

Keeping my attention on the mighty sorceress, I pushed myself off the tree.

Selina lifted her chin and gathered her skirts before giving the order to take away the bodies of—who should have been—the next king and queen.

James dragged the old me away, the me who didn't know my parents weren't actually dead. The me who didn't know I'd come up with a way to save them. I smiled at the thought.

I'd done it.

I'd figured out a way to save my parents.

My heart leapt at the thought. Maybe Selina really was wrong all of these years.

The soldiers moved away from their posts while the remaining people scattered to their houses. My friends—if I could call them as such—remained behind, pressing against the soldiers to get into the palace. I caught a glimpse of Tavia and Keltin with Odette and Ulrich joining the fray to maintain some pressure on the soldiers.

My mother's soul burned and nipped at me.

I hissed and let it go, earlier than I'd hoped, but the soul did just what I wanted it to do—it flew back into her body like a shooting star.

My mother gasped, her spine arching as she gulped in her first, reborn breath.

The soldier who had crouched at her side fell backward, eyes widened in horror.

Hazel scrambled to her hands and knees, looking around with fear as she sucked in breaths. I hadn't taken time to consider what it would feel like to have your soul returned, but Ismae hadn't reacted so aggressively.

My father's soul was growing hotter and hotter, and I wouldn't be able to hold on to it much longer. I jumped over the edge of the staircase and pressed his soul into his chest, making sure it didn't wander off anywhere.

He, too, gasped as he reached his arms and legs out. He grabbed on to my shoulders with a ferocious grip and dragged me close as he took in air.

I withdrew my hood and looked at the soldier. Without uttering a word, I pressed a finger to my lips, then waved for him to run.

He jumped to his feet and took off, tearing down the street without protest.

"We can't be seen," I said to my father, who was still recovering from his resurrection. I reached my free hand out to my mother and grasped her wrist.

She jumped and tried to pull away.

"Mother, it's me. It's Gerard."

"Gerard . . ." Remembrance dawned on her face, and she threw her arms around me. "My son!"

"Oof!" I grunted. "Yes, me. We can't stay here. Selina can't know you survived. And I need to get back inside the palace. I've got to get back inside to save Ismae and fix some other things."

Mother pulled back, leaning on her heels.

My father was finally starting to come around.

I looked at him. "The Ashwryan clans are on their way. Quist and the dragons should arrive at any moment to help, and Odette and James are going to get the pirates."

"Yes . . . Quist would be willing to help." He blinked slowly, his eyes settling into a natural shine, and then his lips spread into a smile. "How did you do it? How did you save us?"

"I did something I probably shouldn't," I said with a little grimace.

He laughed, though it sounded tired. "All magic is something that probably shouldn't be done at first."

"I ripped your souls from your bodies," I said bluntly.

His smile froze. He blinked. "Okay, yes, that is something you probably shouldn't be doing, but then again, it worked."

I shook my head and got to my feet. "I have to do it one last time. Now, get off the steps before we're seen!" I grabbed onto my father's arm and hoisted him to his feet.

He draped his arm around my mother's shoulders, drawing her into his chest, and then he kissed her.

I rolled my eyes. Maybe I might have found it cute if it weren't for the soldiers fighting at the bottom of the stairs with phoenixes, humans, and a wingless fairy—who were sorely losing. But there wasn't time for lingering.

Ushering my parents to move and reluctantly leaving them behind, I jumped off the steps and wormed my way back through the gardens. This time, however, the soldiers were on high alert with the battle happening just feet away. A line of soldiers protected my destination, all of them with their swords drawn and ready to fight me.

"I've got him, gentlemen," a silky voice floated down to me from somewhere in the branches of the tree.

"Nicholas," I said stiffly.

His shadowy form took shape in front of me, his dangerous fangs grinning inches from my face. "I did tell you I would see you again, didn't I?" He reached out to touch my cheek, but I moved my head. "And feisty. You know I prefer it when you fight me."

He expected a fight? Well, he was going to get one. One he wouldn't win.

Not tonight.

I allowed him to make the first move, knowing he was going to spring forth and use his claws to tear into me. It was predictable, though effective. However, when he went to grab onto me, I reached into the core of my heart and felt the warmth of the light spread across my body, sending cool tingling sensations up and down my arms.

Nicholas's claws tore through my shoulders, but he let out a horrible scream as the light spreading across my skin seared his hands. He recoiled, ducking several feet back and holding out his blackened hands. "What is this?" he hissed.

"It's me. The real me. The one Selina and you tried to suppress."

Nicholas attacked me with everything he had in his arsenal. I only saw the shadows move because the moon in the sky shone so brightly. And then they hit me, tearing my jacket, pulling at my face and hair, slicing my arms and back.

I had no sword—it had been taken from me when I'd been placed in the wizard's tower. I had no staff, that had been left behind for the past me to find.

But I had my magic.

I slapped my palms together and called to the moon, "Tunglskin faen!"

Light exploded between my fingers, scattering the shadows. But I didn't allow the light to dissipate. I spread my palms, calling for the light to grow. As I did, the shadows took on a grayish hue, and I realized the shadows Selina had been manipulating were remnants of people. They weren't physical shadows cast from light but were summoned from darkness.

Spirits.

"In all my days," Nicholas said breathlessly. He took a step away from me. "A spirit mage. That's what you've become. Combining light and dark, manipulating both . . . I've seen wizards use spirit magic, but not like this."

"I wonder if I can manipulate you now." My voice sounded powerful, but as if it floated on the wind.

I acted like I was twisting the lid off a jar, grasping the orb of light in my hand, then flicked my top hand to send the orb spinning through the remaining group of shadow beings. Reaching my left hand out, I summoned the beings struck by the light to me, and they shot forth. I curled my fingers, pulling their energy toward me and then manipulating them to my right toward Nicholas.

The demon snarled and dragged his hand across the ground, slicing the earth apart. Most of the shadows fell and were swallowed by the dark fire Nicholas summoned, but a few leapt over the gap and attacked him.

Using the distraction, I decided to play a little bit with my newly discovered spirit power and felt my heart begin to pound. My fingers trembled with anticipation and adrenaline. My shoulders lifted with my deep breath.

Nicholas gripped the final shadow and threw it into the earth, then wheeled around to face me.

I was smart enough to know when to take advantage of a spell and by the time he turned around, I had an army of undead climbing out of the hole he'd made. But not just the undead. I used the spirits still standing in the shadows and forced them back into the bodies. The eyes of the undead soldiers glowed blue and green and ran at Nicholas with a fervor I had never before seen in the undead.

A nearby skeleton soldier stared at his hands, which trembled.

"Go forth," I commanded.

The soldier looked at me with glowing eyes and opened its jaw, letting out a scream that forced me to hold my ears. The spirit exploded into wisps of blue, which slowly dispersed back into the darkness, and the body of the skeleton fell apart and tumbled back into the underworld.

My brows furrowed, and I turned to look at the other creatures I'd created.

A few fell back, standing mutely and looking at each other and then themselves. I realized too late that I had essentially resurrected the spirits by placing them in the skeletons. Doing so must have given them awareness.

Fortunately, those who hadn't caught on to the wonder tore into Nicholas.

The demon roared at me. "You imbecile!"

"Go back to where you belong," I commanded.

He ran for his tear in the earth, then jumped down it. The earth crunched as it slammed closed behind him.

I reached my hand out and pulled the spirits from the corpses, releasing them back into the night. "Be free. No one controls you now. Find your rest."

The spirits faded away into the night.

I waved my hands, moving the skeletons and corpses from my path, and ordered them to return to the underworld. I couldn't afford to leave them roaming freely and risk another accident like Dahlia's death.

Nicholas had wasted much of my time.

The soldiers had been distracted by the undead, giving me a free path to the back door, the same one

I'd used before, and I ran to it, then through the halls. I stopped at the end to catch my breath. Leaning, I peeked ever so discreetly around the corner of the wall.

My past self was already in the throne room yelling at Selina.

My heart began to race.

Slow. Take it slow. Think.

I had to concentrate on breathing as I crept down the hall and to the dining room. I couldn't be near my past self, and no one else could see a second one of me or they would figure it out.

I stepped out from my hiding spot just in time to see Ismae jump over the last three steps on the stairs and to the main floor. My instincts told me to warn her. My heart clenched. She would be dead in just a moment. Yet I stepped back behind a suit of armor.

I had to allow my past self to feel the pain of losing her.

The light from the spell I cast when I had been in the throne room hours before blinded me even in the hallway, and I heard the windows and chandelier shatter.

Without wasting another moment, and using my adrenaline, I ran down the hallway, past the open doorway while doing everything I could not to look at Ismae fall. I found another hiding spot just inside the arch of the dining room doorway.

Focusing on keeping my breath even, I waited for the noise that would call Selina from the throne room. But it didn't come. The seconds stretched.

Cursing myself for not realizing this mistake sooner, I looked for and found a second exit to the room. She'd heard a noise because *I* had been the one to make it. I grabbed a decorative book from the table and pushed it to the floor before I ran and made it through the servant's door, catching the handle before it could click closed.

Selina was in the other room. I could sense her standing in the dining hall, looking for me. My heart was racing so fast I couldn't hold my breath for longer than a few seconds. They felt like they would stretch on forever, and I needed to get to Ismae before she really died.

Slowly letting go of the handle and allowing the door to rest against the frame, I turned away. One wrong move and it would click shut.

Swallowing, I backed up until I finally felt safe enough to turn around and run down the dark corridor. Unfortunately, it dumped me out in the hallway opposite the one I'd used to enter the palace, and I had to go back around the corner into the main hallway with the throne room.

"Sál slite," I whispered, my eyes on Ismae's hair.

Her soul touched my skin, and warmth and familiarity washed over me. I smiled, wanting to hold on to it forever. Somehow, I knew Ismae was aware of me.

"I wondered when you would use your father's magic," Selina said behind me.

TWENTY-SEVEN

When I turned to face Selina, I held Ismae's soul behind my back. I kept my chin high and my gaze narrowed. "Selina."

She gave me a smug smirk. "I would say it's good to see you again so soon, but . . ." She eyed me up and down. "It's been a few hours, hmm?"

I clenched my teeth. She was distracting me. I knew any minute now, the staff would order me to get up and use the staff. If I recalled correctly, the past me had walked into the room by which I stood.

"I may have harmed Nicholas. He didn't seem too happy when I used my light magic to attack him," I said casually.

Her brows shifted, and her eyes darted back and forth between mine.

Ismae's soul tingled across my palm, and I could practically hear her nagging in my ear. *You've got magic, for crying out loud. Use it!*

I slowly pressed my teeth onto my bottom lip and let it slide out. My attention drifted to the sconces on the wall. "Allul sarvont!" I commanded. The flames pulled to my outstretched hand and I redirected them to Selina.

The ball of fire struck her shoulder and she cried out.

I used the distraction to run.

Like my father's soul, Ismae's began to grow hot, and I had to figure out how to get her soul back to her body without letting Selina know what I was doing. She hadn't seen Ismae's soul in my hands.

I ran for a door, assuming it would lead to the ballroom, but when I shoved it open and jumped through, I found myself out on the veranda on the opposite side of the palace. Apparently, the palace wasn't built to mirror the other side.

I hesitated too long, and a bolt of lightning slammed between my shoulder blades. I flew forward, only managing to tuck my shoulder toward the ground so I clumsily rolled on my side. I hadn't moved fast enough to jump back to my feet. I landed rather ungracefully in a bush and scrambled to get out and stand.

Turning to face Selina, I held up both hands in preparation to make a shield and noticed Ismae's soul was no longer in my hands. I gasped and looked around. Out of the corner of my eye, I could have sworn I saw a blur of light, but fireflies were also lighting up the night, not to mention light from the dragons setting trees on fire.

I threw a shield up in Selina's direction and ran after the light, hoping maybe I could catch Ismae's soul and direct it back toward her body, while simultaneously hoping and praying to the gods that she would find it on her own.

I barely made it around the corner of the palace before another bolt of lightning flew at me. This time, however, I managed to dodge it, and the bolt exploded the trunk of a nearby tree, showering me in fragments of bark.

Selina materialized from the shadows in front of me, her eyes as black as the night sky overhead, and I took cautious steps away, careful not to turn my back to her.

Behind her, the battle raged.

The clans from Ashwrya clashed with dragons and my small group of friends. I spotted Keltin with his back pressed up against a wall, doing his best to defend himself with his sword with an unarmed Ulrich at his side. Ferdinand was trying to work his way through the crowd of soldiers to get to him and help.

Overhead, Tavia and Mathias flew with the dragons, aiding them in the sky against women riding flying horses.

"Your friends are losing," Selina purred, noticing my brief distraction.

A roar called my attention to my left where a dragon fell from the sky and struck the ground so hard the ground beneath my feet trembled.

Keltin's sword was knocked from his hand and he held his empty hand up when the soldier pressed his blade to Keltin's throat.

"You can stop this all," Selina said softly.

Looking across the battlefield, at each of the people who had stepped up to help me defend the kingdom against Selina, I knew there was only one choice.

Nearby, a palace soldier lay groaning in agony, blood seeping from his side.

I ran over to him, withdrew the dagger from his boot, then stood and placed the blade to my chest. It was a choice that had always played at the back of my mind. The decision even Chiso in the giant realm mentioned.

Only you know what is best. Only you can discover yourself.

As the tip of the dagger pierced my skin, Selina screamed my name. "Gerard! You would take your own life for these people who have done nothing for you? I taught you everything you know! It was I who trained you! I who helped you find your true power!"

"No," I said defiantly. "I'm doing this *for* you. Because maybe, if I destroy your heart, it will return to you and save your soul. This is the only way I can show you that I love you."

"Don't you dare!"

"No!" Ismae screamed, desperately running to me. Her brown eyes glistened with tears. Those eyes that looked at me with love, that teased with sarcasm, that burned with hope.

Her soul had found its body.

She was the only thing I wanted to see before I died.

I shoved the dagger into me. The blade seared through muscle, across a rib, and straight into my heart. Pain exploded in my chest, stealing my breath.

I collapsed to my knees, a hand still on the dagger's hilt.

Before Ismae could reach me, Selina had dropped to her knees by my side. "Why? Why would you . . . *do* such a thing?" she stammered. "How could you?"

"Is-Ismae told me once . . . everyone deserves s-someone . . ." I tried to gulp in a breath. "Everyone deserves s-someone to love. Y-You're my grandmother. I'll always love you."

Her black eyes softened. She wrapped her arm around my shoulders as I lost my strength, and she drew me to her. Selina wrapped her long fingers around the hilt of the blade and yanked the dagger from my chest, making me gasp and choke on a cry. She placed her hand over the wound as my blood poured between her fingers and down her wrist.

"You foolish, foolish boy," she whispered.

"Get away from him!" Ismae demanded. She stood over Selina, but her face instantly pinched.

It took a moment for my eyes to focus on what it was about Selina that changed. Her eyes were no longer black, but a stunning deep blue. A tear trailed down her cheek as she looked at me. "How could I do this to you?"

I closed my eyes as a wave of nausea washed through me. Needles, thousands of them, pierced my legs. Each breath became shorter until I was gasping.

"No. Please . . . someone, help him!" Ismae cried. She knelt across from Selina and tried to use my shirt to help stifle the bleeding. "Tavia! Mathias! Hold on, Gerard, a phoenix can heal."

Somehow, I managed to raise my hand and touch her arm.

Tears flowed freely down her cheeks. "You can't leave me. You *can't*, Gerard! You're the . . . only one . . . I . . ." She choked on a sob.

"I know," I managed.

She grasped my hands. "You're a necromancer! Do a spell so you can't die."

"Necromancy doesn't work like that," Selina murmured.

My hearing faded away. Their lips moved, phrases echoing in my mind, but I couldn't focus on them. Someone, Mathias or Tavia—I couldn't tell—transformed from a phoenix to a person at my side. The edges of my eyesight grew black as the pain started to fade.

The night sky was beautiful.

Big white pillowy clouds lazily spread across the sea of darkness, and the last of the rays cast gray light on the horizon. I had wanted to sail again. And sled. I had wanted to learn what it would be like to have a romantic relationship. If I had become a real wizard, I wondered what animal my familiar would have been? Then, I wondered if my eternal rest would be up there, in the sky, or below in the underworld.

My eyes closed.

I stood alone in the darkness with light surrounding me. Selina stood before me an old lady, withered far beyond her true years. Blackness dripped from the bridge of her nose and off the tip, plopping to the ground. She sat hunched in a chair. The ooze poured down her shoulders and arms.

I stepped forward, and she shunned away.

The light in the darkness came from me.

I crouched and looked her in the eye. "You know who I am."

"Yes," her voice rasped.

"You know why I am here."

"You cannot give my power to me. It is too late. I am too far gone."

I touched my hand to my chest, then lifted it away. In my palm sat Selina's heart, as decrepit as she appeared. "For a long time, I hated you. I despised what you made me and the actions you forced me to perform on your behalf. I carry guilt and shame with me. While those feelings will never leave me—and they shouldn't—I also can't help but wonder who I would be if you hadn't done what you did. I'll never get the opportunity to know."

Selina lifted her gaze to me. Her eyes were a beautiful shade of blue.

"In spite of all you've done, everyone deserves justice and mercy. Elisa taught me that when she once showed me mercy after I killed her sister. Ismae showed me love when she should have pushed me away. Mathias and Tavia put their trust in me to help their mother. It is time someone shows to you the same kindness shown to me." I held her heart out toward her.

It beat slowly as though it were on the verge of death.

"It is time for you to take it back. To feel what you've long forgotten."

Selina's pitiful gaze dropped to her heart. "How can I after all I've done?" she whispered.

I took her hand and set it over her heart.

She gasped.

I summoned forth my light magic, pouring it into her heart, giving it life, sharing my light with it. The ooze suffocating Selina melted away. Her heart began to shine red and then yellow, and the light trickled up her arm. A silent breeze washed over us, pushing away the evil she'd been consumed by for over sixteen years.

The wrinkles in her hands faded as youth returned to her arms and back. She stood tall. Her face relaxed, and her age showed in the edges of her eyes and lips as it should have all along, and silver streaked her black hair.

Selina sat before me.

The *real* Selina I never knew.

She took the heart and held it against her chest, closing her eyes and allowing the magic and her soul to fill her once again. She smiled at me, light radiating from her face. "Thank you, Gerard."

TWENTY-EIGHT

"Stop! This battle is over!" Selina commands. She lifts her hands in the air above her head, and hundreds of men and women turn to face her. "My heart is returned to me. I have harmed so many of you . . ."

As her speech continues, I see Odette and her crew of pirates on the south side of the city. They are panting and have several soldiers cornered with their arms raised in surrender.

The dragons slowly land on the edges of the battle.

The Ashwryans stand poised with weapons ready to strike—should anyone move.

The soldiers look around, confused.

Selina looks at me, only, not where I stand. She turns and looks at my body lying on the lawn of the palace. I feel new. Distant, yet present.

Ismae holds my hand and sobs into my shirt, her small shoulders shaking. I want to reach out and touch her, comfort her, assure her I am not in pain.

A silver flutter reflecting the moon's light catches my attention. A small owl no bigger than my hand flies a lazy circle before landing on the tree branch near my head.

Our eyes lock.

His feathers are silver starlight and the dust of the moon—pale white with blue and silver natural only to the world beyond ours. His eyes are blue but hold purples and blacks of galaxies.

"My name is—"

"Stjärna," I say for him, already knowing that the *STJ* made a *W* sound before the "arna" in his name. *Warna.* I hold out my hand to him. "You are my familiar. I sense it."

He ruffles his feathers proudly and hops onto my index finger. "And you are Gerard. I have been long waiting for you."

"You've known of me?"

"Certainly. I have followed you for some time, but you were too dark to see me."

I smile, knowing he is right, then turn to assess myself. "What is this magic? This . . . form I am in?" I touch my shirt. I wear a tunic, but not a typical traveling tunic. It is a ceremonial white tunic with a wide dark-blue collar embroidered with silver stars.

"You are in a spirit form, for you are a spirit mage. Like your father, the first of your kind. Though you still have a lot to learn." He looks down his beak at me before tilting his head sideways in a look I almost read as a stern human scowl.

I resist the urge to chuckle at Stjärna. "And just how old are you?"

"Years of life are irrelevant when you are a spirit."

I smile at my new companion. "Stjärna, I think we may just get along well."

He straightens and ruffles his feathers proudly.

"How shall I practice my magic if I am a spirit?"

"I will teach you, but first you must return to your body, and I shall go with you."

I follow the owl's attention and look out at the scene before me, then to Ismae heartbroken and weeping as soldiers lift my body and carry me into the palace. My father and mother exchange worried glances, and my father wraps his arms around my mother.

She pushes away to pull Ismae into her arms as silent tears join in Ismae's grief.

I should feel sadness with them, but I feel no such thing, for I know it is not the end for me.

"How do I return?" I ask.

"You simply walk over and touch your body, just as you did with the soul magic. Don't give me that look, you still have lots to learn, young wizard."

I realize I am giving him an excited smile.

Stjärna lands on my shoulders and ruffles his feathers, excitement building in his small body. "I cannot wait to meet the woman who will be your bride. She is good for you."

I don't bother responding because my own excitement is building as well while I walk to the palace entrance and then through it. Burned debris still litters the room, and I turn to follow the voices of my family.

They laid me on the dinner table—slightly grotesque. Had I been in charge, I would have had them lay me in the sitting room or even ballroom. The black coal around my eyes is smeared, and I appear to be asleep, except my face is pale as death.

"Why hasn't he come back?" Ismae demands, her voice raw from crying. "Mathias cried over him! He should have healed!"

My mother shakes her head. "Perhaps this is magic he cannot return from."

"Perhaps magic wasn't involved at all," Father offers, his brows lined with sorrow. "He may have truly ended his life to save Selina's . . ."

Ismae turns to my grandmother standing off in the corner and staring at my lifeless body. "Do something! Don't just stand there! *You* are the one who taught him dark magic! Bring him back!"

"Dark magic and knowing how to raise people from the dead are different—"

"Gerard told me you had him resurrect an entire graveyard of Ashwryan people. You know undead magic!"

"And he surely told you the results?" Selina counters sharply.

Her husband grabs her by the arm.

Ismae's hands ball into fists.

I cannot wait any longer for their arguments to escalate. As I pass Ismae, I run my hand down her arm and see her turn and look around. I reach out and grip the hand of my body and feel a tingling rush from the top of my head to the tips of my toes.

Blissful silence surrounds me.

Warmth like I've never felt wraps me in its embrace before letting me go.

When I open my eyes and drag myself out of slumber, Ismae's eyes widen.

"G-Gerard?" she stammers.

"Hello," I whisper. My entire body aches, but mostly my chest. It hurts to breathe.

"Gerard!" She scrambles onto the table and wraps her arms around my neck, lifting my head from the table, and then plants a kiss on my lips. She cradles my head. "Don't you ever do that again! Please, please never do that again," she begs more fervently.

I smile, feeling suddenly weary, and touch her arm. "It was accidentally intentional. I don't know how I did it . . ."

My father and mother step up to my side, and I can see Quist leaning on the wall beside the window, smiling proudly at me. Mathias and Tavia must be outside still.

Father chuckles. "How did you pull this off?"

"I am a spirit mage. Stjärna?" I call.

The owl hoots and lands atop Quist's head.

"Ah, old friend!" Quist reaches up and cups Stjärna in his massive hands.

"You know him?" I ask.

Quist smiles at his audience. "Stjärna helped me become a spirit when time here was sealed. It is how

I was able to help Ismae in the underworld and Elisa when she discovered she was a dragon. Stjärna has been by my side all this time. I am pleased he chose such a brave wizard."

"We should announce to the kingdom that you survived," Mother says, raising her eyebrows. She's too relieved to be mad.

I nod my head and let out a heavy breath. My limbs feel tired. Apparently, my body hasn't received the information that I am not dead because it doesn't want to move. I've lost too much blood for it to respond.

My father glances at Selina before he leaves to address the people and tell them I am, in fact, alive. I am a bit surprised he trusts Selina enough to leave her behind. Then again, Quist and Torian remain in the room.

Wanting to stand at my father's side for the announcement, I try to sit up.

"You just died," Quist says quickly, rushing to grab my shoulders before I can topple over.

Ismae frowns at me. "You idiot."

I suck a breath in through my nose and wrap my arms around her. "I want to show everyone I am alive."

"Yes, but you literally just died. Gone. No heartbeat or breath for an hour, Gerard. Where were you?"

I look at Selina. "I was giving her back her heart." I smile at my grandmother. My chest feels lighter than ever.

A ghost of a smile crosses her lips, and there's relief in her eyes, but she remains distant.

I give her an understanding nod. We have been through much together, she and I, but I also understand it will take time for her to recover—if she recovers at all and if anyone wants her near.

"The soldiers going to the southern isles. Were they stopped?" I ask quickly.

Ismae shrugs. "Odette is here, so if anyone sailed to stop them, she would know."

I try to stand, but Quists's hands are heavy on my shoulders.

"You lost a lot of blood," he explains, though I already know. "Should you stand, you will fall."

I frown. "I don't wish to lie on the dining room table."

"Would you prefer a table in the sitting room?" Ismae quips, being a bit sassy.

Torian and Quist burst into laughter while Stjärna's little body bounces with a giggle. Even I can't resist a smile as I nudge her playfully.

"You need to heal. And when you do, we shall learn the difference between spirit magic and soul magic together," Stjärna chimes in.

"The owl is your familiar?" Ismae asks, smiling big.

I nod. "He is Stjärna."

"Wharnya?" she mispronounces.

"No, wh-ar-na." I correct.

She wrinkles her nose. "How is that spelled?"

"S-t-j-a with little dots above it -r-n-a," he chirps in.

She shakes her head. "That makes no sense."

I shrug. "You don't have to understand. It is how we say *star* in the Ashwryan language."

She turns to Stjärna. "I think it is a beautiful name. Forgive me if I mispronounce it. I am Ismae, by the way."

"Hello, Ismae Bytheway."

"No, no. I am Ismae *Pandhurs*."

He rotates his head sideways. "You can't keep changing your name."

She laughs. "I'm not. There was just a little misunderstanding. Ismae Pandhurs is my name." She bows to him.

Stjärna looks to me as he rights his head.

"She speaks the truth," I add.

Quist lets go of my shoulders long enough to make his way around the table.

I attempt to stand on my own, and Ismae catches me. "Gerard, how many times can you be stubborn? At what point will you realize you need a little bit of help?"

I smile down at her. "Perhaps I have realized and wanted your help."

Her lips part as though she is going to scold me again, but her cheeks flush and she closes her lips in an embarrassed smile. "You don't have to fall to get close to me, you know."

"I know." I stroke her hair and wipe a smudge of dirt from her cheek. "I saved your life again. That's twice. If it happens a third time, I'm going to have to lock you in a tower for the rest of your days."

She rolls her eyes at me. "Ha ha."

Mother steps back into the dining room. "Joking about being locked in a tower isn't funny."

"I want you to tell me that whole story someday," I comment.

"Everyone wants to see you," she says, changing the subject. "Are you feeling up to it?"

I nod, and with Quist on one side and Ismae on the other, they manage to get me to my feet. The wound in my chest twists, stealing my breath, but I drag my heavy legs forward anyway.

"We don't have to do this now," Quist says.

Ismae snorts. "Good luck convincing him of that."

Father replaces Ismae, and the two men practically carry me through the front doors of the palace. Many people have exited the safety of their homes and gather around, now the fighting has stopped, and all seem thrilled the skirmish has ended.

"Gerard!" Tavia shouts. She is the first to see me.

Everyone's eyes move to me, and I raise my hand from Father's shoulder just high enough to acknowledge them and let them know I live.

The crowd below applauds loudly for me, and my heart swells.

They are proud of me.

The trees need to be replanted, facades of buildings re-bricked, roads fixed, and walls repaired. I don't know who, if anyone, has died, but it appears none of the royalty have.

The princes and princesses make their way up the stairs to greet me.

Mathias kneels before me.

"No," I say firmly and pull my arm off Father's shoulders to reach out to him. "You do not kneel to me or bow to me. You're my brother. And none of you need to bow."

Mathias takes our Father's hand since I am not able to help him to his feet. As he finds his balance, he wraps our father in a hug.

Relief washes over Tovan Du'Prei's face as he embraces his youngest son.

Mathias's lips relax into a small smile before he leans back and looks at me. "You'll need to catch us up on what you've been doing this whole time. Sleeping while we win the battle?" he jokes.

"Oh, raising people from the dead." I shrug and we both laugh, though I grimace and hold my chest shortly after. I turn to my father. "I think we should have a feast tomorrow and I can help with repairs in the morning."

"You'll help in the morning?" Father eyes me skeptically.

Ismae chuckles. "Oh, Gerard."

Mathias steps up to my side and takes our father's place to help get me into the castle so Father can finish discussing things with the people of the land.

Ismae looks at Tavia. "Will you move here now?" she asks while they follow behind us.

"I don't know. Ferdinand and I wanted to travel, but with everything that has happened, I feel like staying in one place for a little while. It would be nice to get to know my birth parents."

My heart twists at her mention of staying here. I'd forgotten about the mirror Flynn had asked us to break, and we will have to leave soon to do so, but I'll have to figure that out after Servad is back in order.

Mathias and Quist assist me up the stairs and to my bedroom while Michael, who had helped me several days ago, rushes in to run a warm bath so they can wash all the blood and dirt from my body.

Normally, I would have been prideful and refused help, but I am exhausted and just want to be clean enough to sleep. Ismae stops at the door, only to leave with Tavia, but gives me one last look over her shoulder as if she's afraid it may be the last time she sees me.

Mathias asks Quist to leave us be, and Quist complies.

Alone, Mathias hands me the bar of soap. "It's a bit odd thinking this is all over."

"I agree," I admit. "I wonder what will happen with Selina, though."

Mathias studies me. "She's done horrible things."

"So have I."

"Worse than you. Much worse. Stealing the hearts of others to manipulate that power, tearing apart our family, *torturing* you . . . Some things are unforgivable, Gerard."

I can't argue, and instead nod while I scrub my body. It is true. What Selina has done to everyone needs to be corrected by justice. But what sort of punishment should she be handed? I am grateful it isn't my decision to make.

"One good thing has come of this, though," Mathias says casually while dropping a blob of shampoo onto my hair. "I have a brother."

"Does it disappoint you?" I ask.

He stares at the wound on my chest. "At first, it did. I didn't want to be associated with someone like you, someone willing to do anything to steal everything from everyone." His orange eyes lift to mine. "But I also didn't try to know you before. I want us to be brothers, Gerard. I've always wanted one. Maybe you can teach me a little bit of magic?" He offers a smile.

I hold my hand out, and he grips it. "As soon as I have my strength back, I'll teach you to throw a fireball in your human form."

"Now, *that* sounds fun. I'm not washing your hair, though."

I give a weary chuckle. "Should have asked Ismae to stay."

My left arm is too sore to lift very high, and Mathias caves, helping me when he realizes I have to scrub my hair with one hand. He does, however, frown while doing so. I wash off the wounds I can reach from the shadow creatures and leave the biggest wound alone—the one in my heart. Mathias scrubs off the wounds on my back, his fingers stopping briefly over one of the many raised scars before continuing.

When I climb out, he hands me a towel.

I barely have enough strength to stand on my own, and Mathias guides me to my bed.

"I'm not dressing you." Mathias points out.

"Not that loyal, hmm?" I chuckle, but it dies quickly. I'm completely and utterly spent as I fall onto my bed.

Mathias's only effort to get me comfortable is to grab the quilt folded at the foot of the bed and cover me with it. He blows out the candle on the nightstand. "I will see you in the morning."

TWENTY-NINE

I hear hammering through my open window when I come to and drag my eyes open. Judging by the sunlight filling the room, it is late in the day. The breeze from my window is chilly, and a shiver runs through me briefly. I had heard the hammering in my sleep and imagined it to be the shadows knocking on the black door.

But there is no black door here.

When I try and sit up, I find I'm lying on my back and my chest is bandaged, and my entire left side burns the instant I move. I grimace a bit before deciding to stay lying down a little while longer.

My attention drifts to the open window, and to Ismae curled up with her knees to her chest in the chair beside the window. She's got her head on the back of the chair, her head turned toward the light, and a book lies open in her hands. But her brown eyes watch something outside.

Repairs on the city have already begun without me.

"You look positively radiant," I say, aware of how worn my voice sounds.

She turns to me and smiles. "You look like you've seen better days." She closes her book and rushes over to me. She drops onto the bed at my side and kisses my lips. "How are you feeling? You had a fever all night your first night and slept all day yesterday."

My brow twitches. "You mean . . . I have slept two days?"

"Yes. You needed to recover." Her eyes sparkle. "Have you seen yourself a mirror yet?"

"Why would I want to see . . . Oh. I'd forgotten physical changes happen sometimes to wizards when they accept their powers." I purse my lips and accept the hand mirror Ismae grabs from the top of the dresser. I don't want to look. I have always been fond of my chiseled chin, my brown hair that lightened in summer, and my green eyes. I don't even mind the black mark on my face.

"Go on. Look," Ismae urges.

I clear my throat before lifting the mirror to look at myself. I anticipate horns growing from my head, long white hair, or something of that nature. Instead, I am pleasantly surprised to see the dark magic that had marked my cheek is gone now. I still have mismatched eyes, though, and my dark hair now has a white patch at the center of my forehead.

"I suppose I expected something different," I admit, lifting my hand to run it through my hair.

"Gerard, it *is* different."

I lift my gaze to Ismae.

She smiles at me and tilts the mirror down.

My scars . . . are gone.

I climb off the bed, ignoring the burn in my ribs, to stand before the mirror in the corner of the room and turn to assess myself. Every ridge from claws, every gouge from swords, each lightning bolt, fire, and nightmare that had once marked my flesh is gone. I remove the bandages and let them fall to the ground.

There is no scar where I stabbed myself in the heart.

Ismae stands behind me. When she glides her fingers around my stomach, feeling my muscled abdomen, my skin burns with fire. "You're healed. You can make your own choices now. Become your own person."

"I don't miss them," I say before my mind can catch up. I trace my hand down my chest, where the scar from the dagger should have been. "Each held a memory, but not memories of pride. Not memories of mighty battles or victories I won."

"I know," she says and steps around me. "You get to start over. With your family."

I turn to face her, run my fingers through her hair, and lean forward to press my forehead to hers. "And with *you*. I love you, Ismae." I capture her lips in a kiss and draw her against my body so I can feel her tenderness.

She places her hands on either side of my head and rises to her toes.

I bring my hand up her back, under her shirt, and over her soft skin. I can feel her hips against mine and for once she doesn't shy away. This time, she holds her body against me and moves her hands down my chest and across my back.

"I love you, Ismae," I say again, kissing her forehead.

"I love you too, Gerard."

Ismae is my everything.

My sun and moon.

My spirit.

For the first time in my life . . . I am home.

She helps me dress so we can join my family in the dining hall for a late lunch. I had hoped to eat on the veranda, but a thin layer of snow covers the ground beyond the window. My mother is already sitting with Tavia, and both are smiling while eagerly sharing a story. Mathias isn't there yet.

Father steps up behind Ismae and me. "How are you feeling?"

I turn with a big smile. "I feel wonderful. I've never felt so . . . happy before."

He chuckles. "Good. Go on and sit. Mathias was just finishing up the roof on the flower shop."

"Oh, so he gets to help while I lie in bed and sleep," I complain with a smile.

Mother turns to see me and rises to her feet to hug me. "Which is where you needed to be. The repairs are nearly finished anyway. It's amazing how quickly everything gets fixed when everyone helps." She takes her seat again.

"And what has happened?" I ask, sitting at her side.

Tavia nods. "Ferdinand, Ulrich, James, Odette, and Mathias have all been assisting with rebuilding. Odette confirmed there was no attack on Sheblom, there wasn't even a ship launched to attack. The dragons have helped make sure everything is at peace."

"And the Ashwryans?" I ask.

"They met with me yesterday," Father says. "We went over the contract they signed with Selina and ensured we won't be attacking their land. In fact, I would like to have an alliance with them, but they prefer to rule themselves in their familiar clan ways."

I look at Tavia. "Did Athena end up helping?"

She shakes her head. "Grimhilde tried to convince her to help, but she refused. From what Grimhilde says, King Eric pulled her aside and said Queen Athena isn't quite herself yet. She blamed Grimhilde for kidnapping her son and daughter and . . . well, obviously she never came to help."

"All in all, it is done," Mother concludes.

Mathias enters the dining hall, drying his hands on a towel while a servant follows with a bowl of water. He grins when he sees me hands the towel back. "You look well. Like the hair."

I run my fingers through it, knowing he refers to the white now in it. "It will help when I get older, I suppose."

He chuckles and sits beside our father. "Father has been spending a lot of time with us." He glances at Tavia, then back to me. "I would like to stay here, but with no one to rule Zelig, I feel like I should help there."

I nod. "I think that would be appropriate, but do you want to live there alone? Where is Grimhilde?"

Mathias gives a slanted smile. "She wants to travel with Zuri."

"Zuri . . ." My brows furrow. "And what has become of Selina?" I look to Father.

He leans back in his seat, and I realize everyone is silently watching him with anticipation, which means he hasn't divulged his plan yet. He looks at each of us. "In honesty, it is a decision I find difficult to make. I have heard everyone's side, their accounts. The conclusion I've come up with is to banish her through a Windforn mirror. There is a realm with no magic, and I feel that will be a place best suited for her."

I rest my arms on the table. "She will not be able to use magic at all?"

He shakes his head. "Not even a spell to light a fire."

"I am to destroy the Windforn mirrors," I state bluntly, looking at my mother as if she's forgotten. Her expression is mute, which means she's already explained that to Father.

"I know. Which is another reason we feel that is the best option for her. Otherwise, she rots away in a prison here, and I'm not sure what sort of prison would be best."

I glance at Mathias, who gives a satisfied nod.

Tavia leans back in her seat, accepting it as well.

I look up when Ferdinand enters the dining hall and stops at the servant still awkwardly holding the bowl of water and towel.

"We've got the streets finished," he announces when he sees us all looking.

"And what will you do, Tavia?" I ask. "I made a promise to destroy the mirrors. That either banishes you here with us or you to the fairy realm."

She lifts her shoulders in a shrug. "I've been thinking I can help Mathias with Zelig. We were raised to take over, after all."

"Even after you didn't want to rule?" Ismae speaks up.

"I said help, not live." Tavia smiles. "He at least needs help getting started. And he's got to find someone to marry."

He chuckles and shakes his head. "I'll find someone eventually. I'm not in a rush like the rest of you."

"For now, I am fine with the powers of the kingdom being split evenly," Father adds. "Elisa is doing a wonderful job getting her land stronger. I have already sent a message to Arington and Terricina to see how they would like to have their kingdoms move forward. We will reopen trading and get more income to our land."

"And advance the other kingdoms," I press. "You've done many wonderful things here in Servad I would like to see in other areas of our land. Farmers could plow much easier if they had moving machines to help, and there must be ways to assist with the tree harvest for the arborists in Griswil. Zelig will need to reopen mines or something when the snow thaws." I look at my brother and sister.

Mathias nods. "I've already thought of that. It turns out, Tavia met one of the dwarves who used to work in the mines several years ago. I'm going to see if he would like to be a foreman and help us open a new mine. His sons are all too eager to help too."

"His sons?" I ask.

"The boys that Odette and James have had sailing with them," Ismae answers.

I lift my chin. "Oh, I remember them. I met them. Someone called them the lost boys?"

Mathias nods.

I lean back in my seat when the servants bring out food.

This is my family now. This is my life. I am prince of Fidsa, but I know my story is far from over. I still have to get the kingdom back in order, travel to Sheblom and break the mirror for Flynn, and convince myself that maybe it wouldn't be such a bad idea to rule with Ismae at my side.

The thought of spending the rest of my days here with her at my side makes my heart flutter with excitement and peace.

Ismae catches me staring at her and blushes. "What?"

I reach out and take her hand. "I have you to thank for all of this. If you hadn't shown me kindness a few months ago, I wouldn't be here. Not like this.

You showed me being vulnerable doesn't mean being weak."

"I know. And you showed me what it feels like to really be in love."

From the corner of my eye, I see Mathias rolls his eyes before he stands. "I'm going to go back to helping the construction."

"I can help repair the gardens," I offer. "Marigold taught me a couple of things when it comes to growing. And using light magic." I finish the sentence by looking to my mother.

She gives me a knowing, and proud, smile.

Ferdinand rises to his feet. "I'll help. I can help teach you a little more of that light magic."

"I would appreciate that," I answer, knowing that of anyone I've harmed in the past several months, Ferdinand is the one holding on to resentment the hardest.

We walk outside, side by side, heading for the garden. He and I didn't start off on the best of terms, some might even argue they were the worst of terms, but someday I hope to call him *friend.*

A cool breeze brings the scent of burnt wood and cold air across the trampled flowerbeds. Snow flurries down from the sky. If Ferdinand can help me strengthen my light magic, I can find balance inside myself.

Change is coming.

EPILOGUE

Winter spreads across the land, as it should have done every winter for the past sixteen years. Luckily, Mathias knew what to expect and has offered extra bedding from the castle in Zelig to the people in Griswil and Arington. Ismae has been helping, too, by combining her efforts with her oration magic and my father's passion for enchanting objects. They've created looms that do everything manually, save loading the spools of thread. That's easy enough for anyone to handle replacing.

Production of blankets and new clothing is increasing, but we must be most careful with the food as winter impacts the land. Ulrich, in spite of having just moved into Arington's castle with Keltin, has made sure Odette can offer food from trade routes they are establishing in Terricina.

Odette has taken over Terricina's throne, although it doesn't impact her love for the seas, and James remains loyally at her side.

I send a letter through Tavia and Ferdinand to the fairy world and seek to find the dwarves and ask if they would like to open the mines of Zelig again or, better, create new ones. Herock responds immediately, and the reunion with his boys is both warming and heartbreaking since they are still fairies.

I speak with the wizards at the Quinary Academy and ask the wizards if they can help. It will take time, but they believe they can come up with a solution for the fairies to return to dwarves. In the meantime, they still have their father.

The royal families are all present in Zelig when Selina is presented with five mirrors to choose from. Grimhilde has carefully chosen each realm as a possibility for Selina to end her days in. The charms to help her age have faded, and Selina's hair has grayed.

She stands before the second mirror from the right and chooses that—a world with red sand and pine trees. The mirror opens to a quaint village. Selina runs her finger over the heavy metal bracelet around her wrist. It is the same kind of bracelet she forced upon Tavia that stifled her phoenix powers. This one has been specially designed by my father, Tovan, to prevent Selina from using any of her powers so long as she lives.

Selina turns to me. I see she wants to say something and understand. She is begging forgiveness without saying a single word. I wish she had asked, but I don't know what I would have said in response. Mathias was right, some actions are unforgiveable, and the hell she put me through is enough for me to accept her leaving forever.

None of us anticipate Torian, my grandfather, stepping forward with a pack of his own. "She is my wife," he says. "I'll remain loyal to her until the end of our days. It is the promise I made when I took her as mine."

And they leave, hand-in-hand.

The mirror is destroyed.

When we return to Servad, Father is crowned king of Fidsa.

As for me?

My life isn't the same anymore. I sleep on beds instead of the ground. I no longer have nightmares. Selina doesn't control me. I attend the wizard academy, like my father, and as I promised Ismae, I write a letter to the sorceress academy—The Zauberin Akademie. However, my suspicions rise when I receive no response back. The academy is in the Southern Isles. After a letter from the vizier to the sultan, I learn there have been some difficulties in their land and the academy is closed.

Winter gives way to spring.

I have found the perfect ring for Ismae. I wanted to choose the wolf's head, but Mother said that was a horrible choice, so I settled on a gold band split in two and wrapping around the finger like vines. Little rubies shaped like roses adorn the vine. I'm excited as we travel to Griswil for the Spring Equinox celebration. My plan is to propose at the ball.

But Dormir announces his engagement to Elisa, and I know it's bad form to steal the spotlight from the princess of the land.

I hold the ring in my pocket for another time.

And that is the story of how I grew and changed. How I started as a foolish, manipulated, broken boy and turned into a man. How women influenced my life for good and bad, and changed me for good. How I realized opening my heart sometimes means getting hurt, but it also means finding real love that lasts beyond anything one can even dream.

There is still much to come for me, but for now I have one last task to do—propose to Ismae.

THE SECOND EPILOGUE

I'm not as bad as they say I am, you know. You see, my story—the story of Merlin Lokisson—started long before this incident with the staff or my meeting Tavia in the forest. It started back when I accidentally stole a magical artifact.

Okay, stealing the artifact wasn't accidental, but the magic part was. The entire land of Ashwrya was after me, a crazy man claimed I was some long-lost mage, oh, and the girl I was in love with? I turned her into a swan.

Oops.

My story began when I had to take that stolen artifact back from where I stole it or learn how to control its power. Life would never get back to normal otherwise.

Then again, with a dragon on my tail, would anything be normal?

Merlin will reappear in The Knights of Valhalla Saga, beginning with his tale: *The Mage Thief.*

Coming 2021

THE END OF
The Forgotten Kingdom Series

Dear Reader,

Hasn't this series been an incredible adventure?

I had a blast discovering these characters, their world, magic, and more. Ready for some *amazing* news? All of these characters are going to reappear in other series! I left you with a little bit of a cliff hanger about Gerard and Ismae's engagement, didn't I? Well, they show up again in my next series, which is a retelling of 1001 Nights! Want to know more about Hazel? She's getting an exclusive short story that will be part of the boxset for this series.

There is so much in store down the road, I hope you stay in touch by signing up for my newsletter, or even better—my reader group! And let me know who your favorite couple is, I want to know!

Thank you for all of your love and support.

Your new favorite author,
Lichelle Slater

THE FORGOTTEN KINGDOM SERIES

The Four Stones of Tern Tovan
(Prequel to The Forgotten Kingdom Series)

The Dragon Princess
(Sleeping Beauty Reimagined)

The Siren Princess
(Little Mermaid Reimagined)

The Beast Princess
(Beauty and the Beast Reimagined)

The Phoenix Princess
(Snow White Reimagined)

The Crown Prince

Receive the prequel to *The Four Kingdom Series* for FREE by signing up for my newsletter:

https://mailchi.mp/78ba88ee86a2/lichelleslater

ALSO BY LICHELLE SLATER

Urban Fantasy
Curse of a Djinn

Science Fiction/Fantasy
Step Right Up
Come One Come All
Prepare to be Amazed

Christmas Romance Novels
Secret Santa
Accidental Secret Santa

ABOUT THE AUTHOR

Personal dragon trainer, lover of glitter, super nerd.

Lichelle Slater lives in Salt Lake City, Utah, with her adorable King Charles, Perseus. When she's not working full-time as a special education preschool teacher, she's living in the worlds she creates and shares with readers, painting, or doing any other assortment of crafting. One thing is for certain—you'll always find a dragon in her stories.

Sign up for my newsletter here: https://mailchi.mp/78ba88ee86a2/lichelleslater

To join my Facebook reader group, go to Lichelle's Book Wyrms: https://www.facebook.com/groups/753608364988213/

FOLLOW ME HERE

Instagram

https://www.instagram.com/lichelleslater_author/

Twitter

https://twitter.com/LichelleSlater

Amazon

https://www.amazon.com/Lichelle-Slater/e/B01MSU34EN/

Goodreads

https://www.goodreads.com/author/show/16150296.Lichelle_Slater

www.ingramcontent.com/pod-product-compliance
Ingram Content Group UK Ltd.
Pitfield, Milton Keynes, MK11 3LW, UK
UKHW020224250726
13967UKWH00001B/177